CONEY ISLAND

GRAVESEND BAY

CONEY ISLAND CREEK

WEST BRIGHTON

Culver Plaza

Mammon's Alley

the Reverend Dram

Mermaid Avenue

Surf Avenue

Tycho McNulty's dispensary

NORTON'S POINT

Jin doused the flame she carried, and she and Sam crouched in the shadows.

THE
BROKEN LANDS

KATE MILFORD

with illustrations by

ANDREA OFFERMANN

Houghton Mifflin Harcourt
Boston   New York

For information about permission to reproduce selections from this book, write to
trade.permissions@hmhco.com or to Permissions, Houghton Mifflin Harcourt
Publishing Company, 3 Park Avenue, 19th Floor, New York, New York 10016.

www.hmhco.com

The text of this book is set in 11-point Letterpress Text.
The illustrations were executed in pen and ink.
Book design by Sharismar Rodriguez

The Library of Congress has cataloged the hardcover edition as follows:
Milford, Kate.
The Broken Lands / by Kate Milford ; with illustrations by Andrea Offermann.
p. cm.
Prequel to: The Boneshaker.
Summary: In the seedy underworld of nineteenth-century Coney Island
during the construction of the Brooklyn Bridge, two orphans are
determined to stop evil forces from claiming the city of New York.
[1. Supernatural—Fiction. 2. Good and evil—Fiction. 3. Demonology—Fiction. 4.
Orphans—Fiction. 5. Coney Island (New York, N.Y.)—History—19th century—Fiction.
6. New York (N.Y.)—History—1865–1898—Fiction.] I. Offermann, Andrea, ill. II. Title.
PZ7.M594845Br 2012
[Fic]—dc23
2011049466

ISBN: 978-0-547-73966-3 hardcover
ISBN: 978-0-544-43942-9 paperback

Manufactured in the United States of America
DOC 10 9 8 7 6 5
4500786965

To Brooklyn, of course, and the people who made it home:
Alli, Ray, Alfred, Erin, Julie, and the venerable members of
the Paisley Stocking Society, and most especially, Nathan,
Sprocket, and Ed

And to our baby, whoever you turn out to be, we love you
already. Come home soon. Brooklyn is waiting for you.

—K.M.

CONTENTS

ONE

Character, Chance, and Cheating

Coney Island, August 1877

A CROSSROADS can be a place of great power; this should not come as any surprise. It is a place of choosing, of testing, of transition, and there is power in all of those things.

But a crossroads is not always what you think it is. It can sneak up on you. And even if you know to keep your eyes peeled for those two dusty roads, just when you think you know which you will choose and which you will leave behind, that's when your crossroads will turn out to be something else entirely.

A hand of cards, for example. Like the coup of monte Sam Noctiluca was just about to lose.

It may have been because it was a particularly perfect August afternoon—not too hot, with breezes off the water that were just brisk enough to sweep most of the more pungent smells out of Culver Plaza, but not so strong that the cards wouldn't stay put on the table. Maybe it was because it had been a quiet season; the newspapers had been screaming for years about the country being in a depression, but this summer, you could really tell. It could be that Sam had become so grateful for marks that he had forgotten they had to be watched.

Whatever the reason, Sam just hadn't been paying close enough attention.

He saw it coming far too late to try and fix his way out of it. As he realized he was going full chisel into a fairly spectacular loss, he also understood that this fellow he was about to lose to might just be the biggest cheater in all creation. He was certainly the most shameless cheater Sam had ever run across, and that was saying something.

Sam didn't lose at cards often. He was both exceptionally good at the games he played and exceptionally good at cheating if he happened to run into somebody better. Every mark was different, but after a few hands, Sam could usually count on figuring out his particular logic. Whether by character, chance, or cheating, there was a way to beat everyone.

What on earth did I miss? he thought miserably as he stared at the deck of cards in his hand, and the card at the bottom that meant he had just gone broke. He'd missed something for certain, but what that was, he had no idea.

There was precious little skill required to deal monte square, and the odds favored the dealer by so much that Sam almost never bothered to cheat. You dealt one card face-up from the bottom of the deck and one card face-up from the top. Your punters, the marks you were playing against, placed bets on either or both of them. The rest of the deck, the monte, was turned face-up to show the card at the bottom, and if it matched the suit on either of the first two cards, Sam, as the dealer, paid off any bets the punters had made on the matching card.

So if Sam's mark, the fellow in the porkpie hat, bet two bits on a spade Sam had dealt, and Sam turned the monte over to reveal (*Cavolo*, he'd sworn silently, *you have* got *to be joking*) yet *another* spade, Sam had to pay out a quarter dollar of his own bank.

Which would've been fine if the punter had bet two bits, but he hadn't. He'd put down a double eagle, a twenty-dollar coin.

Furthermore, it was the fifth time Sam had turned over the deck to find a spade. Considering there were only ten spades in a monte deck, and that they'd only played six hands, it was pretty impressive. *Impressive*, meaning *impossible*.

And with that, Sam was wiped out.

The punter sat back, tucked his thumbs into his vest, and grinned. "Guess we both learned something today, lad."

Sam forced a friendly smile, even as he mentally let loose a string of hybrid Venetian and gypsy curses that would've made his grandmothers proud, followed by a few choice swear words in German, Irish, and Scots. "Reckon we did." He gathered up the cards they'd played and shuffled them in with the rest of the deck. "We learned I'm a little more naïve than I'd realized."

The punter smiled guilelessly. You'd really never have pegged him for a sharper, let alone the biggest cheater of all time. "Not sure I follow."

Sam leaned back in his chair and considered. He knew better than to judge anybody by the kind of smile he flashed. "Tell you what," he began. "You've got my money, and that's me on my own hook for assuming that if anybody was going to cheat, it would be me, so I took my medicine like a good kid." *Kid*, to emphasize that on a good day Sam could maybe pass for sixteen. Maybe. "Now you've got every penny I had, so indulge me."

The fellow's smile sharpened around the edges, but Sam had already gone too far to change direction now.

"Somehow you stacked the deck, and it had to be when you cut it. How'd you do that?" He smiled eagerly, made his

expression one of admiration rather than accusation. He'd learned lots of tricks with that look, all from adults who couldn't turn
down the opportunity to teach something to a young whipper-
snapper.

It didn't work this time.

This time, the mark hauled off and hit Sam with a sharp
hook that landed just under his eye.

Sam sprawled sideways off the crate he'd been sitting on,
landing hard on his elbow and finally letting loose a few of
those curses. A couple-three passersby paused, but none of them
stopped: another indication that Sam had outgrown his scrappy
kid routine.

Nice while it lasted.

The man watched him get to his feet, still smiling that smile
that was at once as open and friendly as you'd ever wish to see,
and edged. "You usually get away with that, kid? Accusing fellows of cheating?"

Sam spat pink saliva on the ground between them. "You usually get away with such obvious cheating, mister?"

"Usually." The sharper—it was no use pretending he wasn't
a professional—flashed his eyes sideways, and Sam knew he was
about to get hit again. Of course the man would have a sidekick.
Cheating among professionals was like asking for a fight. It paid
to have backup.

And I forgot to look. Stupid, stupid, stupid.

Sam dropped fast and somehow managed to dodge the blow
coming at the back of his head. When he straightened, fists up,
his jaw dropped.

There was no second man, only the same fellow who'd just hit him, but who somehow now stood *behind* him. "Good reflexes," the sharper said.

Sam spent exactly three seconds trying to figure out how the fellow had moved that fast, then decided it didn't matter. He wasted another two seconds wondering what the fellow was up to. He already had Sam's money, so there was no reason to stick around just to give him a whipping.

Any way you sliced it, it was just plain strange. Still, Sam hadn't spent the last year dealing cards in Coney Island without making some friends. He dusted himself off and brought his fingers to his mouth, ready to let loose the piercing whistle that would tell the rest of Culver Plaza that one of their own was in trouble. They might watch him take a single blow from a tourist —sometimes you had to take a punch to soothe a mark's ego and keep him from involving the cops—but they wouldn't stand by while he got knocked into a cocked hat by some out-of-towner.

Then, before he could sound the alarm: "Beg your pardon, gentlemen."

Sam paused, fingers to his lips. He and the sharper turned to regard the old black man who stood politely beside them. "What?" the sharper snapped.

"Wonder if either of you know a saloon called the Reverend Dram." The old man shifted a guitar slung on his back, ignoring the other man's annoyed tone. "Been all over the place and just can't seem to find my way."

The sharper opened his mouth to snarl something in reply. Then he hesitated, and the snarl faded from his face. This was odd. If the fellow was willing to rough up a fifteen-year-old Italian kid, he'd be willing to rough up a black man; even in New York, even more than ten years after the War Between the States, there were folks who practically made a sport out of it. But the sharper hesitated.

"Nope," he said at last. "I'm not from around here." He glanced at Sam, flashing that barbed-wire smile again. "See you around, kid."

Sam resisted the urge to make a rude gesture as the man disappeared into the crowd in the plaza. Then he turned to the newcomer. "I can take you to the Dram, mister." He stuck out his hand. "Sam."

"Well, that's mighty good of you, Sam." The old man took his hand and shook it cheerfully, as if he had no idea he'd just broken up a potential fight. Something told Sam he knew, though.

"Name's Tom," he said. "Tom Guyot."

The arrival of the four o'clock train at the terminus of the New York and Sea Beach Railroad line announced itself with a squeal of brakes battling the forward momentum of two hundred tons of iron. The freckled man in the white linen suit scowled as a fine dust fell onto his cuffs. He looked up at the luggage rack, malevolence in his red-rimmed black eyes, and stared at the carpetbag that had fallen over onto its side.

He brushed the dust from his sleeve with fingers tipped with nails that had been filed to points. It had been about a week since the man had last used those nails to mark a hand of cards, though, so the points were dulling a bit.

With the handle of the bag in one fist and his slim wooden gambler's case under his other arm, he joined the stream of holidaymakers spilling onto the platform at the Sea Beach Palace and surveyed his surroundings. To the west, he knew, were the streets of Norton's Point, full of thieves and gamblers and criminals hiding from the law. A few miles to the east, wealthy guests lounged in the grand new hotels, where piers stretched like manicured fingers into the water. The expanse in between, the bright festal wilderness of West Brighton, was given over to bathers, garish painted banners, grifters, mugs of lager that were two-thirds froth, questionable intentions, and carousels.

Taken all together, this jumble of folks, rich and poor and working and thieving, was Coney Island, the notorious seaside town just south of Gravesend, Long Island.

The black-eyed man leaned on the rail watching, listening, and acclimating while he inhaled the brew of sea air and coal smoke. There was something else in the air, too; a deep note, buried far below the scents and sounds that stirred on the summer breeze. It would've been nearly impossible for anyone else to detect. Humans were notoriously blind to the simmer of violence —which always amused him, considering how like a drug it was to them.

The freckled and black-eyed man, not being human, could smell it as sharply as cologne. It was pervasive here, just like it was everyplace else he'd been in this country in the last twenty years, at least. Maybe more. It was easy to lose track of the passing time. He was far older than the flashy young fellow he appeared to be.

This year, though . . . this year it was *strong*. It had been building through the long years of Reconstruction; it had kept on building during the years of depression; and this summer it was as if it had been incorporated into the very molecules of the air. In the rebuilding South, in the growing West, even here in the North where folks claimed to be so very civilized. Silty, flinty, stony, metallic, the scent was edged with the smell of human sweat . . . and yet sweet, like the perfume of overripe fruit just before it turned and began to rot.

He stood there until the platform cleared, and then he remained a few minutes longer. At last he sighed, picked up the carpetbag and the wooden case, and started in the direction of the beach.

There was still plenty of daylight left, but long shadows were stretching across the sand as he trudged toward the relative dark below the ferry pier, rolling his eyes at the squeals of girls in their woolen bathing costumes and little boys chasing each other through the surf.

In the gloom beside the pilings, the man dropped the carpetbag. He peeled off his suit jacket, draped it carefully over the bag, sat and leaned back against it as if it were a pillow. He removed glittering cuff links and rolled up his sleeves, folded freckled arms across his chest, and closed his eyes.

Then he winced and swore as a blow caught him between the shoulder blades. He sat up straight and punched the bag with his elbow. "Patience, you moldy old bastard," he hissed. Then he sat back against the bag again, harder this time.

Nothing to be done until sunset.

TWO

Wooden Nickels at the Reverend Dram

THE REVEREND DRAM sat on an alley between Mermaid Avenue and the beach, just a bit closer to the dodgy end of Coney Island than most visitors were comfortable with. Unless, of course, they had come to town to visit the rough parts. There were plenty of folks who came just to see why the Brooklyn newspapers liked to rant and rave about how indecent and wicked certain areas of Coney Island were.

Sooner or later, those folks usually wound up here in Mammon's Alley: a string of dancing halls, open-fronted saloons, gaming dens, shooting galleries, dubious hotels, catchpenny amusement stalls, and fakirs' booths all lined up, stacked one on top of the other, and jumbled together, with banners overhanging the lot. It was peopled by hootchy-kootchy dancers in see-through bloomers, short-skirted singers who pestered patrons to buy drinks for them between songs, and bronze-skinned fortunetellers and character readers whose complexions tended to rub off as the night wore on. Local color was provided by assorted confidence men, professional gamblers, hoisters, harlots, and sharpers. If visitors got bored with all this, there were barkers inviting them behind closed doors, and who knew what you might run into there. Nothing you'd want your mother to find you looking at, certainly.

Sam felt a little self-conscious leading the old man named Tom into the alley—it wasn't as bad as, say, Norton's Point, but between the August heat and the drinkers that had been at it since late morning, it already smelled like warm garbage and stale beer; the talkers were already out trying to hustle customers into their dodgy places of business; and a few overpainted ladies propped up at saloon counters were calling out into the streets in search of their next drinks. "Sorry about—hey!" Sam sidestepped a lurching drunk and put out a hand to keep Tom from falling over the man as he sprawled headlong across their path. "Your friend sure picked a rough spot to meet. The Dram's okay, though." Sam nodded up ahead to where a shingle over a relatively quiet doorway depicted a joyful nun dancing on a barrel, her habit hiked up over stocking-clad knees.

Inside, the saloon was not merely quiet; it was basically deserted. Besides the proprietor, the barman polishing the mahogany counter, and the slouching piano player, there was exactly one customer, a bleary-eyed fellow who turned and eyed Tom as he followed Sam in out of the noise and sour reek of the street.

Sam stiffened. You could just tell when someone was about to say something all-fired stupid, and the sole patron didn't disappoint. "Since when did this turn into a watering hole for old buffaloes, Jasper?"

Jasper Wills, the proprietor, sat in a big old chair in the corner. He looked up from his newspaper, took in the situation with one glance, and shook his head with a look of disgust on his face. "I swear, this part of the business makes me sick. I allow a fellow can be forgiven for thinking I'll put up with anything and anyone for a few more nickels in the till, but I swear, for two bits I'll sell the place this minute and be done with the whole thing." He turned to the pianist. "Walt, I'll sell you the place this minute for two bits."

The pianist, craggy-faced and stubble-jawed under a battered old homburg, swiveled on the stool to survey the bar, the man who sat there, and Sam and Tom in the doorway. "Make it a nickel and you're on."

"Fine."

The pianist turned to the barman. "Matty, you got a nickel I can borrow?"

"I think there's a couple nickels in the till," the barman said. He pushed a button and the cash register popped open with a *ding*. He tossed a coin to the pianist. "Here you go."

"Here you go, Jasper." The pianist tossed the coin to Wills. "All yours, Walt."

The pianist stood up, stretched, pushed his hat back on his brow, and straightened his suspenders. Then he faced the customer at the bar. "To answer your question, fella, it's a watering hole for anybody who isn't a complete ass-hat. Now, get out of my place."

Sam snorted in an effort to hold in a shocked laugh.

The man at the bar about fell off his stool. "You can't be serious."

"Mosey off," Walt said, folding his arms and leaning against the piano. "Take your beer if you feel strongly about it. Won't even charge you for the glass."

The customer did not, in the end, choose to take his glass

of beer. He gathered his hat and coat and stalked past Sam and Tom, muttering under his breath about coons getting above themselves in this town. Sam restrained himself from aiming a kick at the man's backside.

"Come on in, mister," Walt said. "Welcome to my fine establishment, and excuse the rabble. The previous owner was a little low-class about who he served."

"Say, Walt." Jasper examined the nickel. "This thing's wooden."

"Hell," Walt muttered. "Gotta add that to the list. Find a barkeep who can spot a wooden nickel." He gave Tom a severe look. "You try to pay with any wooden nickels, mister, you're out on your tail, too. That's where I draw the line."

"Guess that means it's still my place, actually," Jasper said lazily, flipping the nickel over his knuckles. "Get back to the damn piano, Walt. Matty, get this gent a beer, would you? He's looking thirsty."

"Ass-hat?" Sam asked the pianist.

"Made it up myself just now," Walt said. "You like it, Sam? It's yours, anytime you want."

"Used to have some guy who claimed to be a musician around here someplace," Jasper mused from his chair.

Walt sighed, adjusted his battered hat, and turned back to the piano. As he began to play, the man named Tom paused in the act of unslinging the guitar from his shoulder and looked at him sharply.

"Something wrong?" Walt asked without looking up from the keys. Sam glanced from the pianist to the old man and back, trying to figure out how Walt had known his playing had gotten a reaction while he was sitting with his back to the bar.

"I like that song, is all," Tom said slowly. "Didn't realize anybody else knew it."

"Did you write it?" Walt asked casually.

"Nope," Tom answered. "Just sorta picked it up somewheres not too long ago."

"Didn't you figure somebody had to have written it?"

"You saying you did?"

"Nope. Sorta picked it up myself ages back. But I figured somebody had to have made it up, and that there was always the possibility I might run into somebody who'd at least heard it before."

"Well, now you have."

Walt turned to peer over his shoulder, eyes bright under the brim of his hat. "You play?"

Tom nodded at the guitar. "Yep."

Walt looked him over. The moment stretched and threatened to become awkward. Then Walt nodded once and turned back to the keys. "Sometime we should play together, you think?"

Tom smiled with a quick flash of teeth. "Could do," he agreed. "Tom Guyot."

"Walter Mapp." The pianist and the old man shook hands, and whatever it might've been, the awkward moment became companionable instead.

Matty straightened and tried to look like he hadn't been listening. "What'll make you happy, sir?"

"Sure would like a whiskey and quinine."

"Then today's your lucky day."

While Matty poured the drink, Sam slid onto the stool next to Tom. "You said you were meeting somebody, sir?"

"That's right." Tom paused to accept his glass of whiskey and tonic from the bartender. "Ice and all! You're mighty kind, now." He sipped and closed his eyes. "Tastes so much better these days than it used to."

"When?" Sam realized the bartender was giving him a forbidding look. "What?" Matty reached across the bar and smacked him in the forehead. *"What?"*

Tom laughed. "That's all right, I don't mind. In the war, Sam. We took quinine against disease. The whiskey made the medicine go down a little easier, and some of us just got a taste for the two together."

"You fought?" Sam tried to keep the skepticism out of his voice. Tom was *old*. Even twelve years ago he would've had to have been the oldest man on the battlefield.

"That's right. Served an officer till I was allowed to enlist with the United States Colored Troops, but by then I'd already been fighting a goodly time. I was at Shiloh alongside the fellow I'm meeting, then at Resaca; all of that before I was even officially a soldier."

Sam didn't know that much about the War Between the States, but it seemed to him that he'd heard of the battle of Shiloh, which meant it had to have been one of the more bloody ones.

"So, yes, I'm meeting a fellow. If he ever shows up, that is." Tom took another sip from his glass. "Gentleman by the name of Ambrose. Coming out from California, I believe."

"Which is," a voice in the doorway snapped, "a decently

long trip to make. One would imagine there would be some for-giveness if a fellow turned up fifteen minutes late after such a jaunt."

Walt played a little fanfare on the piano while the newcomer, a blond man somewhere in his thirties, dropped a pair of valises and crossed the room to embrace Tom at the bar. "You," he said, holding the older man at arm's length, "haven't changed a bit."

"That ain't so." Tom grinned. "Just, when you get to be my age, nobody can tell how old you are anyhow."

"But it's been ages," Ambrose protested, vague surprise in his voice. "Don't take this the wrong way, Tom, but I was shocked to find out you were still alive."

Walt's fanfare transitioned smoothly into the song he'd been playing earlier. Sam saw the black man's eyes flick briefly toward the pianist. Then he grinned at Ambrose and shook his head. "After what we survived, you thought I'd give up the ghost that quick? Something wrong with you?" He turned to the bar-man. "Say there, how about a drink for my friend?"

"Same thing?" Matty inquired.

"Sure."

Jasper Wills ambled to the bar, reached across without look-ing, and produced a dusty bottle and a glass for himself. "You in town for the bridge, like everybody else?"

"No, for a reunion." Ambrose raised his glass to clink Tom's. "Veterans of Resaca, over at the Broken Land Hotel."

"No fooling. I would've pegged you for a newspaperman."

Ambrose frowned into his glass, sighed, and drained it. "Well, you're not wrong about that," he said bitterly. "What gave me away?"

"Are you kidding? I can smell a newspaperman a mile away," Jasper said. "Used to be one. Then I got the idea that I'd like to run a saloon for my retiracy. You see where that got me."

Sam lingered for a few more minutes, but that thing was happening where the adults in the room slowly began to forget he was there. It was what made him so good at dealing cards, that easy way people had of ignoring you when you were fifteen. You were old enough not to choke on popcorn, but too young to be considered part of a gathering of adults. You were either under-foot or invisible. Until you had their pocket money, of course. Underfoot, invisible, or a thief. Those were the options, basically.

He started for the door, trying not to feel annoyed. As he passed the piano, Walt glanced at him. "Chirk up, Sam." The pi-anist's fingers didn't so much as stumble. "You did a good thing today."

"Because I brought you somebody who'd heard some stupid song before, or because you got to own a saloon for thirty sec-onds thanks to me?"

"You allowed me to invent a brand-new insult," Walt said, "and in return you get free use of it. That ain't nothing, you know."

"Feels like it."

"Most good things do," Walt replied, his fingers weaving a pretty glissando. "Nothing feels like something till after every-thing's over."

"Then what's the point?" Sam asked sourly.

The pianist nodded. "Hard to say."

"Hey, there, Sam." Tom disengaged himself from Ambrose and Jasper and crossed to where Sam stood in the crack of light from the open door. "Thanks for seeing me here. Figure I ought to have a tip for you, something like that—"

Sam shook his head and grinned. "I'll take it off a tourist once I get back to the cards."

"Well, let's say it's a debt unpaid for the moment." The old man held out his hand. "Hope to make good on it when I see you again."

The sun was gone by the time Sam arrived back at the cramped house where he rented an attic room. The front door burst open before he'd managed to reach into his pocket for his key, and Mrs. Ponzi, gaunt and black-haired and severe, wagged her finger, mock-scolding, at him from the front stoop. Sam closed his eyes briefly. He'd forgotten. It was Thursday.

"Saverio, you are late!" his landlady said. Sam submitted to a kiss on each cheek on his way into the parlor; Mrs. Ponzi might have looked like an old schoolteacher, but the second she spoke or smiled, the illusion was spoiled. Even now, though Sam was late for the only actual weekly obligation he had, his landlady couldn't manage a properly angry face.

Thursdays were dancing-lesson days. Mrs. Ponzi, after twenty years in New York, was still under the impression that her daughter, Ilana, had a decent shot at marrying a millionaire and would need to know how to waltz. Ilana Ponzi knew differently. Ilana was twelve, but she had been born and raised in Brooklyn before she and her mother had moved to West Brighton, and Brooklyn twelve was different from Old Country twelve. She knew being able to waltz more likely meant a job at a dance hall as soon as she could pass for sixteen, which probably wasn't that far off. She was tall and big-boned like her mother, and she'd also inherited a single dark gray lock in her black hair, which she wore tucked behind one ear and refused to darken with coloring rinse (discussions about this happened nearly every other week, and Sam had learned to be absent when they did, lest he be dragooned into the debate and asked to provide "a boy's opinion").

Now the girl gave Sam an apologetic roll of her eyes. Sam grinned and shrugged. Dancing lessons were good for a few bits off his rent, and since Ilana was destined to marry an heir to the Astor fortune, he didn't have to worry about Mrs. Ponzi trying to play matchmaker with him.

"I offered to take your place, but evidently I'm too tall." Constantine Liri leaned in from the passage to the dining room with a cup and saucer in his hand. He straightened and walked to one of the parlor's threadbare overstuffed chairs. He was seventeen, the Ponzis' other boarder, and an old friend of Sam's from back in the Brooklyn tenements of Smoky Hollow where the boys had both grown up.

The limp in his left leg, the result of the injury a year ago that had lost him his job working on the New York and Brooklyn Bridge, was barely noticeable today. His straw-colored hair was neatly combed and parted, and Sam recognized the trousers and shirt Constantine wore as his best outfit. He'd been out looking for work.

Sam gave him a questioning tilt of his eyebrow. Almost imperceptibly, his friend shook his head. No luck.

Sam and Constantine, Mrs. Ponzi and Ilana. Four transplants from Brooklyn made family by the strange phenomenon of boarding-house life.

He held out his arms to the girl while his landlady wound her ancient music box, and another day in Coney Island came to a close.

Back on the beach, the black-eyed man stirred among the shadows beneath the pier. It was full sundown. In a few minutes the giant arc lights mounted on poles along the beach would flare to life. It was time.

He got to his feet, dusted himself off, and pulled his jacket back on. As he did, he kicked the clasp of the carpetbag open with the toe of one shoe. Then he bent, picked up the bag, and dumped the contents into the sand. And what fell there was a heap of ancient, crumbling bones.

From his vest the black-eyed man pulled out a battered silver pocket watch that he tossed carelessly in among the pile of remains. He took a look around him to be sure he and the mound of bones were alone. Then he rolled his head on his shoulders as if he was working loose a very unpleasant cramp, looked at the pile for a long moment, and sighed deeply.

"Rise up and shake yourselves, bloody bones," he said at last. "High Walker is here!"

A wind kicked up along the beach, sending hats and skirts and blankets whirling. The man shoved his flying hair out of his face and stepped back. Where the pile of bones had been, a swirling mass of sand was collecting into a shape.

The shape spun like a little tornado, pulling sand and

pebbles and stray bits of seaweed inward, collecting broken shells, snips of paper, and twigs of driftwood, creating a denser and denser cloud that hovered at about the level of the black-eyed man's knees. It began to throb, to shift and pulse and mold itself. Little by little, it began to take shape.

The wind flowing up and down the beach began to diminish. The dark shape, still indistinct and fuzzy at the edges, unbent itself. A tall man stood up.

"Walker," he said, voice gritting. "What is . . ." The man-shape stopped speaking and spat. "Sand? Is this *sand*, you sick bastard?"

"It's what was to hand," the black-eyed man called Walker said easily. He reached into the carpetbag and took out a long blue felt coat. "You want to yell at me for where we are, or you want to get dressed?"

"Where is the crossroads?" The other man extended a sand-colored arm, the hand and fingers still forming as they reached for the coat. "What day is it?"

Walker hesitated. The tall man swirled the garment around his shoulders and slipped the watch into an inside pocket. Then he paused as he buttoned the coat and stared at his companion with eyes the mottled pearl-and-gray color of oyster shells. "Walker?"

"It's Thursday," Walker said slowly. "It's August." He smiled, clenching his teeth together behind his lips. "We have three days, Bones. Jack arrives Sunday night."

"Three days?" Bones interrupted coldly. "Why? I was under the impression that we would get here with at least two weeks to spare before Jack came."

"There was—"

"We took a riverboat," Bones interrupted again, dusty lids lowering dangerously over his oyster-shell eyes. "I could feel the motion of the water. Was there by any chance a *casino* on that riverboat? Possibly some kind of gambling tournament you should have known there was no time for?"

"We don't have time for *this*," Walker snarled. "We need to deliver a city ready for the claiming when Jack gets here. Let's get to moving." He picked up his wooden case and stalked toward the buildings of Culver Plaza.

Bones took the empty carpetbag and followed. "Did you at least win?" he asked in his cold, gritty voice.

Walker smiled thinly. "I always win, don't I?"

"So who dealt you the strawberry?"

Sam touched the bruise on his cheekbone, shrugged, leaned back against the sill of his attic window, and stretched his legs out across the second-floor roof. "Some sharper. Probably get to the beach tomorrow and find myself at the wrong end of a blackjack."

Constantine held out his hand. Sam took a deck of cards from his jacket pocket and passed them to him. He watched Con's fingers as the older boy split the deck, spun the half in his left hand, and shuffled. Some days, usually the same days his limp was worst, Constantine had trouble with cards. Today wasn't one of them, though. The moonlight caught card after card in a perfect fluttering cascade.

"What's the game?" Con shuffled again. "Coteccio, picquet, rumstick, briscola?"

A pale, grasping hand appeared over the edge of the roof, accompanied by a hissing voice. "Sam! Constantine!"

The two boys dove for the edge. Constantine grabbed the hand's bony wrist. Sam leaned over and peered down at Ilana Ponzi, clad in a nightdress and a sweater, balancing on her windowsill and grasping the frame with her free hand. "We're going to have to build her a ladder," he muttered. "Give me your other hand, Illy."

"I do not need a ladder!" came the indignant reply.

Together Sam and Constantine hauled Ilana up onto the roof, wincing at the sounds of her shoes scrabbling for toeholds. "Next time, leave your shoes off," Sam suggested. "If your mother catches us up here—"

"Okay, okay." Ilana crawled along the shingles until she could lean her back against the attic window, then began pulling wax-paper-wrapped sandwiches and cake slices from her sweater pockets. "What's the game?"

The Ponzi house faced northwest, away from West Brighton and toward Brooklyn and New York beyond that. Even now, in the summer, the house was fairly cool. Not like in Smoky Hollow, where as a boy Sam could tell when it was June because that was when the sunlight finally made its way into the room he and his father had shared. Back there, escaping to the rooftops had been just that—escape. You could cook to death on a hot day in one of the windowless back rooms, and most of those rooms held a whole family, sometimes more.

Here, though . . . here, there were only the two boys sharing the clean attic room with its two windows and plenty of ocean breezes to keep it cool. Still, old habits died hard, and the view from the roof was too good to pass up on a nice summer night. As long as they kept Ilana from falling off and breaking limbs, that is.

"What was that game Muhlhaus and his brothers used to play?" Constantine asked, picking through the pile of snacks Ilana had brought up.

"Tysiacha," Sam recalled. "Yeah. You'll like this one, Illy. Take out all the cards lower than nine."

Ilana frowned. "I want to learn one of your games, Sam."

"*My* games?" *Oh, no.*

Constantine slapped his forehead and shook his head. "Your mother's never going to forgive us if we turn you into a card sharp, Illy," he said.

"But—"

"And did you happen to notice that someone nearly broke Sam's face today?" Constantine demanded.

Sam sat quietly and avoided looking at either of them while he picked the low cards out of the shuffled deck.

"I'm not going to start hustling cards," Ilana protested.

"Not tonight you're not, anyway." Con held out his hand for the pared-down deck. "We're going to play Tysiacha. You can play or not. Makes no difference to us."

"Con, want to grab us something to keep score with?" Sam asked. "I'll deal." Constantine nodded shortly and climbed back through the window without another word. Ilana watched with her arms folded and a scowl on her face. "He's just being protective," Sam said quietly. He tapped his bruised cheekbone. "It's this he's bothered by. Not you. Not anything you did. Okay, Illy?"

She clutched her knees to her chest and nodded, but her face was red as a tomato.

Sam handed her the deck. "You deal. Three each, three in the pot, then one each until they're gone. Got it?"

"Yeah."

"Back in a minute."

He swung himself through the window into the attic, where Constantine stood over the desk the two of them shared, staring down at Sam's open gambling kit.

"Are you done?" Sam asked quietly. "There's a kid out there who thinks she just got yelled at."

"So I teach another kid how to be a sharper, send her out so she can come back with a busted-up face while I sit in here with this stupid leg, this stupid arm—"

"Con, knock it off, it isn't your fault. I let my guard down. I know how to—"

"I'm not teaching her, and neither are you." Constantine snatched a pencil off the desk and stalked past Sam to the window. "She can play with us, but no more stocks, no more palming cards, no more sharper tricks. No more talk from you about game logic or how to read a mark. Not until I'm well enough to keep an eye out for both of you. I can't stop you from playing, but I can stop her."

Then he flinched, probably realizing how loud his voice had gotten. He scrambled for the window and went sprawling across the shingles as his foot slid out from under him on the piles of cards Ilana had dealt. Sam followed as quickly as he could, but by the time he was on the roof again, Illy was gone, disappeared over the edge and back through her bedroom window.

❧

"So this is our crossroads, is it?" Bones mused.

He and Walker stood on a darkened street under the wooden walkway that formed the temporary spine of the bridge being constructed between the cities of New York and Brooklyn. Bones looked up at it, taking in the woven-steel cables and the giant stone arches catching the moonlight. Except for the oyster-shell eyes, he looked human now, although that same moonlight on his sallow face reflected just a bit unnaturally off its sandy surface.

"I don't know about this." Walker looked across at the docks of New York on the opposite shore. "I mean, the place is perfect, but . . ." He turned and surveyed the smoking chimneys of the city behind them. "There's only two of us."

"It's perfect," Bones retorted. "Obviously it's perfect." He didn't sound pleased, though.

"Obviously, but it's . . . *ambitious,*" Walker said quietly. "That's the point I wanted to make."

"Yes."

"You think we can do it?"

"He's expecting us to have made significant progress before he arrives," mumbled Bones. "He may understand if we need a bit more time before the taking of the place, but if we can't at least identify the pillars of the cities first, we're in trouble."

The other man didn't look like he entirely agreed. "No. If he arrives and we aren't ready—properly ready, I mean—Jack will never forgive us. Not after last time."

"I don't care about being forgiven," Bones said, his silvery eyes glinting as a ship under sail passed beneath the unfinished bridge. "There are worse things than not being forgiven."

"So this is our crossroads, is it?" Bones mused.

Walker nodded under his hat. "There are, indeed." He pulled a gold silk handkerchief from his pocket, tied it across his nose and mouth, and pulled his hat down low over his eyes. Then he backed into the shelter of a doorway. "Get on with it."

Bones nodded. He turned to the river and faced westward, toward the city of New York. Then he took a deep breath, and a breeze lifted itself off the water and stirred through the empty street.

He sucked mouthful after mouthful of air, and the breeze strengthened into a rough wind, carrying to him the dust and dirt, flotsam and jetsam, and random detritus from the city of New York across the river. Bones breathed it all in, eyes closed.

Walker shrank his lanky frame as far away from the wind as he could. Then the bald man turned eastward, facing into the depths of Brooklyn, and took in three more breaths, hauling the winds to him again. He stood at the center of a whirling vortex of dirt and debris, inhaling and tasting it, while his blue felt coat flapped around his ankles.

Then he opened his eyes and frowned. The air stilled.

"Brick dust and stone dust, riverside muck . . . coal and offal, paper and steel and sewage . . ." Bones spat on the street. "I cannot taste the veins of this city, or the one across the river. There is too much in the way, too many people, too much industry. We will have to find the pillars some other way."

Walker's mumbled curses were muffled by his handkerchief. He yanked it away from his face and snapped it once to shake off the dust. "I don't suppose you have any thoughts on what that other way might be."

Bones gave him a cold look. "Two days is not enough time to do it well. We would be lucky to find even one of the pillars in that time. We certainly can't take all ten." He looked up at the bridge again. "We'll have to do it by cinefaction, I suppose. If we can manage that, we can claim the city for him before he even arrives. Please tell me you have tinder."

Walker reached into his watch pocket and tugged loose the chain. At the end of the fob was a small, cylindrical box of punched tin. "Jack said not to use it if we had any other choice. The coal was small to begin with. He can't go hacking pieces off all the time."

"Well, we had other choices until you wasted two weeks on that idiot riverboat. Any other means of taking the place requires more time than we have."

"Well then, we'd better use it," Walker retorted, stowing the tinderbox back in his pocket.

"Yes, we'd better." The hard-packed sand that made up Bones's face shifted and his mouth cracked into a smile like a break in stone. "And I do like a good fire. We're going to need someone to perform the cinefaction. If we can't find the pillars, but we locate a conflagrationeer . . ." he mused. "Might be time to try digging up a few of Jack's old chums." Then he raised a hand thoughtfully to his chin. "Hang on."

Walker shot him a wary look.

"Speaking of old chums, before we resort to a taking-by-fire, why haven't we talked about going to see *him*?" Bones asked.

Walker's wary look shifted into a red-eyed glare. "Who." It wasn't a question, so he didn't wait for an answer. "Christophel."

"Obviously."

"Why would we talk about going to see him, Bones?" Walker bit the words off sharply.

"Oh, I don't know, remind me again why we got here with only a couple days to spare?" Bones's gray eyes hardened. "If there was ever a time for the two of you to put your grudges aside, this is it. We need to find ten people, fast. He probably knows exactly who we're looking for."

Walker adjusted his immaculate shirt cuffs. "Neither Basile Christophel nor I consider what you are referring to as a mere *grudge*."

"Your pigheaded mutual stupidity, then." Bones rolled his shoulders under the heavy coat, wincing at the grit. "He has . . . tools at his disposal. We should take advantage of them."

"I don't know what he has at his disposal, and neither do you. Nobody does." Walker folded his arms. "And I can't imagine, even if I did know, that it would make up for the fact that he's a conjure-thieving maniac without the sense to be afraid of anything."

"What's he got to be afraid of?"

"Those things he calls up." Now Walker rolled his shoulders, a motion more like a shudder than he would've liked to admit. "What *are* they, even?"

"As long as they do what he tells them, who cares?" Bones laughed, then coughed up sand. "As long as they get the job done, isn't that what matters?"

"You ever consider that maybe he might not think helping us is in his best interests? He *lives* here, after all, and he and Jack aren't precisely blood brothers." Walker shuddered again. "Blood. I had to get *that* image going in my head."

"He'll help us if we pay him," Bones said coldly. "And we can. As for whether he thinks giving the place to Jack is in his best interests, my guess is he won't care. It isn't as if he'll see it as Jack taking charge of *him*." The bald man regarded his colleague for a moment. Then he ripped one of the gold buttons from his coat and held it in his fist. When he opened his hand, a coin lay in his palm. "Shall we?"

Walker's red-rimmed eyes sharpened. "All right," he said casually.

"Call it, then," Bones said curtly. "But if you win, you'd better have an alternative plan." He balanced the coin on his thumb and flipped it.

"Tails," Walker murmured.

Both men watched it tumble over and over, catching the lights of Brooklyn as it rose and fell and bounced on the cobblestone street. Walker waited patiently until it came to rest, then crouched and swore.

"My, my," Bones said mildly. "Did I win?"

Walker plucked the coin from the street and handed it back to Bones. Then he sighed expansively. "Fine. Let's go see Doc Rawhead."

THREE

The Broken Land Hotel

S LOW MORNING."

"Telling me." Sam flipped a card and rolled his eyes. He sighed, leaned back with his hands folded behind his head, and watched gulls circling in Culver Plaza's cloudless sky. "Yours again. Thank God we're playing for shells."

"If we weren't, would I be winning?" Constantine threw down his hand, a very respectable three of a kind. "Hang on. How did you know I won that hand before I showed it?"

"Con, just because I'm not cheating you doesn't mean I don't know what I'm dealing you. It's hard to turn all the instincts off." Sam collected the cards and shuffled them. "This is just the kind of thing you're always taking credit for having taught me. Why so surprised?"

"Yeah, well, maybe I'm flattering myself about how much I actually had to do with it." The other boy stretched, looked around. "Where the heck is everybody?"

"It's Friday. They're still working." Sam dealt them each another five cards. "I won't have any decent business to speak of till this afternoon." He winced, remembering the previous afternoon's business and the bruise still darkening on his cheekbone.

"Yeah," Con said, eyeing the bruise. "That thing's just looking worse and worse."

"So not the rakishly handsome effect I was hoping for, then."

"Not so much, no." Constantine looked over his cards. "Did you see Illy this morning?"

"Nope." Normally Ilana was up early with her mother, starting the day's baking, the first few batches of which were then delivered to a couple of stalls down on Culver Plaza. "She'd already gone by the time I got up."

"Meaning not only is she avoiding us, she's angry enough to actually wake up even earlier to do it."

"Meaning she's really angry," Sam confirmed. He raised his eyes from his hand and took a long look around the plaza.

"Any sign of him?" Constantine asked.

"The sharper from yesterday? No." Sam kept expecting the fellow to appear at any moment, though. He still didn't quite understand what had happened the day before: the unbelievable, invisible way in which the man had cheated, the way he'd almost seemed to be in two places at once when he'd thrown those two punches . . . it was hard to let the incident go just yet.

"Hey." Constantine lifted his head and looked around, too. "You hear that?"

Sam roused himself out of his thoughts and listened. It took a moment, but then he caught it, threading its way through the pound and flow of the surf: the sound of guitar music. Not the kind of music you heard in the saloons, though. This was something totally different.

Sam scooped the cards into a pile and packed them into his kit. "Come on."

"Where?"

With shoes slung over their shoulders by knotted laces, the boys followed the faint sound along the beach: music that rose and crested, crashed, slid, clattered and tumbled. No wonder Sam had missed it at first. It blended with the sounds of the ocean, mimicking the motion of a wave reaching and receding, tumbling stones and sand and shells and making them dance in water that glittered in the sunlight.

By the time they tracked the music to an old boat-rental pavilion, Sam knew who they were going to find, although he had no idea what made him so sure.

The guitar player was perched on an overturned rowboat, trousers rolled up so he could sit with his feet in the water as it came and went. He looked up as the boys approached, and his face broke into a wide grin.

"Mornin', Sam," said Tom Guyot.

Sam grinned back and introduced Constantine. "We heard you playing down the beach, Mr. Guyot. That's some music."

The old man beamed. "Glad you approve. Tom'll do, though. No need to stand on ceremony." He looked up at the sun. "Good thing you two came along just then. I think I might have lost track of the time."

"You got somewhere to be?" Sam asked.

Tom stood and waded onto dry sand, slinging his guitar over his shoulder. "If you can believe it, I'm meant to be meeting someone for a meal. I don't suppose you know the fastest way to get to the Broken Land Hotel, do you?"

"Sure." Sam shrugged. "I'll show you."

The Broken Land had gotten its name in an act of bad translation, something to do with the way the Dutch name that had
become "Brooklyn" sounded a lot like the Dutch translation for
the local Indians' name for Long Island. The builder of the hotel knew this, but he didn't much care. He heard the phrase and
liked it, and after he'd managed to close the dozen or so dubious
deals with the town of Gravesend that had given him the lot out
beyond West Brighton at the far east end of Coney Island, he
constructed himself a hotel worthy of the name. *His* name was
Anders Ganz, and the hotel was only the second building he'd
ever designed. The other one was a mansion halfway across the
country that sat half-hidden in a grove of oaks, but that had been
a long, long time ago.

The hotel was built on boggy ground, bolstered in the
Venetian manner by vertical wooden pilings sunk into the muck.
The whole time it was going up, the Gravesenders placed bets on
how long it would survive before it tumbled into the sea. The
building didn't look sensible or even stable, which might have
been forgivable if it had managed to look fashionable. But the
builder was even less concerned about the styles of the day than
he was about the provenance of the name he'd picked.

The Broken Land was a rambling hodgepodge of architec-
ture. The main building rose in tall chateau-style towers and
spires, with sprawling wings of Tudoresque timber framing
perched on terra-cotta brickwork and topped by French-inspired
mansard roofs and square towers outflung like the arms of a
bizarre and spiny starfish. There were parapets and carved-brick
chimneys, Italianate porches and English baroque domes. Its

wooden-sided Carpenter Gothic bathhouses looked like tiny country churches. There was an iron-and-glass bandstand at the center of the circular drive and another on the great lawn fronting the sea, the acoustics of which were said to have driven a few bandleaders insane.

It was a monstrosity, and only if you let your eyes go slightly out of focus when you looked at it did it coalesce into a rational-seeming whole. But it had a kind of majesty about it.

Constantine, whose leg was bothering him, had decided to stay behind, and the closer Sam got to the hotel, the more out of place he felt. "Your friend's definitely expecting you?" he asked as he and Tom hiked up the circular drive toward the wide pink marble steps to the lobby.

He'd never been inside any of the big hotels, but it hardly seemed likely they'd have anything polite to say to a teenage card sharp and a man who . . . well, who looked like Tom did. He didn't precisely look like a tramp, but he wasn't what most of the highbrow types at the east end would figure for a productive member of society. Not that much of anybody who actually lived or worked in the western parts of Coney Island looked like a productive member of society either, Sam had to admit. Himself included.

"More nervous you look, the less people figure you belong," Tom said. "And yes, for the fifth time, Ambrose is expecting us."

Tom ambled up the stairs, leaning on his cane, and smiled broadly at the doorman. The doorman's face froze at first, furrowing into a scowl, but then it warmed. He grinned and tapped the brim of his hat as he pulled the door open. Tom returned the salute and strolled inside.

Sam stumbled as he followed. It was just the same as with the sharper back on Culver Plaza yesterday. Rightly or wrongly, Sam knew, the doorman's first impulse had been disapproval, just as the sharper's initial impulse must've been to pound Tom into dust. No matter what people said about the evils of slavery now, they generally weren't any nicer to black folks than they were to immigrants. And even though Sam had been born in Brooklyn, he looked Italian enough to know a little about that.

But something happened when Tom looked at people. It happened in the lobby, too. Tom didn't sweep across the floor like the rich folks did, as if they thought they were entitled to the bowing and scraping of the hotel workers and the doffing of every hat in the room. He walked just the same way he'd walked in West Brighton, and yet the room reacted as if he had suddenly grown tall and straight and young and . . . and *white* instead of old and bent and black.

"It's a mystery," Tom said agreeably, as if Sam had been thinking out loud all that time. "But then again, I'm a guest here."

Sam stumbled. "You're a . . . what?"

"I know. Seems awful strange, doesn't it?"

Sam caught himself agreeing before he managed to think about how insulting that would seem, but Tom only laughed. "No offense taken. Look." The old man pointed to a placard on a stand in the middle of the atrium. WELCOME, SOLDIERS OF RESACA. "I gather the owner of the hotel had family on both sides. Just like a lot of folks did."

Now that he was looking, Sam realized there were a number of men and even a few women in the atrium who didn't look like the typical wildly rich guests he was used to seeing at this end of the island. Some wore wild roses in their lapels, and some wore little sprigs of briar, but it wasn't really what they wore that set them apart. There was a sort of . . . well, a *haunted* quality about them, and immediately Sam decided that these must be some of the soldiers of Resaca. With their drawn faces and eyes that appeared sad even when they smiled, they looked like people who had seen some terrible things in their lives.

In fact, they sort of looked like they might still be seeing them.

The blond man named Ambrose sat in the dining room, poring over a newspaper at a table beside a huge window overlooking the waterfront. "There's your friend," Sam said, pointing. "Guess I'll head back."

Tom patted his shoulder. "How about you join us, Sam? You eaten today?"

Sam hadn't, and before he could protest, he found himself sitting between Tom and the newspaperman named Ambrose, feeling very self-conscious as a jacket-and-tie-clad waiter appeared out of nowhere and began depositing a large breakfast on the table before him. Dishes steamed as their domed silver covers were removed. On a cart beside the table a gleaming samovar promised coffee. In each polished surface, Sam saw his face reflected with a look of utter confusion and insecurity. How had he wound up sitting here?

"It's Sam, isn't it?" Ambrose passed him a cup of coffee. "Chat if you like, relax if you don't. Eat, either way. And quit looking like you snuck in under somebody's coat. Neither of us get meals like this usually either, but here we are. You're among friends, and we're glad to have you with us."

"Which is saying a lot," Tom added, "because Ambrose generally isn't what you'd call the warm and friendly type on any given calendar day."

"Very true," Ambrose agreed, taking a flask from his pocket and dosing his coffee with it.

"Thank you, then." Sam picked up the cup Ambrose had offered him, then eyed the creamer and sugar bowl that stood just out of reach. He hesitated. "Can I—could I trouble you for the cream and sugar, sir?"

As he stirred in a scandalous number of sugar lumps, Sam began to relax. He let his gaze wander past the table and across the lawn that stretched between the hotel and the beach.

A gilded cart trundled along one of the garden paths, drawn by a small gray pony and glittering in the morning sun. An old Chinese man in a red silk robe and cap with a long, thin braid hanging down his back led the pony by its halter. There was a name painted on the side of the cart under the gingerbread of the eaves, and a girl perched on the roof.

Her hands were full of fire.

"By God," Ambrose said, following Sam's stare. "Is that the Fata Morgana Company? What on earth are the odds, Burns and Liao turning up here?"

Tom must have replied, but Sam paid no attention to the men at his table, only to the girl outside. There were details he would remember later: her long, black hair falling out from under a newsboy's cap, the name on the cart and the motto painted below it (*Fata Morgana*: *Arte et Marte*), the color of the sparks flying from her palms (blue, a shade only a touch lighter than the water behind her), the fact that they must have been fireworks of some kind and that she appeared to be trying to make them stop.

Just then, however, all that registered was that she was a girl, and there was a world of fire under her fingertips, and she wasn't afraid.

Tom tapped Sam on the shoulder and slid a handbill onto the table in front of him.

The Broken Land Hotel

Presents

FOR A LIMITED ENGAGEMENT OF THREE DAYS ONLY

THE *WORLD-FAMOUS*

FATA MORGANA FIREWORKS COMPANY!

PURVEYORS AND DISPLAYERS OF
WORKS OF CONFLAGRATIONARY ARTISTRY

Combining

Beauty & Legend, History & Science

In a Show of Magical Effects!

See

THE DESTRUCTION OF ATLANTIS
As It Sinks Below an Incendiary Volcanic Sea!

Witness

THE SECOND SIEGE OF CONSTANTINOPLE

Including an Incredible Re-Creation of the Byzantines'
MIRACULOUS GREEK FIRE!

MADE POSSIBLE BY THE SCHOLARSHIP AND ANCIENT
CRAFT OF *THE MYSTERIOUS PROFESSOR*

LIAO,

Master of Methods,

AND HIS PROTÉGÉE,

XIAOMING,

GIRL PRODIGY OF ALL THINGS PYROTECHNIC!

THIS WEEKEND ONLY, AT NIGHTFALL

THE FATA MORGANA FIREWORKS COMPANY
Arte et Marte!

"Perhaps you'd like to come back this evening for the proper show," Ambrose suggested.

Sam fumbled as he tried to give the handbill back. "Oh, I—"

"As my guest, of course."

"Ought to warn you that Ambrose never has anyone's best interests at heart when it seems like he's doing something nice,"

Tom cut in mildly. "Probably just wants to see how much of his paper's expense money he can burn through in a week."

"I *am* just being nice." The journalist put on an offended face. "He's a *boy*. Boys like fireworks. And girls. And probably girls who are fireworkers, especially. Although, admittedly, helping anyone get introduced to a creature of the female persuasion is always a mean-spirited thing to do."

Tom gave Sam a stern look and a little wag of his finger. "You've been warned."

If Jin had known that anyone watching her pass fire from one hand to the other was thinking it was in some way romantic, she would've laughed. If, that is, it also would have occurred to her to stop concentrating on the fire long enough to laugh —and that *never* would have occurred to her. She was too busy trying to keep the entire wagon and its contents from exploding. That, and cursing Mr. Burns for nearly getting them all killed. He would deny it, but she was sure he'd started these fireworks' fuses burning down by smoking carelessly in the wagon. Again.

Of course, until Mr. Burns finished passing crackers with spitting fuses up through the vent in the roof, all things were still possible, including a fiery death.

Jin reached down into the wagon so the owner of the Fata Morgana Fireworks Company could fill her palms with fuse-tipped cylinders. She ground her teeth together and forced herself to hold her hands immobile while he placed the explosives carefully between her fingers with sparking fuses pointing out to keep them from burning her.

As soon as she had four in each hand, Jin straightened and flung the fireworks skyward, where they burst into blue chrysanthemums. Then she knelt and reached back into the wagon for more. It was the only way she could think to get rid of them without revealing how close she and her company were coming to blowing themselves up.

"Last batch," Mr. Burns said, loading her up again. He winced each time he had to touch one of the crackers, which made Jin want to throttle him all the more.

"Good thing," she muttered. By now, the fuses were almost burned down to nothing, and she barely got them out of the wagon in time. The fireworks went off in the air less than a second after she'd let go of them.

The hotel guests that had gathered on the broad front lawn gave a collective murmur of delight and broke into applause. Jin forced a smile and bowed, but behind her lips her teeth were clenched painfully. What she'd just done might've looked like pure spectacle rather than the desperate move it had been, but that last batch had *burned*.

"Jin!" Burns hissed from below. She bowed again and barely got her fingers around the crackers he shoved into her hands, their fuses — good God — *completely* spent.

Jin stifled a scream, shot upright, and somehow managed to launch them far enough away that all she felt beyond the burn in her palms was a little flurry of pinpricks across her cheeks. Then, because she was about to lose her balance anyway, she dropped through the vent into the wagon.

She was prepared for it to hurt, and it did — the old pain in her feet flaring into a red bloom that almost made her forget about the sting in her hands. Almost, but not quite. She dusted herself off and rounded on Mr. Burns, singed hands on her hips.

Outside, the impromptu audience was still applauding what they thought they'd seen: a pretty Chinese girl throwing live fireworks from the roof of a moving wagon; a grand spectacle of entertainment rather than a barely contained pyrotechnical debacle.

Mr. Burns pushed his wire-rimmed spectacles up on the bridge of his nose and gave her a look that he probably meant to be sheepish.

"Again?" Jin snarled.

"Nope, nope, nope," Burns protested. "Not me. Didn't do it. I quit."

Jin narrowed her eyes and sniffed the air. "If you think I can't tell the difference between tobacco smoke and gunpowder, you're mad." She turned, eyed the crates along the wall behind her, bent, and there it was. She straightened with the half-smoked cigar in between her finger and thumb. "All it takes is a bit of smolder to meet a few loose grains of . . . of—" She waved one arm to encompass the entire wagon. "It would be hard to find something in here that *isn't* flammable, which is why you may not smoke in the wagon!"

Burns leaned in and eyed the cigar as if it were an exotic insect. "Well, that is *astonishing*."

"Astonishing," Jin muttered. "When you say you *quit*—"

"Well, I'm in the *process* of quitting, I should have said."

"Does your attempt at quitting by any chance involve incinerating us all?"

The wagon rolled to a stop. Mr. Burns reached out, plucked

the cigar from Jin's fingers, and stuffed it in his pocket as the door behind her opened and the old Chinese man who'd been leading the pony poked his head inside. He jabbed a long-nailed index finger at Mr. Burns. "No smoking in the wagon, *guizi!*"

Guizi: devil. It was Uncle Liao's favorite term for Mr. Burns, although sometimes he mixed it up with *yang guizi*—western devil, if he wanted to allude to Mr. Burns's white European heritage—and occasionally, when he was feeling less annoyed than usual, *laowai*, which just meant old outsider. Somehow it never seemed to occur to Liao—or at least, it seemed not to bother him—that, in the world outside the wagon, he and Jin were the outsiders.

"You know," Burns said calmly, "every now and then we all forget that I own this company."

The old man shoved past him and reached for Jin's hands. "How bad are they?"

"*Hai hao*." She closed her fingers over her burned palms. "I'm fine, Uncle Liao."

"You need those hands for the display tonight." Liao closed his eyes and took a long, deep breath. "If the *yang guizi* had any conscience, he would already have gone for the burn cream," he muttered with forced patience.

Mr. Burns winced and practically sprinted across the wagon for the medical kit. Liao ignored him. "You did well, Xiao Jin. Made crisis look like ballet." The old man tapped her clenched fingers. "Come now, firefly."

Reluctantly she allowed him to examine the damage. Mr. Burns hovered over her shoulder. "I'm sorry, Jin. I really am."

"She's fine," Liao barked, snatching the pot of medicinal

cream from him. "She says she's fine, so she's fine." Despite her annoyance, Jin caught Mr. Burns's eye and grinned as Liao rubbed medicine into her fingers, muttering under his breath, "Therefore even the sage treats some things as difficult."

Then: "What are you standing there for? Get the poor girl some bandages!" and Burns was springing across to the medicine kit again and Liao was giving her one of those little nods he probably thought were comforting.

They made for a strange family, but they were family nonetheless.

Liao had brought the wagon to a halt out of view of the strolling vacationers, behind a row of ornamental bushes that hid the hotel's livery stables. Once Jin's hands were properly bandaged, the three of them filed out into the light to survey the landscape.

"Where are we setting up for the display?" Mr. Burns asked.

"We?" Liao snapped. He narrowed his eyes and took another one of those long, even breaths. Jin stifled a smile; the breathing exercises were real, but when he did them like this, making a production of regaining his calm, it was like a polite way of rolling his eyes. Rolling his eyes, or maybe whacking Mr. Burns in the back of the head. "You think we're going to let *you* anywhere near anything?" He turned to Jin. "You choose."

Jin tried to keep the pride off her face as she turned for a look around. Picking the spot where they set off the display was a critical part of the process. Liao had never let her decide before. "It would be nice to set them so they'll detonate over the water," she mused. "Good reflections."

She followed the beach with her eyes until she found a

sheltered place a short distance to the east, between the Broken Land's two piers. "What about there? No one would see much of what we were doing. Maybe the hotel can move some of those potted trees over and give us a little more cover."

Liao answered by way of a grunt. He had about fifty ways of making noises that weren't quite words yet conveyed meanings, and this was the one that Jin thought of as his pleased-but-trying-not-to-show-it grunt. "Perhaps the owner of the company should see the hotel staff about that."

Mr. Burns sighed and shook his head. "Perhaps I should." He turned to Jin, smoothing down his dark gray hair. "Tie straight?"

"Who cares?" Liao snapped.

"Yes." Jin laughed.

Mr. Burns gave an exaggerated sigh and headed for the hotel. "Time to go to work, firefly," Uncle Liao said, and Jin felt her heart swell the way it only did when it was time to make beautiful things out of explosives.

≫ FOUR ≪

The Conjure Thief

IT WAS DAYTIME, so the town of Red Hook was merely dirty, busy, and loud; seedy, rather than downright squalid. Walker and Bones strolled along the wharves, keeping more or less out of the way of stevedores, sailors, and merchants. In general, the denizens of the port ignored them anyway, despite Walker's natty gambler's getup and Bones's unseasonable felt coat. Most had an honest day's work to do and not enough day in which to do it. Most, but not all.

The ones who did pay the two men notice made up a pretty good cross-section of the local lowlife: a few pickpockets and thieves, a few ladies of questionable intent, a few swindlers trying to pick up marks with shell games. Walker and Bones ignored them. Well, Bones ignored them, despite a few pointed glances at the carpetbag he carried. Walker kept an eye out for anyone who appeared too interested. Once or twice before, someone had tried to pick his pocket and he had seen to it that those would-be pickpockets had lost fingers in the process. He could never decide whether he found these encounters more amusing or frustrating. Bloodstains were hard to get out of the expensive suits he favored.

Past a row of brick warehouses Walker and Bones turned

inland. They picked their way along the ruptured path of cobble-stones that paved the narrow street, stepping over foul puddles of standing water, decomposing crates whose contents had long ago turned to sludge, the occasional scattering of rotted vegetable bits, rats, and the cats streaking after them.

Three blocks in, the shadows held everything but a thin, crooked strip of sky directly overhead. The warehouses gave way to row houses, leaning shanties that lined the cobblestone way. Faces peered out of begrimed windows overlooking the street. Walker and Bones halted where the street became a dead end, and looked up at the building that blocked their path.

It was an old, smoke-stained, gray stone structure with a steeple. It had once been a church, but now its windows were covered over with arches of red brick, all except for the triangle of multicolored glass over the heavy wooden doors. In the mid-day dark of the alley, the stained glass shone with golden light. If not for the grimness of the surroundings, that light might've seemed welcoming.

The name of the church, which had once been carved on the stone over the doors, had long ago been defaced. It had been chipped away to form a new surface for a single word: *Christophel.*

Walker examined the muck on one of his expensive shoes, sighed, climbed the damp stone stairs to the entrance, raised a fist, and pounded on the wood. "There's a bell," Bones observed.

Walker cast a scowl over his shoulder. Then he banged again, harder. "High Walker and Bones for Basile Christophel," he called.

"Well, imagine that," spoke a cultured voice from the open

end of the street. "Visitors from the road. I can't tell you how that delights me."

The approaching man wore his beard in a neatly trimmed V. He was dressed even more sharply than Walker, if such a thing was possible. The fabric of his summer suit gleamed softly, expensively, in the meager light. His hat had been freshly brushed, and his shoes even wore the dirt they were collecting well. The walking stick that casually swept the occasional bits of debris out of his way was made of some heavily burnished wood, and the glint of brass shone from between olive-skinned fingers.

"Basile," Bones said.

"Always a pleasure, Mr. Bones," Basile Christophel said, extending his hand. "Although it never stops being strange, shaking a hand of dust and grit." He glanced over Bones's shoulder at Walker. "Redgore. Or, wait. You go by the other name these days. What was it? Some bindery term, I seem to remember."

"Walker is fine," Walker said coldly. "Were you planning to invite us in?"

Christophel smiled. "Sure thing, friends." He swept past Bones and up the stairs to where Walker stood, arms folded. "Come inside."

"And remind me again why I want to help Jack Hellcoal. In fact, remind me again why *you* want to help him."

Inside the bricked-up church, Basile Christophel leaned back in an overstuffed chair and regarded Walker and Bones over an engraved tea service. Walker stared back across his untouched cup. Bones watched the two of them with a gritty expression that was something akin to amusement.

"You want to help him because this city's going to be his regardless," Walker said, his pointed fingernails scraping the tabletop on either side of his cup and saucer.

"I can't help but notice you ignored my second question, but we'll let that slide for the moment." Christophel showed his teeth. It wasn't quite a smile. "So this place is going to be Jack's one way or the other? I don't believe you'd be here if you really thought that was the case."

"Look for yourself. Jack's coming and you know it." Walker returned the grin, showing not one but *two* rows of teeth, one behind the other. "If it was up to me, we wouldn't be here either way," he continued, "but this softheaded idiot thought you'd want to be part of it, so here we are."

"Ah. Well, isn't that just perfectly politic of you." He tapped his fingers on his knees. "So what is it, exactly, that you need from me?"

"We don't *need*—"

Christophel sighed and turned to Bones. "What do you need, Bones?"

Bones ignored Walker's look of annoyance. "There are several ways to take a town. The best one is to take the pillars, the ones that make a place more than just a cluster of folk by a road. The pillars of a city are the people who hold the place together, and carry it through history."

Christophel's eyes flickered. "Who?"

"You're the local," Walker said. "You tell us. That's why we're—"

"Each city has five," Bones interrupted, "and they shift from generation to generation. There is always a keeper of sanctuary, a keeper of lore, and a smith. The other two could be anyone."

Christophel nodded slowly. "I see. And when you say the best way is to *take* them . . . ?"

"It's what you think. Win them to our cause or remove them by force, and the town loses its center. Then we replace them with pillars of our own."

"And you don't know who you're looking for."

"There are other ways to do it," Walker snapped.

"But your colleague says this is the *best* way," Christophel retorted, "which is why you came to me, so perhaps you could stop acting as if I somehow dragged you here against your will. I'm not passing judgment. I just want to understand the situation."

"We were hoping you might have some insight into who we're looking for," Bones said. "Walker's right—there are other ways to do it, and we're prepared to change our strategy if necessary. But yes, we would prefer this method."

Christophel picked up his cup and took a thoughtful sip. "Well, off the top of my head, no, I don't suppose I know who these pillars are. Let me think about it for a couple of days. Maybe I can puzzle it out. There are . . . people I could ask."

Walker stood up with a growl of frustration and stalked a few paces away. Bones shook his head. "Excuse my colleague, but we have two days in which to do this before Jack arrives. He will be expecting more progress than that. We don't have time to wait." He put sallow hands on the table and stood. "We thank you for your time, Basile."

Christophel regarded him for a moment. "There is a faster way, Mr. Bones."

A few yards away, Walker stiffened. Bones paused as he pushed his chair under the table. "A faster way to do what, exactly?"

"To find the pillars. It could be done as quickly as the end of the day, if you are willing to let them know you're here."

"Why would we do that?" Walker asked stiffly. "To say nothing of how we *could* do that, when we have no idea who they are or how to find them."

"How you make your presence—and by extension, Jack's —known in Brooklyn and New York is up to you. But for my purposes, all you'd have to do is that: make your presence known, and visibly enough to get the pillars of the cities talking about you. Not everyone, mind you. You can't just go on a rampage, or the system won't work. You need to bring yourselves to the attention of your targets, or at least to the kind of people who are likely to get word to them."

"Well, that sounds like no difficulty at all," Walker said sarcastically.

"When you say *system*," Bones interrupted, "what, precisely, are you talking about?"

"What you need," Christophel said slowly, "is a way to search the city quickly. I have . . . things at my disposal that are capable of that. You could think of them as something akin to spies, if you like. But they have a very specific sort of logic— they aren't like human spies who can make decisions about what kind of information is useful and what kind isn't. They need to be told very precisely what to look for, what to listen for. If I set them to listening for certain phrases, certain conversations that you think your pillars would be likely to have, whenever my spies hear any of those conversations or phrases, they'll report back."

"We don't know what they talk about," Walker protested. "We don't even know if they talk to each other."

"But if there was a threat to the city, they'd talk—at least about that threat, wouldn't they?"

"How the hell should *I* know what they'd do?"

"Yes," Bones said. "They would. That's why they exist, to protect the city."

Christophel nodded. "So you get them talking about something we can predict and listen for. *You*."

"But then they know about us," Walker argued.

"But they wouldn't know that you knew about *them*."

Bones was nodding. "This makes sense to me. Then what?"

"What you do with the information is up to you. I'm talking about an engine for searching for the people you need to find, nothing more."

"And how quickly did you say this could work?"

Christophel smiled grimly. "That depends on how quickly you manage to get the right people talking."

Bones smiled back, his oyster-shell eyes glinting. "Does it, now? Well, I'm sold. Walker?"

"What are they?" All of the spite had gone out of Walker's voice. Now he just sounded wary. "This engine, your spies? How is it done? What stolen conjury makes it work?"

"Aha! *Il m'accuse!*" Christophel stabbed a finger at Walker. "You've been waiting all afternoon to bring that up, haven't you, you malicious bastard?"

"Folks steal what they don't know how to build on their

own," Walker said evenly. "You and I have never gotten along, that's true, but all anger aside, what you're describing, these spies of yours . . . this sounds like exactly the sort of thing your kind aren't supposed to be able to do anymore." He looked at Bones. "You don't know this man like I do. We need to be sure he can control what he calls."

"My kind," Christophel repeated, his voice deadly.

Bones put up a hand. "No offense intended, I'm sure. It's a fair point, I suppose. I can't say I particularly care, so long as the thing gets done, but it's a fair point."

"Well. Since time is of the essence"—Christophel rose from his chair—"how about I just go ahead and show you?"

FIVE

The Praxis

I ONCE STUDIED under a great practitioner of conjure," Christophel told Walker and Bones. "It took ages to win her trust, ages more to win her respect. After that, it took a much shorter time to realize that what she could do was a mere shadow of what I sought, and shorter still for her to tell me that what I wanted to learn was mad, impossible, and probably evil. Which, I think you'll agree, was a bit suspect coming from a woman who had ways of killing with candles and coconuts, and charged thirty-five dollars for the service. Surely you can see why I had to kill her after that."

Christophel had led Walker and Bones from the chapel of the former church through a door behind the altar, and now they followed him down a flight of flagstone stairs. Neither responded; they were too busy trying not to slip on the damp stone under their feet.

"I killed her because, given the way she felt about my intentions, she almost certainly would've tried to kill me if I didn't," Christophel continued. "She would've seen it as a moral necessity."

Walker gave a short laugh. "Don't tell me you were worried about some *human* conjuror doing you damage."

Christophel shrugged. "The point is, I didn't kill her for her art. What you say was stolen was given freely. I learned every piece fair and square, just like every practitioner learns. In any case, what I do now isn't conjury. I may have built it on the foundation of what I learned from the woman I killed, but I speak to creatures the conjure doctors know nothing of, and I can do things they could barely imagine."

He reached a door at the bottom of the stairs and turned a key already in the lock. "What I do is something completely new, completely my own. I call it *praxis*."

He pushed open the door to reveal a room full of glass jars twinkling in the light of scores of lit candles: containers of powders, metal filings, fibrous bulbs and roots, glittering mounds of salt, snakeskins, the occasional liquid something. There were a few pieces of furniture holding it all up: a barrel, a rolltop desk, and a huge cabinet of the kind used to sort mail. This cabinet was full of little pigeonholes stuffed with dried roots, sheets of paper, envelopes, inkwells, jars of pins and tacks and nails, bowls of keys, bundles of freshly made candles in every conceivable color, tufts of feathers, bottles of alcohol and vinegar and patent perfumes, balls of string, assorted bits of crockery, jawbones. Potted plants and strings of onions and garlic hung from the rafters. The candles smelled faintly of animal fat, and their flickering flames trailed thick gray lines of smoke toward the ceiling.

In the center of it all was a table. It had been scrubbed smooth as marble, but there were still dark stains and burn marks visible on the surface.

Christophel took a narrow sheet of parchment and a fountain pen from the desk and stood in front of the table. He handed

He pushed open the door to reveal a room full of glass
jars twinkling in the light of scores of lit candles.

the pen to Walker. "Write everything you want my spies to listen for on this page and give it back to me."

Jack Hellcoal. Pillars of the City. Cinefaction. Walker frowned as he wrote, adding the phrase *by blood, by naming, and by fire,* and looked at Bones. "What else do you figure?"

"Looks good to me."

Walker passed the page across the table. Christophel glanced over the list and nodded. "Very good." He stared at it for a moment more, then set it aside. From the barrel next to the desk he pulled out a large roll of paper. "Next part takes tallow," he said, unrolling the paper to reveal a map of Brooklyn, Long Island, and New York. "Lots of it. Bring candles and pour the melt over the map."

Walker and Bones took burning tapers of all different colors from the sconces and candlesticks scattered around the room and held them so that the tallow dripped down. Christophel spread the mixture across the map with his palms, flattening it and securing it to the tabletop. Candle by candle, they coated the table.

At last, Christophel peeled the residue from his left palm. "Beeswax for Mass, tallow for this work." He looked at Walker. "Where's that fancy smokes case you used to carry?" Walker put a hand protectively to his jacket pocket. The conjuror chuckled. "I don't want the case, Walker. What've you got inside it these days?"

"Kentucky cheroots. Why?"

"Let me have one."

Walker produced his case, and handed Christophel one of the cheroots. He took the parchment with Walker's list of words and wrapped it around the little cigar. Then he lit and smoked them both almost completely down to ash in a single, impossibly long pull. He let the ash crumble into a saucer. After that, Christophel dropped the smoldering end into his still-coated right hand, peeled the tallow from his palm, and folded it around the remains of the cheroot. He placed the odd little parcel in the center of the table.

Inside the tallow envelope, the red butt of the cigar glowed for a moment, threatening to melt through its enclosure, then died.

"Hoodoo conjurors do much of their work through the offices of spirits," Christophel said as he watched the embers go out. "When a spirit does a conjure doctor's bidding, it's because the doctor has a relationship with the spirit. He's asked for the spirit's good graces and, having received them, can bid that spirit to do good works or bad, so long as the bidding's done with complete faith. Mr. Bones, be so kind as to bring me that purple candle by your elbow."

Christophel took another thin china saucer from one of the pigeonholes in the cabinet and two bottles from another. "But faith is a slippery thing. I never did like the idea of trusting in spirits that way. Mr. Walker, you should find a feathered monstrosity of a hat somewhere on the desk over there that I believe has a hatpin stuck through it. I need the hatpin."

Walker retrieved the pin, and he and Bones looked on as Christophel uncorked the bottles and poured liquid from each onto the dish. The smells made them easy to identify: vinegar and bitters.

"Hatpin, please," Christophel said to Walker, and rolled it in the vinegar-and-bitters mixture. "What I wanted was something I could control completely, something with a logic that would make its workings perfectly predictable. Candle, please."

"Is there such a thing?" Bones asked, handing him the purple taper. "Seems rather a lot to ask of anyone or anything, that kind of obedience."

Christophel ran the length of the pin through the candle flame, making it spark and sputter. "There's a trick to it, of course," he replied. "The key that sets praxis apart from conjury. The thing, Walker, that enables *my kind* to work this sort of art."

He circled the table, drawing jagged boundaries in the tallow surface with the hatpin, boundaries that slowly resolved themselves into a rough outline of the map beneath. "The key is not to let the daemon know it's being asked."

"The demon?" Bones demanded. "You're talking about messing with demons? Are you utterly mad?"

Christophel shook his head. "These are not the sort of thing you mean when you use the word."

"I told you," Walker said tightly to Bones. "I warned you."

"Stop behaving like children," Christophel snapped. He pointed the pin at Walker. "You're one of the last of the race of the High Walkers. He's a goddamn . . . what the hell *are* you, anyway, Bones? And I've been roaming this earth since before the walls of Pandemonium were built. We aren't humans, afraid of our shadows."

The pin shook in Christophel's hand, but neither Walker nor Bones noticed. Something else was happening to the conjuror. Across his brow, beads of dampness, like sweat, had begun to form. Only it wasn't sweat. The beads were watery red.

"It's a fair question," Bones said softly, staring at the red droplets on Christophel's skin.

"Do you know who I *am?*" Christophel snarled. A large drop slid down his face, leaving a crimson line between his eyes and down his nose. "*Messing* with daemons? I *command* daemons! And I have the right, because I figured out how. I answer to myself and no one else, no matter how anyone tries to bind my *kind*."

"We know who you are, Basile," Walker said quickly as another runnel of bloody sweat trickled from Christophel's temple to the corner of his mouth.

Christophel's tongue darted out, tasted the drop. Abruptly, he stilled. "Blast and damn," he muttered, yanking a handkerchief from his pocket. He ran it over his face and neck, mopping the blood away. Then he turned to the desk and rifled through the drawers until he found a mirror and examined the slick of red still popping up across his skin.

"Damn, damn, damn." He blotted his face again and examined the coppery stain around his collar. When he spoke next, his voice was tightly controlled. "Excuse me for a moment, gentlemen. I would rather not let this stain set."

When Basile Christophel's footsteps on the stone stairs had faded from earshot, Walker turned to Bones and folded his arms. "And that, Bones, is why, behind his evil, evil back, we call him Doc Rawhead."

"It isn't possible," Bones mused. "I really thought you were overstating the matter."

"Overstating which bit, exactly?" Walker asked casually. "The sweating blood bit, or the bit about calling up . . . whatever it is he's going to call up?"

"Either. Both." Bones put the plum-colored candle back into its sconce and peered up the stairs after Christophel. "The other part, too. What he said about having been roaming since before Pandemonium, about having the right?"

"Are you asking what he meant, or whether or not he was lying about it?"

"I know what he *meant*. You never told me that part. Is it true?"

"I never told you because I only suspected it. Until now. He rather completely admitted to it." Walker took a deep breath. "Yes. Despite how twisted it seems, yes. Basile Christophel's a jumper."

Quick footsteps sounded on the stairs. Christophel appeared in the doorway wearing a crisp new shirt, a thin scarlet sheen just barely visible across his nose and cheekbones. He regarded Walker and Bones calmly. "So, you fellows want to finish this or not?"

The pin was redressed with vinegar and bitters, and Christophel ran it through the candle flame again. He scratched four letters into the surface of the tallow packet holding the cheroot ash at the center of the table: *INIT*.

The second he finished crossing the *T*, the little packet began to move. "Let the deal go down," Christophel said as he poked the hatpin into the table so that it stood upright a few inches away.

"Now watch," he whispered.

The letters took on a cold green glow, but they were only

legible for a moment before the shifting of the multicolored tallow stretched them beyond recognition. The packet arched upward, curved into itself, uncurled, twitched, and writhed, and suddenly what had been a small, amorphous thing was now a hunched but recognizably human form. Its arms reached for the head of the hatpin, and leaning on it like a cane, the form slowly unbent itself.

It stood nearly two feet tall. The many colors of its skin had mixed into a fairly uniform, oily shade of gray, and it was now stretched so thin that it was almost transparent, like blown glass. Otherwise, it looked like something fashioned from clay by a child, human-shaped in the sense that it had two legs, two arms, and a head. The hands that gripped the hat-pin were fingerless mittens. It didn't seem to have feet—the legs disappeared into the layer of fatty tallow coating the table, as if it was wading in shallow water that came up to its ankles.

Inside the transparent head, a dull, uneven glow came to life: the stub of the cheroot. On the creature's forehead, the four letters Christophel had scratched into the packet were neat and legible again, black against the gray skin.

Walker opened his mouth, but Christophel raised a hand to silence him. In his other hand the conjuror held the saucer of ash. He watched the tallow creature intently.

After a moment, another detail appeared on its head: a wide mouth. It opened, and the thing began to speak. The sounds were indistinct mutterings at first.

Then it spoke a single audible word. "Root," it mumbled.

"Root. *Root.*" Each repetition of the word made the voice stronger, until at last its first sentence emerged. "I am the root," it said experimentally.

The creature paused, turned its head and body in a circle —although it had no eyes, the motion was plainly that of *looking around*. The tallow around its ankles swirled in little eddies like moving water as it turned.

"Can it see—" Bones began. Christophel put a finger to his lips and shook his head.

"I am the root," the tallow figure said again, more confidently.

Watching it closely, Christophel poured some of the ash from the saucer into his palm and curled his hand into a fist.

"I am the root," the thing said once more. This time the words rang like a declamation. It raised the hatpin like a staff. Christophel took a deep breath and brought his fist with the ashes to his face.

"I am the root, the root of the tree," it announced, "and thou shalt have no gods other than me!" And then it shouted something that sounded like "*Syn!*"

The moment the creature finished its declamation, Christophel took a deep breath and blew the ashes in his fist across the table before the tallow-work figure. "Synack," he whispered. The ashes settling across the table smoldered briefly, a little nebula of red cinder stars, and faded to gray again.

The figure replied with another syllable, "*Ack*," turned to face the opposite corner of the table, and raised its arms again. Christophel moved around to that corner and poured more ash into his hand.

"I am the root, the root of the tree, and thou shalt have no gods other than me," it called again. *"Syn!"*

Christophel blew another puff of ash across the table. "Synack," he repeated, and once again the dead ashes flared to life for a moment as they settled. The tallow creature replied again, *"Ack!"* and turned to the next corner.

At each corner the figure repeated its proclamation. Each time, Christophel responded with a puff of ash and the whispered word that brought the cinders to life. And when they had faded again, the creature spoke its reply.

When all the ash had been distributed, the creature stuck the point of the hatpin into the tabletop and spoke the word written on its forehead. *"Init."*

Immediately, a smattering of cinders across the table lit up like tiny gaslights, and one by one, lines of dull gold light radiated from them back to where the hatpin's point rested in the tallow. The pin glowed with the same shade of gold each time this happened. So did the smoldering cheroot in the tallow creature's head.

Christophel brushed off his hands. "It's begun. We can leave it to its work. Come."

Back in the sanctuary, Walker folded his arms and fixed Christophel with a wary glare. "You said you were raising a demon, not some kind of . . . some kind of *god*."

"Its name is Bios. And it isn't a god," Christophel said dismissively. "It only thinks it is. It has to, or it wouldn't do the work we want it to do. The creature has to think the process it is undertaking is its own idea. That table is its domain, its universe. It doesn't know we exist."

He poured himself a cup of lukewarm tea from the pot they had left behind and took a sip. "If there is some kind of god in the system, some mystical root in the tree," he mused with a cold smile, "*I* am that root. I'm the one who brought Bios into being, who created in it the wish to seek out your pillars. But Bios doesn't need to know that. It *can't*. Particularly since, as you pointed out, according to the accepted wisdom of the world, *I* should not be commanding it to do *anything*."

"So what is it doing, exactly?" Bones asked.

"It will create new daemons. We told it to search for conversations within the boundaries of the map on the table involving the words you wrote on that parchment. The first time someone speaks one of those words, Bios creates a lesser daemon to follow that person and report back whenever he or she says something else that your list defines as significant. Each of those lesser daemons is represented by a live cinder on the tabletop. With enough of them listening, Bios will be able to show us who your pillars are."

"There were already cinders coming to life," Walker said. "Does that mean Bios is already figuring it out?"

"Yes, but slowly," Christophel warned. "You saw maybe thirty cinders, thirty people speaking words of meaning. That may sound like a lot, but you must remember there are somewhere near one million people in New York and nearly half that again in Brooklyn and the neighboring towns. To make anything more than a haphazard guess as to which of them we want, we need more people talking about you, and quickly."

"Which means we need to get moving," Bones said with a cold smile.

Christophel held up a hand. "There's one thing I want to know first," he said. "I want an answer to the question Walker ignored earlier."

Walker eyed him icily. "Why we're working with Jack."

"Well, I was going to say working *for* him, but yes."

"Why? You want to come aboard?"

The conjuror hitched up an eyebrow. "I'm satisfied with my situation, but I'll admit I'm curious."

Walker and Bones looked at each other. Then Walker shrugged and gestured toward his companion. "Be my guest."

"You have this," Bones said to Christophel. "This sanctuary, this town. A place that's yours. A place where you belong."

"*Belonging* might be stretching it a touch," Christophel admitted.

"We have *nothing*," Bones continued, an edge of bitterness tingeing his raspy voice. "No sanctuary, no home. And we belong nowhere. The humans are everywhere, like rats and roaches, only louder and messier and generally more unpleasant. We want to be able to stop roaming if we choose. We want a haven to come home to. And Jack . . . Jack has the means to build one for us."

"He has the means to claim a place by raining destruction down on a human city," Christophel corrected. "He has the means to invade, not to build anything new."

Bones shrugged. "Humans breed, they migrate, they colonize, they take every inch for themselves. When there is no country left unclaimed because they have taken it all, then the only option left is to take something back. We believe Jack can do this. He's the only hope we've had for a very long time. This is why we have chosen to throw our lots in with his."

"Well," Christophel said after a moment, "it's a reason."

"So glad you approve," Walker said dryly.

The conjuror gave him a long look. "I didn't say I approved. But you have satisfied my curiosity, and for that, I thank you."

"Fair enough," Bones said. "Now, because time is short, we'll take our leave, Basile. Time to get this place talking."

"This next bit should be more to your liking, Redgore," Christophel observed nonchalantly, a little smile twitching around his mouth.

Walker's red-rimmed eyes glittered malevolently. "Oh, yes. I suspect that this much, at least, I'm going to enjoy."

≈ SIX ≈

Jiŋ

S AVERIO!"

It was uncanny how well Ilana Ponzi could mimic her mother's voice. Sam leaned around the punter sitting opposite him. Sure enough, there she was, waving as she made her way across Culver Plaza with a blue dinner pail swinging from her hand.

"That your girlfriend, kid?"

Sam grinned at the punter, who had already lost three dollars and looked to be good for at least another two. In fact, this mark might as well have been wearing his entire card-playing philosophy pinned to his vest. It was a huge relief, after the debacle with the card sharp from the day before, to discover he hadn't suddenly lost his ability to read another player's logic. "Nah," he said airily. "I get my meals delivered. The girls line up for the privilege. But I suspect we've got time for another coup or two before she gets here, if you'd like to try and win back a few bits."

No surprise, the guy lost; in fact, he lost another three dollars in the short time it took Ilana to reach them. But if he'd been in any mood to complain, it only lasted a minute.

"Oh, I didn't think to ask if I should bring anything for your friend," Ilana said cheerfully. "How could I be so thoughtless?" She popped open the lid of the pail and beamed at the punter as she handed him a paper-wrapped sandwich. "Here you go!"

It was impossible, even for a punter who'd just lost a decent amount of cash, to be angry when Ilana Ponzi was doing her adorable routine. The mark accepted the sandwich with a rueful shake of his head and left his money behind.

"Thanks, pard," Sam said as Ilana dropped onto the crate the mark had been using for a seat.

"See how good my timing's getting?" she demanded. "Admit it. I'd make a *perfect* partner. I'm simply too charming to get mad at."

"You're a natural."

"Wait." Ilana slapped his fingers as he reached for the cards. "Here." She handed him the pail and swept up the deck. "Watch. I've been practicing." Sam leaned back, balancing on one edge of his own crate, and tried not to smile while Ilana demonstrated her card-shuffling prowess. "I've pretty much got this one down. What's that other one you showed me . . . Wait, Sam, keep looking . . ."

Several yards beyond Ilana's dark head, a slim figure was walking awkwardly across Culver Plaza. The face was hidden by a wide-brimmed black slouch hat, and although the person was dressed in brown trousers and a jacket and had both hands shoved into the pockets, Sam was immediately certain it was a girl. And it was pretty obvious he wasn't the only one who could tell. There was a pair of older boys, maybe eighteen or nineteen, trailing along behind her, muttering to themselves and nodding in her direction. Bad news.

"You're not looking," Ilana protested, turning to see what had stolen Sam's attention.

Then something made the figure in the hat turn to face the boys at her heels. They burst into laughter. One of them must've said something fairly awful.

"Horrible boys," Ilana said indignantly. "Why are all boys horrible?"

Sam put up his hands and opened his mouth to protest, but then as the girl turned her back on the hecklers and started stalking off, her plodding gait even more ungainly the faster she walked, one of the boys reached out and flipped the hat off her head. A long, black braid tumbled out as the hat went flying. It was the Chinese girl from the Broken Land Hotel.

"Sam," Ilana yelped, hopping up and down and pointing at the horrible boys, and scattering cards all over the ground in the process.

"Wait here." He shoved the lunch pail back into Ilana's hands. "Don't let anybody run off with my stuff and don't take any bets. *No. Bets.*"

He took off across the plaza, completely without a guess about what he could possibly do besides put himself squarely between the girl and the troublemakers. In fact, he was pretty certain that probably all that was going to come out of this was a black eye to match the bruise on his cheekbone. Sam could work some halfway decent miracles with a deck of cards, but he was still a fairly unassuming fifteen-year-old kid, and no pair of self-respecting roughneck rowdies were going to pause more than half a second before they pummeled him flat.

Then, when he was still a few yards away, something utterly unexpected happened, almost too quickly for Sam to catch.

The girl put one red-slippered foot down on the brim of her hat to keep it from escaping, a motion that looked almost balletic compared to her awkward walk, and that brought a fresh set of guffaws from the boys. By now Sam was close enough to see her face, which slid into a half-smile, shy and flirtatious.

The leering boys took the little smile as an invitation to sidle closer. The girl dipped forward, one hand behind her back, and reached long fingers into the collar of her shirt. Eyes goggling, they leaned closer still.

Then she threw the hand that had been inside her collar toward the boys, flinging a fine dust into the air between them, and swept the hand behind her back up after it. A blue flame appeared between her fingers. The flame met the dust and ignited, and a flurry of sizzling sparks popped in the air in front of the girl.

She scooped up her hat, turned toward Sam, and shoved it unceremoniously in his face as he reached her side, covering his eyes just as the sparks erupted with a muted *boom* into a ball of green fire.

The boys, who'd been leaning in way too close, probably trying to get a look down her shirt, flung their hands up over their eyes and howled in pain.

The girl took hold of Sam's arm and turned him away from the stinging vapor left by the explosion. "Thanks for trying," she said with a thin smile as she tucked her braid back up into the hat.

"Sorry, I . . . I meant to . . . are you . . . are you all right?"

"Am *I* all right?" For a moment her thin smile widened and she actually looked amused. "Yes, thank you. I am." She glanced over her shoulder at the two older boys stumbling toward the nearest saloon to wash out their eyes. "Best I get going, though, before they can see again."

"Can I . . . do you need . . ." Oh, this was mortifying, but Sam couldn't bring himself to cut his losses and shut up. "Can I walk you somewhere?"

She stopped walking and folded her arms. "Why?"

"It's only that . . ." Sam willed himself not to blush. "Just to make sure nobody else gives you any trouble? You see what just happened, and you were in probably the best-behaved part of West Brighton. I don't know where you're headed, but basically anywhere farther west it gets way, way worse."

"And you were so helpful with those last two," she added, deadpan. "Seeing as how I've *never* been in a tough town before . . ." Then she hesitated and eyed Sam for a minute. "Thank you," she said, finally. "It's very good of you to offer, and I appreciate that you mean it. But I try very hard to take care of myself, so I'm going to decline."

Sam nodded. "I guess I can understand that."

She looked at him for just a moment longer. "My name's Jin."

"Sam."

"Thank you, Sam."

He nodded again and took a step back. She turned toward

the west side of the plaza and started off with the same awkward gait he had noticed before. "Jin. Hold up."

She stopped, folded her arms, and waited wordlessly for him to catch up.

Sam ignored her impatient look. If she insisted on wandering off by herself, there was at least one thing he could offer. "If you get into any kind of a fix around here, the best place to go is the saloon called the Reverend Dram. It's on a rough street, but they're good people there. They've helped me out of a ton of scrapes. If you ask for directions to it, most anybody will tell you, and even most of the troublemakers'll leave you alone if you say you're a friend of the folks at the Dram."

Jin gave him another of those long, uncomfortable looks. "There's a fireworks pageant tonight out at the Broken Land Hotel," she said at last. "It's my display. If you're going to keep worrying, you should come tonight. If the show happens, you'll know I made it back safely."

"Done," Sam said, almost before she'd finished speaking. She gave him the barest shadow of a smile and disappeared into the milling crowds on the plaza. When he couldn't see her hat any longer, he returned to find Ilana Ponzi where he'd left her with his table and kit, grinning her little face off. "What?" he snapped.

"Who's the *girl?*" Ilana said in her best schoolyard singsong voice.

"Illy, don't start with me or I'll tell your mother I saw you kiss a newsboy."

Ilana gave an indignant squeal. "I *never* . . . well." She twirled the lunch pail around her fingers and pretended to consider. "Maybe you're right. Maybe I do have a newsie boyfriend, and maybe Mama packed this lunch for *him*."

"Hang on—"

"Too bad, too. It was a good lunch." Ilana Ponzi skipped away laughing, swinging the pail like a girl on holiday.

"So what is it with you and Christophel? He seems to be rather our sort of fellow, all things considered."

Walker hesitated as the horse-drawn cabriolet carrying the two of them back to Coney Island hit a particularly nasty hole in the road. "There is," he said carefully, "a lot you don't know, Bones. I say this with utter respect for you and your age and the wisdom of the dust you carry. But . . ." He glanced meaningfully at the carpetbag on the floor by his feet.

The oyster-shell eyes glittered. "But there are gaps. Yes."

Walker nodded. "Gaps. Precisely. How much, exactly, do you know about jumpers?"

"Only the folklore. I've never met one before today."

He sighed. "Jumpers, as a class of folk, set me on edge. Part of it, I admit, is the whole not-picking-sides thing. I don't care whether you're for a man or against him, but I like to deal with fellows who can make up their minds. Who have some kind of convictions. I like to be able to tell where they stand."

"But what do you care, as long as Christophel does what you want?"

"Well, then there's the other matter," Walker continued, taking his smokes from his pocket and lighting one. "There's how they see, how they think. They're far-seers; time works differently for them. Even if they do what you want, it's impossible to know why they're doing it. You can't know if they're really trying to help you, if they share your motives, or if they're just going along with you now in order to work some kind of unforeseeable betrayal of you and your plans in a decade or two. They're just impossible to know. It's like trying to work out what a cat's thinking when it looks at you." He paused for a pull on the cheroot. "And then I've also heard . . ."

He hesitated. Bones waited while Walker smoked and put his thoughts in order.

"I've heard they can . . . they can make mistakes," Walker said carefully. "Because of the way they see, the way they remember; because of how time works for them. I've heard they can get . . . confused. I always understood that to be the reason they weren't supposed to work any kind of conjury."

"The folklore goes that they gave up that right when they refused to choose sides, back in the old days."

"That's folklore. I think it has less to do with punishing them for their indecision and more to do with practicality. If it's true that they get confused, not having conjury . . . well, that limits their ability to cause trouble."

He stared at the cheroot smoking in his fingers. "Of course, Doc Rawhead seems to have found a way around that." He dropped the cigar to the carriage floor and crushed it under his shoe with a look of distaste. "I just think it's a bad, bad idea to get involved with jumpers. But we have, so that's that. *Jacta alea est.* Let the die be cast. But I'm crossing my fingers." He grinned. "In any case, at least we've come to a place I'm comfortable with."

Bones regarded him thoughtfully. "I suppose, then, you'll be handling this portion of the process?"

"The claiming by blood." Walker's grin curled even more. "Yes. And you'd do well to stay out of my way."

⋙ SEVEN ⋘

Norton's Point

T HE TRUTH was that Jin had a pretty good idea just how bad the part of town she was headed to was. She'd figured that out when she'd first asked the concierge at the Broken Land Hotel how to get there. A grown man, and he'd actually blushed.

Of course, he was also the one who'd suggested she go to Norton's Point in the first place. Hotel concierges not only knew everything; they could find anything. So when Jin, poring through Fata Morgana's little library of pyrotechnics manuals, had realized she could try something remarkable in the display that night if she could only get her hands on a few uncommon chemicals, she'd gone straight to the concierge.

"I need to find some things," she began, and rattled off what must've sounded like the kind of shopping list only an embalmer or somebody mixing up knockout drops would assemble. The poor fellow had turned about five shades of red and purple, then told her to try Norton's Point.

"You can get p-pretty much anything there," he'd stammered. "I'd go soon, though — it's at the opposite end of Coney Island, and it isn't what I'd call safe for a . . . a young lady . . . in the evenings."

So Jin went.

Every place is the sum of its parts, most of which are its inhabitants; and navigating any place is all about figuring out how to walk among those people. But there are also certain tricks to moving safely through the rough parts of most towns. Jin knew them all.

Of course, it's always best not to find yourself in those areas in the first place. When that can't be avoided, the second best thing is not to look like a stranger. Strangers draw attention. Jin, of course, looked like a stranger everywhere, so she had to settle for the third best strategy: look as much at ease as possible, while still very clearly not letting your guard down. Look aware. Look ready, without appearing to anticipate trouble. Look confident, without showing swagger. Swagger just begs to be proven wrong. And while eye contact sometimes helped and sometimes didn't, Jin had long ago decided that keeping her head up and her eyes open was always safer than the alternative.

Still, she was pretty sure there was nothing this breezy seaside island could throw at her that could top *Jiu Jinshan,* "Old Gold Mountain," San Francisco. The neighborhood where she'd grown up there had given her a pretty thorough grounding in squalor and iniquity.

As she walked on, West Brighton dwindled, sandy streets diving into beach grass and gnarled trees. Buildings began to look a little more haphazard and temporary as they leaned into the breeze off the water. Jin angled her hat over her eyes and wished, for the fifteenth time, that she'd brought her bicycle. Four miles out and four miles back . . . her feet were going to mutiny. Already, they were starting to ache.

The ramshackle houses became a ramshackle cluster, and

then suddenly the cluster became a claustrophobic little pile of hotels, restaurants, and saloons. The area smelled of sour beer and garbage and old oyster shells and fish heads left to be picked over by scavengers, and something familiar that Jin couldn't quite identify—but it was always in a place like this that she smelled it, a place where her guard went up instinctively and where she always felt the memory of *Jiu Jinshan* poking fingers down her throat. She rubbed her jade bracelet, the only thing she had taken with her when she'd left. The gesture always helped to boost her confidence.

The muttered insults from the boys back near the middle of town were endearments compared to anything anyone was likely to say to her here. The respectable types would ignore her, but they were vastly outnumbered.

There were sideways looks and ugly smiles from the men she passed, many of them reeling already, and uncomfortable glances from the occasional women. Jin knew what those glances meant. The kind of women who lived or worked in places like this might put up brave and saucy fronts for their neighbors and customers and each other, but they were still human and female. Whatever protective instincts they refused to feel for themselves still crept out from time to time. She could see them hesitate over whether they should try to warn her about where she was.

Confident, without swagger. Eyes open, head up. Jin reached one hand into the bag she wore slung across her shoulder and touched the familiar shapes inside until she found her list of chemicals and a little glass tube with a bulb at one end. When she took her hand out of the bag and unfolded the list, the tube was nestled in her palm, invisible but ready.

The vague information she'd pestered out of the concierge amounted to little more than a name. "I don't know the man myself," he'd said. "Our guests don't tend to be after the sort of things he sells. But everybody in Coney Island knows who he is."

Jin sighed and put the paper with the name and her list back in her pocket. She was going to have to break another of her many rules for rough parts of town: never ask for directions.

She waited until a woman in a bustled dress slipped out of an unmarked doorway next to a saloon. The lady and her dress both had the same look to them: beautiful, but worn. Jin forced down a quick flutter of panic at the thought of what kind of business that unmarked door probably led to, and crossed the street.

"Excuse me," she whispered.

The woman looked up sharply. "What is it?"

"Do you know where I can find a man named Tycho McNulty?" Jin spoke quickly, before the woman could work through the preconceptions people always had when a strange foreign girl addressed them. Sometimes they got angry at being spoken to. Sometimes they assumed talking to you was going to be too difficult to bother with.

But this woman hesitated and gave Jin a long look. She was trying to hide it, but there was concern there. "What for?"

"I need chemicals." It was absolutely true, but Jin knew perfectly well that the lady would assume she needed the chemicals for something far more frightening than explosives.

The lady would probably also figure that she and Jin had something in common. Jin forced that thought down deep and met the woman's now openly concerned gaze.

"Are you all right?" she asked quietly.

Jin nodded. "Do you know where I can find this McNulty?"

The lady took a deep breath. "Take your next right. Look for a door with green paint and a brass plaque." Then she did something shocking. She reached out one gloved hand and clasped Jin's shoulder. "Take care of yourself."

Jin had just enough time to stare, startled, at the broken stitching on the thumb of the woman's glove before she was gone, hurrying up the street in her tired dress.

Jin watched her for a moment, utterly stunned by the gesture. She could still feel where the woman had touched her shoulder. The first few tears fell before she even realized she was crying, then she swiped her sleeve over her eyes and stumbled toward the alley where Tycho McNulty kept shop.

The green door was at the far end, where the ocean scent almost broke through the smell of alcohol and rotting things and where Jin thought she might actually be able to hear the occasional wave crash on the unseen beach. The plaque was tarnished, but the engraving was even and all the words were spelled right: T. MCNULTY, PHARMACIST.

She squared her shoulders, lifted the bronze door knocker, and let it fall. After a moment, the peephole under the plaque darkened. Jin waited until the eye behind it disappeared. She knew there were other eyes in the street watching, wondering what she was up to. She could feel them.

She knocked again, harder. This time, when the eye appeared behind the peephole, she held up her carefully lettered shopping list.

The door opened and the man who stood on the threshold

looked her over and folded his arms across his chest. The pharmacist wasn't much taller than she was, and although he obviously wasn't a young man, Jin got the sense that his gray hair, like Mr. Burns's, had come a little on the early side. A pair of old rimless spectacles perched on his nose, and the look he gave her through them was shrewd but curious. "I want it to be very clear that the only reason I'm considering serving you is that I can't stand not knowing what you plan to do with all that. Come on in, and give me that list."

"Goodness," Jin said as she stepped inside and stared at the spotless counters and cabinets and scales of Tycho McNulty's dispensary. "It's so . . . so . . . ."

"*Clean* is the word I believe you're trying politely not to use." McNulty retrieved a perfectly sharpened pencil from a neat desk and tapped it against the nosepiece of his spectacles while he scanned Jin's list for the third time. "Now, don't tell me. I want to figure this out on my own. And you can put away whatever that ampule in your palm is," he added, waving at her with the business end of the pencil. "It's a point of personal pride for me that nobody gets mugged in my place."

Jin gave him a sharp look while he examined the piece of paper. He was hardened, his face made rough by this town or whatever had brought him here, but he had let her into his place of business and now she was a customer. She slid the glass tube back into her bag.

"Do you stock all that?"

"Can you pay for it if I do?" McNulty was making notes now, scrawling and drawing lines and doing quick bits of math in the margins of the page. "Eh, there's a thing or two here that could be a problem," he muttered. "Depends on what—oh, stupid me." He looked up at her, a triumphant smile glancing across his face for a moment before he could put his stern expression back on. "Explosives."

Jin frowned. "Not just explosives, sir."

"No, of course not." He smiled again, a brief flash that came and went like a spark. "Fireworks."

Nothing like fireworks to make grown men behave like little boys. Jin grinned. "Yes, sir. I work for the Fata Morgana Fireworks Company. We're in town for a show at the Broken Land Hotel."

"And what, you didn't pack for the trip? There are proper suppliers in New York, you know."

"There's not enough time for that. We have a display tonight. I want to make some changes to it." She hesitated. "Those changes—what those supplies are for—they're my crazy idea. If it doesn't work, we'll do our standard program, but—"

McNulty held up a hand. "Wait. Your idea, meaning *you* came up with this list? Figured out the chemicals, worked out the quantities? Some of these are terribly dangerous, you know. Especially in combination."

Jin pursed her lips and looked at him silently, trying to decide if he was joking or not.

"Really?" she said finally. "Could you tell me a little bit more? You don't think they might, say, *explode* or anything, do you?"

McNulty stared back at her for a moment, then burst into what sounded like long-unpracticed laughter. "All right, all right. Let's see what we've got here."

McNulty, it turned out, was a natural fireworker. He had

nearly everything on the list, and for the chemicals he didn't have, he had alternative suggestions. A combination to deepen the color Jin wanted; an idea about how to treat the paper she used for handmade tubes so they would be more water-resistant; additives to change the color of the smoke that remained in the sky after the sparks went out. The longer they worked, and the more elaborate their concoctions got, the more McNulty seemed to shed his stony demeanor.

Jin leaned on her elbows while he poured a batch of flash powder they had mixed up into a pan. "Why are you here?" she asked. "You don't really seem . . . to fit."

"I fit here just fine." He kept his eyes on the match as he dropped it into the pan. The powder ignited with a sudden shimmering flare and a soft *whoosh*. "I came here to hide from the police."

"Why?"

"I'll answer that if you tell me what's in the ampule you had in your hand when you came inside."

"Something for protection," she admitted. "I was told it was a rough part of town." McNulty waited. "If I were to run into danger, there's a bulb that can be emptied into the tube," Jin explained. "The mixture explodes on impact."

"Like a grenade?"

"Yes, only made of glass and with a prettier fire. Why are you hiding from the police?"

"They think I killed my wife."

He didn't so much as glance up to gauge her reaction. Jin stiffened. "And . . . did you?"

McNulty shook his head. "No. She was sick. At heart, not

in body. And she knew there were things in my dispensary that could stop the pain she was feeling more permanently than anything I would give her if she asked for my help." He stared at the dying sparks in the pan and sighed. "It must never have occurred to her that it would look like I had poisoned her. But that's how it looked, so here I am."

"Oh." Jin didn't know how else to respond to that.

He rose from his chair and began wrapping up her parcels. "You'd better get on your way back, hadn't you?"

"I should, I suppose." Jin took the packages and tucked them one by one into her bag. McNulty had been almost cheerful for a while, but now . . .

"Why don't you . . . come out to the display tonight?" she asked at last, haltingly. "You could see how everything turns out."

He smiled halfheartedly. "You're an odd girl, you know that? Here you are, in arguably the worst square mileage outside of the Five Points, shopping for explosives as if it was as ordinary as shopping for bread and milk, and when I tell you I had to flee the police on suspicion of murdering my wife, you just shrug and invite me to come see fireworks."

"I'm also a Chinese girl, which is fairly uncommon in this country," Jin added seriously. "You may not have noticed that, what with the explosives."

The pharmacist gave a reluctant laugh. "I did sort of forget. No, I can't come to see your fireworks. If the police happen to notice me and care, I'd be hauled off to jail quicker than you could wave goodbye." He handed over the last of her packages.

"But maybe I'll find my way out onto one of the piers. Might see it from there, mightn't I?"

"You might." She slung the bag over her shoulder, then paused. "Oh, I nearly forgot." She knelt, unpinned a little billfold from the inside of her trouser cuff, and held it out.

McNulty took the bills, peeled off the top two, and handed the rest back. "Get yourself home safe, Jin. Make sure I can see those fireworks."

EIGHT

Claimed by Blood

WHEN THE HORRIBLE thing happened, it wasn't in Norton's Point at all. It was in West Brighton, and Jin almost tripped over it.

She'd gotten turned around and found herself in an alley behind a saloon, from the sound of it. *Is there anything in this place but alleys and saloons?* she'd thought in annoyance. Then she'd tripped over the body.

She took a wary step back, sure she'd fallen over a drunk. When the figure didn't move, she spun to make sure she wasn't about to get mugged. Nothing stirred. Jin waited for her pulse to settle down, stepped around the impediment, and got on her way again.

Then she stopped. She turned back to the lump on the ground. She reached with the toe of one slipper to nudge the pile of newspapers covering it. The paper slid sideways, reluctant and clumped, stiff, not the way paper should slide. It was stained, but by then all Jin could do was stare at what it had been concealing.

She screamed. And she kept screaming until her hands, clenching and unclenching mindlessly, dropped the little glass tube she was still carrying. It hit the ground at her feet and burst into a blinding red fireball edged with glass shards that stung when they hit. But Jin, unaware, kept on screaming until the black at the edges of her vision overtook her and she crumpled to the filthy ground.

"Well, well."

English. Faces shimmered. She'd been somewhere once where things had shimmered and people spoke English. Jin licked her lips. "Am I in the desert?"

"The desert?" The face with the hat laughed hoarsely. "No, sunshine. You're in Coney Island."

She felt for her eyes, tried to rub away the shimmer. Another face leaned in. "You feel like sitting up?"

Jin nodded. Careful hands, respectful hands, lifted her upright and into a chair. The faces and the room around her came little by little into focus. An upright piano with a shabby velvet-topped stool; walls decorated with nondescript lithographs of landscapes, and the same print of Custer's Last Stand that hung in every hotel, saloon, and restaurant she'd seen in the last year; mismatched tables, mismatched chairs. A long mahogany bar with a spotted mirror behind it and assorted glasses hanging above. The vague smell of alcohol and wood polish and sawdust.

A mostly empty saloon. Of course. "There are saloons everywhere here," she said shakily.

"You know how you got here?" the man with the hat asked. Jin shook her head and winced as the edges of her vision started collapsing into blackness again.

"Just a minute now," the second man said, and disappeared.

The man in the hat pulled a chair over and sat beside her.

"The fellow that brought you here said he heard screams and an explosion and then more screaming. When he found you, all he could get out of you was 'Sam said to go to the Reverend Dram.'"

"Take a breath." The second man reappeared with a bundle of fabric in one hand and a glass in the other. "Drink this, but don't breathe the fumes."

The sharp alcohol vapor shot up her nose anyhow. "Smells like whiskey."

"It is."

Jin drank the glass in a gulp and sputtered while her throat and stomach blazed. "It's not *good* whiskey," she managed.

The two men, who were in the midst of exchanging a meaningful look, turned and stared at her. "What on earth do you know about whiskey, young lady?" the hatless man demanded.

"I know the good stuff doesn't burn your eyebrows off before you drink it. I've been to Kentucky." She put a hand to the side of her head and winced as her fingers found a knot that felt, impossibly, to be about the size of an egg.

"I *told* you not to breathe the fumes, and this'll do just fine for medicinal purposes." He held out the fabric bundle. "Put this on your head."

The bundle was full of ice. Jin sighed and closed her eyes. "Thank you."

The two men stood, hands in their pockets, having whole silent conversations with their faces while Jin held the ice pack to her head. She opened her eyes, about to ask what had happened, when she remembered.

"There was . . ." She licked her lips again and steadied her voice. "There was a body in the alley. That's why I was screaming."

The hatless man turned on his heel and headed back to the bar. "Bring the good stuff this time," the other one called. Then he turned back to Jin and leaned his elbows on his knees.

"My name's Walter Mapp," he said. "That's Jasper. This is his place."

Jin nodded, but she wasn't listening; she was just seeing clumped newspapers slide from a mangled, vaguely human shape. Over and over.

"Stop picturing it," Mapp said sharply. "Don't do that."

"You didn't see it," she said thickly.

"Yes, I did," he told her. "I went back with the fellow who brought you in. He didn't want to get involved with the police himself. You were out for nearly an hour, sunshine. A lot's happened."

"It was terrible." Another glass materialized in her hand. She stared into it. "It was torn up so badly — couldn't tell if it was wearing ripped clothes or ripped skin." She looked up at Mapp. "What did that? What *could?*"

Before Mapp could answer, the door of the saloon burst open and Uncle Liao and Mr. Burns all but sprinted across the room.

"Is she all right?" Mr. Burns demanded. "Jin, are you all right?"

"Yes, sir. Wait — where did *you* —?"

"Don't bother with *sir* while we're ascertaining whether

you're alive or not!" Liao ordered. "Xiao Jin, *ni shou shangle ma?*" He took her head between his gnarled hands, tilted it so that he could peer into her eyes.

"*Wo toutong.* I hit my head," she added for Mr. Burns's benefit.

Liao moved the ice pack away from her scalp and examined the knot. Then he plucked the glass from her fingers, sniffed, turned to Jasper, and gave him an approving grunt. "Drink, firefly. Little sips, while we talk to these men."

Mr. Burns managed a pat on her knee before Liao swept him away to where Walter Mapp and Jasper now stood a little distance off. Jin took a sip from the glass and looked up to find the boy named Sam, the one from Culver Plaza, lingering near the door.

He came to sit in the chair Mapp had vacated. "You remembered what I said."

Jin looked over to where the four men stood deep in conversation. "How did Uncle Liao and Mr. Burns get here?"

"You mentioned my name," Sam told her. "When you asked for the Reverend Dram. The fellow who found you brought you here and then came to find me."

She snorted. "In all of Coney Island there's only one Sam?"

"It's a small place," Sam replied with a shrug. "They know me here."

"And I told you where the display was going to be tonight. That's how you knew where to look for them." Jin nodded at Liao and Mr. Burns.

"Well, yes, you did, but I already knew." He gave her a sheepish smile and pulled a folded page from his pocket. Jin recognized it immediately as one of Fata Morgana's handbills. "I was at the hotel this morning when your wagon arrived. I saw you when you were . . . Actually," he admitted, "I have no idea what you were doing. You looked like you were trying not to set yourself on fire."

"Close. I was trying to keep *him* from setting me on fire," Jin said, jerking her head at Mr. Burns. The motion made it throb all over again. "Oh, that is not going to feel good tonight." She closed her eyes against the pain and immediately the image of the body swam into view. She felt herself starting to shake, and forced herself to open her eyes, even though she knew the shaking meant she might cry.

The boy named Sam was hovering, all concern and awkwardness. She couldn't bear it. "Did you see?" she whispered harshly, scrubbing at her face with her sleeve.

He shook his head. "I didn't see it. Mr. Mapp was the only one who went."

"Did he *tell* you?"

He hesitated and glanced over at the huddled men, plainly willing them to finish their conversation and come to his rescue.

Jin grabbed his arm. "He did. What did he say? What was it?"

"It's no good, dwelling on it."

"I can't get it out of my head anyhow. At least help me make sense of it. What could . . ." Jin took a deep breath. "What could *do* that to someone?"

He looked like he was trying to figure out something comforting to say. Jin put on her most forbidding face and stared him down. There was no comfort for this. There was only the hope of making sense of it. That's how it felt, at least.

"It was pretty bad, huh?" he said at last.

She sighed and took another little sip from her glass. There was no way to answer that. No way that would convey what she had seen, anyhow.

"Walt didn't say anything about what he thought happened," Sam said quietly. "But he told me about the body, and the writing."

This was new. "What writing?"

"You didn't see it? It was on the wall, where the—where it was lying. Let me remember and get it right. It said—"

"That's enough talk of this wretchedness." Uncle Liao swooped in, waving his hands like a man trying to stop a fight. He pointed a finger at Jin's mostly untouched glass. "Little sips, I said!"

Jin ignored him. "What was the writing?"

"Xiao Jin!" Liao thundered.

"*Zhe shi shenme yisi?*" Jin shouted back, astounded by her own anger. "I'm not leaving until you tell me what this means!"

"It means that a creature may walk like a man and still have a beast's heart, Xiao Jin," Liao retorted. "That's all it means. No more."

"That isn't enough! If you had seen it, what I saw . . . If you knew what I have caught behind my eyes—" She banged a fist against her forehead. "If you did, you'd do whatever it took to give me some kind of peace!"

"How will knowing what a murderer wrote on a wall give you peace?" Sam asked softly.

Jin shrugged, suddenly exhausted. "I don't know. I only

know I'm going to be thinking about it every moment of the day and night no matter what."

Everyone in the room turned to Liao. He gave her a long look, then turned to where Walter Mapp leaned on the back of the piano and gave him a curt nod.

Mapp tapped the fingers of one hand on the piano. "It said, *Claimed by blood for Jack Hellcoal.*"

Jin began to shake again. Tears pricked at her eyes for the third time in a single day. It was absurd. The words clarified nothing for her. Why, why the tears again?

"What does it mean?" she whispered.

Mapp shrugged. "Darlin', I haven't the foggiest."

Jin nodded. Then, unable to hold it back any longer, she burst into tears.

"*Lai he yi he.* Little sips," Liao said again, much more gently.

Obediently, Jin took another sip and tried not to cough. Fiery liquid slid down her throat, burned away some of the desperate aching sobs.

"Good girl, firefly." Liao patted her shoulder. His knotty old hand was shaking, too. "Now again."

Jin sniffled and wiped her eyes. "Can't imagine you really want me drunk and setting off rockets, Uncle Liao," she mumbled. Panic hit, quick and sharp. "My bag—what time is it?"

"Don't be absurd. It's for recovery, not for boozing you up."

"My bag," Jin said again, shoving the ice pack into Mr. Burns's hand and the glass into Sam's. The second she was on her feet, a wave of nausea hit and she nearly fell back into the chair. "Mr. Mapp! I had a bag with me. Did it—"

"Sit right back down, young lady," Mapp ordered. "Your gear's safe and sound. It's right there, on the bar."

"Oh, thank goodness." She allowed herself to be guided back into the chair while Sam rushed to retrieve the bag.

Liao plucked it from his hands. "Yes, and what, precisely, is this errand that takes you into some kind of shantytown hellpit? And why did you not at least take the *laowai* with you? It isn't as if he has anything better to do than keep you company."

"Hey," Mr. Burns protested weakly.

"You disagree?" Liao snapped. "You would have told our Jin no, you have no time to make sure she doesn't get herself killed?" Burns opened his mouth, but then thought better of answering. Liao took one of his long breaths, then turned back to Jin, holding up the bag like an indictment. "What kind of cat are you keeping in this bag?"

"Atlantis. But different than we usually do it." Despite everything, Jin smiled and settled back in her chair. "If we get back in time for me to build it before tonight."

Liao looked like he was trying hard to maintain his expression of disapproval, but at this his face cracked into a reluctant smile. "Spoken like a true *daoyao ren*." He glanced at Mr. Burns. "Our Jin has a cinnabar heart," he said. "It is too brave for her own good." He gently took Jin's bag from her. "Little sips, now. Then we will go to work so that you may build your Atlantis."

The creek that bordered Coney Island to the north and separated it from the rest of Gravesend had huge stretches of empty banks on both sides, overhung with stunted trees and lined with weeds. Less than a quarter of a mile from civilization, yet certain spots along that creek felt like wilderness. In one of those isolated little pockets of marshy ground, Bones stood a few yards up the bank while Walker, stripped to the waist, rinsed blood from his arms.

The freckles there were black as ink, and angry red lines connected them, raised marks like scratches or welts. His back, too, was a network, an elaborate tracery of those same welts. If they hadn't been so geometrically precise, they would've resembled whip marks.

Walker's face, reflected in the scarlet-scummed water, looked utterly disfigured. The freckles there stood out black now, as well, forming a swirling and jagged pattern around his eyes and across his nose, scored by more of the lines. His red-rimmed eyes burned, but he was smiling.

"That," he said cheerfully, scrubbing gore out from under his fingernails, "was fun."

"That," Bones corrected, "was possibly excessive."

"Not if the point is to get people talking," Walker retorted. He dunked his head under and yanked it out again, shaking the water off and finger-combing his hair back. "Do you know how many people are lying dead somewhere, waiting to be found? Can't have our work blending in with the rest."

"You're the expert." Bones held out Walker's shirt and jacket. "What now? Can we stop our hell-raising for an hour and get ourselves dinner before the next bout of carnage?"

"Dinner?" Walker laughed. "How can you be hungry at a time like this?"

"We haven't eaten today. My needs are simple, but I have them. Let's go get ourselves a beefsteak or some such."

"Suit yourself." The red marks were fading now, and the ink-black pointillism across his face had faded, too. Now he just looked massively freckled.

"Not hungry?" Bones asked dryly.

By way of an answer, Walker merely tweaked the bow of his neat ribbon tie, straightened his collar, and grinned.

NINE

The Conflagrationeer's Port-fire Book

JIN, LIAO, and Mr. Burns departed the Reverend Dram with the afternoon sun just beginning to sink in the sky. When they had disappeared from Mammon's Alley and were on their way back to the swank east end, Sam slid onto a barstool alongside Walter Mapp, facing Jasper Wills across the long mahogany. "What's it mean, really? The scrawl about this Jack person?"

Mapp swiveled on his seat and regarded Sam with affronted eyes. "You accusing me of lying to that poor girl when she asked me a direct question?"

"You avoiding mine?"

"That was the general idea, yes. I don't know what it meant, Sam. I'd have told her if I did. She's right, poor kid. Everything matters when you're trying to make sense of something senseless. I'd have given her whatever I had, if I had anything at all."

Jasper Wills poured something into a glass and passed it across to Sam. Remembering Jin's glass of whiskey, he took a slug, doing his best to look like it was no great thing. Then he gave Jasper a withering look. It was sarsaparilla.

"You like this girl?" Mapp asked, turning his own glass on the bar.

"Some boys were hassling her and she . . ." He gestured,

trying to find words for the beautiful puff of fire that had driven the boys off. "It was like a dandelion, only it was this fireball."

"Okay, Sam." Mapp straightened and pushed away his glass. "Look, this is probably just another bit of the same old nastiness."

The same old nastiness, meaning the periodic violence that sometimes seeped eastward out of Norton's Point. It wasn't, though, and they both knew it. The words on the wall made it not the same old anything.

"Probably nothing more," Mapp went on. "Still, if it isn't . . ." He turned to face Sam. "You know who would be a good person to talk to? That Tom Guyot fellow."

Sam had been nodding along. Now he stopped, confused. "Why?"

"He isn't what you think he is, for one thing." The piano player stood. "And he knows the roads, and if the Jack on the wall is the Jack I think he is, Tom might just be able to tell us something. If he's still in town, that is."

"He's in town." For the second time, Sam unfolded the handbill. *The Fata Morgana Fireworks Company, Arte et Marte!* "I think I know where he'll be tonight."

At the other end of the island on the grounds of the Broken Land Hotel, near the livery stables and well out of view of any of the guests, Jin took out Tycho McNulty's parcels and explained to Liao what she wanted.

Side by side they worked, grinding the ingredients of Jin's special formulas in mortars and blending them gently with one of the big white feathers Liao kept in his workbench drawer.

Then they began the task of making up new explosives from their old stock, with Liao painstakingly emptying the contents of tubes and rockets and Jin making new stars, the little wrapped packets holding the incendiary compounds inside each firework. After that they started stringing individual fireworks, stars and cases, tourbillions and port-fires, together into more complicated things: furilonas, caprices, chequer pieces, and devils-among-the-tailors. All the different sorts of combustible artistry that would come together to form Jin's program of miracles.

"Xiao Jin, *gande hao!* Did you do this on purpose?" Liao called as he began stringing a fuse onto a double guilloche, a huge spinning windmill. "I am so pleased that none of these formulations will need to dry."

Jin smiled from the workbench where she was building a compound firework that, when lit, would erupt like a water fountain. Of course she had done it on purpose; anything that needed to dry would take hours, and would be useless for the evening's display. But Uncle Liao didn't really need to be told that. He already knew.

Liao's gnarled hands manipulated the fuse like a spider weaving a web, his long, thin braid hanging over his shoulder and his face folded into a scowl of concentration. Jin watched him for a moment. "You think it will do what I want?" she asked. "Tell me, truly."

He answered without looking up. "You think I would let you proceed with it if I did not? Xiao Jin, it is not such an outlandish idea. Water-fires have been made before."

That, of course, she knew—artificiers from hundreds of years ago wrote of rockets that skipped like a stone across the

Side by side they worked, grinding the ingredients of Jin's special
formulas in mortars and blending them gently with one of the
big white feathers Liao kept in his workbench drawer.

water, or even dove under and resurfaced, still burning, to rise into the air and explode.

"But not by us." Their usual Atlantis program was beautiful, but it didn't use water-fires. And she certainly didn't need to point out to Uncle Liao that what they were now planning—what she had figured out how to do—was something far more complicated, something she'd never heard of anyone doing before.

"Indeed," Liao said. "It is a high form of artifice, to blend opposites like fire and water in this way. Which reminds me: where did you find the formulas? For the powder, for treating the fuses, for the spur-fires and the rest?"

Jin glanced at the bowl that held what was left of the special black powder they had used: gunpowder she'd compounded using one of the unusual ingredients she'd bought from Tycho McNulty. "They're based on a recipe out of the book," she said slowly. "But I made some changes."

"Is that so?" His fingers hesitated for just a moment, and Jin knew why.

The book. More properly, *The Conflagrationeer's Port-fire Book, Being a Compendium of the Chemistry and Design of Infernal Devices, for the Artificer of Displays Entertaining and Educational, or the Purveyor of Mayhem of Any Sort*. Author unknown, but, as far as Jin could tell, probably insane.

She watched Liao as he secured four cylindrical explosive cases to one arm of the guilloche. She tried to read his silence.

The book wasn't precisely off-limits; they kept it with the rest of the pyrotechnics manuals on the communal bookshelf, right alongside Jin's much-abused copy of Comstock's *Natural Philosophy*, Liao's *Tao Te Ching* and the writings of Meng Chiao and Chuang Tzu, and whatever popular fiction Mr. Burns was reading that week. They just didn't use it. Ever. And Jin had always understood that there must be a reason for that. She had just never figured out what that reason was.

"It is not easy to find meaning in the formulas in the book," Liao said at last, dusting off his hands and reaching for the hammered yellow-metal cup of wine by his elbow. "Not everyone is able to read it. I am curious as to how you managed it."

"Not easy to find meaning is putting it mildly," Jin mumbled, still not sure if she was in trouble or not. The *Port-fire Book* read as if it had been written to annoy potential readers right into giving up. Formulas had names like The Calling, Five Winds and a Fire Bring Winter, the Graven Sky, and Ascension, Part the Eighth. Ingredients generally included some kind of elaborately named mud and a list of things that logic dictated had to be the rest of the components, if you could only figure out what they were. *Drops of autumn, tincture of bitter-and-gray, horizon red (refined), salts of age* . . . Not a single thing about the book was obvious or straightforward.

How she had figured out the formulas she'd used—what they did and what the instructions really were—was no easier to explain.

"It's . . . I think I recognized the proportions first," she said after a moment's thought. "Black powder is usually always made with the same proportions of saltpeter, charcoal, and sulfur. So I realized I could make spur-fires first, because there were ingredients in those same proportions. That helped me figure out what some of the ingredients were, and then I could sort of, I don't know, see the sense of how things were written." But that made it sound like she'd worked out some kind of code. It hadn't really been quite like that.

She tried again. "Do you remember when I was younger and learning English?" Liao nodded. "There was a time when I knew a few words here and there, and then a time when I understood more of them and could work out what an English speaker was trying to say if I put the words together like clues. And then, one day, I suddenly realized I wasn't doing that anymore. Putting clues together, I mean. I *understood* what I was hearing, really understood it."

She paused, remembering how strange it had been when that realization had hit. "It was more like that. I knew what I was reading. I just *understood* it."

"Spoken like a true *fangshi*," Liao said with an odd smile. "Perhaps you are not destined to be a mere grinder of powders for long."

Fangshi . . . a master of methods. Uncle Liao's term for a pyrotechnician who was a true artificier. It was his name for what *he* was, a word borrowed from *waidan*, the ancient Chinese art of compounding elixirs.

It was high praise.

"Come." He nodded to the basket of spur-fires they'd made according to Jin's specifications. "Let us go and see what magic you have worked." Jin picked up the basket and followed him out of the tent where they'd been working.

Every time they set up shop, Fata Morgana erected three tents beside the wagon. The first was the tent they left now: the *danshi*, Uncle Liao's laboratory tent, and there was always a bit of ritual to setting it up. He was very particular about it.

The first consideration was location, and Jin had seen her uncle demand to move the entire encampment for the sake of putting his tent just where he wanted it. They had to dig down a foot or so into the ground where the *danshi* was to go, which — Liao had once impatiently explained — was to make sure there was neither an old well nor a tomb concealed below. The best Jin had been able to figure was that a hidden well might've made for unpredictable humidity above. But she had never come up with a reason why Uncle Liao would be concerned with an un-marked grave.

Yet, it was this concern that had caused the most trouble in the past. There were parts of the country where you couldn't dig in a field without unearthing hidden burial places, and Jin had come to learn that the greener and more verdant the ground, the more likely it was to be nourished by the dead. Tall nettles, in particular, were always best avoided. After passing through Gettysburg, which she'd since learned was the site of one of the bloodiest battles of the War Between the States, Jin had devel-oped a healthy fear of open fields.

Once they found a good spot without bodies or wells, they assembled a low wooden platform and built the tent on it; Uncle Liao's laboratory had to be off the ground. The tent had flap doors on three walls, which had to face south, east, and west. His stove went in the middle, facing the east door and insulated by white clay bricks. His chest of ingredients, his workbench, and his favorite tools made of burnished yellow metals went on the northern wall. Last of all, Liao hung four flags that he called his talismans, one at each corner of the tent. He kept the furnace going religiously from the moment the erection of the tent was complete until the night before Fata Morgana packed up and moved on—just long enough for it to cool down before they left.

The second tent, which they also built on a platform, became a storage and staging space. The third was made of heavy black, oiled fabric to shut out the light, and this was where Jin and Liao took her freshly made spur-fires.

They slipped into the dim interior. Jin took a pair of goggles from a rack beside the door and pulled them over her eyes. She dragged a table to the center of the tent, took one spur-fire case from the basket, and set it there. Then she lit the fuse with the pocket-sized flint lighter Liao had made for her, and backed away as her uncle drew the curtained doorway closed and plunged the tent into darkness.

The fuse burned down fast, and the case erupted into a hemisphere of scattering stars in a shade of deep violet Jin had never seen before, with a smell like fresh pine needles that definitely wasn't normal.

"*Hen piaoliang*," Liao murmured. *Very pretty*.

The violet cinders danced themselves out, and the tent went black again, but Jin's heart was so full and bright she felt like laughing. *I did that. I made that, and I worked out how to do it on my own.*

After dark, the Broken Land Hotel was a mania of lights. Even the lawn was aglitter: there were lanterns in the trees and on posts that overhung the paths, and even a pair of croquet courts with candlelit wickets.

Sam joined a cluster of folks walking from the hotel toward

the water, trying to look like he belonged as he kept an eye out for Ambrose or Tom. He stepped around groups of guests busy spreading blankets on the grass, until he heard the drifting sound of familiar music. He followed the tune across the boardwalk that ringed the lawn and onto the beach, where Tom Guyot sat plucking the strings of his tin guitar. "Hey, now." The old man grinned. "Glad you decided to come on out. You run into any trouble with the hotel folks?"

"Nah." Sam kicked off his shoes and dropped into the sand. "I did what you said and just acted like I wasn't worried about getting stopped. Also I . . . er . . . ran into the girl from the fireworks company earlier today," he added as nonchalantly as possible. "We happened to have a little conversation." *Just a little conversation, after she defended herself with explosives from some rowdies. And just another little conversation, after that business with the dead body in the alley.*

Tom nodded equally nonchalantly, fingers nimble on the strings. "I see. That wouldn't have anything to do with why you're wearing such a snappy outfit, would it?"

Sam smoothed down the front of his best shirt. "I was trying to look less like a scruffy card player so they'd let me on the grounds here," he said defensively. "But . . . about her. There was something else." He swallowed. "She . . . Jin—the girl— she found a body. Somebody murdered and dumped in the rough end of town."

Tom set down the guitar and looked at Sam. "That poor thing. She all right, you figure?"

"She seemed to be. She's . . . well, she's pretty strong, I think. Still . . ."

"Still." Tom nodded and began quietly plucking the strings again. "Ain't easy, coming across something like that. 'Specially when you're someplace civilized, like the middle of town."

"You remember the pianist at the Dram? Walter Mapp?"

Tom's song faltered. He tapped the metal body of his guitar with his fingernails, staring out at the water. When he started playing again, Sam felt a little thrill of recognition: it was the song Mapp had played that Tom had reacted to so oddly the day before.

The music stopped again. "Sure," Tom said easily. "Nice fellow."

"He wants to talk to you about it. What . . . what Jin found. Tonight, after the fireworks."

"Why's that?"

Sam still wasn't sure why Walter Mapp thought Tom could help. "Well, there was writing over the . . ." He lowered his voice. Tom leaned closer. " . . . over the body. It said *Claimed by blood for Jack Hellcoal*. I think he thought . . . you might know what that meant. I don't know why."

Tom drummed his fingers on the guitar again. "I suppose I'm part of the roaming world now," he said softly. "Guess I got to start acting like it sometime."

Sam frowned, wondering if he was supposed to understand what that meant. "Sorry?"

By way of answer, Tom just went back to picking gently at the strings. "Getting dark," he said at last. "Should be starting soon."

"You couldn't find a spot on the grass?" Ambrose appeared suddenly, standing over them with a scowl on his face, and dropped a picnic hamper into the sand between Sam and Tom. "These are fancy sandwiches, and they will not be improved by sand, I'll have you know."

While the newspaperman unpacked paper-wrapped sand-wiches and cold bottles of beer, Sam leaned back and stared sky-ward. Then Tom said something that snapped Sam to attention. "Ambrose, you remember those Jack tales you used to tell?"

"Sure," Ambrose said. "What about them?"

"Jack . . . tales?" Sam asked, confused. "You know about this guy?"

Ambrose glanced up from the picnic. "What guy? There are dozens, scores of tales about Jack. Gets mixed up with kings and giants a lot. You might've heard one about a beanstalk."

"That's the same Jack?"

"The same Jack as what?" The newspaperman lowered the sandwich he'd been about to bite into. "It's a *character*. When folks want to tell a story and they need a trickster for it, they talk about Jack."

Sam frowned. "So . . . this isn't even a real person?"

Ambrose laughed. "You think there are magic beans out there, Sam?" But then he hesitated. "Well, that's not to say that *some* of the stories might not have some truth to them."

Tom spoke up again. "Ambrose, you ever heard one about Jack and a hellcoal?"

"Sure," Ambrose said, still looking vaguely confused by the conversation. "The one where he beats the Devil."

"Ah." Tom sat back, thoughtfully. "That sounds like the kinda thing might be useful to hear. You mind coming along with Sam and me after the show, maybe tell what you know of the story to a couple folks?"

"Sure, I suppose," Ambrose said. "You mind if I eat this sandwich now?"

There was a sudden, piercing whistle, and a single streak shot into the sky like a falling star going the wrong way. The whistle trailed off, and the shooting star dwindled to nothingness. And then the sky caught on fire. The crowds on the beach and the lawn stopped moving and turned their heads up with a murmur of wonder.

A dome of light exploded over the Atlantic, turning night into day and illuminating a platform that floated fifty or so yards out on the water. Sam just barely had time to notice that most of the platform was hidden by a curtain before the curtain dropped, revealing a framework structure that looked like the skeleton of a castle.

From the center of the framework came a spark. Four fuses rushed the spark to the bottom corners of the skeletal castle, and the thing came to life.

Golden fire broke out at the corners, sped along the base of the structure, and began to pour upward. Before the dome of light in the sky from the first rocket had entirely died out, the fire had charged over the entirety of the edifice on the platform, replacing the skeleton with a palace built of flame. It looked, apart from the gentle, just barely visible motion of the fire, like a grand stone building caught by the red-gold of sunset.

Then, from the ramparts of the castle, the fireworks began. There were rockets that sailed overhead and burst, alone and in clusters, into a wild array of shapes and colors. There were some that whined and hissed and undulated across the sky. Some flew up in pairs or in threes that twisted around one another, leaving braided vapors of smoke behind them before they exploded. Others rose like tailed comets and burst into constellations of falling stars. And still there were more: rockets that spiraled like springs as they flew heavenward, shooting so high that when they finally burst into gigantic spheres or domes, the resulting fingers of light and trailing sparks seemed to be falling like rain over the people below.

Sam tore his eyes away from the sky for just a moment to look around at the upturned faces of the audience. There was scattered applause and murmuring here and there, but for the most part folks just stared, wonderstruck, as the fireworks tinted their cheeks blue and green and violet and scarlet and gold.

In between outbursts above, things were happening on the platform: a spray of blue-violet rose in front of the castle, like an ornamental fountain; a line of rotating candles, red and yellow and blue and orange, came to life around the base of the walls one after the other, like a row of blossoms in a flowerbed; green shapes sprouted and grew into fir trees. Soon there was a garden there, spread out at the foot of the blazing palace.

"Well, if that isn't something," Tom murmured. Sam could only nod. It was more than *something*. It was *astounding*.

From another part of the waterfront, off to the left, a sudden inferno of red and orange erupted. On a second floating platform, another curtain dropped to reveal the conical shape of a volcano. The fireworks pouring from its mouth increased and shot higher. The crimson reflections crept across the water toward the castle.

A panic of rockets flew from the first platform like an exodus of fleeing fire creatures—only instead of skyward, these rockets shot away horizontally and skipped across the water, diving under and resurfacing and spitting color and sparks all the while.

And then the palace began to sink.

Thick jets of blue and white sparks erupted along its base like foamy water as it went under, first the beautiful garden with its trees and fountains, then the walls of the castle itself as the structure descended, leaving the platform undisturbed at its center.

With a final volley of rockets and fleeing water sprites, the castle was gone. The scarlet reflection of the erupting volcano covered everything. Then, it, too, ceased.

There was a moment of quiet, and a few scattered claps. It seemed nobody was quite sure if they wanted to applaud the sinking of the castle. It had been so beautiful, and now it was gone.

There was another spark from the now-empty platform, and the unmistakable figure of Jin appeared, holding a ball of violet flame cupped in her hands. She knelt at the edge of the platform and touched the flame to the surface of the water, with the air of someone releasing a captive creature back into the wild.

She leaned back, still on her knees. The flame floated for a moment. And then, unbelievably, it dove. From where Sam sat on the beach he could just follow its progress beneath the water.

It touched something that began to glow with the same violet light.

The glowing shape started to rise. It grew larger and brighter as it did, until it broke the surface.

"Will you look at that?" Tom murmured.

"How is that *possible?*" Ambrose leaned forward, elbows on his knees. "I've seen plenty of fireworks, but *this*—"

Sam watched silently, enthralled. The castle, impossibly on fire *underwater*, was lifting itself up again.

Now the audience broke into *ooh*s and *aah*s, and a wave of clapping swept across the lawn. The castle kept rising until the entire skeletal framework, defined by deep violet sparks, had emerged. Jin was nowhere to be seen. Sam burst into applause right along with everyone else.

Then the whole thing blew up.

It fragmented with a world-shaking boom into a hundred separate rockets that sailed in all directions: arching overhead and shooting sideways and skittering over the water, spiraling and whistling and weaving ghostly and beautiful ribbons of vapor and smoke. Then the lot of them detonated, painting the sky and the sea below it with layers upon layers of glittering color.

And then, at last, the sky fell silent and only drifting smoke remained.

The platform was empty. Jin was gone. The whole thing had lasted just under an hour.

Sam gave his best, most earsplitting whistle and applauded until his hands hurt, hollering all the while.

Beaming, he got to his feet and dusted himself off. "I'm going to go say hi to Jin. I'll meet you in the hotel's lounge in a bit, Tom. Hopefully Mr. Mapp's there waiting for you."

Jin could barely conceal her delight as Liao rowed her back to shore in one of the hotel's little dories. She was still brimming with joy as she jumped out to haul the boat up onto the sand, still babbling to her amused but visibly proud uncle as she began taking crates from it and piling them on the beach.

"Jin!"

She looked up and spotted Sam waving. Uncle Liao cleared his throat. "I see Mr. Burns over there," he said, nodding toward one of the piers, where the owner of Fata Morgana was accepting the congratulations of some hotel official. "I'll be there with him."

Jin nodded and turned back to the boy trotting toward her. Ordinarily she would have carefully controlled her face so as to look perfectly composed, but the triumph of the resurrected Atlantis was too fresh. "Sam!" she called delightedly. "Did you *see?*"

"I . . . it was . . ." Sam hesitated. Jin tried not to laugh while his mental calculations were displayed quite clearly across his face. "Brilliant."

Jin blinked, then chuckled. "Good one, that."

He went an amusing shade of pink, dark enough to see even in the dim light from the ferry pier. "I wasn't trying to be clever," he admitted. "I meant it. How did you learn to do that?"

"Uncle Liao." Still beaming, Jin tucked a coil of match

cord into the crate. "He met Mr. Burns in Chicago. Mr. Burns had just inherited Fata Morgana and he knew nothing about fireworks, but the relative who'd left it to him also left a cookbook full of recipes which, not being a pyrotechnician, he couldn't make heads or tails of. So he hired Uncle Liao."

"And that's how you wound up with the company, too?"

Jin's smile faltered. She could feel the delight draining off her face. "No, I came along later."

Sam seemed to know he'd said something wrong. He grabbed Jin's bag from the boat as she reached for it, and slung it over his shoulder. "I got it. That, too," he added as she shrugged and went for one of the crates. "Just tell me where to take it."

Jin gave him a long, appraising look. Then she shrugged again. "The wagon's up near the stables. Let me just tell Uncle Liao where I'm going." She turned toward the pier. "Uncle Liao," she called. *"Wo jiang dao che."* Then she struck off past Sam and up the beach.

They walked most of the way in silence, although she made a point of slowing her pace after a moment or two. What he had said wasn't his fault, she told herself. He didn't know how much she hated thinking about how she'd come to be part of Fata Morgana.

Beneath their feet, sand gave way to boardwalk, boardwalk to lawn, and lawn to gravel. Someone had to speak again. "It is not clear to me," Jin said at last, forcing herself to say what was on her mind, "why you are here. This bothers me."

"Here?" Sam glanced sideways. Jin kept her eyes carefully on the ground in front of her. "You mean here in Coney Island, or here at the Broken Land?" Sam shrugged and grinned. "I like fireworks. Also . . . hang on a tick . . . yes, *you* invited me, if you recall."

"That was to get you to stop fussing over me," she said with a dismissive wave of her hand. They reached the wagon and the three fluttering tents alongside it. She stopped walking and faced him, arms folded. "I mean *here*, Sam. Now. Carrying boxes for me. What are you doing?"

Sam set the box down and put his hands in his pockets. "If it's the box-carrying that's bothering you—"

"It's not."

"I really and truly have no idea how to answer you. Are you angry about something?"

"Like what?" she shot back. She *was* angry now, but only at herself for starting this awful conversation.

He laughed shortly and rubbed his face. "I'm working on that problem myself, and I'm not coming up with anything that makes sense. If I was playing cards, this is where I'd call for you to just show your hand. Why is it," he added thoughtfully, sounding like he was speaking more to himself than to her, "that people get so much more complex when they *aren't* trying to take my money?"

Jin unfolded her arms with a little sigh of impatience. "I'm going to open the wagon door, and you're going to offer to carry the box inside." He frowned, clearly without a clue as to where this was going. Her face felt hot, but she forced herself to explain. "I want to know if you're going to mistake that for an invitation."

"An . . . invitation?" Sam stared at her, uncomprehending. Then, right before her eyes, it dawned on him, and a flush swept over his face once more. "Wait a minute. No. *No*. Are you out of your—why would you . . . why would you think *that?*"

Now that he'd utterly lost his composure, Jin's miraculously returned. She shrugged. "It's not unheard of."

"Did *I* do something to make you think that? I mean—well, *did* I?"

She held his shocked stare for a moment, then let her face soften just a little. "No. You didn't. But that would've made it particularly disappointing if . . ." She sighed, turned, climbed the stairs, and opened the wagon door, tossing the words "You didn't do anything, Sam," over her shoulder.

Inside, she took a deep breath. Outside, he hadn't moved. Jin would've heard it if he had. He was waiting for her to decide whether or not to let him in.

She lit the lamp beside the door. "Bring the box up."

"Jin." Sam waited until she returned to the doorway. "When you said it's not unheard of . . . ?"

She said nothing, just stood there, afraid of what he was going to ask.

"Has that actually happened to you?"

Another long moment passed. "Not," she said quietly, "in a long time."

She waited uncomfortably while several questions and emotions flashed across his face. Then, after a moment, he picked up the box and carried it inside. Jin pointed to an empty space under a bench opposite the entrance. "The box can go there. I'll take my bag."

Sam slid the box under the bench, handed over Jin's rucksack, and turned to go. "The display really was awfully good, Jin. Maybe I'll see you around the island."

"Thank you," she said. "Maybe so."

Out on the gravel, Sam paused and looked back at the wagon. Jin stood in the entrance, her hand on the doorframe, and watched him.

"Are you finished for the night?" he asked. "With the fireworks, I mean. Are you finished?"

Jin nodded. "Why?"

"Because . . ." He hesitated. "There's a fellow here named Tom, and Walter Mapp, one of the folks you met today, he thinks Tom might know something about Jack."

"Jack?" She stiffened. "The one in the . . . the writing?"

Sam nodded. "I'm supposed to meet them in the hotel right now. Do you want to come, or do you want to be done with it?"

Her hand tightened on the frame. "I want to come. Will they mind?"

"Well, you're going to stick out like a sore thumb, but Tom's a guest here. If you can stand a few stares . . ." He shrugged. "I figure you deserve to know, if that's what you want. If they kick you out, I'll make them kick me out, too."

"I have to tell Uncle Liao where I'm going." She shut the door and darted past him, toward the water. "Wait here."

She sprinted to the beach, ignoring the ache in her feet that running always brought, and made excuses to Uncle Liao and Mr. Burns. Then she sprinted back. "This way," she said to Sam, heading across the gravel lot between the stables and the back of the hotel. "It's dark, but it's a shorter walk around to the main entrance."

Light from windows on the upper floors cast bright pools on the gravel to their left as Jin led Sam through the shadows and along a row of ornamental potted junipers. Eventually they came around to the wide circular drive with the glass bandstand at its center.

From here, the Broken Land, with all its lights blazing, was something straight out of a lithograph print. The odd angles and glass cupolas and mismatched puzzle-piece dormer windows of the strange, sprawling hotel somehow managed to come together under the moon.

"Wow," Jin said, trying not to sound too impressed. It was the first time she'd seen it from the front at night. "Are they even going to let us in there?"

"We're invited," Sam said. "Just try and look like you belong."

Sam's confidence notwithstanding, the doorman gave them a dubious look as they came up the stairs to the main entrance. "Hotel guests and their guests only, young man."

At his side, Jin flinched. "I knew it," she mumbled.

"Wait a minute," Sam said. "We're invited," he told the doorman. "We're meeting friends."

The doorman's doubtful expression didn't change. He looked from Sam to Jin and back. Jin tried not to fidget. Then she started feeling a vague anger stirring in her gut on Sam's behalf. They weren't trying to trespass. They *were* invited.

"There are folks waiting for us," Sam continued. "And if *you're* not going to open the door for this young lady, at least get out of my way so *I* can open it for her." Then, before the doorman could reply, Sam shouldered the heavy door open and stepped aside for Jin. "After you."

"Er. Thank you," she said quietly.

"Don't be embarrassed," Sam said as the door swung shut behind them. "That guy was just being difficult."

She nodded and tried not to look as uncomfortable as she felt. The doorman was behind them, but now everybody in the atrium was staring. This made the long walk across the huge atrium seem even longer.

Sam was acutely aware of the girl at his side.

They were just about the same height, but he was sure that if he really stood straight he would have an inch on her. Her long braid was pinned up, probably the better to stay out of the way of sparking fuses. It had clearly been done without a thought for appearances, yet somehow it managed to make her look bizarrely elegant. Strangest and most fascinating of all, she was close enough for him to smell the gunpowder and smoke that still lingered from the fireworks display.

At last, the green tiles and gilt paint of the atrium gave way to the Turkish carpets and brass rails of the saloon. Walter Mapp waved from a booth in the corner where he sat with Tom Guyot and the newspaperman.

The three men exchanged brief glances when they spotted Jin, but they stood up when the pair reached the table, and before it had even occurred to Sam to wonder if she would be comfortable in the close confines of the booth, a waiter appeared with a chair.

When the five of them were seated, introductions made, and fresh glasses had been brought and poured for Sam and Jin, Ambrose spoke up. "So this is Liao's prodigy, the girl from San Francisco?"

Jin, who had just that moment reached for her glass, stopped as if she had been turned to stone. The look she gave Ambrose was almost belligerent. "How do you know that?"

"I lived in San Francisco for a long time," Ambrose replied. If he noticed her odd look, he ignored it. "Your uncle and I crossed paths once or twice out there, and have done so once or twice since."

Tom Guyot reached across and patted Jin's hand. "Ambrose has spent some time on the road, too, darlin'. That's all."

Walter Mapp cleared his throat and raised his beer. "Young lady, that was a hell of a show you put on. I've never seen the like of it."

"Your uncle must be proud," Tom added.

Sam raised his glass, too. "Congratulations."

Jin smiled briefly and murmured, "Thank you." Little by little, she seemed to relax again.

"Well, friends," Walter Mapp said at last, "it pains me to bring the conversation around to unpleasant topics, but this matter of Jack . . ." He looked at Jin. "You all right talking about this, now?"

She nodded. "Yes, sir."

"All right, then." He turned to Tom Guyot. "I've been off the roads a long time. I'm hoping you can shed some light."

The old black man nodded. "I've heard the story, but that's all. The real expert is Ambrose here. Apart from what he writes for the papers, he's a proper fiction writer, and he knows quite a lot about what goes on in the roaming world."

They all turned to look at the newspaperman, who shifted uncomfortably in his seat. "Jack tales—well, I don't know how many of them really refer to the man we're talking about, but people do tell lots of stories about a man named Jack. I may have collected a few of them in my time."

"You know the one these folks mean, though," Tom persisted.

"I think so," Ambrose admitted. "The one about the coal of hellfire, I believe."

"Do you mind recounting it?" Mapp asked with exaggerated patience. "It could be a matter of some importance. Anyway, we've got no place else to start."

"I suspect I can call it back up." Ambrose tapped his fingers on his knees. "And yes, I suppose I do know more about it than I'd like to." He glanced at Sam, then at Jin, considering each for a moment or two. "You've spent your life on the road," he said to Jin at last. "I'm going to guess this won't shock you as much as it'll shock Sam."

"What?" Sam demanded. "What kind of narrow-brained kid do you take me for?"

"It's not that. It's just life in a city makes you believe in certain things, a certain order. A certain reality." He paused to take a sip from his glass. "The world is not simple. The world is not one *place*. It's the sum of an impossible number of incomprehensible things, and if you start out on any road in the world and follow it for any distance at all, sooner or later you enter into strange country."

The journalist paused to empty his glass and call for another.

"So," he finally continued, "the world is not simple, but it would be much, much better for us if it was. And we can sense that, even if we do not understand or perceive the full complexity of things. So we look for order." He gave Sam a short smile. "My point, Sam, is that for this to sound like anything other than a folktale, you are going to have to adjust your thinking."

He took another sip of his drink and looked out the window for a moment. "And so we come to Jack."

TEN

The Tale of Jack

I N DAYS of yore," Ambrose began, "there was a sort of man we might call a woodsman pioneer. These were days in which only the shortest of paths had been cut into the wilderness, and these woodsmen made a living carving homesteads and farmland from the unknown for less intrepid souls, who would make their homes in the spaces the woodsmen cleared, then applaud themselves for their adventuresome spirit. Jack was one of these woodsmen, and one winter he found himself so far into the hills that, rather than trying to return home before the first snows, he decided to build himself a cabin and winter there.

"Now, in those days, uncanny beings walked the roads and woods of the country." Ambrose paused after this weighty declaration while Walter Mapp and Tom Guyot stifled chuckles.

"Did they, now?" Mapp asked, faux incredulous. "What a world it must've been."

"Gentlemen, do you wish me to tell the story or not?"

"We do. By all means, continue."

"Excuse me," Sam interrupted, "but . . . uncanny beings? What's that mean?"

"In those days," Ambrose went on with a final sharp look at Mapp, "there were peculiar creatures roaming the land. These were uncanny beings. Some looked like men. Some thought that worrying about whether they could pass unnoticed among humanity was a waste of time, and they wore stranger shapes.

"Not long after Jack had built his cabin in the wilderness, a nightmare blizzard fell upon the hills. Now it's hard—particularly in a city, particularly in the summer—to imagine what these snows are like, Sam, the great snows of the middle country. In only one day, Jack was trapped. The drifts piled against his door, buried him in a white silence that rose almost to the eaves. And on that first night, only hours after Jack had tried his door and discovered he couldn't open it because of the weight of the snow outside, he heard a sound. Someone was rapping upon the door.

"Although he knew, because of the ten-foot drifts, that it was impossible, he took hold of the latch and turned it. Miraculously, the door swept open at the lightest touch.

"The land outside was white with snow, shining with ice, knife-sharp with bitter wind, but the snowdrift that had buried the cabin was gone. And standing in the doorway was . . ."

Ambrose hesitated and leaned his elbows thoughtfully on the table. "Now, here I must confess to some uncertainty. I've heard this story from a number of sources, and *shockingly*"—he paused again for the slightest lift of his eyebrow—"there are some few details that have not been consistent. The first of these details is the identity of Jack's visitor."

He took another drink, ice clinking in his glass. "I've heard it was Saint Peter, out on a tour to be sure mankind was behaving in a civilized manner. I've heard it was some kind of native prince or Indian shaman. But the version that seems most reasonable to me"—he gave Jin a wink—"is the one I'm about to tell you, because in my not inconsequential experience, there is nothing quite so likely to plaster something up wrong as a woman." Ambrose shook his head apologetically.

"The woman who stood on the threshold was, obviously, beautiful. It would've been the end of the story if she wasn't. This fact, the fact of her unbelievable sweetness of face and figure, should have tipped Jack off to her thoroughly untrustworthy nature." He turned to Sam. "Mark my words, homely girls are the only ones worth trusting. I, for one, suspect that all beautiful girls are, in fact, wicked creatures with evil intentions." He gave Jin a pointed glance. "Present company, et cetera."

"I have never been guilty of being a beautiful girl," Jin observed archly, "so I will choose not to take offense. And I know at least one poet who would agree with you. *Keep away from sharp swords. Don't go near a lovely woman.*"

"Wise poetical words," Ambrose agreed, "although I suspect some of us"—his eyes flicked over to Sam—"might argue with the rest of what you said. Anyhow. Back to Jack.

"Being an adult male, Jack was perfectly familiar with the diabolical nature of beautiful women. He should have been able to make a better judgment of the character of his guest and slammed the door in her face. He didn't, of course; Jack was many things even then and has since been accused of many more, but he was never inhospitable.

"She was shivering; shivering so hard she couldn't speak. She was a hair's-breadth from hypothermia, and her hands and lips were blue. And although Jack's cabin was scores of miles deep in the wilderness, the only luggage she carried was a violin case.

"Jack brought her inside, near to the fire. He helped her out of her frozen coat, more like an icicle than fur or wool, wrapped her in two blankets, and left her to warm while he looked for a set of clean clothes. Then he occupied himself at the other end of the cabin, giving her as much privacy as the tiny room would permit while she changed out of her wet garments and into the dry ones he had offered her. When she stopped shaking and the blue had gone out of her lips and fingers, Jack made soup and coffee. When she had eaten and drunk all she could, he dragged the cot where he slept over near to the fire and tucked her into it, under every blanket he owned. When at last Jack fell asleep himself, sitting against the wall and covered only by his coat, the woman had still not spoken a word.

"For three days, the wind and snow raged outside. Inside the cabin, Jack fed his visitor, mended her threadbare clothes, and let her sleep in his bed and under his blankets while he slept against the cold wall." Ambrose gave Sam another sharp look. "Together in the freezing wilderness in that cabin for three days. And let me remind you again, this woman was *beautiful*. Whatever else Jack might've been, he was at least capable of acting the gentleman when he felt like it.

"The woman would smile at him in thanks when he would pour her a tin cup of coffee, and that smile would come close to crushing his heart, it was a thing of such glory. She would smile a good night before she covered herself with the blankets to go to sleep, and that smile would finish the job of breaking him, it was a thing of such splendor. And heaven help him if he looked too long into her eyes."

"What do papers pay per word for that kind of prose?" Mapp cut in. Jin snickered.

Ambrose rolled his eyes. "I'm keeping my audience in mind. It's a *skill*, Mapp. Do you want to take over?"

"No, sir. Pray carry on."

"Then pray keep quiet, if you don't mind. For three long days this went on. For three days, the woman refused to speak. But each night, before they retired to their respective sleeping places, she would open her case and produce a beautiful violin. She would rub the bow with a chunk of red rosin she wore on a pendant around her neck, and she would play. For an hour she would speak through those strings, and each night Jack fell asleep believing he knew her just a little bit better than he had the night before."

"Ain't that just true?" Tom said. "My old guitar's always better at saying what I want to say. It's a sight easier to just let the instrument do your talking. Wouldn't you say, Mr. Mapp?"

"I would," Mapp agreed.

Sam willed himself not to look at Jin. He didn't know music, but watching her paint the skies that night he'd had the same thought—that he had caught a truer glimpse of her in the glare of the rockets over the water than she had allowed him any of the times they had spoken face-to-face.

"On the fourth day, Jack awoke, not on the floor where he knew he had fallen asleep shivering beneath his coat, but under a blanket on his cot. He rolled over to find coffee already boiling on the fire, and the woman watching him from a chair beside it. She was dressed in her own clothes, and she held her coat on her lap.

"And then, at long last, the beautiful woman spoke.

"'The time has come for me to leave, Jack.' You might imagine what hearing her speak his name did to his already-aching heart. 'In gratitude for your courtesy, I am going to make you a gift of three wishes. Save them for when you truly need them.' Before Jack could decide whether to protest her leaving, beg to know her name, or ask about her gift, she leaned over to kiss him. And before he could recover from that, she had crossed the room, swirled her coat around her shoulders, and disappeared through the door. Naturally, Jack came to his wits, sprang across the cabin, and attempted to give chase. When he tried to fling the door open, however, he found himself confounded. It would not so much as budge an inch. Only with great effort did he force it wide enough to see the ten-foot snowdrift holding it closed from the other side.

"She was gone. Only later, many hours after she had left him in the silence of the snowed-in cabin, did he find her necklace, the one with the red rosin pendant, hanging from a nail by the fireplace. It was the only proof that she had ever been there at all."

It was a good story, and Ambrose was definitely a good storyteller, but this didn't sound like the world Sam knew. It must have shown on his face, because the newspaperman gave him a sharp look and said, "You look like you wish you could tell me we aren't here to listen to ghost tales."

"I . . . well, yeah," Sam said defensively. "What Jin saw

—well, that was real. You said yourself this is just a story you heard. How do you know any of it's true?"

"I don't pretend to know anything," Ambrose replied. "I know the story, that's all. What you make of it is entirely up to you. But it's going to get stranger before it's over."

"I'd like to hear the rest," Jin said quietly. "If no one minds."

Ambrose swirled his glass. "Well, the snows melted, and the time came when Jack should've moved on from that slapdash shack in the hills. But he didn't go. First he started walking the woods in search of any signs of the mysterious woman. There were none. Weeks passed. Months.

"Then, in June, a wild rose vine appeared along one corner of the house and burst into bloom. To Jack, these flowers seemed like a sign. Little by little, he began to hope that she might come back. The second that thought came into his mind, he was as good as lost. He was never moving on."

He paused and looked at Sam. "Here's a thing you would never know, living in a city. Men are like trees."

"Trees?"

Ambrose nodded. "In a city, in a forest of others like him, a man will grow straight—taking into account his type, his temperament, and the unique blights upon his personality. But alone on the plain, alone in the desert, alone in the wilderness where he is the only tall thing to mar the horizon, to bear the pressures of the wind . . . *alone*, Sam, with the raging storms, the starving rocks, the alkaline soil . . . alone, a man may yield and become deformed by his environment. And Jack was alone for a very, very long time."

Jin and Tom were nodding, as if all of this made perfect sense. Sam tried to imagine ever being that kind of alone and found he couldn't fathom it. Anytime he had ever been by himself, there had been a wall somewhere close by with someone on the other side of it.

"In the wide world," Ambrose continued, "it is natural to seek out the paths others have blazed, if one is lucky enough to find them. Well, in that manner, those strange roamers I mentioned before began to find their ways to Jack's cabin."

"Mr. Ambrose, sir, excuse me," Sam interrupted again. "I don't know what you mean when you say 'strange roamers' . . ."

Ambrose opened his mouth, then closed it again and turned to Tom Guyot and Walter Mapp. "Would you like to field this one, gentlemen?"

Tom and Mapp exchanged a glance. "Sam," Mapp said, pushing his old hat back on his head, "you and I've known each other a while. Tell me the truth, kid. You think I'm a little odd?"

Sam nodded. Then common sense and politeness kicked in. "I mean—"

"Sure, sure, everybody in Coney Island's an oddity." Mapp waved his hand carelessly. "Hell with parlor manners. Point is, I'm one of those strange roamers—or at least I have been, in my life; though, like I said, it's been a long time. So's Tom, and trust me when I tell you, we're probably the most normal of 'em. Take the most bizarre freak in West Brighton, multiply him by whatever big number you want, and put what you get on the road. That's what we're talking about."

Sam thought back to earlier that evening, right before the

fireworks. *I suppose I'm part of the roaming world now,* Tom had said. So *this* was what he had meant.

"But what—what does that mean?" Sam frowned at Mapp. "You don't *roam* anywhere."

"I did for a long time before I came here, and someday I'll leave for the road again."

"So it just means being strange and being on the road? Like . . . like a tramp or something?" It was sort of an awkward question. People generally didn't like tramps. Another thing newspapers were fond of screaming about, along with the depression and strikes and riots and anarchists, was what they liked to call the tramp scare.

Mapp shook his head. "When you think of tramps, you're probably thinking about vagrants or folks walking from town to town looking for work. What we're talking about is something different." He looked to Tom. "How do I explain this?"

"Far as I go," Tom said thoughtfully, "it's sort of a matter of feeling more at home on the roads than the places they lead to. You get to be at the edge of things, walking the borders of the world. How it feels to me, anyhow."

"Did you always feel that way?" Jin asked. For the second time, Sam had the feeling that she understood what was being discussed far better than he did.

Tom shook his head. "No, ma'am. There was . . ." His voice trailed off. "There were a couple of things happened to change the way I looked at the world. One of 'em was the war. The other . . ." He glanced at Mapp again. "Well, that's a story for another time." Then he turned back to Jin. "But you know what I mean about the roads, don't you, darlin'?"

She nodded. "Sometimes, out in between cities with all those big stretches of the country and all that sky . . ." She smiled wistfully. *"For a while the dust weighs lightly on my coat. These times, the traveler's heart is a flag a hundred feet high in the wind.* That's the same poet I mentioned before, and it's as if he saw right into my heart when he wrote that."

Tom smiled at her. "That's just exactly it. You have a roamer's soul."

Across the table, Ambrose cleared his throat. Mapp gestured grandiosely at him. "As you were."

"Thank you, Mr. Mapp. To continue. By the time the uncanny roamers began to arrive at Jack's door, he had already gone a little ways around the bend.

"The first one to knock arrived in the spring, in the midst of a thunderstorm. Jack answered, certain it was the woman with the violin. Instead, a small, raggedy man in a torn coat stood there, dripping on the doorstep. Jack was crushed, of course, but he let the stranger in. The little man was all gratitude, and Jack, though disappointed, was gracious. This changed, however, the moment the man had made himself comfortable by the fire and asked Jack if he could perhaps borrow one of his blankets. Jack refused.

"The blankets, you see, whether in reality or only in Jack's tortured mind, still retained the scent of the woman with the violin, and he could not bear the loss of that small comfort. He did not explain this, of course—how could he? So his guest assumed he was simply being mean-spirited, and the second Jack's eyes began to droop, the stranger snuck one of the blankets and wrapped it around himself.

"Jack woke with a start, and I'm sorry to tell you I can't repeat much of what he said to the stranger before he yanked away the blanket and tossed the fellow back out into the rain. Suffice it to say, the stranger thought Jack had quite seriously overreacted, and he was angry. He turned to the door Jack had slammed shut behind him and scratched a small sign into the frame, just beside the doorknob. It was a warning to others like him, and it was the beginning of Jack's reputation as a troublemaker.

"Meanwhile, Jack was about to make his second mistake, and this one had to do with those three wishes he hadn't yet used."

"About those," Jin interrupted. "Why didn't he just wish for the woman to come back? Or to know where she was, or something like that?"

"Ah. Well, that's a good question." Ambrose tapped his chin and thought. "I was never given a specific reason, but I can make a pretty good guess, because if there's one thing men who have loved and been left are likely to be, it's *stubborn*. I suspect Jack knew that wishing for her to come back wouldn't be the same, or as good, as having her come back of her own will."

"But maybe she didn't know whether he wanted her to come back at all," Jin protested. "How could she possibly know that?"

"Oh, please," Sam muttered. "Girls always know."

"That is absolutely *not* true. Who on earth told you that?"

"The girl who lives downstairs from me," Sam retorted. "And she's assured me several times that she knows everything."

"In any case," Ambrose said with a touch of a smile, "Jack had not used any of his wishes in the many months that had gone by since the woman's visit, but after he had thrown out the stranger, he made his first one. He wished that if anyone other than himself ever again touched those blankets, they would cling to that person's hands and burn like hot coal until Jack himself ordered the punishment to stop."

"Over a *blanket?*" Jin asked. "You weren't fooling about him having gone around the bend."

"Over how the blanket *smelled,*" Ambrose corrected her. "Being a female yourself, you cannot possibly have any concept of how obnoxiously potent a woman's scent is, particularly when the woman in question is not present. Don't give me that look, young lady. I'm twice as old as you are and married to a woman I'm often absent from. I know whereof I speak."

"That's just plain crazy," Jin muttered. "Am I wrong?"

"Sounds crazy to me," Sam said quickly, which was a complete lie. Actually, after this evening he thought it made a perfect kind of sense.

Ambrose shook his head. "That's nothing. Another strange roamer appeared at the cabin, this time in the summer. This one was an old, stooped woman, and although she saw the mark on the doorframe, she was too tired to go any farther that day. She knocked on the door, and while she waited for someone to open it, she made her mistake. She picked a rose from the flowering vine.

"Jack opened the door just in time to see her do it, and he flew into an even greater fury than he had about the borrowed blanket. He ordered the woman off his land and stood there to make sure she really left. At the edge of the woods, however, she paused to carve her own warning mark on a tree beside the path that led to Jack's house.

"Meanwhile, Jack was busy using his second wish. The land he had cleared, the place where the cabin sat, was ugly, forbidding. All except that rosebush, the only beautiful thing that remained in Jack's world while he waited in vain for the woman to return. You can perhaps imagine why he was protective of it.

"'If anyone touches this rose vine,' he said angrily, 'may it wind that person up in thorny branches and scratch and squeeze them until I call a stop to the pain.' And that was summer.

"Over the next few months, many roamers saw the marks on the tree and the door, and one by one they passed Jack's house, muttering about the strange hermit in his lonely cabin. It wasn't until the autumn that any of them was desperate enough to knock again. This time it was a small boy with golden eyes, and he was being pursued.

"The thing that chased him was huge, fast, and deadly. The boy couldn't see it, couldn't smell it, couldn't hear it. But they were the only living things in the woods now; every bird, every beast, everything else had fled, so the boy knew his pursuer was close. He also knew that if he didn't find sanctuary, he would be dead in a matter of minutes.

"He saw the old woman's warning as he raced up the path. He saw the small man's warning as he came to a panting, trembling halt at the door. He knocked, and Jack opened the door just a sliver, but it was enough.

The boy slipped through. He hauled on the door, slamming it shut before Jack could react. A moment later there was a thump on the other side, the impact of something heavy that made the entire cabin shudder. Then, stillness. And Jack turned from the door to stare at the boy with the wild golden eyes.

"'Please,' the boy said. 'It's waiting for me. Please don't send me away.'

"Jack had changed, certainly. But while he was no longer the hospitable woodsman pioneer of his youth, he had felt the cabin lurch, and he was no monster. 'Don't touch the blankets,' he warned, 'and when we are able to venture outside again, do not touch the rose vine. Sit by the fire. I'll make us coffee while we wait for whatever is out there to leave.'

"They waited, and the boy sat silently until the coffee was done. 'What is it?' Jack asked at last.

"'I don't know,' the boy said. 'No one has ever seen one. Only what they leave behind when they are finished with their prey.'

"'And how did it come to be after you?'

"The boy shrugged. 'I must've done something. A creature like that doesn't come after you for no reason.' He looked with imploring eyes at Jack. 'That's true, isn't it? I must've done *something*.'"

Ambrose paused to pour himself another glass of beer. "I'm not sure I could have answered that question. Jack nodded, but only because that seemed to be the answer the boy hoped to hear."

"Wait," Sam interrupted. "Why?" Like most boys he knew, he'd spent his entire life trying to avoid doing anything—or at least, getting caught at anything—that might get him in trouble. Why would anyone want to be told that they deserved to be chased by some invisible, murderous being?

It was Jin who answered. "I think it's much worse to think awful things just happen without any good reason," she said quietly, worrying the single green bangle around her wrist. "If you . . . if you can believe you deserve to be hurt, then there's always the possibility that you can figure out what you did to deserve it, and you can stop doing that, and then . . ." She swallowed. "And then you can imagine that things might get better."

Tom Guyot patted Jin's hand, rigid and motionless as stone on her knee.

"You know that isn't the world we live in, darlin'," he said softly. "Would make life all sorts of easier, but things aren't that way."

Jin nodded without looking at him. "Yes, I know."

Abruptly Sam was ashamed that he hadn't done something, spoken comforting words or patted her shoulder or the like. But the moment had passed.

Ambrose drummed his fingers on the table. "Shall I carry on?"

"Yes, please," Jin said gratefully.

"Jack and the boy sat in the cabin, trying to wait out the invisible thing. When Jack went to sleep, the boy obediently leaned against the wall without a blanket, shivering from cold and fear. He couldn't sleep a wink, and sometime during the night, he noticed the rosin pendant that still hung from the nail beside the hearth."

"Oh, no," Sam muttered. "Don't do it, kid."

Ambrose nodded sadly. "Of course he took it down, but only to see it better. And of course, that's when Jack woke up and screamed at the boy to give it back, and in his panic the boy dropped the necklace into what remained of the fire."

"Rosin is a kind of pitch," Jin said softly. "Pitch burns."

Ambrose nodded again. "Jack dove and managed to save it before the piece burned up entirely, but the damage was done. He turned on the trembling boy, who was crying his apologies, and ordered him from the house.

"'But what if it's still out there?' the boy asked.

"That, of course, was the question. Jack looked at the strange child who wore such terror on his small face and for a moment he almost relented. But he was too far gone, and in the end, his twisted anger and hurt won out.

"He opened the door and the boy, who knew perfectly well that the damned thing was still out there seeking him, walked out of the cabin, shaking all over.

"It was upon him before Jack could shut the door.

"The boy dropped to his hands and knees with a shriek. It was as if something huge, something unseen, had come flying at him from behind and knocked him flat. Then the boy was upright again, but plainly not under his own power. He flailed violently back and forth and from side to side, feet occasionally leaving the ground, entire body occasionally being—how else to put it?—*blotted out*, as if some larger creature had passed between the boy under attack and the man watching.

"Jack managed to pull himself together long enough to realize he ought to go for his gun. By the time he had gotten it and come back to the door, the golden-eyed boy was dead. The last thing Jack saw was his shredded body sliding along the ground toward the woods, dragged by the unseen thing that had chased him there. And Jack made his last wish: that anyone else who touched that pendant would feel the full weight of all his loss and all his sadness and all his loneliness, as well as all his horror and guilt for what he had done to the boy. And that was the autumn."

Despite his skepticism about the story itself, Sam discovered he was shocked and horrified. He glanced at Jin. She held her fists curled tightly in her lap, and her fingers were so tense that a little network of shiny scars on her hands that Sam hadn't noticed before stood out white against her skin.

"Winter came and went and came again. The death of the strange boy marked Jack's cabin as an evil place, and there were no roamers desperate enough to venture there any longer. Years passed and Jack lived on, alone and unaging as he waited for the woman to return and suffered the memory of the boy's death over and over. Perhaps his long life came from his dealings with the uncanny roamers; perhaps the world of men had just forgotten him as completely as he had forgotten it.

"But the otherworld had not forgotten Jack and what he had done. Poor hospitality was bad enough, but there were very few children among the uncanny, and the death of the boy with the golden eyes was something they could not forgive. They watched Jack's life lengthen as if he had no intention of dying, and finally they decided that if he would not die like the mortal he was, someone would have to go and carry him to Hell where he belonged.

"The first one turned up in the winter. When Jack opened

the door, he found a man in a striped suit waiting there. 'Jack, I'm here to carry you to Hell,' the man said, 'and I'm not taking no for an answer. Get your things together and let's go.'

"Jack stared at the man in the suit for a long minute. Then he laughed. 'Fine. I guess it's about my time. Come on in while I pack. There are some blankets there if you'd like to warm up.'

"'Don't mind if I do,' the man said. And he went straight to where the blankets sat on a chair by the fire. Jack stood there and laughed and laughed while the blanket the man had reached for clung to his fingers, burning them and refusing to be let go, no matter how the stranger shook his hands and howled.

"'I'll set you free,' Jack laughed, 'but I'm certainly not going with you to Hell.' What could the fellow do but agree? So Jack ordered the blankets to stop their torture and the man in the suit slunk out of the cabin and into the woods.

"The next one came in the summer. This was a bigger man, shaggy-headed as a bear. 'I'm here to carry you to Hell,' he growled when Jack opened the door, 'so get your things together and let's go. And I know all about your cursed blankets, so don't bother trying that trick on me.'

"This time Jack didn't laugh. He took a deep breath and nodded. 'I can see I'm not going to be able to change your mind,' he said sadly. 'Come on in while I pack.'

"'No, thank you,' said the shaggy-headed man. 'I'll wait right here. Make it quick.'

"'Well, I suppose there isn't really much I need,' Jack admitted. 'Truthfully, the only thing I really care about is that rose vine. It reminds me of someone I used to know. Since you're

right there, break me off a branch of roses and I'll be ready
to go.'

"The shaggy-headed man was so pleased with how well Jack
was cooperating, he didn't bother to wonder about the strange
request. He reached right into the roses, and immediately—
too quickly for the man to escape—the vine wrapped him in
its thorns. The stranger screeched in pain while it twisted and
tightened, and Jack just laughed and laughed.

"'I'm not going with you,' Jack said finally. 'I'll let you go,
but then off with you and leave me in peace.' The man held out
as long as he could, but in the end there was nothing for him to
do but agree.

"The last one came in the autumn, and it was a girl. When
Jack opened the door and found her there, he nearly fainted dead
away—she was the very image of the golden-eyed boy, only her
eyes were the silver of the winter moon.

"'You have worn out your welcome in this place,' she told
him. 'Cut me with your thorns, burn me with your blankets, it
makes no difference. There is no torture you can show me that I
don't already feel without my brother. I am here to carry you to
Hell or tear you to pieces myself.'

"Jack looked at her and knew that she was telling the truth.
'Fine,' he said. 'Bring me my necklace, the one by the hearth,
and I'll go with you willingly.' And I think there was a part of
him that hoped this last ruse would fail. He held his breath as the
girl with the silver eyes crossed the cabin and took hold of the
rosin pendant.

"Her scream was worse than any sound he had ever heard,

full of more pain than he would have believed possible. It was the sound of murder witnessed; it was the sound of humanity dying; it was the sound of hope frozen and thrown against a rock to be crushed like an icicle. It was everything Jack had wished. Before his eyes the girl was rapidly going mad with anguish. It was too much to witness, even for him.

"'Stop,' he shouted. 'Stop, and set her free!' But he had forgotten to include that bit in his wish, and all he could do was try to hold her down and keep her from hurting herself until she reached a momentary calm, like an eye in the storm of torment. The girl stared at him with her red-rimmed silver eyes. 'I see now,' she said in a voice broken by screaming. 'You are already in Hell.' And then she flung him aside like a rag doll as the pain and agony began to build in her body again. She staggered out of the house screeching, leaving Jack alone with his precious possessions. For a long time, he heard her ravaged voice echoing through the trees.

"More years went by, and at last Jack began to tire of his long life. The woman with the violin was clearly never coming back—there was no way to know if she was even alive. Worse, he had the death of the boy with the golden eyes and the madness of his silver-eyed sister on his conscience, and these memories never stopped tormenting him. So finally he packed up his things, put the pendant around his neck, cut a rose from the vine for his lapel, and went in search of Hell for himself.

"From time to time, he encountered other strange roamers—for naturally, that is what Jack himself became the second he started out on the road—and after all the trouble he had caused, they were glad to help him find his way. But when he at last found his way to the Gates of the Underworld and rang the Infernal Doorbell, something impossible happened.

"The Devil himself came to the door, looked Jack over as if he were some form of livestock, and pronounced these words: 'No, I don't think so.' Then the Devil paused, fished about in his waistcoat pocket, and held out his hand. In it was a live coal.

"'Take this,' he suggested, 'and go find your own place. I suppose you know Heaven isn't going to let you in, either.' And with that, the Gates of the Underworld clanged shut in Jack's face.

"And that," Ambrose finished, "is how Jack came to be wandering the earth, looking for somewhere to start his own place."

"Stepped on a pin, the pin bent, and that's the way the story went." Tom lifted his glass. "That's the proper way to finish a tale like that where I come from."

"That's a story," Sam protested after a long moment's silence. "That's not real. It isn't possible."

"I told you you'd have a hard time believing it," Ambrose said. "A city is chaotic, but it's at least predictable. The country is wide and strange, and full of wonders that have to be seen to be believed. This is who is meant by Jack Hellcoal."

"So the message," Mapp said grimly. "The words that were on the wall. They said *Claimed by blood for Jack Hellcoal.* What is it he's claiming, exactly?"

"Well," Ambrose said thoughtfully, "I think you have to consider the worst-case possibility, Mr. Mapp. That he's decided on New York."

Then the Devil paused, fished about in his
waistcoat pocket, and held out his hand.

Sam stared. "He's . . . decided on New York for what? For his own . . . what, his own personal Hell?"

"Looks that way," Ambrose said, draining what remained in his glass.

Jin turned her glass in circles on the tabletop. "How does it work? Making a place into Hell?"

Ambrose shrugged. "No idea." He looked at Tom, then at Mapp. "You?"

Mapp shook his head. "Nope," Tom said thoughtfully. "But I can't say as I think it sounds like a good thing for the folks who already live here."

Silence fell over the table.

"He must be stopped," Ambrose said finally. "He absolutely must. You understand, this isn't about New York. I like New York, but there's more at stake than that." He looked at Tom. "That's true, isn't it?"

The old man nodded. "The country isn't in what you'd call a safe place. Folks are angry, still. Folks are scared, and folks feel like punishing each other, and I don't think many of 'em are clear about what they're mad for. They're just mad."

"That's because they're the *other* kind of mad," Ambrose muttered. "All of them. They're less than a score of years removed from the worst thing that has ever happened to this country, and frankly, a lot of things that many of us hoped a Union victory would change went right back to the way they were. The number of lynchings this year . . . the strikes, the bombings . . . the number of people who are out of work . . . and a lot of people seem to be working rather diligently to make sure Emancipation turns out to be a change in terminology rather than a new life for men like Tom." He looked at the old guitar player. "Would you agree?"

Tom sighed. "Being free is better than the alternative. But just saying the word isn't enough. There's a lot of places in the country where folks will still do mighty nasty things to a body, free or not." He rubbed a hand across his face, which wore an expression that reminded Sam a lot of the haunted gazes of some of the other soldier-guests of the hotel. "So many people died for us to be able to have a right to that word, *free*."

Ambrose nodded. His eyes were glazed over in recollection. "It was just bodies falling," he murmured. "Whatever got you there in the first place, in the end it was bodies falling and dying long, slow deaths. They weren't even people. They were just bodies, bodies that fell and foamed and bled and froze and starved and died. And no one has forgotten, or forgiven, a moment of it."

He smiled thinly at Sam. "The point is, the country is angry and afraid and I swear to you, not one city, not one town is safe from the possibility of exploding into violence at the slightest touch. Nothing would provide a swifter impetus back into chaos than some kind of inexplicable terror erupting in a place as visible as New York. Frankly, I don't think I'm alone in believing the United States would plunge headlong into panic at far less. Just think about what happened only last month with all the railroad strikes. Dozens and dozens of people dead. Whole streets, whole districts burned to the ground. Hell, if a strike in Pittsburgh can almost start a war, well—" Ambrose shook his head and shuddered. "This country is fragile. If New York or any city of the North or South falls . . . What we're discussing would tear this country to pieces once and for all."

"*Brambles grow where an army has been*," Jin said quietly. "*Bad years follow a great war*." She looked at Tom. "So what do we do? What *can* we do?"

Tom gave her a sad smile. "It should never fall to the children," he said. "Ain't right that you found that body, ain't right that it's painted in your head, sweetheart. We'll find some way."

Walter Mapp looked evenly at Tom. "Then you're willing to help."

"'Course I am. Any which way I can."

Mapp cleared his throat. "I have an idea about *how* you could help."

A moment's quiet followed then, while the two musicians looked at each other across the tabletop. Then Tom Guyot reached into his pocket and pulled out his watch. He laid the old timepiece on the table. "You're talking about this."

Walter Mapp nodded.

Sam glanced at Jin, utterly confused. An old watch?

Tom sighed. "Anything but that."

"I used mine five or six lifetimes back," Mapp said quietly. "Otherwise I'd lay it down right this minute."

"Now, I don't think that's true," Tom said, a note of reproach in his voice. "You've been walking longer than I have, so I figure you thought long and hard before you spent yours. I bet you used it on just the right thing at just the right time. And I bet, Mr. Mapp, I just *bet* you gave it all the best thinking you had before you did."

Before you spent yours? How did you spend a watch? Sam glanced at Ambrose. The newspaperman was watching the exchange with a look of horrified fascination on his face. He caught Sam looking at him, rearranged his expression into one of not-very-convincing confusion, and shrugged. No help from that quarter.

Then Sam looked again at the timepiece on its coiled fob and spotted something he hadn't noticed before. There was a coin hanging like a charm from the fob's clip: greenish, with a hole in the center and uneven edges.

Mapp shoved back his hat, folded his arms, and glared at Tom. "Do you really think you'll ever find a better reason to use it than this?"

"I don't rightly know," Tom retorted, "but I 'spect I deserve a minute to think it over."

"What is that?" Sam interrupted, pointing at the coin.

Both Tom and Mapp jumped as if they'd forgotten there was anyone else in the room. "A favor," Tom said at last. He slid the watch off the table and pocketed it. Walter Mapp made a noise of frustration.

"A favor from . . . who?" Sam persisted. "Can it help?"

Instead of answering, Tom looked to Walter Mapp. "It . . . could," Mapp said reluctantly.

Tom nodded. "Ain't no way to know until we try. Thing is, once we try calling in this favor, well, the rest of it's out of our hands and into somebody else's."

"Whose?"

"Somebody even Mr. Mapp ain't sure we want involved," Tom said. "Not if we can find another way." He looked across the table at the pianist. "Look here, I'm not going anyplace. If it comes down to it, heck, I won't say no. But at least let's try finding some other means aforehand. You and I both know using a favor ain't as simple as making a wish and having it come true just so."

Mapp sighed again. "Can't call that a lie. All right. It'll be our last-ditch effort, if it comes to it—and if, when it's time, you agree."

"I want to help," Jin interrupted. "It's the only way I'll be able to stop seeing it."

Her voice was even, unhesitating, but her hands were still curled into those tight fists that made her scars shine white as bone.

Jin caught Sam looking. Before she could hide her hand in her lap, he caught hold of it. She flinched, but allowed him to uncurl her fingers on the tabletop. Momentarily forgetting that there were three pairs of eyes watching, he left his palm over hers for just a moment, wishing he could find a way to make it seem casual somehow.

He couldn't, of course, so he took his hand back.

Ambrose's eyes were on the glass he was refilling, but Tom smiled and Walter Mapp gave him a little nod of approval before glancing around the table.

"All right, then." The pianist raised his glass. "We save New York in order to save the country. Anybody see any problems with that?"

"Do you feel better about things at all?"

The lights of the hotel cast long shadows before them as

Sam and Jin descended the pink marble stairs to the circular drive. "It's something," Jin said carefully. She didn't actually feel any better at all, but she didn't want to admit it, nor lie outright. "It's better than nothing. And what was all that with Mr. Guyot and Mr. Mapp and the favor?"

"No idea." Sam shrugged. "Can I walk you to the wagon?"

"I suppose."

They took the same route back, through the shadows between the ornamental trees and the light falling from the upper windows. They walked in silence, until Sam stepped on something.

Jin caught his arm as he stumbled. "Are you all right?"

The gesture must've surprised him as much as it did her. He didn't even look to see what he had tripped over. "I'm okay, thanks."

Then she glanced over his shoulder, squinting at the dark shape at the base of one of the potted trees. Her heart started hammering. Sam turned, too, and took a step back toward it.

Jin's hand tightened on his arm. "Stop."

The shape was a foot.

"Don't," she whispered. "Don't go any closer."

Sam unwound her fingers carefully from his elbow. "Stay here."

"Sam, *don't—*"

"Just wait here." He took a step toward the trees, just close enough to see what she had already noticed: the foot was bare. "Jin, go on to the wagon," he said unsteadily. "Get your uncle. I'll go get someone from the hotel. It's probably nothing, probably some drunk fellow passed out."

Jin nodded, stumbled backwards. "Hurry," she said, then took off at a run.

She sprinted across the gravel to the Fata Morgana wagon and flung open the door. Uncle Liao and Mr. Burns were sitting at the little dining table over their evening cups of tea. "C-come quick," she stammered. "There's a—"

The look on her face must've been horrible, because they were moving before she could manage the word *body*. Jin led them back to the row of trees, where they met Sam leading Walter Mapp, Tom Guyot, and Ambrose from the opposite direction.

Jin and Sam stood a short distance away as the rest of them clustered around their grim discovery. She wrapped her arms about herself silently, her face stony.

Walter Mapp stumbled backwards, then sprinted around to the front of the hotel. Tom Guyot turned toward them, his dark face gone ashy and his eyes haunted. "You two stay back, now," he said, voice cracking.

"What is it?" Sam asked. "I didn't really—"

"A riddle," Ambrose said leadenly, turning away from the trees to face Sam and Jin. He was pale. "How might a man be naked and still wear rags?"

Jin made a whimpering noise. She barely recognized her own voice as she murmured, "Rags . . ."

Mr. Burns lurched away from the potted trees and disappeared around the corner. From the other side of the building came the sound of retching as Walter Mapp reappeared with two men in hotel livery. "Right there," he said, pointing.

Almost immediately, one of the two wavered on his feet. It

actually looked like he might faint. The other took one look and turned, waving his arms weakly. "Okay, folks. Clear the . . . aw, hell. Go. Just go."

Jin caught Walter Mapp's sleeve and pulled him closer. "Is it . . . ?"

Mapp's face was haunted. "Same thing. Yes. Right down to the writing on the wall." He turned to Tom Guyot, who was worrying the green coin on his watch fob with shaking fingers. "Don't you think about it. What you said before was right, Tom, and I was wrong to push you. We have some time before we start thinking about using that. Put it away."

Liao strode toward Sam and gave him a sharp once-over. "You are the boy from this afternoon, yes?"

Jin tore her eyes away from the naked, protruding foot as Sam swallowed and answered, "Yes, sir. Sam Noctiluca."

The old man nodded once. "Take Jin and go."

Jin started. "Uncle Liao—"

"No arguing. I will send our signal when I wish you to come back." Liao put a gnarled hand on her shoulder. "There is much in your life I could not protect you from, firefly, and I know you will never believe you need my protection. Do this because it makes my heart easier. Do it for me, because I wish I could keep you from seeing the evils of the world. It is a little thing, to humor an old man, *shi bu shi*?"

Jin nodded. "*Shi.*" She turned to Sam, wiping her eyes. "Let's go."

ELEVEN

The First Pillar

THE DOOR of the old church opened before Walker had finished knocking. "My, my," Basile Christophel drawled, leaning on the doorframe. "You have been busy, haven't you?"

"Show us," Walker said shortly.

"With pleasure. Come right in."

In the basement room, the tallow-coated table shone like a starry sky. Clusters of glowing ash like nebulae had sprouted south of Brooklyn, with golden webbing reaching back to where the daemon Bios waded through the tallow with its hatpin and smoldering cheroot brain.

Christophel gestured at the two glowing clusters. "I presume these are the sites of whatever mayhem you undertook. You can likely disregard the activity there — people are talking locally. What you want to see are the conversations that aren't just local concern and gossip."

He pointed to a smaller cluster to the north. "This one, for instance. Now, it could be this is nothing more than a Brooklyn newspaper discussing yet another case of bad behavior in that wretched den of iniquity that is Coney Island . . . but news doesn't usually travel that quickly. I think this is worth investigating."

"How do we find it?"

Christophel produced a pincushion from one of the compartments in the letterbox cabinet and drove a pin through the center of the glowing ash to spear the map beneath it. The red-gold glow intensified to a cold white and burned away an irregular circle of tallow to reveal the place the pin had marked.

"Atlantic Avenue and Court Street," Christophel remarked. "I can't give you a more precise location than that, but somewhere right thereabouts, you should find one of your pillars."

Bones had wandered to the other side of the table. "What about this one?" he asked, nodding at a cluster of cinders still farther north in New York.

Christophel grinned. "Ah. Yes. Now this one is *very* interesting."

"Well, don't keep us waiting," Walker grumbled. "Do your pin trick, show us where it is."

"I don't have to do the pin trick to tell you where *that* is," Christophel said with a smirk. But he pushed a second pin into the cluster anyway and the three of them watched the tallow melt away. "It's Tammany Hall. Looks like one of your pillars is a Democrat."

"Tammany Hall," Bones mused. "All I know about Tammany is that it's where that Tweed fellow had his headquarters."

"Tweed's in jail," Christophel told him. "The current boss is Honest John Kelly. Probably no better or worse than Tweed, but for the moment playing it smarter." He tapped the pin. "I think this ought to be your first stop. If you have any chance to, shall we say, win any of the pillars over to your cause, this one is your best bet. It takes a certain amount of . . . pragmatism . . . to work for Tammany. You may find you can do business with this fellow, whoever he is."

"Two out of ten," Bones murmured. "One from each city. That's not bad for half a day's work."

"Especially if one of them can be convinced to help us find the rest," Walker added.

"I've been thinking about that." Christophel leaned back against the desk and folded his arms. "I don't think you're looking for ten. I think you're looking for five."

"Five per city," Walker corrected.

"I understand that, but I also understand Brooklyn and New York." Christophel nodded at the outlines drawn in the tallow. "You're really not talking about two cities. You're talking about one city cut in two by a river, and that river is about to be bridged. It's only a matter of time before the two are consolidated."

Walker and Bones exchanged a glance. "Are you saying this," Walker said carefully, "because it's logical, or because you know it to be true?"

Christophel grinned. "Both. Of course, anything is possible, and I can see all of those possibilities, but there just aren't that many versions in which it doesn't occur. The probability of your . . . experience . . . being one of the versions in which consolidation *doesn't* happen . . ." His eyes glazed over.

Walker gave Bones a warning look. Bones put up a hand and waited.

"Oh . . . so very unlikely," Christophel murmured. His expression sharpened, and he smiled at Walker. "No. You're looking for five. I'm certain."

"Well, that would make life easier," Bones said. He looked at Walker, who still had a rigid expression on his face, and spoke with deliberate casualness. "Wouldn't you say?"

Walker forced a twitch of a smile. "I'll say it would."

Bones nodded his head once. "Tammany Hall it is. Where do we go?"

"East Fourteenth Street. I'd get right on your way." Christophel looked at the cinder stars glittering in the tallow. "The cluster's still growing. Your man's there, and talking. You could perhaps catch a couple birds in one stop."

"It'll take us hours to get there," Walker protested. "Won't the place be empty this late, anyhow?"

Christophel shook his head. "It might take you an hour, but you can go to the docks right here in Red Hook and hire someone to ferry you across to New York. Tammany headquarters has restaurants and entertainment open every day till midnight. You have time."

Bones slapped Walker on the shoulder, leaving a yellow-dust handprint on the gambler's suit. "Let's be off."

Walker twisted his head to look at the print, sighed, and brushed at it in annoyance. "No rest for the wicked."

Jin stopped at the wagon long enough to throw some things in her rucksack and hand a bicycle wheel and a metal stake out to Sam. Then she led him back down to the beach and eastward, beyond the two iron piers to an open stretch of sand mostly out of reach of the lights of the hotel.

Beside a huge piece of driftwood, she unslung her bag from her shoulder and began pulling what Sam assumed were explosives from it. "Go sit," she said over her shoulder. "This will take me a minute to set up."

Sam lowered himself onto the wood. He was just about to kick off his shoes when he spotted the lantern bobbing its way up the beach toward them.

"Who's there?" called a voice.

Sam could just make out the dark shape of a man in the dim glow. "Who's that?" he called back.

The man with the lantern stopped a few paces away. Now Sam could see that he was wearing one of the Broken Land's red and silver uniforms. "Hotel staff," he retorted, glaring from Sam to Jin and back. "And you? This is private property."

Jin waved. "We're with Fata Morgana, your fireworks purveyors. Just testing some things for tomorrow's display."

The uniformed man did not look impressed. "How do I know that? I warn you, this hotel does not tolerate trespassers."

"I'm not a trespasser," Jin said calmly. "And this is how you know I am who I say I am." She reached into her bag, took out two small leather pouches, and poured a bit of powder from each onto her palm. Then she set the pouches aside and rubbed her palms together in fast circles. Golden-green sparks flew from between her hands.

Now he looked a little impressed. "That's something," the uniformed man said admiringly. "Doesn't it burn?"

"Only a little," Jin said, brushing off the remaining powder. "I'm sorry, we didn't mean to startle you. I just needed some open space to practice."

"That's all right. I won't chase you off." He gave Sam a big wink and went on his way.

Jin rolled her eyes at his back. "What's he think he's winking at?" she grumbled as she turned back to her bag and continued unpacking her gear.

"That didn't really burn, did it?" Sam asked, forcing himself not to reach for her hands to look for himself. It had seemed pretty convincing.

"Only a little, just like I said," she replied, not looking up. "You get used to it. It's not so bad."

She buried the stake in the sand and secured the bicycle wheel to the end that pointed skyward, then she took a length of fuse and a handful of little cylindrical explosive cases from her bag. With short, sure knots she ran the fuse around the rim and placed the rockets at precise intervals.

"How can you see to do that?" Sam asked. She made it look like instinct, even in the near-complete dark between the piers.

"I can do this with my eyes shut," she said. "This is my favorite kind of firework." A few more moments, and she stood back to examine her handiwork. "Ready?"

"Sure."

She took from her pocket the same contraption she'd used that afternoon to light the fireball in Culver Plaza, flicked it to life, and touched its flame to the end of the fuse. The glowing end raced around the rim, touching off the fuses of each of the individual explosives one by one, and the wheel began to rotate, driven by the flaming rockets. It picked up speed until the rockets blended into a single hoop of golden flame.

"This is a simple one," Jin said, backing away and lowering herself onto the log beside Sam. "I can do fancier versions."

"It's beautiful. What is it?"

"It's a catherine wheel."

"Who's Catherine?"

"Saint Catherine," Jin said. "She was martyred. Broken on the wheel." Sam looked at her blankly. "You don't know what that means? Not a very good Catholic, are you? Aren't most Italians Catholic?"

"I never said *I* was."

Jin watched the wheel spark as it turned. When she spoke again her voice was flat. "They strapped you to a wheel and hit you with cudgels. Beat you to death. It doesn't sound like much, I guess, but it was bad enough that sometimes people were strangled out of mercy after the first two hits."

Sam looked at the fiery wheel as it went on sputtering golden sparks. "Sounds dreadful."

"It used to be a torture device, and now it's a beautiful flower of light." She smiled a little. "A very religious woman once told me that it was wrong to name something so frivolous after the wheel Catherine was martyred on. That it was disrespectful to the memory of the saint. But I think that's unfair to the wheel. It didn't choose to be an instrument of pain. I think all things, if they could choose, would decide to be instruments of joy. But people put them to terrible uses, and then it's a part of them forever."

Sam watched the sparks flying from Jin's beautiful flower of light, wondering how the heck he was supposed to respond. "Are you really looking at that and thinking of torture?" he asked quietly. "Why?"

"Because it's part of the wheel," Jin said. "Part of the past of every catherine wheel." She turned and Sam felt her eyes pin him. "Because it's been years since I saw a dead body, and today I saw two."

The reflection of the golden sparks made her eyes look as if they were full of fire and pain at the same time. She held his gaze for a long time, and then she turned away.

"Sometimes it's hard to forget those things, even in the face of beauty," she said quietly. "I never do. Uncle Liao says that's why I'm so good at fireworks. I know they grew out of violence and war. The first pyrotechnicians—many of them, anyway—were gunners. Believe it or not, that's where Liao learned about explosives—aboard a ship. All fireworks, even ones like these . . . they are flowers grown on a battlefield. That's where we got our slogan."

"*Arte et marte*," Sam murmured, remembering the phrase at the bottom of the handbill.

"Art and war." Jin nodded fiercely. "And I want to do everything I can to help my works overcome the destruction in their past. Some people, like that woman I mentioned before, cannot see beyond the evils. But I want to make them so beautiful even someone like that can forget what they have done."

She looked back at him, and her eyes were full of night and flame and the brightness of what he thought might've been tears. There was wariness there also, threatening to drop between them; that same wariness that he had seen her pull on like armor whenever there was any mention of her past.

To his shock, he knew exactly what he wanted to say to her, and he knew how he wanted to say it. "There is nothing that your past could have in it that would make you anything but lovely to me." The words were awkward coming out, but for some reason that didn't seem like a bad thing.

"You don't know that," Jin said savagely. Her gaze was utterly, inhumanly beautiful. Never before had he wanted to kiss a girl so badly. Of course, this had to be the worst time in the world to have those kinds of thoughts.

Now that he'd said the hardest words, the rest were easier. "You don't ever have to tell me. I promise not to ask, Jin, but whatever it is, I promise you I wouldn't care."

Jin laughed, a sharp, bitter sound. "Forgive me if I don't sound impressed by your gentlemanly spirit. Anyone can curb their curiosity for a weekend, Sam. After that you'll never see me again."

"*You* don't know that," Sam retorted. "And I'm not a gentleman, I'm a card sharp. I'm not some sport who makes a habit of saying nice things to girls. In fact, this might be the longest conversation I've had with a girl who wasn't a relative or a landlady, ever."

Another moment of silence. A few yards away, the catherine wheel sputtered to stillness and left them in the dark.

Jin swiveled and reached for him. Sam's chest clenched and he pulled her close without a second thought. It was then, as he felt her freeze in his arms, that he realized she'd only been reaching for the bag of explosives tucked behind the driftwood log they were sitting on.

"*Cavolo,*" Sam muttered, dropping his arms. "Sorry."

"Fine." Jin was already on her feet with the bag in her hands. She pulled on a pair of gloves, stilled the spinning bicycle wheel, and began stripping away the shredded remnants of the rockets with a pocketknife.

Sam watched her reset more explosives, stringing the fuse first, then selecting new rockets and attaching them to the rim. He decided this was a good sign. If he'd really fouled things up beyond repair, she certainly wouldn't have wanted to stick around to set up another wheel.

It took longer this time. It was impossible to say whether she wanted to do something fancier or if she was avoiding returning to his side, but finally her blue-flamed lighter flared and fired the fuse.

"Watch," she whispered as she backed toward the driftwood bench again. The glow raced around the wheel and sent it into motion. This time, the rockets erupted into blue and silver, and as the spinning accelerated, the sparks of four more fuses raced inward and a delicate filigree of sparkles burst to life at the center.

"I came to America, to San Francisco, when I was just a baby." Jin stared at the wheel as she spoke. "I don't know how it happened. I have no memory of it. I was maybe two years old."

San Francisco. Of course. Sam's heart sank. Why hadn't he realized it before? That was why she had gone so strange and defensive when Ambrose had called her *the girl from San Francisco.* To be a Chinese girl growing up there . . . whatever she was about to tell him, it wasn't going to be good.

It wasn't going to be easy for her to say, either.

"You don't have to—"

"I know." Jin's gloved fingers flexed by her side, and she continued. "I was raised in a house owned by one of the tongs.

The tongs run San Francisco, at least as far as the Chinese are concerned."

"It's the same here," Sam said quietly, but that wasn't quite true. The tongs in New York were nowhere near as powerful as they were out West.

"And there aren't many Chinese women in America." She looked at him out of the corner of her eye. "You know that, too?"

Sam nodded without speaking. It was the way things often went with immigrants; fathers, sons, and brothers went first. His own grandfather had come to New York alone, then he had brought Sam's grandmother over later, when he had saved up enough for the passage.

"Most of the Chinese women who make it here are smuggled in," Jin said flatly, as if she was reciting something she didn't want to have to think about. "They don't always make it to their families, if there are families waiting for them at all. There are ways to make money off a cargo of people, especially girls, especially in a community where there are tens of thousands of males and only a few score of females. You understand what I mean?"

Sam looked down at his knees and nodded again. The tongs did this kind of business in New York, too.

"When I was eight," Jin continued quietly, "they brought a woman to the house to bind my feet. The pain was . . ." She stopped talking for a moment and took a deep breath. "I had always planned to try and escape, but after that, I couldn't do it by running or climbing."

"I don't really know what that means, actually."

She glanced at his bare feet. "Curl your toes under, but not the big one." He did. "Curl them further. Put some weight on the knuckles if you have to. The knuckles should be all the way out of sight."

It was basically impossible for Sam to do as she asked, but he tried. "How's that?"

"Dreadful, but I see you get the idea. You can relax your foot. What you just did can't even approximate what binding is like. The foot is broken at the arch and pretty much folded in half. The idea is to get the length of the foot down to three inches from the toe to the heel." She held up her forefinger and thumb a short distance apart. "That big."

Sam stared. "How is that even possible?"

Jin shrugged. "Break the toes, break the arch, fold them where you want them, wrap them in wet cloth, tie them up. Then you have to stand up and walk around, because body weight helps the compression. When the cloth dries, it tightens. You rewrap the feet every few days or so. Or rather, someone else rewraps them, someone who isn't bothered by screaming. The woman who first bound mine bragged that back in China she had been much sought after because she was basically deaf and there was no amount of screaming a girl could do that would make her show mercy."

He swallowed. "I'm so sorry."

Jin shrugged again. "It's what's done. It's what has been done for centuries. It's a mark of status, really, although it's also . . . well, some men find it attractive. This is why it was done in the house where I lived. Someone got the idea that a few of us—the ones who weren't as pretty as the others—would fetch higher prices with bound feet. And we wouldn't be able to run away. So they made me a small-foot girl, along with a few others, even though I was eight then, which is older than usual and so it was . . ." She swallowed. "It was very bad. The pain, I mean."

Another long silence stretched. Finally Jin spoke again. "I think perhaps if I had been a normal girl, if I could have run to my mother's arms afterward and she could have told me all the reasons it was important, all the tradition and meaning, whatever had made her decide to put me through that pain . . . it might've been different. But it wasn't like that, not in the house in San Francisco. It was done because someone thought the men who visited the house would like to see a girl tottering around on tiny lotus feet, and I didn't have a mother to run to, and I couldn't run anymore, anyhow."

If it had been another boy talking about his awful past in the tenements, Sam would've tossed an arm over the kid's shoulder or thumped him on the back, but it didn't seem like the right thing to do now. Also, he suspected that Jin might take a dim view of any fellow who put his hands on her uninvited for the second time in less than fifteen minutes.

"How did you get away?" he asked at last.

"There was a man who was a miner. He had an old . . . injury, and when he came to the house, he would talk, that's all. So I asked him about explosives. I pretended to be amazed by them —I was much younger, a little girl. He would bring firecrackers and squibs, little things he could set off in the courtyard without burning the place down. I asked questions, and little by little I learned, and then I started stealing the powder and fuses."

The catherine wheel had gone out some time ago. Jin began removing more supplies from her explosives bag as she continued.

"Somewhere along the way I think he figured out what I was up to. I think he might even have brought certain things just so I could take them. Perhaps I could've told him, but I thought if I let him help me escape he might expect me to leave with him. Then, when I had saved up enough and thought I knew enough to try, I set the explosives off. I blew up half the house and left in the chaos."

"You blew up the house to escape?" Sam didn't even try to keep the admiration out of his voice. "When you were eight?"

"I was nine by then." But she smiled just a little as she corrected him. "Blowing it up wasn't hard. The hard bit was getting everyone out of the part I wanted to demolish."

"Still."

"I managed to hobble three blocks from the house before a wagon pulled up in front of me. It was Liao and Mr. Burns, of course." Jin pulled a pair of jars from her bag, unscrewed the caps, and sifted the contents together in a metal pan. "They'd been passing through San Francisco, and they happened to have been close enough to see the explosion I'd set. Liao jumped down and chased after me and of course I couldn't run. He took one look at my hands and knew I'd been messing around with powders."

She turned and held out one hand to Sam so that he could see. Her gloved fingers were touched with dark smudges of ash. Then she pulled off the gloves and held out her hand again. It bore the marks of old and still-healing burns: shiny skin on the knuckle of her index finger and the end of her thumb, and a scar near her wrist that stood out pinkish against the golden tone of the rest of her hand. She rose, set the pan a few feet from them, and poured a few drops of oil over the powder mixture. A sharp waft of cinnamon drifted up.

"I thought for certain they would take me to the police, but Uncle Liao said if I could do that with stolen firecrackers, I might be worth teaching. The explosion had particularly difficult-to-achieve shades of crimson and gold, you see. I had somehow managed to blow up my prison with flair. And that's how I got my names: Jin means 'gold,' and my stage name, Xiaoming, was the name of an emperor's daughter from old myth. It means 'shines in the night.'"

She shook the concoction gently, like a prospector panning for precious metals, and placed it carefully on a flat stretch of sand. "The first thing he did was cut the binding off. He said a proper fireworker has to be able to run if things go wrong. You can imagine I didn't argue. Of course, some of the damage was already done. We discovered we had to wrap them up again and allow my feet to adjust to looser and looser bindings, a bit at a time. We let my feet out like that, little by little. It took years before I could teach myself how to run again."

Jin lit the mixture in the pan with her pocket lighter, and it flared into a neat little blaze. "Instant bonfire," Sam said with a smile.

Jin nodded and sat beside him again, arranging the cuffs of her trousers so they covered her shoes. She didn't say anything more.

The bonfire had a silvery tone to it, and the smell of cinnamon still hung in the air. Sam's chest was tight with a dull ache.

Somewhere across the lawns behind them, despite the horror that had just been discovered on the hotel grounds, an orchestra at the Broken Land was playing a waltz. The sound carried through the night as clearly as if they were only a few yards away from the bandstand.

"I know how this is going to sound," Sam said at last, "and I'm sorry for it, but I think I'm right." He took a deep breath. "I think you should take off your shoes."

She glared at him. "I beg your pardon?"

He hadn't suggested she shuck off her clothes, but it wasn't all that far off. "I know this is an utterly inappropriate thing for me to say, but you should do it. Everyone should feel the sand between their toes when they can."

For a long moment he watched her debate it, the glare firmly ensconced on her face all the while. In the end, though, the frown between her eyes faded. "All right."

She reached down, fumbled under the wide cuffs of her cotton trousers, and produced a pair of embroidered red shoes with pointed toes, which she set neatly to one side.

Sam waited. "Well?"

"Well what?"

"How is it?"

She considered. "Very nice, actually."

"You can't tell just from sitting there like that. Get up, walk around. And would you quit worrying?" he added as she shifted her weight awkwardly. "I didn't suggest it so I could try and sneak a look."

She muttered something in Chinese, stood, squared her shoulders, and took a few steps. Despite what he'd just said, Sam wondered whether she would notice if he tried to catch a glimpse of the feet she was so worried about. It was dark, after all . . . but somehow, he managed to keep his eyes away from the ground.

"It's nice," Jin said again, and this time her voice was softer. She walked farther. "Feels good, actually. You're right."

Sam watched her circle back around the fire. He had begun to suspect that the awkward gait he'd noticed on Culver Plaza was something that she fell into when she, herself, felt awkward. She'd had it again when they'd crossed the hotel's atrium, but earlier, just after the fireworks when she'd been so happy, it was as if she'd forgotten all about her damaged feet, and her body had forgotten along with her. He watched for the awkwardness now, but her steps merely looked deliberate as she strode across the sand toward him again.

The faraway waltz drifted in the air, and the breeze made her clothes ripple and her hair catch brief glimmers of light from the fire. The ache in his chest was threatening to make him say something stupid. But then, he wondered, how would he feel if he didn't say anything at all? What was the worst that could happen?

So he said it. "Would you dance with me?"

Jin stopped walking. "I can't dance, Sam." No wariness this time, and no coyness either. She spoke as if she thought she was saying something obvious.

"Because of the binding or because you never learned?"

"Both."

"But you can run."

"Yes, but it hurts. It always hurts."

"Then I have another suggestion." He got to his feet and

held out his arms. "Trust me. Think how well the last one turned out."

She looked at him for a long time. "I came out here with you, and we sat here in the dark, alone. I told you things I never tell anyone. I took off my shoes. I know how this must appear. You might be thinking . . . but please don't get the wrong idea. I couldn't bear it."

The ache twisted. There it was, exactly what he'd been afraid of. What had she said earlier? *I want to know if you're going to mistake that for an invitation.*

"I don't think that," Sam protested. "You know I don't think that, don't you?"

"Then why are you here?" she asked wildly. "And you want to *dance?* White boys don't dance with girls who look like me."

"That's only because there are about five girls in the country who look like you," Sam retorted. "And because people are stupid." He dropped his arms. "I don't know what to say to you. I'm not good at talking to people, not like this. But I know how to dance, and it makes me sad to see you sad. Please dance with me."

She looked back at the fire, as if it had advice to offer. Then she nodded once and stepped closer.

Sam put an arm lightly around her waist. "You know what a waltz is?"

"That's the one that goes *one, two, three, one, two, three?*"

"That's the one. Now, about the part where it hurts your feet. Do you trust me?"

Jin gave him a wary glance. "Not remotely."

Sam smiled. "I don't think that's true." *And I hope I'm right about that.* "This is how we get around the pain." He stepped closer still and tightened his arm, bringing her body right up against his and lifting her almost, but not quite, off her feet.

Jin's eyes snapped wide. "What are you doing?"

"Just reducing the weight you're putting on your feet, that's all." Of course, that wasn't all. They were nose-to-nose now, and he could feel her heart hammering against his chest. "Put your hand back on my shoulder, like this. Ready? And—"

"Sam."

"Yes?"

"If you put one finger out of line, I will kill you. You believe that?"

"Yes, actually, I do. Now, one . . . two . . . three . . ."

It didn't happen easily, but he managed to get them waltzing.

Somewhere on their second turn around the bonfire, the tension began to melt out of her. Not long after that, Sam realized the hand she'd rested on his shoulder had crept around his neck to hold on to him. She smelled like gunpowder and cinnamon, and he couldn't breathe in the scent deeply enough. He kept on counting steps, whispering numbers as the silver-and-red bonfire threw wild reflections into the eyes that looked past his shoulder into the night.

They danced until the faraway music faded, leaving them standing beside the fire, arms wrapped around each other. Jin had never looked up at him, had never met his eyes, but her head rested on his shoulder now. Sam turned just enough to see the plane of her face and felt her cheek against his chin.

They danced until the

faraway music faded.

"Jin . . ." he said quietly. "How are your feet?"

She smiled and spoke against his neck. "I feel as light as a spark."

"Good," he said. "That's all that matters."

From somewhere in the dark, a barking explosion sounded, followed by a loud whining whistle. A shaft of white light shot heavenward and exploded into a shower of pink stars overhead.

Jin looked to the sky. "That's Uncle Liao's signal."

"I'll take you back."

She turned in his arms to watch the last of the pink sparks fall, and he watched her with his heart in his throat. Then she nodded once, slid out of his grasp, and returned to the driftwood and her rucksack. Sam stood awkwardly by the fire in its pan, unsure whether he ought to say something now or not.

Jin took her little knife from the bag and pulled the gloves back on. Then she stripped the darkened catherine wheel and returned to the fire just long enough to drown it in sand. While she slid her feet back into her shoes, Sam dug the pan out. This, of course, was a stupid thing to do.

"Holy Mary, Mother of—" The metal, naturally enough, was searing hot from the fire. He flung it away and jammed his burned fingers in his mouth. Jin appeared at his side, yanked his hand away from his face, and examined the red marks already coming up on his fingertips. She sighed.

So the evening ended with Sam back outside the Fata Morgana wagon, looking stupid while Jin coated his hand in burn cream and her uncle watched with his arms folded and his eyebrows raised, muttering something about what had possessed him to send Jin away in the company of this idiot boy.

At that, she raised her eyes to Sam's and gave him the slightest, smallest conspiratorial smile, which sent a blush over his face that he could only hope the old man would interpret as appropriate shame for being a stupid boy who burned himself on obviously hot pans.

"If you can, put ice on it when you get home," she told him.

"Yes, ma'am."

"Take the jar with you," Liao instructed. "Use more tomorrow."

"I'll bring it back," Sam promised. Liao waved his hand dismissively and disappeared into the wagon.

"Can you come find me tomorrow?" Sam asked Jin the second her uncle was out of earshot.

"On the plaza, same as today?"

"Yes."

She gave him one of her long, thoughtful looks. Then her face broke into a grin that made his stomach flip. "Yes, I think so."

And then she was gone, up the stairs and into the wagon, and despite the pain in his hand and the horrible things that had happened earlier, Sam spent the long trek back to West Brighton feeling as though he were walking on air.

He let himself into Mrs. Ponzi's house and found Constantine playing solitaire on the parlor floor. Ilana was stretched out on the sofa, asleep.

"We tried to wait up for you," Con said quietly, throwing down a five of clubs. "Some of us failed."

"What time is it?" Sam squinted at the clock on the mantelpiece.

"It's one in the morning," the other boy told him. "Where the heck have you been?"

"You waited up this late? What's wrong with you?"

Constantine stretched. "Nothing's wrong with me. What's wrong with you?" He jabbed a finger at Sam. "You owe me some information. What's this I hear about you and a Chinese girl?"

On the couch, Ilana stretched and rubbed her eyes. "Is that Sam?"

"More important," Con continued, "what's this I hear about you getting invited to watch fireworks at the Broken Land Hotel and you didn't take us?"

Sam glared at Ilana. "You."

"Was it a secret?" she asked sleepily.

"I only told you so you'd tell your ma not to expect me for supper."

"You didn't say I couldn't tell Con." She sat up and brightened. "How were the fireworks? Did you see—what's her name—Jin?"

"Who's Jin, and why does Ilana know so much that I don't?" Constantine grumbled.

"Jin's the Chinese girl," Ilana supplied, "the one who made the air explode when the horrible boys were bothering her. Sam, how were the fireworks?"

Sam ignored her question. "Something happened." He hesitated, not sure he wanted to talk about it. "Illy, maybe you should go up to bed."

The girl's mouth dropped open with such a show of indignation that Sam actually flinched. "I beg your pardon," she said icily. "But this is *my house*."

"It's your mama's house," Constantine pointed out mildly.

"That's right, which makes it *my house*, too."

"All right, all right," Sam cut in. He told them about the body behind the hotel, which then prompted him to tell them about the body Jin had found near Mammon's Alley earlier, a detail he'd neglected to mention when he'd told Ilana he wouldn't be home for supper. Then he told them about Jack.

"That sounds like a folktale," Con said.

Sam nodded. "That's what I said."

"But you think this is real?"

"Well, I think someone killed two people because of that story, whether it's real or not." He sighed. "Yes, I think it's real. I don't know how to explain it."

Ilana tugged her sweater closer around her. "So . . . what are you going to do?"

"I have no idea."

The three of them sat silently for a moment. "How were Jin's fireworks?" Ilana asked again at last.

Sam closed his eyes for a minute and pictured the sinking castle and the spinning catherine wheel. "I wish you could've seen them," he said. "She's amazing."

Ilana gave a happy sigh. Constantine flicked a card at her and hit her square on the forehead. "Sappy little fool."

"Hey," she said, fumbling for the card, "I've been practicing that, too. Watch. I can hit Sam from here. Sam, hold still."

Cards flew, some more accurately than others, and another night came to an end.

TWELVE

Tammany Hall

Ir was well after midnight when the cabriolet drew to a bumpy stop on East Fourteenth Street and the driver thumped on the roof, but the red brick and white marble Tammany Society building hadn't emptied out yet. Walker and Bones climbed down to the curb and regarded the huge edifice looming overhead and the stream of bodies—mostly men, but more than a few women—pouring forth from the double doors. Bright arched windows, three stories' worth, threw light down onto the street.

"And you thought the place would be deserted," Bones drawled, easing himself into a spike of shadow between two windows, out of the way of the departing masses. "I bet we can still get ourselves a steak if we're persuasive."

"Needle in a haystack," Walker muttered, dodging through the crowd to join Bones. "Time to see if Doc Rawhead's trick works, or if he's just making me stick myself with pins to be funny."

On his lapels, Walker wore the two pins Christophel had used to mark the tallow-coated map back in Red Hook. He removed the one on the left and used it to break the skin on the pad of his thumb. He jabbed the pin deep, but no blood welled up to mark the spot.

"Interesting," Bones said. "So far, so good."

"This is the part where it just gets silly," Walker muttered. He stepped up to the marble trim of the nearest window and drew his thumb across it.

He started, stared. "Well, I'll be damned!" He looked at his thumb. It was still unmarked, showing no evidence of being jabbed with a pin, but there was now a broad smear of fresh blood marring the ivory-colored marble where Walker had touched the building.

"Looks like our man's still inside," he observed.

They fought against the tide of exiting people and into the hall. A young man in livery tried to tell them the place was closing, but a hard glare from Bones made the kid back away and avert his eyes. Nobody else paid them any attention.

Walker took the pin from his lapel again and jabbed the rest of the fingers on his left hand. Just as before, the pin left no marks and brought no blood to the surface. He strode to the wall and followed the perimeter of the room, drawing his hand along the paneling, the jambs of the doorways that led to auditoriums, and the banisters of the staircases until Bones grabbed his shoulder. Walker turned to find he'd left a smeared and bloody handprint on the wall beside a stair leading down.

They elbowed their way into the basement, where some kind of show had just disgorged its audience, most of whom were trying to enter a saloon that was trying just as hard to close for the night. Walker strolled along the wall, trailing his hands across every entrance and exit, until he reached the saloon and found his fingers leaving bloody trails across one of the panes of the interior windows beside the door.

"Walker." Bones nodded at the window. On the other side of the glass, past the throng of people entering and exiting, a pair of men—one with silver-gray hair, the other with brown—sat deep in conversation in a booth at the far end of the saloon.

Walker and Bones shoved their way inside, ignoring the protests of the patrons and the employees, and stalked over to the table. The two men looked up in surprise.

"Beg your pardon, gentlemen, but—"

Walker ignored the younger man's protests and put his hand flat on the table. It left a perfect bloody handprint.

"Make room," Bones said coldly. "We'll be joining you for a moment. There's something we'd very much like to discuss."

A waiter appeared beside the table, but the older man waved him off. "Please," he said, sliding deeper into the booth and gesturing for them to sit. Bones sat beside him, and Walker grinned evilly at the younger fellow until he made room on his side.

Bones looked from the older man to the younger. "Which of you is tasked with protecting the city?" he asked.

The two men exchanged a glance. There was panic in the younger man's eyes, resolve in the elder's.

"I see," Bones murmured. Then he rolled up the sleeve of his coat and reached for the face of the man beside him.

It was a bizarre thing to watch, even for Walker, who had seen it happen once or twice before. Bones's entire forearm seemed to disappear into the older man's mouth, and then the man began to cough. He fought spasmodically against Bones, and his cough changed swiftly to a harsh and racking choking noise as the gritty arm was forced further down his throat.

He turned red. Then he turned blue. Then he fell over onto the tabletop. Sand spilled from his mouth.

The waiter, on his way back over to try to hustle these lingering guests out the door, stopped dead in his tracks a few feet away, then backpedaled and nearly fell headlong in his haste to get away from the booth. He plunged out the door, shrieking at the top of his lungs, followed by the saloon's panicked remaining patrons.

"Bring us a beer when you come back," Walker called after him.

Meanwhile, the brown-haired man had begun to shake. He made a motion as if he thought he could shove his way past Walker, who warned, "Don't even think about it." And then, while the young man looked on in stunned terror, Walker's face underwent a horrifying change.

The freckles across his face deepened to black, and angry red welts shot out from each inky spot until his face was a webwork of scarlet marks. His red-rimmed eyes darkened and went bloodshot. Then Walker snarled, baring not one but two rows of teeth, the front set straight and normal and human, the back set jagged and made for tearing.

"Sit down, sir," Bones said evenly. "We are here to discuss the surrender of the cities of New York and Brooklyn to Jack Hellcoal. I believe you are one of the five men authorized to speak for the cities."

"Four," Walker corrected. The word emerged as a growl.

Bones glanced at the dead man sprawled across the table. "Yes, of course. Four."

"What do you want?" The fellow had gone shock-pale to the roots of his hair. "How could you . . . do you know who that *was?*"

"Do you know who we represent?" Bones demanded.

The man nodded without taking his eyes off of his lifeless companion.

"Then you know that no one is beyond his reach."

"What do you want?" the brown-haired man asked again.

"As I said before, your city. And we can take it with your help, or we can just kill you, now that we know who you are."

"And who are you, by the way?" Walker asked with the air of a man introducing himself to a new business associate. The young pillar turned to look at Walker's black-and-red face in disbelief.

"You don't know? How did you find us, then?"

Walker grinned and raised the hand he had punctured with Basile Christophel's pin, holding the palm a mere inch from the pillar's face. Blood began to seep from his fingertips. "The blood tells."

"Oh, God." The man dropped his head into his hands. "Frederick . . . Frederick Overcaste. I'm the keeper of the roads."

"And your friend?"

"Henry Van Ossinick."

"There's a Van Ossinick ironworks, isn't there?" Walker asked. "Van Ossinick was the smith?"

"Yes." Overcaste shuddered and peered up through his fingers. "What now?"

"You have two options." Walker reached across the table to grasp one of the bright gold buttons on Bones's coat. He gave it a sharp twist, plucking it free, and flipped it gracefully over his knuckles. "We can kill you, or you can trade us a bit of information for the privilege of our letting you live. It's entirely your choice. Unless you'd like to let the coin decide. I'll even let you call it."

Overcaste watched the gold flash over Walker's knuckles. What had been a button now looked very much like a coin. Then he looked at the dead man across the table. Bones reached over and thumped Van Ossinick's back, and another cascade of sand spilled from his mouth.

It didn't take long for Overcaste to make up his mind. He opened his mouth, hesitated, and reached into his pocket. When he opened his hand a huge gold coin sat in his palm. Walker held up his own now-empty palm.

"Good choice," Bones said, "and it's a fair payment, I think. Now, about the other three."

On the other side of the glass window that bore Walker's bloody fingerprints, two men watched the exchange in the saloon. They were not men you would ordinarily expect to see keeping company with each other, but that was the point of meeting at Tammany Hall. It was a place for all sorts, and if there was no better answer for why men from such different walks of life might arrange to meet there, the simplest assumption—that one of them was paying off the other — could always be relied upon to answer any observer's curiosity.

One was a blond, broad-shouldered fellow scarcely out of his twenties. He wore a plain and sober sack suit and worried the brim of a derby hat with rough fingers. The other, closer in age to forty, was tall and gaunt and flamboyant in a blue velvet tailcoat, plaid trousers, and a top hat that added a full extra foot to his height.

The man in the sack suit turned without a word and joined the crowd making its way up the stairs. The man in the top hat took a silver toothpick from his waistcoat pocket and chewed it thoughtfully for a moment before he followed at a more leisurely pace back to street level.

They met again on the sidewalk. "Van Ossinick's dead," the younger man said wonderingly.

"He knew the risk." The man in the tailcoat took a gold cigarette case from his pocket and offered one to his companion. "They came here, which means they either knew we were meeting or knew about Overcaste and simply got lucky in their timing."

He flicked a match to life and lit the other man's cigarette, and then his own. Then the two of them began walking east, toward the docks.

"Overcaste will break," the man with the derby muttered.

"Obviously." The word carried so much venom the younger man turned to look sharply at his companion, who smiled grimly and added, "He's a politician. Politicians are pragmatists. When power shifts, they cannot help but shift as well. It was always a risk with Overcaste." He shrugged his velvet-covered shoulders. "But this means they know who we are now, Sawyer."

Sawyer nodded. "My preparations are ready." He cleared his throat. "And we—"

"*Someone* has to warn Arabella," the flamboyant man interrupted. "It can't be you. Or me, for that matter. From now on, we cannot be found in the same place. We speak only through our seconds." He shot Sawyer a sharp look. "In all seriousness, Sawyer, you cannot go. I'll make the arrangements. I'll see to it she's safe. Do not, do *not* play the hero."

Sawyer nodded, but the older man gave him a long look before he resumed smoking. They walked in silence until they reached the cluster of wharves facing the dark mass of Brooklyn. The river was still alive with the lights of ferries, but the wharf here was mostly quiet—the sailors, stevedores, and longshoremen having retired to saloons and whorehouses and rooming houses for the evening—so that only the lap of water, the creak of wood, and the soft thudding of hull against pier were audible.

"If you don't mind," the man in the top hat said, "before we go our separate ways I'll invite myself along with you this one last time. My territory's closest, so if they're any kind of smart, they're headed to the Bowery to look for me already."

Sawyer looked over the other man's shoulder into the dark street beyond. "Will your . . . your fellows be joining us?"

"If your boat'll carry us all."

"Should do."

The older man nodded, turned, and gave a sharp whistle. Four shadows dressed in outlandish coats and tall hats detached themselves from the darkness and sauntered forward. "I thought they were doing better this time," he mused. "They're unaccustomed to being . . . unobtrusive."

Sawyer led the group along the waterfront until they reached a little dock so cluttered with crates that the gig tied up at the end was nearly hidden from view. He tipped his hat to the two men waiting with oars at the ready, and one by one they piled aboard.

"Hawks, you'll let me know when you've gotten word to Arabella?" Sawyer asked when the boat was cast off and under way.

"I will, and I'll do it first thing of all, but you have got to keep your distance. I mean that, Sawyer. No matter what. Our responsibilities to the city are more important than our personal attachments. You cannot go to her. If anything should happen to you and me, she is the city's only hope." He gave the young man a hard look. "And if you doubt how serious I am about this, I beg you to remember that there is also a woman waiting for me back home on the Bowery whom I am not likely to ever see again."

The oarsmen pulled the gig across the river in a southerly crossing, until they reached a dock under the skeletal neck of the Great Bridge. They made the boat fast, and Sawyer, Hawks, and the four rowdies from the Five Points disembarked.

Now Sawyer and Hawks shook hands again, and without another word the younger man stalked up the darkened street and into Brooklyn.

Hawks turned to his crew and clasped his hands in front of him. "It's time, boys," he declared, a slow grin spreading across his face. "You didn't believe me when I told you there were bigger battles to fight than the petty squabbles that pass for wars back in the Points. Well, you're about to see the truth of it for yourselves."

"Well, the woman wasn't lying." Stripped to the waist, his torso spattered with red, Walker strode across the sloping floor of the apartment above the Bowery saloon called the Blind Tiger's Milk to where Bones stood next to a quaking Frederick Overcaste. "There's no one else here."

"Of *course* she was telling the truth," Overcaste protested, his voice rising in poorly controlled panic. A trickle of blood ran under his boot. He made a gagging noise and scraped his foot on the wall, leaving a broken red smear.

Overcaste had led them south from Tammany Hall straight to the light-strewn thoroughfare that was the Bowery. There they wound their way through the evening crowds and past brilliantly gaslit theaters, policy shops and bucket shops, and dubious pawnshops that were probably fronts for confidence men. Even at this hour, vendors lined the road with carts, selling cigars, fruit, candy. Then Overcaste had turned down a side street, one that led straight toward the conjunction of roads known as the Five Points. Almost immediately the street had fallen apart under their feet. Stolen cobblestones left gaping holes. The ground was marshy, uneven, and the gutters ran with unidentifiable, stinking sludge. Walker had whipped a handkerchief from his suit coat and held it over his nose as he and Bones followed Overcaste to the saloon's entrance.

They hadn't been able to actually enter the saloon itself.

The door could not possibly have been locked—they could see through the windows that the bar was thronged inside—but it wouldn't budge for any of them.

"So that's the sanctuary," Walker had grumbled. "Find us a way in, Bones."

Bones had held up a palm and blown across it, and his entire hand had disintegrated and spun on a sudden gust of wind, up over their heads to scrape against the sagging glass of the second floor. "The saloon is protected," Bones had intoned. "His quarters above are not."

Now he and Overcaste stood in that upper flat, watching Walker stalk like a predator from room to room. "I *told* you Hawks and Sawyer were supposed to meet Van Ossinick and me at Tammany Hall," Overcaste continued. "They didn't show up, so they had to have spotted you. If they spotted you, if they saw what . . . what happened to Van Ossinick, they would never have come back to . . . to . . ."

"To anyplace you could lead us to this quickly," Bones finished. Overcaste put a hand to his face and wiped away sweat. "Say it," Bones suggested coldly. "It'll get easier every time you do."

"Yes," Overcaste whispered dully. "To anyplace I could lead you to this quickly."

Bones smiled thinly. "Easier every time."

Overcaste turned to glance into the hallway behind him. "My point," he said, his voice cracking, "is that his woman was telling the truth, and you knew it." He looked at Walker. "You didn't have to . . . to—"

Walker tilted his head and fixed Overcaste with red-rimmed

eyes. He smiled, and it was terrible enough to make the pillar take a step back. Then Walker turned and went into the next room, where a pitcher and basin sat on a washstand beside Hawks's bed.

"It was unlikely we would find him here," Bones said as Walker started scrubbing his body clean. "But it would have been unacceptable not to check. Presumably Hawks has a hidey-hole nearby, somewhere he can go and still keep an eye on this place." He nodded his head toward the hallway. "Walker was trying to draw him out."

"Obviously." Drying his neck with a rag, Walker returned and took his shirt and jacket from Overcaste with another of those grim smiles. "But I also just enjoy the hell out of my work. Everyone should, don't you agree?"

The politician squatted, his elbows on his knees. He was beginning to look sick.

"Just say yes," Bones suggested.

"Now"—Walker finished buttoning his shirt and yanked on his jacket—"what about this Sawyer fellow?"

"He lives in Brooklyn," Overcaste muttered toward the floor. "I don't know where."

"Oh, we don't need you to tell us where to look," Bones told him. "We just need you to get us there as fast as possible. The rest we can do ourselves."

Overcaste raised his head, sweat on his forehead. "How?"

Walker took the pin from his right lapel and flexed the fingers of his other hand. "By the pricking of my thumbs, Overcaste. By the pricking of my thumbs."

THIRTEEN

The Gentleman from the Bowery

SAM STROLLED ALONG the track, eyes on the blue of the water in the near distance, just beyond the smoking chimney of the train pulling into Culver Plaza. It was early, and the plaza was pretty well deserted. Sam waved at the fellows sweeping out the front of Bauer's hotel and casino and attempted a jaunty nod at a pair of girls trying to keep their hats on in the morning breeze. They giggled, and although Sam never could tell when a girl's giggling meant she was laughing at him and when it didn't, he decided to interpret it today as a positive sign and grinned back. It was a beautiful Saturday. All in all, probably a good day for cards.

That was what he thought, at least until he saw the man sitting where Sam had been accustomed to setting up his table for the last year and a half. Porkpie hat and all, it was the same sharper who'd miraculously stacked a monte deck full of spades right under his nose. There he was, just like he belonged there, already working up a push of beachcombers who thought they could beat the odds and win themselves money for a fancy lunch.

Sam stopped dead, blinked to make sure he wasn't imagining it, and made an abrupt change of direction. When he got to the counter of Toftmann's, the open-fronted saloon on the east side of Culver Plaza, the barman had a cup of coffee and a milk roll waiting. "Sorry, Sam. I don't know where he came from."

"Thanks, Oliver." He took a bite of the roll and drummed his fingers on the bar. "How long's he been there?"

"About an hour. Sam, a couple of fellows tried to move him for you. Eamon Fowler, first, then Benny the Cooler. Evidently he challenged each of them to beat him at any game they wanted, and if they won he'd leave. They both lost."

"He beat Eamon and Benny?" Sam asked incredulously. "How the heck did he manage that?" He swiveled on his chair, coffee cup in hand, for a better look at the sharper. "I've never even *heard* of anybody beating the Cooler."

He watched for a minute, thinking hard. The man was playing three-card monte, not the same game he'd cheated Sam with, but one that everybody knew how to play. Some hustlers played it with three cards, where the object was to keep track of a specific one—the ace of clubs, say. Others played it with walnut shells, where the idea was to keep track of the shell with a coin or some such thing hidden under it.

Marks loved the game because they figured it couldn't be all that hard to follow the card you were supposed to be keeping an eye on. Of course, no hustler played a game like three-card monte as anything but a brace game—one that was fixed. And after what Sam had seen of this particular sharper's capability, he figured this fellow was either preternaturally fast with his fingers, or cheating, or both.

The man in the porkpie hat moved three slightly bent cards around on the table quickly, but not so quickly that Sam, even at a distance, couldn't follow the movements. The mark pointed confidently at the left-hand card, and the sharper, with a few words that Sam couldn't hear (but was pretty sure went something along the lines of *Are you sure, fella?*), flipped it over.

The crowd cheered. The fellow swept a few dollars into his pocket. The sharper had lost.

"If that's cheating, he's pretty bad at it," Oliver observed.

"No, it's a brace game, for sure. That's just the first act. If a mark doesn't believe he can win, he's got no reason to play." Sam shook his head and took another bite of the roll. "I guess if he can beat a proper gambler like the Cooler, fleecing me would be easy. But for the life of me, I still can't figure out how he braced up my own deck without me spotting it. That really burns me up."

"To say nothing of the fact that that's *your* spot."

"Well, yeah. That, too."

"What are you going to do?"

That was the fundamental question. Sam actually had no idea what he *could* do about it. A momentary dream of rousing all of Culver Plaza to oust the interloper flitted through his mind, but that was impractical and unlikely. He was a local, but he was a kid, and so far he hadn't even been made to pay a fix for the privilege of playing cards here. Until he was contributing to someone's income, he had no right to expect protection from anybody. Furthermore, the sharper would surely be carrying enough money to pay a fix of his own if the law showed up, so calling the cops on him was pointless, too.

Anything Sam did was going to result in him losing face or money or — most likely — both. He sighed. "It was good while it lasted. I'm just going to have to find another spot."

"Sam." Oliver nodded in the opposite direction, away from the waterfront. Sam turned and willed the broad smile that plastered itself immediately across his face down to something less moronic. Jin was crossing the plaza toward them.

He turned to Oliver and punched him in the arm. "Quit staring, idiot."

"That's a girl, right? She's coming this way."

"I know, stupid. Quit staring."

"I kinda can't," the barman said helplessly.

Sam scowled at him. "Try." Then he waved at the approaching figure. "Morning," he called. "Come have a cup of coffee."

"Good morning." Jin glanced at his hand as he pulled out one of the barstools for her. "How are your fingers?"

They hurt like hell, and frankly he hadn't been sure how he was going to shuffle a deck, to say nothing about dealing cards all day. He certainly wasn't going to admit any of *that*, though.

"Not so bad," he said, holding them out for her to inspect. "That stuff your uncle gave me was pretty amazing."

She took his hand in both of hers and examined the blisters on his fingertips. "Those look dreadful," she said, her tone making it perfectly clear that any bravado he tried to pass off on her was pointless.

Behind the bar, Oliver coughed. Sam gave him a grateful look. "Jin, this is my friend Oliver. Oliver, Jin."

Oliver nodded. "Pleasure. How does your friend take her coffee, Sam? Or . . ." He frowned and scratched his head, plainly trying to remember anything he knew about the Chinese. Jin's face took on a guarded look. "Or do you prefer tea?" he finished, a touch awkwardly.

Jin tilted her head and gave him a hesitant smile, her guard relaxing. "I prefer coffee, if you don't mind. But . . . thank you. Just plain coffee."

"Anything to eat? We've got some pastries, or I can fry up something."

"The pastries are good," Sam interjected. "Oliver does the baking."

"Then I will try those. Thank you."

Oliver disappeared into the kitchen behind the bar. Jin took off her hat, allowing her long ponytail to fall over one shoulder, unslung her rucksack, slid onto the barstool, and turned to take in the view across Culver Plaza and down to the waterfront. "This is very nice."

"Not so bad in the morning, is it?" *In the morning,* by which Sam actually meant *without obnoxious boys calling you names, or savaged bodies turning up in the hedges, or uncanny folks trying to take over the city.*

"Mmm." She folded her hands primly while Oliver set an empty cup and saucer on the bar before her. Sam stared at him. He had put Jin's coffee in an actual coffeepot, and was now pouring it out for her like a proper waiter. Then he presented her with a plate of rolls and scones and tea cakes arranged with what looked like an attempt at artful placement. And then, while Sam watched in utter disbelief, he set out little matching pots of butter, honey, and red jam, and a little silver butter knife and coffee spoon on an honest-to-God folded linen napkin.

"What?" Oliver demanded.

"I didn't know this place had silverware, is all," Sam observed mildly.

By way of reply, Oliver sniffed and put a pair of tongs in the bowl of sugar cubes. "I don't bring it out for heathens like you, is all, Sam." He waved his hand at Jin as she dug a little purse out of her bag. "It's on the house. Sam's a regular. Yell if you want anything." He walked to a chair at the opposite end of the bar where he promptly disappeared behind a newspaper.

"A regular?" Jin said, eyeing Sam dubiously. "This is a pretty fancy breakfast to have every day."

"It's not my usual." Sam refilled his cup from the coffeepot. "Oliver's just trying to impress you."

"What on earth for?" she asked, spreading jam on a scone.

Because he's my friend and he can tell that I like you. "Darned if I know. What kind of jam is that?"

"Strawberry, I think. When do you usually start playing cards?"

"Normally I'd be set up already, but today, who knows?" Sam nodded across the plaza. "There's a guy who's trying to take over my spot. We're working out what to do about it."

Jin turned and followed Sam's gaze. "In the crowd over there?"

"Yep. The guy in the porkpie hat."

"Shall I blow him up?" Jin asked, eyeing the sharper while she took a bite of scone.

Sam turned to stare at her. In the corner, Oliver dropped his newspaper and any pretense that he hadn't been listening in. "Can you do that?" he asked incredulously.

Jin patted her pockets, then reached for the rucksack and peered inside. "Well, no," she admitted. "Probably not with what I have on me right now."

"Thanks for the offer anyhow," Sam said, reaching for a roll.

"Wait a minute," Oliver interrupted. "What *could* you do with what you've got on you right now?"

"Let's see." She peered into the rucksack again. "I have the fixings for several sorts of loud noises, a few good flares and flashes, and a fair quantity of smoke. Can you think of any way that might be useful?"

Sam considered for a moment. An idea began to take shape. It wouldn't get his spot back, but it would cause some trouble and humiliation for the sharper, which was something.

"Hmm. Maybe."

They ate their breakfast, then Sam strolled casually over to the betting table, hands in his pockets, and waited until the sharper looked up at him and smiled a self-satisfied grin. "You here to play, kid?"

"Yeah," Sam replied. "You got a minute for a game?"

"Sure, sure. Have a seat."

Sam let go of the little cluster of firecrackers he'd been holding through the lining of the left pocket. He shook his foot unobtrusively as he slid onto the stool opposite the dealer and felt the crackers slide down his pant leg and out onto the ground. He toed them into place under the table.

"Good of you to stop by and say hello. Guess you know a few of your colleagues stopped by this morning, too," the man said, flipping the three creased cards face-up on the table to show the queen of spades, ace of hearts, and ten of clubs, then flipping them back over. "Thought you might do something stupid like get bent out of shape."

"Nah." Sam sat with his arms folded while the dealer manipulated the cards in a halfhearted effort to hide the queen, the first-round move that was meant to let the mark win easily. "Best man wins." Sam tapped the left card when the dealer finished.

"*Jacta alea est,*" the sharper said with a grin. He flipped it over to reveal the jack of clubs—which hadn't even been one of the original three he'd put on the table.

Holy Mother of . . . Sam could only hope he managed to hide his shock. *When on earth had he performed that switch?* Sam had actually been watching for it, but when he hadn't seen it, he'd just figured the dealer was going through the standard routine, allowing Sam to choose correctly in the first round of play.

The outrageous way he'd stacked Sam's deck the day before yesterday had been impressive. But *this* . . .

The sharper gave him a narrow smile. "You got one thing right, kid. Best man wins. Now, did you want something?"

Sam swallowed his disbelief and leaned across the table. "I came to warn you. There's going to be a sweep of West Brighton today. The cops are doing a nice big visible roundup of suspects for some big bugs from Gravesend. You picked a bad day to set up."

"And why on earth would you possibly want to warn me?" He swept up the cards and tossed them back down. Queen of spades, ace of hearts, ten of clubs, just like before. "That's baloney."

"This was my spot, and I haven't given up on it," Sam hissed. That much, at least, was true. "You get pinched here, everyone's watching whoever deals here from now on. It's spoiled for everyone." He looked down at the table and rolled his eyes. "You really need me to go through the motions? There's no queen to find."

The dealer grinned and flipped over all three cards to reveal three queens of spades. Then he hid them and flipped them once more: queen of spades, ace of hearts, ten of clubs.

He'd done it so fast, any of the five or so folks watching would have doubted their own eyes, wondering if they'd even seen the row of queens in the first place.

"Now you're just showing off," Sam protested, dumbfounded.

"Yeah. Look, kid, thanks for the warning, but no thanks. I'm pretty sure you're full of it." The sharper sat back again, eyeing Sam from under the narrow brim of his hat. "Now, put down a bet or get up and let somebody who wants to win some money in. I'm here to play cards, and you're no challenge."

"I'm no challenge, but some guy on holiday's gonna be?" Sam shrugged and stood. "I tried." Then he turned and left, playing out a whisper-thin length of fuse through a hole in his pocket and down his pant leg as he went.

Fifteen yards from the betting table, Jin passed behind Sam, heading for the waterfront, and as she did, he felt a tug on the fuse he was still playing out. He let go of the end he was holding and kept on walking. When he reached the nearest bench, he sat and leaned back to watch the proceedings.

At the betting table, another player was just sitting down

to try his luck. Midway between the sharper's table and the spot where Sam sat, Jin crouched. She appeared to be making an adjustment to her shoe. Her bent knee would keep the sharper and his marks from seeing what she was really up to, but from his angle Sam could see her pocket lighter flare as she touched it to the end of the fuse.

She straightened and kept walking toward the water. Sam began to count silently. *One one thousand, two one thousand, three one thousand, four one thousand . . .*

The spark burning its way along the fuse toward the table was all but invisible.

Eight one thousand, nine one thousand, ten one thousand.

Sam stood up and stretched. In the saloon across the plaza, Oliver let out an earsplitting whistle.

The holidaymakers and honest customers just clapped hands over their ears or shot glares of annoyance toward the saloon, but the man in the porkpie hat knew a warning call when he heard one. Right about now, he would be wondering if Sam could possibly have been telling the truth about the police raid.

Sure the sharper would look at him first, Sam hammed up a panicked reaction and sprinted into an alley. He looked back just in time to see the payoff: the spark reached the end of the fuse, and the little cluster of crackers exploded into a burst of smoky staccato reports that sounded exactly like gunshots.

Never mind that the "gunshots" were coming from under the table, or that smoke was pouring from there, too, and a lot of it. The sharper reacted to the sound and confusion just as Sam had figured he would. He plunged out of the smoke, sprinted through the crowds, and disappeared into the alleys west of Culver Plaza, leaving his abandoned mark and a few onlookers staring after him and coughing in confusion.

Jin, who'd had to make an about-face to run after Sam, caught up a moment later. "It worked!" she said delightedly, grabbing his hands gleefully and without thinking.

Sam smiled and winced at the same time. Of course, she realized a second too late, she'd just squeezed his burned fingers, which was only very slightly more embarrassing than the fact that she'd grabbed them in the first place.

She let go and composed herself. "Well. You do find interesting ways to entertain a girl."

Sam bowed. "I do what I can. Of course, now we're going to have to avoid Culver Plaza for a bit. How about a walk by the water? The beach isn't far."

She smiled, remembering the wonderful feel of sand under her bare feet. "All right."

They cut between two buildings and through a little grove of painted bathhouses. When they reached the spot where the wooden walkway ended and the sand began, Jin stopped. "Sam. Is it permissible . . . do people walk there without shoes?"

By way of answer, he just held out his hand.

She took off her slippers. Then she hesitated. "You want to look, don't you?" she asked quietly.

He did—she could tell he did—but he lied and shook his head. "Nope. I just want you to enjoy the sand while you're here."

"I'm missing toes," she said casually. "Still curious?"

"I'm not going to—" Sam stared at her. "*What?*"

"It's a result of the binding."

Sam stopped in his tracks and looked at her. "Why would you tell me that?"

Jin balked. "I . . . well—" It occurred to her a moment too late that what she should've said was "I said it because it's true." The problem was that it *wasn't* true.

"Are you really?" he persisted.

"Missing toes?"

"Yes," he said patiently.

She hesitated again. "I said it," she began, "because I wanted to make you ashamed if you thought of looking."

"And I am. I was trying to be polite, but of course I thought of looking, and I'm properly ashamed now. So tell me, are you really missing toes?"

She took a deep breath. "No. I'm not," she admitted. "Girls do lose toes to bound feet, but I didn't. I'm sorry. I just wanted . . . I wanted to make sure you—after last night . . . I'm sorry. I shouldn't have lied—"

"It's okay," Sam interrupted. "Give me your shoes. I'll carry them for you."

Jin stared at him. "That's all?"

He shrugged. "What else am I going to say? I won't look. I told you I wouldn't. I will, however, carry your shoes if you let me."

Jin did, and they walked on.

"By the bye, you should probably not mention to my uncle what I've been up to," she said as they threaded a path through beachgoers in woolen bathing costumes and other folks in summer suits and dresses strolling to the water's edge.

"You mean he wouldn't approve of your being barefoot on the beach, or he's really convinced I'm too big a fool to be trusted with anyone's safety?"

Jin gave a little snort. "He absolutely thinks you're a fool, but that isn't what I meant. The explosives. The way I used them today, and yesterday with those boys."

"I won't tell him anything. I guess today's adventure might've been a little questionable, but why yesterday? You were defending yourself. Sort of."

"Sort of." Jin hopped out of the way of a wave, and her feet sank into the delightfully cool, wet sand. "But Uncle Liao would not be proud of how much I enjoy doing things like that, so it's probably best not to mention it at all. When one is forced to use weapons, one isn't supposed to do it with relish. Uncle Liao already loves to tell me about what a disappointment I would be to Lao Tzu. Anyway, don't mention it."

"Who's Lao Tzu?"

"Uncle Liao's favorite philosopher." Jin let the next wave wash across her ankles and smiled down at the receding water. Then the smile faded. "Should we check in with your friends at the Reverend Dram? In case they have any sort of news?"

Sam looked at her sadly. "I was really hoping to keep you from thinking about all of that."

"I know you were. But you can't take that memory away." Jin met his gaze. "That isn't the only reason I came to meet you today, though."

"Really?" Sam asked, smiling a little foolishly.

"I also felt like blowing something up," she said, keeping her face perfectly straight.

Sam blinked. Then he burst into laughter. "Fine. Come on. But I'm telling your uncle you said that."

Mammon's Alley was quiet, almost peaceful—but then again, Jin thought as Sam shouldered open the door of the Reverend Dram, it was early by saloon standards.

"Hello?" he called.

Walter Mapp looked up from where he sat, leaning against the piano and reading the paper. "Ahoy there. You two looking for a beer already?"

"We got customers?" Jasper Wills called from behind the bar.

"No, Jasper. Stay where you are. Someone," Mapp said, winking at Sam and Jin, "dropped a case of bottled beer back there, and now has a bit of a mess to clean up."

"We were hoping for news," Sam told him.

Mapp folded the paper and leaned on his knees. "I wish I had news for you, Sam."

Jin tried to keep the disappointment from her face. "Is there something . . . anything we could be doing?" she asked.

"I think what you mean is, what are *we* doing? And I'm sorry to tell you, despite hours of discussion after you two left last night, we still haven't got a clue. But don't you worry a hair," he said. "We are tenacious folks. We'll come up with a plan."

Suddenly, the door of the saloon burst open and two young men dressed in long-tailed coats and unusually tall top hats strolled in like they owned the place.

Rough fellows, Jin recognized. The style might vary from city to city, but if you knew what to look for, you could always spot the hoodlum types. To further confirm what she already knew, Sam pushed her behind him.

"Jasper," Mapp barked over his shoulder.

The two rowdies took long looks around the room, then one turned on his heel and called out the door, "All's clear, Jim."

The man who entered then was tall and thin and deadly-looking, and it was obvious to Jin that everyone in the room —everyone but her—knew exactly who he was. Sam recognized the newcomer immediately, right along with Jasper Wills and Walter Mapp. "James Hawks," he said quietly.

Sam didn't know much about the crime-ridden New York district called the Five Points. Then again, you didn't have to know much about the Points to have heard of James Hawks, keeper of the Bowery saloon called the Blind Tiger's Milk. When newspapers in the state wanted to rail about the evils of violence in the city of New York, they wrote about the Five Points. And when the bosses of the various gangs there needed to be reined in, it wasn't city police who came knocking on their doors. It was James Hawks, the only man even the most vicious thugs in the city doffed their hats to out of honest respect, which most folks figured really meant he was the only man they were truly afraid of.

Hawks glanced around the room, taking in Sam, Jin, and Mapp, before his eyes fell on Jasper Wills, who was already on his way out from behind the bar.

Hawks's eyes crinkled. He swept his beaver-skin top hat from his oiled hair and smiled. "Jasper. Always a pleasure."

Wills shook Hawks's outstretched hand with a smile that

The man who entered then was tall and thin and deadly-looking.

managed to be only a little bit wary. "Welcome to West Brighton, Jim. To what do we owe the pleasure?"

Hawks handed his hat to one of his boys and clasped his hands behind his back. "Well, I'll tell you, Jasper, it seems you've got some odd happenings going on hereabouts. I heard, for instance, that a young lady"—his eyes flicked sideways at Jin—"discovered a fairly gruesome message not two streets from here only yesterday."

"You know a thing or two about finding gruesome things in your neck of the woods, I suppose," Jasper said, folding his arms. "I'd never insult you by asking what business it is of yours, but I admit I'm curious to know what brings you yourself out here to investigate."

Sam's eyes widened. Jasper Wills had just, more or less, told James Hawks that what went on in West Brighton was none of his business. This was the stuff of nightmares, the kind of thing that got innocent bystanders killed. He took a deep breath and tried to figure what the best course of action would be if things started going south.

Hawks, however, only smiled wider. "Fair point, Jasper." He turned to his backup. "Boys, outside with you. We'll be needing some privacy."

Sam held that breath until the door had shut behind the two rowdies. Even then, he half-expected Hawks to casually pull out a knife and announce that he was going to kill them all with his own hands for the insult.

Instead, the tall saloonkeeper nodded at the nearest table. "May I invite myself to sit? And could I prevail upon the lot of you to join me?"

"We should . . ." Sam gestured halfheartedly toward the door, knowing that trying to leave was futile. Apart from the fact that *the lot of you* plainly included them, Jin was certainly not going to leave of her own will — not now that it was clear that Hawks's appearance had something to do with the body she'd found.

James Hawks lifted an eyebrow. "You should . . . what? Are you the kids who found the bodies?" Sam nodded reluctantly. Hawks turned his eyes on Jin. "And you're the girl from Fata Morgana? Liao's protégée?"

Jin's eyes widened. "How do you know that? How is it that *everyone* knows that?"

"You should join us," Hawks said easily.

Brow furrowed, Jin allowed him to pull a chair out for her, and the matter was settled.

When Sam, Mapp, and Jasper Wills had taken seats as well, Hawks put his elbows on the table and rubbed a hand over his face. Suddenly he looked old, exhausted.

"Thank you," he said tiredly. "I apologize for the theatrics. I'm accustomed to ordering people around, and usually it's necessary. But it wastes so much time, and we have so little to begin with."

"What's this about, Jim?" Jasper asked.

Hawks sighed. "I'm here to speak to you about the man whose name was written on the walls."

Sam opened his mouth, the name *Jack* on his lips, and Hawks held up his hand. "Don't, if you please. In ages past, they believed that naming a thing calls it, and while I pride myself on being a man of reason, in desperate times we may perhaps forgive ourselves our superstitions. We will not speak his name. I came here because of you," Hawks continued, turning to Walter Mapp. "They tell me you're a headcutter, one of the oldest. Is this true?"

Jin elbowed Sam. *Headcutter?* she mouthed. Sam could only shrug.

"They say that, do they?" Mapp folded his arms. "They talk a lot, for being a nameless *they*."

"Certainly you know there are many, many roamers in the city."

"Certainly."

"Well," Hawks said patiently, "are you or are you not Walter Mapp the Liar, who bested the Devil and won a favor?"

A silence stretched over the table. *Who bested the Devil and won a favor?* Thinking immediately of the conversation from the night before and the strange coin on Tom Guyot's watch fob, Sam stared from Hawks to Mapp. He couldn't decide if he thought Hawks had lost his mind or if he was simply losing his. Had the two musicians actually been discussing calling in a favor from the *Devil* to defeat the man he'd refused to let into Hell?

Jasper Wills broke the stalemate first. He sighed, shoved his chair back, and stalked to the bar, muttering, "Plainly, I need a beer if I'm going to be able to handle this conversation."

FOURTEEN

The Headcutter

I F I'M TALKING to the wrong man," James Hawks spoke calmly, as if he hadn't just said something completely insane, "I had better be on my way and find the right one."

"Nope," Mapp said, leaning his chin on his palm. "When you put it like that, I suppose I have to say you're in the right place. Haven't been called the Liar in ages, but I'm Mapp. I'm the one you're looking for."

"Pleasure to meet you," Hawks said. "This man, whose name we will not use, is it fair to assume you have also learned who he is, what he wants?"

"We think we understand the stakes," Mapp said. "Can't say we've figured out what to do about it. You?"

"Sure," Hawks said with an easy smile. "I think you ought to use your favor and stop him."

Mapp sighed and pushed back his chair. "If I hadn't spent it several lifetimes back, I'd do that in a minute." He spread his empty palms helplessly. "But I did, so I can't."

Sam waited for him to mention that there was another man in Coney Island who was owed a favor from the Devil. Then he realized he was hoping Mapp wouldn't do it. Now that he knew Tom had been talking about the Devil when he said using the favor would mean turning the whole thing over to someone they didn't necessarily want involved, he could see the sense in Tom's decision. Somehow, though, he couldn't picture Jim Hawks understanding Tom's reluctance.

Hawks looked closely at Mapp, as if trying to decide if he believed him or not. Then he nodded once, shortly. "Then I suppose we'll have to come up with another plan of attack."

"Know much about this fellow?" Mapp asked. "The one we're not calling by his name, I mean."

"I know of him only from stories from the road. From others like him and like you." Hawks smiled coldly.

Mapp looked mildly offended. "Don't like the uncanny in your town, Hawks?"

The saloonkeeper's smile grew even more brittle. "Humans cause enough trouble all by themselves, I find."

"We were all human once," Mapp said with a shrug.

"Not all of you," Hawks retorted. "Not all, not by a long shot. I've seen the two he sent, and I promise you they are not part of any race that lays claim to being human." He cleared his throat. "Let me tell you what I know. Then, I ask that you return the favor."

Mapp eyed him for a moment, then nodded. "Sounds fair to me."

"There were five of us," Hawks began. "Five people, five mortal humans out of every generation whose task it is to hold together the soul of the city. There is a term for our office, which I also will not use. While we stand, the city stands. It takes its character from us, imperfect and human though we are." For a moment, his voice sounded almost humble. "Suffice it to say, the best, the most sure way for a creature like the man we are discussing to capture a city, to take it for his own, is through the five of us."

"You said there *were* five?" Sam got up the courage to ask.

"*His* fixers, the murderers of the two men you found, have also killed one of our own. And I suspect they have won another over to their cause."

At the end of the table, Mapp stirred. "When you say *through the five of us*, what are you talking about, exactly?"

"If he cannot convince us to share his vision for the city, he cannot remake it into what he needs. But he can kill us, claim the city before it finds its soul again, and replace us with stewards of his own."

"Claim it how?" Jasper asked.

"By blood, by naming, and by fire." Now Hawks looked at Jin. "The last, the claiming by fire, is called cinefaction. There used to be those who claimed cinefaction alone could take a city, but that required a particular type of artificier. In the old days, those artificiers were called conflagrationeers."

Jin stiffened. Hawks smiled thinly. "You know the word."

She shook her head, but the gesture lacked her usual confidence. "I may have heard it."

"Your uncle —"

"No. My uncle would *never* —"

"Let me finish," Hawks snapped. "Your uncle works for a company that can trace its roots back to one of the great conflagrationeers of old. The original Fata Morgana Company was formed by a partnership between a man named Burns and a conflagrationeer by the name of Ignis Blister."

Jin opened her mouth again, and Hawks cut her off. "I don't know how you came to be here at the same time as these two, the fixers, but it cannot be coincidence."

A faint flicker of a memory twitched in Sam's head. He looked at Jin, but she was still sitting rigidly, staring at James Hawks with a mixture of confusion and defiance.

Sam turned his attention back to Hawks. "How do you know all this?"

"We cannot uphold the city if we aren't educated in the things that threaten it," Hawks told him. "The point is, it's a bad time for Fata Morgana to be in the neighborhood, if they are here innocently."

He turned back to Jin. "They are going to come for you, girl. They are going to believe either your uncle or his partner can perform the cinefaction. And if they refuse or claim ignorance, these fixers will likely kill you all, beginning with *you*, with the very reasonable expectation that, if either man has the knowledge to perform the process, the sight of your suffering will convince him to do the work. And you've seen the suffering they're capable of inflicting."

Jin's scarred hands began to shake on the table. She curled them into fists. "What about that?" she asked. "Who were the two men they killed?"

"I don't know." James Hawks's expression softened. "I'm sorry to tell you I think they were killed in order to draw us out and bring us together—the five who stand for the city. They were killed to call attention to what was written over their bodies. Nothing more."

Jin shoved her chair back from the table and stalked rigidly away across the room. Sam glanced from Hawks to Walter Mapp. The pianist nodded for him to go to her.

She stood by a shuttered window, arms folded across her chest, staring blankly at it as if there were a view to be seen. Sam came to stand beside her, hands in his pockets, and waited.

"All that, and we don't even know who they were," Jin said dully. "They didn't do anything to deserve it, they had no idea what was happening, they just—" Her voice broke, and she stared silently at the flaking paint on the shutters. "And my uncle would never—even Mr. Burns, not even if he could . . . Anyhow, it isn't as if *anyone* could make sense of it."

The book. Of course. The one Burns had inherited, but that he couldn't make heads or tails of. The one Jin's uncle was hired to interpret. That had been the memory nagging at Sam.

"You mean that book," Sam whispered. "The one you told me about." Jin nodded shortly. "You think either of them knows what's really in it?" Sam asked quietly.

"No, of course not."

But her hands were still clenched tightly, a gesture Sam was coming to realize meant she was holding something back. "Jin, what is it?"

She hesitated, glanced over her shoulder at the three men waiting at the table behind them. "I used a formula out of it for the display last night," she whispered. "A few formulas, actually. I read through that stupid book all the time, and I found a formula that I thought I could make sense of, and it worked. They all worked. That's how I got the fireworks to burn underwater." Her voice was beginning to take on an edge of panic.

"What does that matter?" Sam whispered.

"I don't believe for a minute that either Uncle Liao or Mr. Burns knows what that book is. But both Uncle Liao and I have made some of the formulas in it work." She paused, looking at him expectantly. "Sam, *what if that makes us . . . ?*"

"Makes you what? Conflagrationeers, whatever that means?"

She exhaled, hard. "I don't know. But it can't be good, knowing what I know; that I've made some of those formulas work. It just feels . . . wrong somehow, now that I know what sorts of things that book is used for."

He understood why she was worried. Still, Sam felt she was missing a major point—namely, the fact that all three members of Fata Morgana were in mortal danger as long as they stayed in the vicinity of the city of New York. "You have to warn your uncle," he said, trying to keep his voice gentle. He swallowed. "You have to leave town."

Jin said nothing. She stared at the shutters a moment longer, then strode back to the table and took her seat. "Please excuse me for disrupting," she said evenly. "I would like to hear the rest of what you have to say."

James Hawks shrugged and folded his hands on the table. "I have nothing more," Hawks announced. "Mr. Mapp? How say you? I have few people I can trust. Many of the city's uncanny will side with him, if it comes to that. But I would like to trust you."

Walter Mapp sighed. "It had better not come to that." He took off his hat and scratched his head and chin. "Yeah, Jim, I'm with you. There's another headcutter in Coney Island, too, Tom Guyot. He'll help us, so far as he can, but he's an old man. And he has a friend, a newspaperman, who knows a thing or two about Ja—about *him*. Might know more than he's told so far."

"Another headcutter?" Hawks mused. "Well, well. The co-incidences just carry on, don't they? I suppose you'd have told me if he had a favor to spare."

Mapp gave a noncommittal lift of his shoulders. "Could be that it's not a coincidence he's here, but that doesn't necessarily mean it's bad news."

"What's a headcutter?" Sam asked, unable to keep quiet any longer.

Mapp chuckled. "Among musicians, we call a contest a *head-cutting*. There are a lot of us among the roamers on the roads, and somewhere along the way, a contest with the Devil came to be called by the same name."

"Well . . ." Sam looked from Mapp to Hawks. "So, which one are we talking about? A musical duel, or a literal contest with the Devil?"

"Funnily enough," Mapp said, grinning, "in Tom's case and mine alike, the answer is . . . both."

"So what now?" Jin cut in, impatiently.

"I presume someone needs to warn Fata Morgana," Mapp said. "Probably best you don't go, sunshine. If their most logical move is to use you to force your uncle's hand, you'd better stay out of sight."

"I could go," Sam volunteered. "Can Jin stay here?"

"I don't need a nursemaid," Jin muttered.

"Jin—"

She flung up her hand. "Point taken, Sam. But it's insult-ing. You should expect me to grumble about it."

"I need to send messages to the remaining two of my . . . colleagues," Hawks said. "They are both here in Brooklyn."

Jin spoke up immediately. "I can do that, can't I?"

Mapp turned to her with raised eyebrows. "You know your way around Brooklyn, do you?"

"I *meant*—"

"I *know* what you meant. Let me explain to you what *I* meant when I said you'd better stay out of sight."

Jin dropped her head onto the tabletop in frustration.

"Sam's the best choice for delivering any messages," Jasper suggested. "He's at the invisible age, and he knows how to conduct himself."

"The invisible age?" Sam mumbled. "Oddly, I know exactly what you mean by that. Sure, I'll do whatever you need."

"All right, then." Mapp stretched in his chair. "What say we send Sam with a warning to Fata Morgana first, and maybe see if he can find Tom Guyot." He turned to Hawks. "That sound like a plan to you?"

Hawks nodded. "Go quickly. Mr. Mapp, do you think the newspaperman could tell us more if he wanted to?"

"Hard to say. Maybe. No harm in asking."

"All right." Hawks turned back to Sam. "If you can, see about finding him, too. When you get back I'll have more messages ready for you, and one of my boys can drive you to Brooklyn."

"Will do." Sam took Jin's arm and drew her a little distance away from the table. "Anything you want me to say, in particular?"

She sighed. "Tell Uncle Liao I'm safe. Tell him I said to be safe, too, and not do anything stupid. And Sam?" Her voice dropped so that he had to lean in close, close enough for the scent of resins and gunpowder to waft over him again. "Get the book," she whispered. "It's in a little cabinet with glass doors in the wagon, next to the workbench. It has a pebbly green leather cover, you can't miss it. Bring it back with you."

Her eyes were wide and worried. Sam reached for her fingers and squeezed them. "It's going to be fine. Anybody who tries to play rough with your uncle's going to regret it."

She cracked the smallest of smiles and squeezed his hand back. "Go."

Sam was at the door when Hawks's voice stopped him. "Sam. Just a moment. In case I forget when you come back." The man from the Bowery strode to his side, drawing a billfold from his pocket. "You are going to have to travel as quickly as you can. Got someplace you can carry this?"

Sam tried not to look shocked at the amount of greenbacks the saloonkeeper had with him. He'd never seen that much cash in one place in his entire life. He fumbled in his pockets and came up with a little bag he used when he didn't want to haul his whole kit around, just big enough for a deck of cards and some dice.

Hawks took a sheaf of bills from the mass of greenbacks. "Find Liao," he said quietly as he tucked the money into Sam's bag and then added a handful of coins from his pocket. "*Not Burns*. You understand?"

Sam frowned. "The instruction, yes. The reason, no."

"That's good enough for me. Off you go."

Sam trotted into the hotel and up to the concierge's desk, remembering Tom's words and willing himself to look like he belonged.

The concierge wasn't remotely fooled.

"I . . . er . . . need to leave a message for two of your guests," Sam mumbled, trying not to be intimidated by the man's arched eyebrows.

"For whom?"

"For a man named Tom Guyot. And a fellow called Ambrose."

"Are you acquainted with Mr. Guyot?" the concierge asked severely. "We try not to disturb our guests unnecessarily."

"I'm—well, yeah, we're acquainted," Sam said, starting to get annoyed. He straightened up and worked on looking insulted. "I had lunch here with the two of them just yesterday."

Eyebrows still dubiously arched, the concierge passed two sheets of paper across the desk and waited while Sam scrawled, *Mr. Guyot, please come to the Reverend Dram right away! Very important. Sam Noctiluca and Walter Mapp.* He wrote out a similar message for Ambrose, then folded the pages and handed them back. The concierge took them with an expression that clearly said he was surprised Sam could write at all.

But there was no time to waste, so Sam ignored it. "It's really important. Can you, I don't know, rush them along?"

The concierge simply raised his eyebrows, impossibly, another quarter inch and slid the messages into one of the letter cubbies on the wall behind his desk. Sam stared at him, cursed silently to himself, then turned on his heel and stalked across the atrium toward the door.

About halfway across the room, someone stopped him. "You're the boy I saw at the fireworks with Sergeant Guyot and Major Bierce, aren't you?"

It was one of the haunted-looking men Sam assumed were the Resaca veterans, a man with bright blue eyes and heavy sideburns and maps of old worry lines around his mouth and eyes. He wore a little sprig of briar in his lapel. The military ranks threw Sam for a minute, but it wasn't hard to figure out who the fellow was talking about. "Er. Yeah."

"And did I hear that you're looking for them now?"

His eyes were eerily sharp. Sam flinched. "Er. Yeah," he repeated.

"I know where to find them. Would you like me to pass your letter along?"

"Oh. Sure. Thank you." Sam begged another two sheets of paper from the concierge and wrote out his messages again while the soldier waited. "Did you . . . did you serve with them?"

"Yes." A look of sorrow crossed the man's face. "At Shiloh, and then at Resaca, back when Major Bierce was a first lieutenant and Sergeant Guyot was just Tom."

After he finished writing and folded the pages, Sam tried to think of something else to say. For the second time he realized that he didn't actually know much about the war. "A lot of people died at Shiloh, huh?"

Of course, the moment he said that, he wanted to slap himself on the forehead. This man had survived the carnage, but he had probably seen a lot of his friends die. Why would he want to talk about it with a stupid kid who didn't really even understand what, apart from slavery, the fighting had been about?

But if the soldier was bothered, he didn't show it. "Twenty-five thousand killed, wounded, or missing at Shiloh," he answered, his words vaguely singsong, like the way someone might recite a litany in church. "Another eight thousand at Resaca."

Twenty-five thousand in casualties and losses? That was like wiping all of Gravesend and Coney Island off the map on a busy summer Sunday, when it seemed like the whole world was crowded into town. It was shocking, absolutely impossible to understand.

The soldier held out his callused hand for the messages. "I'll see it done," he said with a shadow of a smile, and then he was gone, leaving Sam to wonder what it meant to have witnessed that kind of bloodshed. Jin could barely wipe the memory of the body in the alley from her mind, even for a minute. Just the thought of the bare foot he'd tripped over made Sam sick to his stomach, and he hadn't even seen any of the gory bits.

Behind the hotel, the Fata Morgana wagon was quiet, and appeared deserted. Sam knocked on the door and waited. No answer. He peered inside each of the three tents, but they were empty, too. Sam knocked at the wagon again, then jogged down toward the water, where Jin and Liao had set off the previous night's display. Still no sign of anyone.

He tried the livery stable next. The only person inside the huge barn was a kid working on the axle of a carriage. "'Scuse me," Sam called. "You seen the fireworks people around lately?"

The kid leaned out from behind one of the wheels. "Yeah. They hired a coach and driver about an hour ago."

"Any idea where they were going?"

"New York, somewhere. All I know."

Sam cursed quietly. Even the quickest route to Manhattan

took a couple of hours. They'd be gone until late afternoon at the earliest. "Thanks."

Well, they'd have to be back in time for that evening's display, anyhow. In the meantime, Sam wandered back to the wagon. There was still the matter of Jin's book.

Feeling a bit like a thief, he tried the door. Locked, of course. He walked around the wagon, eyeing the curtained windows in the hopes of finding one open. Still no luck—until he found a window on the back, opposite the door, with curtains that were parted enough for him to peer in. It wasn't unlocked, but it gave Sam a glimpse of the ceiling inside.

Or, more accurately, it gave him a glimpse of the *hatch* in the ceiling, the one Jin had been perched over the morning Sam had first seen her, tossing fire into the air.

"Well," he murmured to himself, "it's something to try." And with a glance around to make sure there was no one to see him acting like a burglar, he jumped up, grabbed the overhanging cornice, and levered himself over it and onto the top of the wagon. He crept over the pitched roof, curled his fingers around the edges of the hatch door, and pulled.

It moved.

"Oh, thank God," he muttered. Then, with one last look around, he opened it just far enough for him to slip through, and dropped inside.

It was not the most graceful landing, but since there was no one there, it didn't much matter. Sam picked himself up and took in his surroundings. There was the workbench under the window with the parted curtains, flanked on each side by cabinets bolted to the walls. There was a note addressed to Jin on the workbench. Sam paused to read the first line — *Gone for supplies; will return by afternoon* — and picked it up to take back with him.

To the right of the workbench and cabinets, exactly where Jin had told him to look, was a glass-fronted bookcase held closed with little hooks. The green pebbly leatherbound volume Jin had told him to look for was on the second shelf.

He stuck the note between its pages and tucked it into the back of his trousers. He shifted the rest of the books on the shelf just enough to hide the gap where *The Conflagrationeer's Port-fire Book* had been; then, before climbing out again, he paused to take a quick look through the front window to make sure he was still alone.

He wasn't. Two men were crossing the gravel drive toward the wagon. There was absolutely nothing to justify the sudden sense of ill ease that swept over Sam at the sight of them, but it was undeniable.

Something about the way the redheaded man moved, maybe? Even at a distance Sam could tell he was dressed in expensive clothes; he looked right at home on the grounds of the Broken Land, except for the fact that no guests would venture back here by the stables. There was something about his gait, though, that just didn't look right. It was too smooth — there were none of the little human motions and gestures that people made when they walked. Those subtle gestures let you read a fellow when he sat down to play cards, and everyone made them — but not this man. He didn't flex his fingers or put his hands in his pockets or scratch his head or fiddle with his suit cuffs or do anything but walk with coiled elegance straight for the wagon.

The other man looked odd, too — if only because he wore a long felt coat that was entirely inappropriate for a beautiful summer morning. His sallow skin glittered slightly in the sun, as if a fine sweat covered his bald head.

There was no way out, not without being seen. Sam eased himself away from the window, crossed the wagon, and closed the curtain on the other side to keep them from spotting the open roof hatch the way he had.

Bang bang bang bang bang. "Hello?" a voice barked. "Anyone at home?"

More quietly, a second voice: "I'll check the tents."

"Fine." *BANG BANG BANG BANG BANG.* "Burns! Open up!"

Sam blinked, remembering what James Hawks had said. *Find Liao, not Burns. You understand?*

The door rattled, making Sam's heart stop for a moment. One more round of banging, then the knocker's grumbling voice drifted away to join the second man, just barely within earshot but not close enough for Sam to make out what they were saying.

They could be anyone, Sam told himself. *They could work for the hotel. You have no reason to think they have anything to do with this.*

He crept to a different window and slowly pushed one corner of the curtain aside. The redheaded man was smoking and pacing just outside the second of the three tents that surrounded the wagon. A moment later his companion emerged, shaking his head. Then he pointed at the tent nearest the wagon, which stood on a low wooden platform.

When the man in the coat went to push open the flap, something strange happened. It wouldn't budge.

The two men looked at each other. The one with the cigarette elbowed past the other and yanked at the tent flap. Nothing happened. He shoved at it, throwing one shoulder into it as if it were a proper door. The oiled fabric gave just enough for him to bounce off it, as if it had been made of India rubber.

A hushed conversation took place. The bald man bent and tried to lift up the hem of the tent, with no more success. The two separated, walking around it in opposite directions. A few moments later, they reappeared. This time the conversation was louder and more heated.

The man in the white suit dropped his head back and stared at the sky, exhaling a mouthful of smoke. Then they strode back the way they had come and disappeared out of sight.

Sam took two breaths to work up his nerve, double-checked to make sure they were gone, then jumped for the hatch and pulled himself out and onto the roof. He slid the hatch closed, dropped back to the ground, and sprinted for West Brighton.

FIFTEEN

Red Hook

WELL, THIS IS inconvenient." Bones settled back into one of the plush velvet couches in the Broken Land's atrium. "Would you stop that, please?"

Walker stopped pacing and rolled his head on his neck. "We only have until tomorrow night."

"Yes, Walker, I'm aware. So we come back tonight for the fireworks show, and we talk to Burns afterward. It's inconvenient, but it isn't world-ending."

"I don't like this place," Walker said, casting a dark-circled eye around the room and sizing up the guests strolling in and out in their summer finery. "There's something off about it."

"Stop fidgeting."

"It feels—"

"Walker," Bones hissed, "you're attracting attention."

Walker followed Bones's gaze to the foot of the wide marble stairs, where a blond man in a suit was watching them. He returned the man's stare with an insolent tilt of his head until the fellow stalked out of the hotel.

"This place is getting to me," he muttered.

"We'll have to come back here tonight for the show." Bones stood and stretched. "In the meantime, we need to speak to Christophel."

Walker groaned.

"There's nothing for it," Bones pointed out. "Hawks has disappeared. Sawyer has disappeared. Overcaste doesn't know who the fifth is. We need Bios again. It's worked so far."

"So far," Walker repeated shortly. "And we still have a long way to go." But he shrugged and followed Bones out of the atrium to a waiting carriage in the driveway.

Frederick Overcaste looked down from the driver's box. "Where now?"

"Red Hook," Bones replied. "The docks."

Sam burst onto Mammon's Alley, where the sheer volume of pedestrians forced him to stop running just seconds before his lungs burst into flame.

Three Five Points b'hoys lazed out in front of the Reverend Dram. They watched him with amused expressions as he limped up to the door. "Pleasant constitutional?" the one on the left inquired.

"Shove off," Sam mumbled, wiping the sweat from his face.

The fellow on the right whistled through a broken front tooth. "Good thing we're on your side, kid."

And who knew how long that state of affairs would last? *Don't bait the ruffians*, Sam told himself as he slipped inside.

Walter Mapp and James Hawks looked up from the table as he entered. "I think I almost got caught by Ja—by his guys,"

Sam said before either one could speak. He glanced around. "Where's Jin?"

Hawks ignored that. "The Fata Morgana people?"

"Nobody was there. Then I—" Sam hesitated, leaning his hands on his knees and gulping air to make it look like he was just catching his breath. *The Conflagrationeer's Port-fire Book* was still hidden under his shirt in the waistband of his trousers. He didn't know if he wanted to tell anyone he'd taken it.

"Sorry," he said breathlessly. "I just ran something like three miles."

"Jasper," Mapp called, "get the kid some water, will you? Go on, Sam."

"I talked to a fellow in the stable, and he said someone drove them out to New York," Sam continued. "I figured they wouldn't be back for hours, so I was about to leave, and then I saw these two men. I hid—I guess I was feeling like I looked suspicious." That much, at least, was true. "They went right up to the wagon, knocked a bunch of times, and . . ."

"And?"

Sam hesitated again, and looked at Hawks. "And one of them called for Mr. Burns by name."

Hawks gave Mapp a look. "What did they look like?"

"One's got dark red hair and freckles. The other one's bald and he was wearing a long coat."

Hawks banged his hand on the table, then got up and paced a few steps away and back. "I take it those are the same ones you saw?" Mapp asked.

"Indeed," Hawks said. "What about that Tom Guyot fellow?"

"I left a message," Sam said. "It was all I could do." Jasper Wills handed him a glass of water. He gulped half of it down, choked, sputtered, and drank the rest. "Where's Jin?"

"Upstairs. Said she wanted to take a nap," Mapp told him.

"Where?"

The pianist shook his head. "She said not to wake her up. Not even when you got back, not even if you asked."

"But she—wait a—*what?*"

"Not joking, Sam. I think she's more bothered than she wants to admit."

He felt thwarted. Why would Jin have told them that? And there was no way to insist to see her, no way to explain himself, without giving up the book.

Bang bang bang! Sam just about jumped out of his skin, half-expecting the harsh voice of the redheaded man to follow the knock, but it was only a fourth b'hoy, rapping at the door before peering inside and catching Hawks's eye.

"It is here?" Hawks asked.

"Yes, sir."

"I've arranged a carriage." Hawks rose, picked up three envelopes that had been sitting on the table, and held them out to Sam. "Instructions for you, and messages for the others. Mike will drive you."

The fellow peering through the door touched his knuckles to the slick, oiled hair at his temple in a little salute.

"But if Jin's that bothered, I really should—"

Walter Mapp put a hand on his shoulder. "Sam, she'll be fine. She's not fragile, and we don't have time to waste."

"Let's go, Captain," Mike called from the doorway. "We're blocking the street. Not exactly inconspicuous."

Sam sighed and took Hawks's envelopes. "Fine. When she wakes up tell her . . . tell her I'll have something for her when I get back."

Mapp raised an eyebrow, but he nodded. "Go."

He got as far as the doorway, then did a double take at the fancy little runabout blocking traffic. "Where the heck did you get this?"

The fellow called Mike sprang up into the coachman's seat. "Mr. Hawks said we might be in neighborhoods where it would be best to look sharp." He glanced dubiously around, letting Sam know this was not one of the neighborhoods Mr. Hawks had been referring to. He was probably only about Constantine's age, seventeen or eighteen, and, Sam guessed, Irish, although there wasn't much of a brogue to give him away.

Odd, Sam thought, what different worlds they came from.

He opened the envelope with his instructions and checked the addresses. "Seems that way." Then he looked from the posh carriage and its two gleaming bays to the older boy's outlandish clothes.

"I got another coat," Mike said patiently. "We aren't complete heathens in the Points. Now, where the hell are we going?"

"Brooklyn," Sam answered, clambering into the runabout. "Looks like the first stop's Columbia Heights."

With the other three b'hoys clearing folks out of the way, Mike guided the carriage onto Surf Avenue, heading east for the toll road that connected Coney Island to the mainland. Just before the turn onto the shell-paved thoroughfare, a bigger, four-in-hand carriage came barreling full-tilt at them.

Mike yanked on the reins, hauling the bays to a protesting halt just in time to avoid being run off the road, and causing something to go flying off the roof.

The coach was tearing along so fast that when it took the turn onto the shell road it nearly overturned. Sam leaned out for a look just in time to catch in the four-in-hand's window the face of the red-haired man he'd seen behind the Broken Land.

"That's him," he yelped.

"Well, if that ain't the strangest." Mike turned with an odd look on his face. "I could swear that was Frederick Overcaste driving that thing."

"Who's that?"

"Tammany heeler. He's a . . ." Mike paused. ". . . a colleague of Mr. Hawks's."

"A colleague? Like the kind of colleague we're going to deliver messages to?"

Mike nodded and gathered the reins to get the horses moving again.

"Something fell off the roof," Sam called. "Was it anything we should—"

"Nothing up there but traveling blankets. Leave them."

He snapped the reins, and just as the bays started trotting along again, a very aggravated-looking Jin climbed in next to Sam. "Ouch, by the way," she mumbled, dusting herself off.

"What are—how on earth did you get onto the *roof?*"

The horses stopped again. "Where the hell did she come from?" Mike demanded.

"I guess we have another passenger." Sam grinned. He leaned out the window again, watched the four-in-hand plowing through the toll gate, and considered. "Follow them," he said at last. "We'll go to Columbia Heights afterward."

Mike shot him a disgruntled look. "Is that what Mr. Hawks told you to do?"

"Mr. Hawks didn't know we were going to get this kind of chance," Sam countered. "What did he tell *you* to do?"

The older boy mumbled an elaborate series of swear words, from which Sam understood that Hawks had basically instructed Mike to do whatever Sam told him, and flicked the reins.

"Nobody was there at your wagon, but I snuck in and found this for you." Sam took Jin's book from under his shirt and held it out. "One of the grooms in the stable said they went into New York," he added. "They left a note. It's in there."

She read the message quickly and nodded. "There's a place in New York where you can get decent fireworking supplies." She pocketed it, opened the book on her lap, and started flipping through.

"There's something else, though." Sam told her about the two men who'd come knocking, about how the red-haired man had called for Mr. Burns. Jin listened with wide eyes.

"That doesn't mean anything," she protested. "He could just . . . everybody we work for always asks for Mr. Burns, either because they want to deal with the owner or because they want to deal with the one who's white. It doesn't mean he's in with Ja— with *his* men."

"All that's true, Jin, and I'm not saying I think anything,

one way or the other," Sam said. "How well do you really know him, though?"

"How well do I know Mr. Burns?" Jin gave him an utterly disgusted look. "I've known him as long as I've known Uncle Liao. They're my family. *Both* of them. Just because Mr. Burns isn't Chinese—"

Sam put up his hands. "Jin, you call one *uncle* and one *mister*. That does sound like two different things."

"That's only because—"

"Jin. Stop. I believe you."

"Fine, then." She gave him one last sharp look and turned her attention back to the book. "Now let me read for a while."

A while turned out to be the rest of the trip, which took them all the way to Red Hook. Sam searched his pockets for a deck of cards. Thinking about the incredible feats of the sharper in the porkpie hat, he worked his way through his repertoire of stocks and slips and false shuffles and cuts. But even with that to occupy him, it was a long way to ride in silence.

Mike followed the coach all the way to the docks, then he pulled the horses to a stop and let the four-in-hand disappear around a corner. "Any farther and they'll know they're being followed," he said. "If they don't already. What do you want to do now?"

"I want to know what they're up to. They can't go much farther in that huge coach, anyway." Sam glanced at Jin. "Let's go on foot, see what we can find out."

"This is a bad idea," Mike said in a tone that sounded like he wasn't really expecting them to listen.

Sam hopped to the cobbled pavement with Jin on his heels. "Just be ready to go in a hurry."

"You think I should? Really?" Mike snorted. "Good plan, kid."

"I'd make a properly crushing answer if I wasn't sure he already wants to bash my teeth in," Sam muttered as he and Jin strode after the four-in-hand.

"Good plan, kid," Jin replied.

The docks were noisy and thronged, but the route the carriage had taken was fairly obvious. The crowds that had been forced to part like the Red Sea for it to pass had not quite filled back in, and Sam and Jin were able to follow in its tracks without too much difficulty.

They turned away from the docks and onto a narrow street between two warehouses, and immediately flattened themselves against a shadowy wall. The four-in-hand carriage was less than a block ahead.

Moving slowly, it turned another corner into an alley. A moment later, the red-haired man and the bald fellow in the long coat stepped back into the street. Leaving the carriage behind, the two men headed deeper into Red Hook.

Sam started after them, keeping to the shadows, but Jin grabbed his arm. She put a finger to her lips and pointed toward where the carriage waited. They would have to pass the entrance to the alley, and the driver would still be there.

Sam nodded and followed as Jin crept silently to the corner and poked her head cautiously around it. She waved for Sam to go ahead. He took a quick look as he passed, but the man Mike had called Overcaste was not in sight.

At the end of the street, the two strange men stopped in front of an old stone church. A moment later the door opened, and they disappeared inside.

"Now what?" Jin whispered.

"That's probably not the only door. Just about every place has some kind of service entrance." Sam skirted around the side of the building, under the bricked-in arches that had once been windows.

He found what he was looking for at the very back, almost hidden beneath a pile of cast-off building material and refuse. Under a dory with a gaping hole in its hull, a scattering of bricks, rotting planks, and what looked like a pair of pews was a short stone stair leading down to a wooden door.

As quietly as they could, they shifted the debris off the boat. Sam lifted it so Jin could scramble underneath, then she held it up for him to follow.

Pale beams of light filtered through onto the door at the bottom of the flight of stairs and illuminated a word burned into the wood.

"'Christophel,'" Jin read. "What's that mean?"

"Maybe it's the name of the church."

Jin tried the latch. The door opened easily.

"It's unlocked?"

"Yes." She looked at him uncomfortably. "I'm starting to think Mike was right, and this is a bad idea."

"Want to go back?"

She sighed. "No." Gingerly, she slipped inside. Sam mumbled a wordless prayer to whatever saint watched over kids who snuck into places they knew they shouldn't, and followed.

The room was dark, damp, and smelled of dirt. After allowing the silence to settle around them for a moment, there was a *snick* and Jin's blue-flamed lighter flared to life, flickering just brightly enough to reveal the pale round shapes of skulls set in niches along one wall and the dusty backs of wine bottles stacked along another. In between, there was an inky-dark hallway.

With a quick glance over her shoulder at Sam, Jin headed into the passage, her flint lighter held aloft. Mercifully, the dirt floor absorbed their footfalls.

They heard the voices just as they turned a corner to find themselves at the bottom of a set of flagstone steps. Light fell from a half-open door opposite the stairs.

"It's slowed down, certainly."

Jin doused the flame she carried, and she and Sam crouched in the shadows.

"What do you mean, slowed down?" Sam recognized the red-haired man's voice.

"I mean, there are fewer daemons coming alive. Bios is not hearing the key words as much." That wasn't a voice he'd heard before.

"So . . . what? Walker needs to mangle a few more people, get them talking again?" The bald man.

"You could do that," the voice of the third, unknown man said.

There was a moment of silence, and then, "There's really nothing?" the red-haired man demanded. "Ten hours gone, and nothing from the daemons in all that time?"

"Well, look at the map," the third man said. "There's activity in Coney Island"—Jin's fingers dug into Sam's wrist—"but we have to dismiss that as local chatter because that's where your first two kills were, and there's activity in Brooklyn, but you already knew about that, and you told me the pillar there had already fled."

"This one in Brooklyn," the bald man said. "It's not quite in the same place, is it?"

"Close enough," the red-haired man grumbled.

"And when did it happen? That's more recent than last night."

The third man answered, thoughtfully, "It was earlier this morning, but you're right, it must have been well after you left Tammany Hall. It's hard to be exact. Maybe around eight or nine?"

"And Overcaste said four of the five pillars had planned to meet there last night, but Sawyer and Hawks didn't show up," the red-haired man said thoughtfully. "We searched Hawks's home on the Bowery last night, then Sawyer's home and stone-works in Brooklyn this morning, sometime around eight or nine. Sawyer certainly wasn't there then. But that's when you think these daemons were created?"

"Then this is the fifth pillar," the bald man said. "Either Sawyer or Hawks went to the fifth pillar, the one whose identity Overcaste doesn't know, the one who didn't have to go into hiding because the other two knew Overcaste couldn't give him up."

"Her," the red-haired man corrected. "Overcaste said all he knew was that she's a woman."

There was another moment's silence, then the third man spoke again. "That's Columbia Heights. If there's someone of interest there, she ought to be easy enough to find. Most of the rich muckety-mucks are out of town for the summer."

Sam grabbed Jin's arm and hauled her back down the passageway toward the door. They were making noise this time, too much, Sam thought as they reached the room lined with skulls and wine, but speed seemed more important now than silence.

They burst through the door and fought their way clear of the refuse. Sam started for the waterfront the second they were safely aboveground, but then he heard Jin hiss his name. She was dragging back the pieces of refuse they'd pushed aside to be able to move the dory. Sam cursed, dashed back, and helped her pile the two heavy wooden pews on top of the hull. "Just in case," she said breathlessly. "Okay. Let's get out of here."

They rounded the corner of the church and hit the cobbled street just in time to run full-tilt into the man who'd been driving the carriage, the one called Overcaste.

He got ahold of Jin, who'd been in the lead. Before Sam could so much as consider what to do about it, however, Overcaste howled and shoved Jin away, cradling his left hand. Jin pocketed the lighter she'd just burned him with, grabbed Sam's arm, and ran.

They reached the waterfront and zigzagged their way through the crowds on the docks until they came to the street where, thankfully, Mike was still waiting with the runabout.

The coachman watched Sam and Jin sprint for the carriage with a nonplussed look on his face. "Go," Sam panted as they flung themselves inside. "Go, go, *go!* Columbia Heights, as fast as you can."

Mike rolled his eyes and snapped the reins, and the horses leaped into motion. Sam turned to watch the street behind them, but the four-in-hand didn't make an appearance.

"Was it worth it?" Mike called.

"I think so." Sam collapsed back into the corner of the padded seat. "I thought Hawks sounded a little crazy when he said naming a thing calls it, but now I'm not so sure."

Jin sat with her feet drawn up on the bench, her arms wrapped around her shins, and her chin on her knees. "Remember he said the two bodies we found—that they were only killed for the sake of what the killer wrote on the walls? I didn't want to believe anyone could die that senselessly, but he was right. They were killed to get people talking—to make them talk about specific things. And that somehow helped whoever's in that basement figure out where they were."

"They're ignoring us, though," Sam said thoughtfully. "Even without naming names, it's still hearing the group at the Reverend Dram, but they think that's just people in the neighborhood where the murders took place spoiling the results somehow. So at least Hawks is safe for a while longer."

"You know what would be useful?" Jin chewed on her thumbnail, eyes unfocused. "If we could find a way to *really* ruin their results. If we could keep them from being able to find Hawks or the other two. That's all we need, isn't it?"

Sam looked at the green leather book sitting on the opposite bench. "That, and keeping anyone from doing that claiming-by-fire thing."

Jin shot him a reproachful look. "I told you—"

"I'm not talking about Mr. Burns, Jin. I told you I believe

you about that. But it's true, isn't it? The fire, that's the other thing they need."

She leaned across and picked up the book. "Don't talk to me."

Sam banged his head twice against the wall of the carriage, closed his eyes briefly, and reached into his pocket. Back to the cards.

Frantic footsteps sounded on the stairs. Walker, Bones, and Christophel looked up from the tallow-coated table as Frederick Overcaste burst breathlessly into the basement room.

He opened his mouth, then caught sight of the daemon Bios wading across the star-strewn surface of the table. His eyes popped. He screamed.

Bones reached out a hand and slapped him once across the face. "Haul yourself together, sir."

Overcaste clapped a palm to his red cheek and stared. "What *is* that?"

"Why, if it isn't the distinguished Mr. Overcaste," Christophel drawled. "I confess myself disappointed. Didn't you learn anything at Tammany? Never walk into a room and ask a question that everyone else obviously already knows the answer to. It makes you look like an idiot. Worse, it makes you look like an *amateur*."

"Can we help you?" Walker asked coldly.

Eyes flicking from Walker to the daemon and back, Overcaste composed himself. "There were two children sneaking around the church."

"Red Hook's full of urchins," Christophel said dismissively.

"One of them was a Chinese girl," Overcaste retorted, his voice growing stronger. "Got a lot of Chinese kids in Red Hook, have you?"

"Liao and Burns travel with a Chinese girl," Bones mused.

Overcaste nodded vigorously. "And when I tried to stop her, she burned me with something. I never even saw what it was."

"Hell. We haven't got time to go chasing kids around Red Hook." Walker reached across the table and plucked the pin that marked the most recent activity on the map. "All right. Enough wasting time. We know where the fifth pillar is. Let's go find her. Then we'll go back to Coney bloody Island and deal with Fata Morgana."

SIXTEEN

The Fifth Pillar

T HE STREET CALLED Columbia Heights ran parallel to the waterfront and looked out over the great unfinished bridge across the East River. While the runabout drove past one staggeringly beautiful house after another and Sam and Mike worked out how to get to the address Hawks had provided, Jin examined the bridge.

It was a beautiful thing, with its arched stone and spun-steel bones stretching across the water so far above the roofs on either shore and the constant traffic of steamers and tall ships in between. Sun glittered on the cables. She could just barely make out the wooden footpath that stretched from the anchorage in Brooklyn up to the top of the nearer tower. It extended toward the other tower and disappeared from view, looking like nothing more than a faint line drawn by a pencil. She was only sure it was a footpath because she could see the tiny shapes of people on it.

By the time the carriage pulled to a halt before a grand house several stories tall, a vague idea was beginning to take shape in her mind.

"Jin, are you coming?" Sam asked, clambering down to the street. "Hurry up."

"Yes, I'm coming." Tucking the green leather book under one arm, she followed him up the walk, studying the bridge over her shoulder all the way up the stoop to the front door.

Sam rang the doorbell and they waited. Jin glanced at the street behind them, expecting the four-in-hand coach to turn the corner onto Columbia Heights at any moment. Beside her Sam fidgeted, straightening his cuffs and checking to be sure that he had Hawks's envelopes in his pocket and trying to impose order on his unruly hair until Jin elbowed him to make him stop.

At last, the door opened, and a man in an impeccable suit peered out at them. "The tradesman's entrance is to the left and around the back."

It was all Jin could do not to grab his perfect lapels and screech at him to get out of their way, that two killers were coming and they were all going to die badly if they didn't get out of that house fast.

To his credit, Sam managed not to fidget under the doorman's gaze or burst into the panicked warnings Jin was barely managing to hold in. He stood up a little straighter and recited what he'd been practicing in the carriage for the last twenty minutes. "We're here with a personal message for Miss Arabella van Cortelen. We are to deliver it to her, and to her alone. I understand that this is unusual, and that your job is to tell us it isn't possible, but if you would please check with Miss van Cortelen before you turn us away, we would be very grateful."

During this speech, Jin watched the doorman's face go from doubtful to indignant to curious. He glanced over their shoulder at the handsome runabout, now a bit dustier thanks to its mad dash from Red Hook, and its livery-coated coachman (at some point before arriving in Columbia Heights, Mike had changed his weird tailcoat for a plain driving coat with a little gold braid at the shoulders).

"What shall I tell Miss van Cortelen about . . . the nature of this message?" the doorman asked cautiously.

Jin bit her lip to keep from saying, *Tell her it's about freakish murderers coming to tear her to pieces.*

"Please tell her we are here on behalf of the city," Sam said with unnerving calm, repeating the second bit of Hawks's instructions.

The doorman gave the two of them another long, searching look — while the words *They're coming, they're coming, they're coming* looped in Jin's brain — then nodded and closed the door.

They weren't kept waiting long. The door opened again a moment later, and this time, a girl of about eighteen stood on the other side. She was dressed in a domestic's plain and neat calico dress and apron. She had beautiful gray eyes and light red-brown ringlets, and she was black.

"Miss Arabella will be glad to see you." She smiled. "Please come along this way."

They followed the girl inside, through a foyer full of freshly cut flowers and antiques to a lush parlor facing the street.

"Miss Arabella, Mr. Sawyer, excuse me," the girl in the calico said with a little curtsy, "but these are Miss Arabella's visitors."

A young woman and a blond man who had been deep in conversation on a tufted sofa fell silent and rose to their feet. "You have a message for me?" The woman was lovely and willowy, and wore her reddish-blond hair in an elegant pile of curls. "Why don't you sit down," she suggested. "You look like you've had a long day already."

Well, *that* was a surprise. Whatever she'd been expecting, Jin hadn't thought she'd be invited in like a guest. She trailed behind Sam as he crossed the gorgeous room to the couch opposite where the two had been sitting.

"I think," Sam said, his voice awkward and apologetic, "that we're supposed to give this message to you alone. And we have to hurry."

"You said you speak for the city." Arabella van Cortelen lowered herself gracefully back to her seat. "Mr. Sawyer does as well. It's possible you've come to give me the same warning he has."

Sawyer. The name had sounded familiar, and now Jin remembered where she'd heard it. "Mr. Hawks mentioned a man named Sawyer, didn't he?"

Sam took Hawks's envelopes from his pocket. He handed one to the young woman and glanced at the blond man. "There's one here for you, too. I guess you were going to be my next stop."

Sawyer leaned forward to take his letter. "You came from Hawks? Took him long enough. He said he'd warn her about Jack's men first thing, and here it is the next day . . ."

Jin flinched at the mention of the name, and beside her she felt Sam do the same.

Miss van Cortelen put a hand on Sawyer's arm to silence him. "You mentioned that time was short," she said to Sam.

"You can speak in front of Mr. Sawyer. He saw Jack's creatures for himself last night."

"They're coming here," Jin blurted. "They're on their way, and every time you say his name you help them find you."

"It's true," Sam said quickly. "They're on their way here. We left well before they did—we think—but they're tracking you, all of you, by somehow *hearing* when anyone talks about him. They killed people just to make you say his name, and you've been saying it today and now they know where you are."

Sawyer blanched. "Oh, good Lord—"

Arabella van Cortelen gave him a sharp glare. "I suppose the mystery of why Hawks said to stay away is solved."

"You both have to get out of this house," Jin insisted. "Are you listening? They're coming here, *now*."

"I know a place we can go," Sawyer said.

The young woman shook her head. "No. We can't be found together. You should never have come here in the first place."

"Take our carriage," Sam suggested. "We'll find another way back."

"No." Arabella folded up her letter. "Susannah?"

The maid strode across the room to her side. Jin had entirely forgotten she was still there.

"Take this," Arabella said, handing her the letter. "Go with these two back to Hawks and let him know we're safe. The letter will prove you came from me."

Then she stood and hugged the girl tightly. To her surprise, Jin realized both women were crying.

"Thank you," Susannah whispered.

"It's my honor," Arabella whispered back. "Now go. Get on your way." She glanced at Sawyer. "You, too, as soon as they're gone."

Wiping her eyes, Susannah headed for the foyer with Sam and Jin on her heels. Jin took one last look out the front window as she passed out of the room, just in time to see the four-in-hand carriage pull up to the curb behind the runabout.

"Stop!" Jin shoved past Sam and grabbed Susannah's wrist as she was about to open the door. "They're here!"

Susannah made an about-face and headed down the hall. "Cellar."

In the front parlor, Sam heard Arabella van Cortelen hurriedly directing Sawyer to the tradesman's door.

"We can't just leave them," Jin protested as the first tattoo of surprisingly polite knocking sounded behind them.

"We must," the other girl said over her shoulder as they passed through a dining room and into the kitchen.

"But shouldn't we—shouldn't we do something? Try and protect them?"

"With what?" Sam asked, trying not to sound unkind. "Did you happen to bring explosives with you?"

"No, but . . . shouldn't we at least try to help them hide?"

"No." The maid darted around a huge worktable and opened a door beside the stove. "And we must hope Miss Arabella can convince Sawyer to leave without attempting anything too heroic. He should've been right behind us if he was leaving by the tradesman's door."

The next round of knocks was louder, so much so that they

were audible even in the kitchen. Sam hesitated. It did seem wrong to abandon the two when so much rested on keeping them safe from Jack's men.

Then from the front of the house came a dreadful crash and clatter: the door being driven in by an unimaginably strong blow.

With a single choked sob, Susannah hiked up her skirts and plunged into the cellar.

There was no more time; they had to hope Arabella had known what she was doing when she sent them away. Sam grabbed Jin's arm and shoved her after Susannah, then followed and pulled the door shut behind him.

At the bottom of the stairs they found themselves surrounded by kegs and row after row of shelves of liquor. "This way," Susannah whispered. "Try not to knock anything over." Then she slipped sideways between one of the racks and the wall behind it and disappeared with Jin close on her heels.

From somewhere above, loud voices. Sam swallowed, tried not to think too hard about whether they were more like screams than shouts, and followed.

They edged along in a single file behind the shelves until Susannah, and then Jin, disappeared again. A moment later, just before he reached the back wall, Sam came upon a narrow brick passage just tall enough for them to walk upright. He moved around the corner into it. There, the two girls were having a brief, whispered conference, and when they'd moved few yards further in, Jin took out her pocket lighter to give them a bit of illumination.

They followed the passage to a set of uneven stone stairs

that took them down and down and down, then ended at a pile of rubble and stone that looked like some sort of cave-in. "What happened?" Sam whispered. "Are we trapped?"

"Behind you," Susannah answered. "Under the stairs."

It was almost invisible in the flickering light; just another deep shadow in a dark place. Susannah brushed past them, crouched, and climbed down, feet first, into what turned out to be a small hole. "There's a ladder," she said. "Find it with your toes." And then she was gone.

Sam turned to Jin, standing behind him with her book clutched against her chest and the tiny flame flitting back and forth over her face as she breathed in and out. "You first."

"I really don't know what we're doing anymore," she murmured. She doused the light, pocketed it, and climbed awkwardly into the hole after Susannah.

By the time Sam reached the bottom of the ladder, it felt like the temperature had gone up a good ten degrees. A few yards away, a light flared. Susannah handed a lantern to Jin and lit a second one for herself. It was just enough light to show that they were in a cylindrical space with red brick walls and a dirt floor ribbed with evenly spaced ridges.

"Where are we?" Sam whispered.

"Arabella's father built it as part of an underground train thoroughfare, but he didn't manage to acquire the right-of-way, so it never became more than a mile or so of tunnel. Be careful," Susannah warned as he nearly went sprawling. "There used to be railroad ties there. If you walk in the middle, it's smoother."

"Why didn't she—Miss van Cortelen—why didn't she come

with us?" Jin asked. "The lanterns—she must've been planning for this kind of emergency."

"We aren't here to hide," Susannah's voice drifted back. "There's a grate about a mile down that will let us out near the docks at Fulton Street." She glanced over her shoulder at Sam and Jin, her face miserable in the lantern light. "And the plan was never for Miss Arabella to use this."

Of course. Sam nearly sprawled headlong again as the sudden realization made him forget to pay attention to the rippled ground underfoot.

"It's you, isn't it?" he asked, eyes wide. "Arabella van Cortelen doesn't speak for the city, does she? *You do*."

"Yes."

"But you're . . . I mean . . ." Jin turned back to Sam, a helpless expression on her face.

"I'm a Negro," Susannah said quietly. "Yes. I promise you, if the people of the city had been in a position to vote on it, things might've gone much differently, but here we are."

"Did Mr. Sawyer know?" Jin asked.

Susannah shook her head. "No one knew but Arabella and me, and anyhow Sawyer didn't stay behind because of who he thought she was. He's in love with her, and thanks to that, he's probably dead." She sighed. "We should have told him the truth. Now it's down to Hawks and me, and I can't think of what to do except make the same stupid mistake Sawyer did. We shouldn't be in the same place until this is over, but I don't know where else to go. I can't stay down here when they're right over my head, and I can't hide while the city's in danger. I'm not sure what I'm supposed to do."

They walked on, following the vague promise of fresh air and Susannah's swishing skirts, until light dawned at the far end of the passage.

Early-afternoon sun sliced through an iron grate before them. Sam pushed it open, lowered himself down a brick wall until his feet came to rest on the bank of the East River, and reached up to help Susannah and Jin out. They stood on a short section of weedy ground beside a rickety, overgrown pier. The wall rose up behind them, its face broken only by the opening they'd just climbed through.

"I think the Fulton ferry house should be just a little ways up to our right," Sam said, peering northward. "We can hire somebody there to take us to Coney."

But Susannah pointed south. "This way."

"I'm sure we're below Fulton Street. We should go right."

"This way," she repeated sharply, and stepped carefully across the crumbling pier to a tiny, hidden inlet grown over with rushes. A mast was just visible among them. "We can sail down to Coney Island in this." She began pulling grasses away to reveal a little skiff with furled sails.

"I don't know how to work a boat," Sam warned.

"*I* know how to sail it," Susannah said patiently. "It isn't much of an escape plan if I can't work the parts, is it? I just need a moment or two to ready it." She went to work, and a few minutes later she was hauling up the first canvas sail.

Jin stood facing upriver, the *Conflagrationeer's Port-fire Book* wrapped in her arms, and her eyes on the huge, skeletal form of the bridge and its two huge stone towers.

"What are you thinking about?" Sam asked.

"I was thinking about whatever it is that lets them find people based on what they're speaking of." Her eyes flitted along the length of the cables. "I was thinking about how to break it."

"How?" Sam followed her gaze, but all he saw was the unfinished bridge. "With . . . that?"

She nodded. "It seems to me that all you'd have to do, really, is get enough people talking about the right things."

On the little boat, Susannah looked up from the rigging to listen.

"Well, for starters," Sam observed, "we don't know what they're listening for."

"Not exactly, but we can make some pretty good guesses. *His* name. Whatever the proper term is for what Hawks and Susannah are." She opened the book and tapped the word *Conflagrationeer* on the title page. "Maybe this? Something we were saying at the Reverend Dram registered, even though we were being so careful. If we could come up with a . . . a *message* or something, using enough of the words they're listening for, a message thousands of people could see and read, that would make them talk . . ."

It wasn't a bad idea, but there was one major problem. "But how on earth could we possibly get enough people saying those words at once to make any difference?"

"That's where the bridge comes in," Jin said thoughtfully. Her eyes flitted back and forth along the length of the glittering galvanized wire being spun into the strands that would form the massive suspension cables. "It's moving, isn't it?"

"The wire?"

"Yes."

"Yeah. They're using the bridge like a spinning machine. The wire goes back and forth between the anchorages." The Brooklyn anchorage was too far inland for them to see from where they stood, but Sam pointed toward it anyway. "Each time it goes across, another length of wire is added. So many wires make up a strand, and so many strands make up a cable."

"How do you know all that?"

"Constantine—a fellow I board with—used to work on the crew that assembled the engines in the anchorages. And my father worked on the bridge, too."

"Hmm." Jin scratched her head. "So something could be pulled across fairly easily, then."

"I don't follow—"

She waved her hand. "Let me think about it for a bit. Looks like Susannah's ready for us."

They climbed aboard and Susannah cast off the boat from its hidden mooring. Ships were thick out on the river as she and Sam rowed the little craft into the channel. Then she let out the sails expertly and they were on their way.

The trip downriver to Norton's Point took about an hour. Jin stared up at the towers of the bridge until they were out of sight, then she buried her nose in her book. She refused to talk any further about thwarting whatever method Jack's men were using to search the city. So Sam spent the trip sitting with Susannah at the helm of the little skiff.

"How does it work?" he asked. "How do you become . . . whatever it is you call what you are?"

"I don't think it always happens this way, but I inherited it. Sawyer did, too, and Frederick Overcaste. We all took on the

The trip downriver to Norton's Point took about an hour.

positions at about the same time: Sawyer in 'sixty-two, Overcaste in 'sixty-four, and me last of all five years ago. I inherited from my father, and Arabella's father passed on at the same time, while I was working in her house. That's how we managed to hide the truth."

"Three of you in such a short time? How did that happen?" She gave him an odd look. "The war, Sam."

"Of course." Then he did some math. "But when you . . . the war had been over for, what, six or seven years when you inherited, hadn't it?"

"So they tell me," Susannah said quietly. "But not everyone behaves as though it's been over that long. My parents died at the same time, and I blame both of their deaths on the war. My mother, particularly. I prefer to think she died as part of a struggle for our country and not just because someone was angry and chose the first Negro woman whose behavior he didn't like as the target of that anger."

They sailed on, and Sam thought back to what Ambrose and Tom had said about why the city was so vulnerable to Jack's plan. *Folks are angry, still,* Tom had told him. *Folks are scared, and folks feel like punishing each other, and I don't think many of 'em are clear about what they're mad for.* Then Ambrose: *They're the* other *kind of mad. All of them. They're less than a score of years removed from the worst thing that has ever happened to this country.*

"What does it mean to be a . . . what you and Hawks are?" he asked after a while. "What will you do to stop the city from falling?"

Susannah sighed. "That's just the problem. I really have no idea."

He gaped at her. "You . . . you don't know?"

She shook her head. "This," she said shortly, "appears to be the flaw in the grand plan to keep one of us hidden. I don't think it occurred to anyone that, when the attack came, it would happen so fast there would be no chance for the five of us to come together and form a strategy."

"But how is that possible, if you exist to protect the city?" Sam protested. "If that's the one thing you're supposed to do?"

"Well, it isn't the only thing." She reached up to touch the taut canvas of one sail. "Each of us has a role in holding the city together, even in peace. We each have something we keep all our lives, so that it is never lost, and then we pass it on. My role is to be the keeper of lore." She smiled faintly. "Ever since my father died, all of the stories of New York and Brooklyn have filled me up like water in a jug. Sometimes they overflow, and I see them even when I'm not looking."

Susannah peered at him then, and Sam saw something happen to her gray eyes: they slipped out of focus just a little, and although she was staring directly at him, he had the sense that she was seeing something more.

"You sit on a rooftop in Smoky Hollow with a blond boy, playing cards," she said softly. "The wind picks them up and up they go, swirling away. An owl swoops down and plucks a jack out of the air, and flies away with it to the south. The blond boy tells you that's him, flying away from the tenement. You pick up a black-haired jack and fling it into the wind after the owl."

"That happened," Sam whispered in wonder. "That was the night I decided to move to Coney Island with Constantine."

"You play cards with a man in a blue summer suit who tries

to cheat you, but you see what he is doing and you switch the cards on him, so that when he plays the card he stole, it wins the game for you."

"And that was how I won the money for Con and me to board with Mrs. Ponzi," Sam told her, eyes wide. "I remember every hand I played against that fellow."

Susannah nodded. She blinked, and her eyes focused on him again. "It's one of your stories; and your stories, and your friend's stories, and mine, and those of all the others who live here—those are the things that make up the city's history. And I'm the keeper of those tales. They live in me."

"So you know . . . everything that's ever happened here? To everyone who's ever lived here?" He stared. "How can you keep all that in your head?"

"It's not in my head," she said with a shrug. "It's in my body and my blood. It is who I am. That part of my role I understand. The matter of how I can protect myself and the city from this assault is what worries me now.

"The city has never been under this kind of attack before. It's possible Hawks will simply send me back into hiding, figuring if at least one of us stays out of view, the city could stand—but," she mused, "how long would it take, waiting out such creatures? Creatures like that don't give up easily, and they found me so quickly . . ."

She shook her head. "No, it doesn't make sense. There must be something I can do. Unfortunately, the only person who can tell me is Hawks, and the last thing we should do is be in the same place . . ."

Susannah beached the skiff just north of Norton's Point,

and Sam hopped out and dragged the prow of the boat up onto the sand. "Little bit of a walk now," he said, "but we're almost there."

Jin caught his arm. "You go on ahead. There's someone here I need to see before I come back to the saloon."

"Does this have to do with the plan you're cooking up?"

"Yes. I'll explain later."

He looked at her dubiously. "You really think I'm going to leave you in Norton's Point, Jin?"

"Yes, because right now you need to get Susannah to safety, and I'm not going with you." She smiled. "Don't be a pest. I will need some of Hawks's money, though."

"Jin—"

Susannah put up a hand to silence him. "Excuse me if this sounds snappish, Sam, but time's too short for you to waste it being chivalrous. We all have bigger things to worry about than getting set upon by everyday crooks. Jin will be fine. Let's go."

This, of course, was perfectly true. Vaguely embarrassed, Sam nodded, dug in his pocket for the bag of greenbacks and coins, and handed it to Jin. "Fine. You win. Hurry. Meet us at the Reverend Dram."

He glanced over his shoulder once as he and Susannah began their hike across the dunes toward West Brighton, but Jin had already disappeared into the waving grasses that bordered Norton's Point to the north.

SEVENTEEN

The Cinnabar Heart

JAMES HAWKS was pacing. Jasper Wills was cleaning the mahogany bar obsessively, working around Ambrose while the newspaperman leaned on his elbows and drank his way through a bottle of rye. Tom Guyot sat next to Walter Mapp's piano with his tin guitar, and the two were improvising something that sounded as though it was based very loosely on "Aura Lea" when one of Hawks's boys opened the door for Sam and Susannah.

"Well, well, well." Mapp swiveled on his piano stool and faced Sam with arms folded. "We figured Jin would turn up with you, seeing as how she's been missing ever since you left, but I don't believe I've met this young lady."

"This is Susannah . . ." Sam frowned. "Sorry, Susannah, I didn't ask your last name."

"Susannah Asher." She glanced around the room, found Hawks. She took his letter from the pocket of her apron and held it out. "You sent this to Arabella van Cortelen, but I believe it was intended for me."

Hawks took the letter, opened it, closed it again, and eyed Susannah. "Asher? I don't know that name, I'm afraid. Arabella's predecessor was a friend of mine."

"Asher was my mother's surname, and I've used it my entire

life, but I inherited my post from my father." Susannah waited, watching Hawks steadily as the tall man examined her face, her gray eyes, her light skin and hair.

"Thomas van Cortelen," he murmured. "Thomas was your father?"

"Yes." Susannah's voice cracked just a little.

Hawks's expression softened. "I can see it now," he said quietly. "You do take after him."

Abruptly Sam remembered how Susannah and Arabella had embraced, both of them crying, just before Susannah had fled the house. Her voice wasn't breaking for her father. It was breaking for the sister she'd lost only hours before.

"Well, this is heartwarming," Mapp drawled. "Where's Jin, Sam?"

"Norton's Point. But before I explain that, I have to tell you about Red Hook."

The group clustered around the table again while Sam narrated the afternoon's events, from nearly being run off the road by the four-in-hand to the sprint to Columbia Heights and the flight through the tunnel to the river. Then he told them about Jin's musings on the possibility of breaking the strange listening mechanism that had led Jack's men so easily and so neatly to the van Cortelen house. "She thinks she has a way, but she wouldn't tell me much," he finished. "Whatever she's up to in Norton's Point, it has something to do with it, though."

"It's not a bad idea," Hawks said thoughtfully, "if she can actually figure out how to do it. Although I wish she had trusted us enough to tell us before she snuck off to Brooklyn with you."

Tom chuckled. "Would you have let her go?"

"Probably not," Hawks admitted. "And I don't suppose you know what became of Mike, do you?"

Sam shook his head. "I'm sure he got clear. He was in the carriage."

Hawks rubbed the back of his neck. "I don't know that we can count on that."

At the piano, Mapp nodded in agreement. "And if they get ahold of Mike, they'll have ways of making him give up our location. Anyhow, from what you overheard in Red Hook, it's probably only a matter of time before they realize what they're seeing in Coney Island is more than just neighborhood gossip about the killings." He stood and stretched. "We need a new base of operations."

"We'll go back to the hotel." Ambrose drained his glass and clapped it down on the mahogany. "Obviously." He stood just a bit unsteadily and waved his arm. "Let's go."

"He ran out of Ja—of stories about the fellow in question about two hours back," Tom said to Sam under his breath. "Been working on that bottle ever since."

"The Broken Land?" Jasper frowned and turned to Sam. "Isn't the young lady's fireworks company booked there for a while? If those two malcontents are looking for fireworks, why would you want to go where they're likely going to look first?"

"Have you seen it?" Ambrose retorted. "It's a huge, monstrous, *gigantic* hotel. There's no reason for us to accidentally cross paths with them. I'm not suggesting we sit at the bar and hope they don't suddenly have an urge for a cocktail. I have a suite of rooms. Hell, we can rent another one and keep Hawks and Susannah separate if we want to. When Jin surfaces, she can have her own room in a whole other *wing*."

"Who's paying for all these suites?" Hawks asked idly. "Out of curiosity."

"Please. I have an *expense account*. And I'm just drunk enough to use it."

Hawks gave Ambrose an appraising look. "I wondered if you were going to turn out to be good for something other than sopping up a bottle of old orchard."

"I'm a *journalist*," Ambrose said with exaggerated dignity. "This is part of my *process*."

"I'll wait here with Sam," Tom offered. "I'm guessing he isn't gonna want to leave just yet."

Hawks turned to Jasper Wills. "You're going to have to clear out for a while, too, Jasper. You got somewhere to go?"

Jasper drew himself up tall. "My dear sir, I have lived in this town my entire life. Of course I have somewhere to go."

"And it's not, well, just *upstairs* or anything?"

"I'll take a ferry over to Richmond if it'll make you feel better. Just as soon as Sam and Tom and Jin are on their way."

Just then, the door of the saloon burst open. Sawyer, the man Sam had last seen in the flowery parlor on Columbia Heights, stood in the doorway. He looked battered; his face was bruised and his blond hair was matted down with what Sam hoped—but doubted—was dirt.

His eyes settled on Hawks. Mike hovered behind him in the doorway. They must have escaped together.

"Sawyer? What are you doing here?" Hawks rose from his

seat, scowling. "We can't be in the same place, man. You know that."

The younger man's busted-up face twisted in pain. He glanced from Hawks to Susannah. "Arabella's dead."

"So I've been given to understand." Hawks put a hand on Sawyer's shoulder, but his face was hard. "And I'm sorry for it, for you and for the fact that we haven't got time for mourning." He gestured at Susannah. "But Arabella, it seems, was not the inheritor. Miss Asher is."

"*What?*" Sawyer turned to glare at her. Recognition dawned on his face, then fury. "*You?*"

Susannah's expression was full of sorrow, but she stood tall as she faced him. "I loved her too, Mr. Sawyer."

From the look Sawyer gave her, his reply was not about to be pleasant. Hawks interrupted before he could get a word out and spoke deliberately. "Sawyer, there are still three of us left. We have that, at least, to be glad of."

"To be glad of," he repeated. He shook his head. "That's what you think? That *this* should make her death somehow *fair?*" He rounded on Susannah. "Is that what you think as well?" he spat.

"Sawyer!" Hawks barked. "Pull yourself together! She's dead and it's a shame, and although I am well aware of your feelings for her, I feel bound to point out that you brought it on her yourself when you disobeyed my instructions, and worse, you nearly got yourself killed at the same time!"

"If it's anyone's fault, it's yours!" Sawyer snarled back. "You said you would send someone. It took you nearly a whole day to do it!" He shot a hateful look at Susannah. "And *you*. She died for *you*."

"My timing was not to blame," Hawks said coldly. "Nor was Susannah. What Arabella did for her is between the two of them. What the blazes has gotten into you? Do you have any idea how much trouble we're in?"

"Yes, of course I do," Sawyer snarled. "The difficulty is, I simply don't care anymore. The Devil take this place. Arabella's dead, and someone needs to pay."

There was a new current in the air, something in his voice as he spoke the last sentence that made Sam want to run.

Hawks sensed it, too. "The ones who killed her will pay, Sawyer," he said carefully.

"That's too much to trust, and too long to wait." The blond man put his hand into his pocket. When he pulled it back out, he held a small pistol. "I think I'd rather *you* paid, Hawks. You and that mulatto."

It happened so fast, Sam barely had time to yank Susannah to the ground before four shots erupted, shattering the air. They seemed to come from everywhere.

Then the smoke was clearing, and Mike was lowering his gun in the doorway, and James Hawks and Sawyer lay coughing and bleeding and dying on the floor. And just that quickly, only one of the five protectors of the cities remained: Susannah Asher, who fought her way out of Sam's grip, shoved herself to her feet, and stumbled across the room to retch behind the bar.

⊱≒≈≒⊰

Jin came up on Mammon's Alley from the beach, only half paying attention to her surroundings. She had the *Conflagrationeer's Portfire Book* open in one hand; she had picked a formula at random and was reading it over and over, unable to decide if she was hoping it would suddenly make sense the way the others had, or if she wanted it to remain incomprehensible. With her gaze on the book, she'd nearly walked right past Sam, Mike, and Tom Guyot without noticing them.

"Jin," Sam called, jumping down from where they sat on a pile of empty barrels. Tom looked up from the strings of his guitar and nodded a hello, then went back to his plucking.

"Oh. Hello." Unforgivable. At a time like this, to have broken one of her cardinal rules for wandering unfamiliar places . . . she was so annoyed with herself that it took her another beat to notice the looks on their faces. "What is it?"

"Hawks and Sawyer are dead," Sam said dully. "Shot each other. Right in front of us."

"*What?*"

Mike rose abruptly from his barrel and stalked around the corner of the building without a word. Sam went red faster than Jin had known was possible, and he buried his face in his hands. "What a mess," he muttered. "All the rest of Hawks's b'hoys went running for the Points practically before his body hit the ground. Mike stayed, 'cause he said Hawks's last instructions were to do whatever he could to help me." He ground his palms against his eyes and groaned.

Jin looked from Sam to Tom—who said nothing—to the corner where Mike had disappeared. "Why did he just leave like that?"

"Mike shot Sawyer, I guess," Sam said indistinctly, his face still hidden. "Trying to save Hawks. And Sawyer wanted to kill Susannah, too."

Jin stared at him. After all that, after all they had done to warn Sawyer, to get Susannah to safety. "But . . . why?"

"Sounded like he blamed them for Arabella van Cortelen dying."

"But that's . . . that's . . ."

"Stupid, I know." Sam rubbed his face and looked up. "But now Susannah's the only one left."

"Where is she? Is she all right?"

"I think she's a little shocked. We all were. She's safe, though. Did you get what you needed?"

She shook her head. "The man I went to see wasn't there. I'm going to have to go back to the wagon after all. But I spent the walk here figuring out exactly what I want to do, and I think it'll work." She hesitated. "Well, the fireworks part'll work. Whether it will accomplish what I want it to . . . well, I guess there's no way to know until we try."

"The fireworks part? What, exactly, is it you're planning?"

Despite everything, Jin smiled. "I want to write a giant message for both cities to read, a message that will get thousands of people talking and ruin this thing those two creatures are using to search for Susannah." Her smile widened a little as she pictured it. "A giant, burning message in the sky over the river."

"And you can do that? Write actual words with fireworks?"

"Sure. Words are easy, although I'm going to need a big space and some extra hands to help me assemble everything." Jin looked up at the late-afternoon sky and watched a trio of seagulls wheeling overhead. "There isn't time to do it before nightfall, but we can have it ready for tomorrow evening." She glanced at Sam. He wasn't going to like the next part. "And I'm going back for the display tonight."

"It's not safe," Sam protested. "Not that I expect it'll stop you, but they're going to be there looking for anyone associated with Fata Morgana."

"I know it, but no one's warned Mr. Burns or Uncle Liao." That was only part of it, though. She hesitated, not sure how what she had to say was going to sound. "I need to see something good, Sam. I need it, or I think I might break." Tom Guyot hadn't spoken in all this time. Jin dropped onto a barrel next to him and watched his shaking fingers as they ran over the strings. "Are you all right, sir?"

"Bit of a . . ." His fingers stumbled on the strings and he winced at the discord. He clenched his quaking hands. "Just didn't expect to see that kind of thing again, that's all."

"That kind of thing?" she repeated softly.

"The hate. The violence, that close." He lowered the guitar so that the rounded end of it sat on the ground, and he stared, unseeing, at a spot at the top of its neck. When he didn't continue, she followed his gaze and saw the little metal piece that held the strings away from the wood. It was a bronze color that didn't match the rest of the tin guitar, and when she looked closer, she could just make out flattened letters on its surface. It had once been something else, and had been remade to become a piece of this guitar.

A medal.

"That's from the war, isn't it?" she asked hesitantly.

He smiled a little. "Sure is. Medal of Honor. There were three of us who were given this award. Three Negroes, I mean."

Sam came to stand on Tom's other side for a look. "Wow. I didn't know you won a medal."

"I don't know about it being the kind of thing you win," Tom said sadly. "Must seem right foolish, to break it up and make it into a piece of a guitar."

The gesture didn't come easily, but Jin put an arm around him and leaned her head on his shoulder. "No," she whispered. "I think it makes perfect, beautiful sense. I think if that bit of metal had a choice, it would rather be part of something that makes you happy than something that reminds you of a time you were sad."

Tom reached up to pat her hand. "That's how I figured it, darlin'." He sighed. "All right, then. Sam, you best go apologize to Mike. Let's get on our way."

Mike pulled the horses to a stop in the circular drive at the Broken Land and hopped down to help Tom out and up the hotel stairs. Then he drove Sam and Jin around the building to Fata Morgana's little camp near the stables.

Sam leaned out. "Doesn't look like anyone's home."

"Meaning, at first glance you don't see any maniacal evil-doers. That doesn't really tell us much." Jin watched the quiet encampment for a moment, then sighed. "Mike, do you mind staying with the coach, so we can get out of here in a hurry?"

"Not a bit."

She nodded to Sam. "I think I should be able to find everything I need in the storage tent."

They dashed to the shadows of the tents. Sam followed Jin to the center one, pulled open the door flap so she could slip inside, then ducked after her and immediately scrambled so as not to sprawl onto the plank floor.

Jin winced and turned to look at him apologetically. "Watch that step up."

"Thanks."

"There should be some empty crates over along that wall. If you can find them, bring us two."

The tent was full of piles of boxes labeled with odd mishmashes of words and Chinese characters and shedding bits of the straw and sawdust that had been used as packing material. Sam left Jin wandering among them and went in search of the empties. The odor in the room made his heart speed up just a touch: gunpowder and sweetness, the same scent he caught when he was close to Jin.

He found a stack of huge, empty crates and brought them back just as she returned with an armful of thin metal letters, each about a yard tall. He reached out to take them from her and yelped as his good intentions were rewarded with five distinct jabs in his burned hand. It was like getting stuck with a fork.

"Careful, careful. There are spikes on them. That's where the explosives go." She piled the letters gently into one of the crates. Shaking her head, she reached for Sam's hand and examined it. "Please stop injuring yourself in stupid ways."

"I don't know how I was supposed to know there were spikes," he grumbled.

"Well, looking first would've done it, I think. At least they didn't break the skin." She ran her fingers across the burns one last time, sending goose flesh up his arms. "Just wait here and don't touch anything."

He obeyed, watching and feeling rather useless as Jin came and went, adding items to the crates and to her rucksack and then going back for more. Finally she brushed straw and sawdust from her clothes and slung the bag over her shoulder. "Ready?"

"Ready."

She picked up one of the crates, stuck her head out of the tent, and peered both ways.

"Anything?" Sam whispered.

"I don't see a single person. I think we're okay." She elbowed her way through the flap and held it open with one shoulder for Sam.

"*Xiao Jin!*"

A few yards away, the wagon door burst open and Liao stood there, arms folded across his chest.

"Well, this wasn't supposed to happen," Jin observed. Sam held very still and tried very hard to be invisible.

Liao gave the two of them a long, angry look, barked something in Chinese, and stepped back inside the wagon. Jin sighed, then set down her crate. "Come on."

They trailed in after Liao. The second the door had shut behind them, he snapped, "Explain."

Jin pulled a stool out from under the workbench, sat, and regarded her uncle. "I'm sorry if I worried you, Uncle Liao, and I'm sorry to have taken supplies without asking, but I need to tell you something, and I can't perform the display tonight."

"You need to tell me something? Like, perhaps, about the book that is suddenly missing from our shelves?" Liao asked.

For the second time, Sam wished he could become invisible.

"Like . . . well, yes," Jin admitted. "Like that. Uncle Liao, the men who killed the person we found in the bushes behind the hotel, they're looking for a conflagrationeer. Sam took the book for me because I asked him to."

Liao's face hardened. An awkward moment passed, and Sam decided there wasn't much point in trying to hide in plain sight. "I'm sorry, sir. I apologize."

"It is not easy to say no to my niece," Liao said coldly.

"It's really not," Sam mumbled.

"Uncle, what is a conflagrationeer?" Jin asked. "What is it they want you to do? These folks who are trying to stop what's happening, they think I need to stay away, or the killers might try to hurt me to make you do what they want. Do you know? Does Mr. Burns?"

Liao's scowl disappeared. "How are you involved with these men? And who are they?"

"They work for . . . for the man whose name was on the wall," Jin said carefully. "And they can hear when we talk about him. They want a conflagrationeer, and they are coming after you and Mr. Burns."

He nodded. "Then we will leave. Right now. Tonight."

"No," Jin protested. Sam's heart sank, but it was so obviously what had to happen that he nodded in agreement with Liao. Jin stared at him in disbelief. "I'm not leaving now!"

"I beg your pardon?" Liao thundered. "We leave immediately! Or at least as soon as the *yang guizi* returns. Don't be absurd. Why on earth would we stay here when this sort of creature is creeping about in the shadows?" His voice softened. "Your friend knows I am right."

"My *friend* should—"

Sam flinched. "Jin, he *is* right. You know he's right. I'm sorry, but there's no reason for you to be here, in danger."

"Yes, there is!" she snapped.

"What is that reason?" Liao demanded.

"Uncle Liao," Jin said at last, "what if I could stop them?"

The old man folded his arms into his sleeves. "How, if you please?"

Jin likewise folded her arms into her sleeves and returned his skeptical look with a defiant one of her own. The two of them stared at each other for a moment. There was nothing for Sam to do but watch and wait.

"If we run," Jin said at last, "if you and I and Mr. Burns pack up tonight and go away, nothing changes for the city." She glanced at Sam over her shoulder. He shook his head. *Please, please,* he wished silently, *don't say what you're about to say. Please don't bring me into this. Please leave. Please be safe.* But of course, she did bring him into it. "Nothing changes for my friend, Uncle Liao."

"Your friend, who you met only a day ago," he said slowly.

She nodded. "My friend, Uncle. And it doesn't matter for how long. You taught me that, when you gave me Meng Chiao to read. A single evening can leave its wound in the soul."

"Jin," Sam said quietly. "You've got to leave town."

Neither of them looked at him.

"My friend has a cinnabar heart, too," Jin said at last. "And when have you ever, *ever* heard me call anyone my friend?"

Liao frowned. "Xiao Jin, I have always wished for you to have friends, but they are no good to you if you are dead."

"Uncle, please."

Sam cleared his throat. "You folks really ought to—" Both of them held up their hands: Jin's small and delicate, Liao's gnarled and long-nailed. Then they started speaking to each other in rapid Chinese. Sam tried to act like it didn't bother him that he had no idea what they were talking about.

It went on for a while.

At last, Liao's mouth curled up. "Too brave for her own good, my Jin. What is your idea, firefly?"

Once more, Jin outlined her plan for the message over the river. When she finished, Liao made a little noise that Sam couldn't interpret but Jin obviously took for approval. Then he looked at Sam. "It is not easy to say no to my niece," he repeated. Then, to Jin, "And it does not seem right to me, if you wish to attempt to do something great to help so many people, to discourage you."

Jin exhaled. "Thank you." Then she frowned. "But what is a conflagrationeer, Uncle?"

The old man shook his head. "Xiao Jin, I know that word only from the book, the same way you do."

"What about Mr. Burns?"

"Mr. Burns may well know more than I do, as that book comes from his grandfather."

"So you aren't a conflagrationeer?" Jin asked. "*I'm* not a conflagrationeer?"

He laughed. "After all your brave talk, of all things, you are

[274]

afraid of *yourself?*" Liao put his hand over hers. "Xiao Jin, you are a brilliant fireworker. More than a fireworker—you are a true artificier, an artist in the realm of pyrotechnics. You should be proud of who you are and what you can do."

She nodded but said nothing, waiting as if she thought there was more. Sure enough, after a moment, Liao spoke again. "I have never been called by this name, *conflagrationeer*, but I suspect it is another kind of master of methods, a *fangshi* of a different sort. If I am right, then being a conflagrationeer is like being any kind of artificier or adept—all depends on what the master chooses to do with his skills."

Jin frowned, as if this was less satisfactory than his first answer. The old man sighed. "I wish I could give you more comforting words. *You* have a cinnabar heart, my firefly, and while it is possible that you would be a terrible disappointment to the great sage, there has never been a time that you have not made me proud."

Jin's eyes glittered. "*Xiexie*, Uncle Liao."

"I can do the display tonight. That is no great thing. It will not be your beautiful reborn Atlantis, but I will make you proud." He patted her arm. "You must, of course, not be here if these men are looking for fireworkers."

"Mr. Liao," Sam said cautiously, "do you think it's a good idea to even do the display? It's you they're looking for, after all."

Liao gave him a short, narrow smile. His eyes were hard. "You have no need to fear for me. This I promise." He looked to Jin. "How shall we reach each other?"

"In the sky," Jin said. "The way you always call me."

Liao nodded. "And the boxes? You have all that you need?"

"I think so."

"And where will you stay?" Sam might've imagined it, but he was pretty sure he saw the old man's eyes flick sideways at him forbiddingly.

"You can stay with Susannah," Sam said quickly. "Right upstairs in the hotel. I think Mike said she's in suite five fifty-seven. That way you're nearby, but out of sight. You'll feel better if you can look out the window to see if your uncle and Mr. Burns are all right."

"And she will see that we are fine," Liao said with an approving nod. He looked to Jin. "You believe that, my firefly? I promise these men will not harm us. You need not worry."

She nodded back. "I believe you."

"But you two . . ." Liao wagged a finger at Jin and then, maybe just a bit more forcefully, at Sam. "*You* I do not trust without defenses. Come, please."

They followed him out of the wagon and across the gravel to the nearest tent, the one Walker and Bones hadn't been able to enter.

"This is Uncle's laboratory," Jin whispered over her shoulder. "Mind the step." Sam rolled his eyes and followed her through the door flap and up onto the wooden platform.

Inside, this tent was nothing like the last one. It looked more like a temple than a laboratory, except for the big iron furnace in the middle of the room. Sam stared, taking in the strangeness around him, while Liao went straight to the workbench on the north wall with Jin at his heels.

"Move your braid," the old man said. Jin pushed her hair aside. Liao took a red grease pencil and drew a symbol made of angles on the back of her neck. "A *shenyin* for you, my firefly: the talisman for Opening Up the Mountain. It is said to give the means to control demons and spirits, and it is said to open one's eyes to the scriptures of *taiqing*, the Great Clarity, that one might know the ingredients of the great elixirs of *waidan*, even when they are hidden."

"Well, these men are plenty demonic," Jin murmured.

Liao grunted as he finished the talisman. He looked over at Sam. "You, too, young man. A talisman for you, as well."

Sam walked self-consciously over to the workbench. Liao took a piece of yellow paper from a drawer and drew another red symbol on it. "A *shenyin* for you," he said, "a divine seal for warding off harm." He poured water from a pitcher on the bench into a yellow metal cup and held the paper over it. Abruptly, the bottom edge began to smolder. Black-red ashes fell into the water.

When the entire page had burned, Liao handed the glass to Sam. "Drink."

Sam glanced at Jin. She nodded. He did as he was told. It had a piny-cinnamon flavor, and the bits of charred paper felt strange when they hit his tongue. It seemed almost as if the ashes were effervescing, like the bubbles in mineral water or phosphate soda. The fizzing feeling continued as the last swallow slid down his throat and into his stomach.

"What was that?" he asked as he handed the cup back to Liao.

"Talismanic water. Jin's braid will hide her mark. On you it would stand out." The old man regarded Sam over the cup clasped in his gnarled hands. "It is a gift of protection, but you must think of it as luck, not as a guarantee of safety."

"I understand," Sam replied, although it was a bit of an overstatement.

The old man knew it, too. "I am sure you do not." He patted Sam's shoulder. "But I appreciate your courage." He turned back to Jin. "Go now, Xiao Jin. Call upon me if you need me."

When they returned to the carriage, Mike took charge. It turned out that he had done a bit of scouting earlier that afternoon, after driving Mapp and Ambrose and Susannah to the Broken Land but before going back to Mammon's Alley for Sam, Jin, and Tom. Now he led them to a tradesman's entrance, and a little fast talking and a quarter eagle coin from what was left of Hawks's money got them into a lift that carried them up to the fifth floor, crates and all, with no questions asked. Then Mike led the way down the halls to a door marked 557 and pressed the bell.

The peephole darkened, and a moment later Susannah Asher opened the door. "Thank heaven," she said. "It was giving me the twitches, being the only person in this suite."

"Good," Jin said, shouldering past with her crate. "Because we might need to bring in a few extra hands in the morning."

"In the morning?" Susannah asked with a little frown. "Can't we do anything now?"

Jin sighed. "I wish we could, but I need one more chemical, something to keep the charges from burning out too quickly." She explained to Susannah what she planned to do. "I can get what I need from a pharmacist I met yesterday, but he was out and not expected back before morning. There's really nothing that can be done until I have that ingredient."

This was only partly true; there were things that *could've* been done, but none that *had* to be done quite yet. Jin told herself it wasn't selfish to want to spend an hour watching the sky. *I need it*, a childish part of her mind insisted. *I need it, or I'll go mad.*

She set down her crate against the far wall and peered out the window just in time to see Liao duck into the storage tent. There was so much work for him to do. She wondered where Mr. Burns was. Probably raking the sand on the beach so there would be a flat surface from which Liao could fire the rockets. It was one of the very few things Liao and Jin trusted him to do to prepare for a display.

Sam came to stand beside her. "Jin," he said quietly, and nodded over her shoulder.

Susannah sat on the sofa, staring at the crates of explosive supplies. Her face was drawn tight as a drum.

"Susannah?" Jin lowered herself onto the sofa beside her. "What is it?"

"What does this do besides buy us some time?" the other girl asked quietly. "Even if it works and we keep them from being able to find me, they'll still be out there. They'll never stop trying, unless I find a way to stop them. There has to be something I can do. Otherwise, what's the point of all this?"

"I have a question," Sam said, perching on the coffee table before the two girls. "With Hawks and the other two gone, there's only you and the fellow who went over to the . . . the other side left. How do the three empty spots get filled again?"

"Well, I inherited it from my father, and so did Sawyer and Overcaste." Susannah leaned back and stared hard at the ceiling, thinking. "But I don't think it *has* to happen that way. If it did, we'd have problems whenever one of us died childless. Furthermore, the inheritor is permitted to accept or decline the task. Also, I don't think the . . . the stewardships we fill are always the same. I know there is always a keeper of lore — that's me — and a smith, and a keeper of sanctuary." She ticked off fingers on one hand. "Van Ossinick was the smith, and Hawks was the sanctuary keeper. The Sawyers were stonemasons, and Overcaste was the keeper of roads."

"The reason I ask," Sam said, "is that Hawks claimed they needed to remove you, then take the city, then replace you with creatures loyal to them. Could you replace the missing ones before they do? Even temporarily?"

Susannah frowned. "You know, I don't know the answer to that. There must be a way to create new stewards. Otherwise, you're right — *he* wouldn't be able to do it."

"If it had ever been done before," Sam pointed out, "you would have that story inside you somewhere, wouldn't you?"

She looked up. "Yes." Then her expression sharpened. "But it will take me some time. There are a lot of tales to sift through."

"You'd best get going, then, I guess." Jin patted her shoulder and stood up. "We'll worry about buying you the time."

EIGHTEEN

Foxes and Tigers

SUNSET REDDENED the water to the west as Sam and Jin wound their way through the people setting out blankets and chairs on the lawn in preparation for the evening's fireworks. They got a few stares, but by and large the crowd was only concerned with finding the best places to sit.

Despite the vague guilt she had about being out there rather than up in the hotel suite, Jin felt a tiny glow of satisfaction. The audience was far bigger than the night before. Word of her Atlantis must have circulated among the guests all day.

She and Sam ducked through the ornamental trees and crossed the space between the piers. Closer to the water, she could see two familiar figures setting up rows of rockets and squibs. Jin resisted the urge to call out and wish them good luck. They'd demand to know why she wasn't hidden away someplace safe, and she didn't feel like arguing about it.

They crossed behind the far pier, passed the second row of potted trees, and found themselves on the same deserted stretch of beach where they had danced by the light of her chemical bonfire.

Sam sat in the sand with his back against the driftwood trunk. "How are you feeling?"

She turned, surprised. "Fine."

He was looking at her with concern in his eyes. They were so very green—the kind of green that was almost impossible to replicate in the sky. "I figured you'd be worried. About your uncle and Mr. Burns."

"Oh." She sat a short distance away and wrapped her arms around her knees. "I am, but I suppose I believe Uncle Liao." She put a hand to the back of her neck, touched the stickiness of the red grease pencil he had used to draw the talisman. "I don't know why I should, but somehow it makes sense to me."

"That thing he drew on you. The paper he made me drink. Does it feel—should we feel different, somehow?"

She had been trying to figure that out herself. "I'm not sure."

"Because the symbol looked a lot—to me, at least—like the one on the banner in one of the corners of your uncle's tent."

Jin pictured the flags Liao always hung up after they raised the laboratory. "It might be, now that I think about it." She started with a sudden realization. "In the carriage, when you were telling me about seeing the two men lurking around the wagon, you said they couldn't go into that tent, didn't you?"

"Yeah. You think it was because of that symbol?"

"I'm not sure. The talismans are supposed to give protection, but I always figured that was more like a tradition than anything real." She rubbed the scarlet pigment between her fingers, and wondered.

They sat in silence for a moment or two and watched the sun fall below the western horizon. It occurred to Jin that just because she didn't like talking about her past didn't mean that other people felt the same way. "Would you like to tell me about your father?" she asked hesitantly.

Sam had been staring up at the first few stars. Now he looked at her for a moment. Then he shrugged. "I don't want to bore you."

Which wasn't quite the same as a no, Jin realized. "I think I would like to hear. But only if you want to tell." The look he gave her was dubious, but not evasive. "Really," she added.

"He worked on the bridge," Sam said. "When the caissons for the towers were still being sunk."

"What is a *caisson*?"

"It's what they used for the foundations of the towers. They were boxes without bottoms, kind of like diving bells, only the size of a city block and made out of pine and iron and oakum." Sam held his hand out, palm down and cupped into a sort of bell shape.

"They built the towers bit by bit on the top of the boxes, which weighted them down and sent them to the bottom. Then they took compressed air and filled the boxes, which drove out the water. Then a crew went down into the box through an air lock and started digging out the floor while another crew piled stone for the tower on top, and little by little, the caissons sank deeper. The crew inside kept digging until they reached bedrock, so the foundations would sit on solid ground. Then, when they had them where they wanted them, they filled the caissons with cement and the foundations were done."

"So your dad was on the crew digging out the floor?"

Sam nodded. "He worked in the Brooklyn caisson until it

was done, then he went to work on the New York caisson. Right up until he died."

"Oh." Sam had never said his father was dead, of course, but somehow Jin felt she ought to have figured out that much before now. Playing cards on the waterfront probably wasn't something kids with proper families did, even here, so close to New York. "I'm sorry, I didn't—"

"No, it's okay. I don't mind. It's nice to talk about him." Sam stretched out his legs and looked across the water. "The air pressure gets higher, the deeper you go, and the New York tower had to be sent really deep into the riverbed. On the Brooklyn side they only had to sink it down forty-five feet or so. On the New York side, they had to sink it almost twice as far." He shrugged again. "People were getting sick the whole time, of course. Everybody knew spending time under pressure wasn't good for you, but usually it just meant some pain for a few hours. The men in charge were very careful, and nobody died working on the Brooklyn side, or even for a long time on the other one. It was when they hit around seventy feet, that's when my dad started feeling sick." He paused. "You really want to hear about this?"

She nodded. "If you want to tell me. Only if you want."

"Well, you told me your story." Sam folded his arms. "They call the caisson disease the Grecian bends, or sometimes just *the bends* for short. For Dad, it started with cramps in his legs after he'd come up. He said working in the caisson was bizarre and frightening sometimes, but the pain didn't happen until after he was back on the surface. When it did, he said it hurt like some giant was tearing him apart at the joints." He shuddered. "I saw it come on, once. I would meet him in a saloon off Fulton Street when he would come back across to Brooklyn after work."

"Your dad met you in a saloon every day?" Jin asked. "How old were you?"

"I guess by then I was almost thirteen, although we'd been meeting there since I was eight or nine, all the way back when Dad started working on the first caisson. My usual was a glass of milk." He gave her a little smile. "Dad wasn't a big drinker. The doctor had all kinds of rules for keeping healthy under pressure, and he didn't like the men to drink, but they all did. Every one of them believed a shot of whiskey would do more to help them recover at the end of the day than any of the coffee and bunk rest the doctor prescribed. And that saloon was as good a place to meet as any. A friend of Dad's tended the bar there. He used to pay me a nickel a week to clean up while I waited. Then one day Dad just . . ."

He frowned. "I remember his face going gray, like lead, before he started throwing up. By the time he fell over, he was sweating like I'd never seen a man sweat. Huge cold drops all over. He said something, but I didn't understand what it was. Then he started screaming. Someone went for a doctor, and the doctor knocked him out with morphine.

"We got him back to the house where we were rooming," Sam continued, his voice going a little dull, "and everybody told me he'd be fine in a few hours. The doctor said the pain had to run its course, so it was best that he just sleep through it. But then a few hours after that he went into convulsions, and an hour later he was dead."

"That's terrible," Jin said quietly. But Sam had a faraway look, and she wasn't sure that he heard her.

"I'd learned some card games from the men Dad worked with." He smiled dimly. "Cards, and a pretty good collection of German and Irish curses to go along with the Italian ones I knew. A couple years ago, a kid from the tenements, a fellow I played cards with a lot, told me he was going to Coney Island. He'd worked on the engines that they're using now to spin the cables up until he got hurt, and he figured Coney was a good place to try next. I mean, lots of fellows are out of work in Brooklyn, just like everywhere. But *here*—well, Constantine knows how to sail, plus we figured there were hotels like this one being built that would need waiters and cooks and shoeshine boys, there were restaurants that would pay you to dig clams on the beach, there was talk about racetracks and Tammany Hall hacks who would pay a kid a dollar to carry picnic baskets for them. Dad was gone, and my mother had been gone since . . . I think she died when I was three or four, so there was really no reason not to pick up and give this place a try. Plus I basically only survived that first year without Dad because of what Constantine taught me about cards. So we came here together."

He rubbed his face hard. "My dad made two twenty-five a day in the caisson just to die in the most unbelievable pain imaginable, so this place sounded pretty good to me. And here I am. I will say this, I live a lot better than we did in Brooklyn, although I'm not sure how Dad would feel about the way I do it."

"You play games with people who want to play games, in a town by the sea."

"It sounds nice when you say it that way, but you left out

the part where I take their money. So many folks are out of work, and the ones who aren't are having wages cut, or are on strike to keep their wages from being cut. . . . It feels like the wrong time to be living off people who really don't have money to be gambling with."

Jin watched him as he stared out at the water. "I think your father would be glad that you make a living that doesn't require you to work in pain," she said quietly. "And he might point out that you aren't stealing money from those people. They want to play, so they're choosing to take the risk."

"My dad was never in pain while he worked," Sam said quietly. "You saw the towers, Jin. When this bridge is finished, it's going to be one of the great wonders of the world. And my dad gave his life for it. His blood's in that bridge. That *means* something." He shook his head. "I'm proud of him, that's all. I'd like to believe he'd be proud of me, but even if I manage to do more good than evil in the world, it isn't likely I'll have anything to show for it. Not like *that*." His face was solemn, but his eyes glittered with pride for his father's accomplishment.

"It really is beautiful," Jin said at last. "The bridge. It's a thing of wonder, you're right."

He scratched his head. "You know, Constantine would make a good . . . whatever you call what Susannah is," he mused. "The friend who brought me out here. You'll never meet another kid who feels so responsible for so many people. And his blood's in that bridge, too. That's where he got injured." Sam sat thoughtfully for a moment, then turned back to her with a smile. "Your turn."

"To do what?"

"Tell me something. But something that makes you happy this time."

"Oh." She thought for a moment, then announced, "I can tell where I am in the country based on what kind of hotcakes they have for breakfast." Sam burst into laughter, which made Jin smile, too. "Last year at a display we did in Chicago a man accidentally set a lady's bustle on fire with a handheld sparkler," she added, just to see Sam laugh some more. "Her backside went up in flames faster than a pile of hay, thanks to all the horsehair in her dress. That was pretty good entertainment."

This time he laughed with his head thrown back and his eyes squeezed shut, and Jin watched, delighted.

She told him about seeing the lines of prairie schooners, the covered wagons carrying settlers out West, each time Fata Morgana crossed the great open spaces of the middle country. She told him about those vast wide lands, the tall grasses that undulated across them like waves on the sea, the skies so big they seemed as endless as the ocean itself. And as she spoke, other recollections came back to her like lost treasures that had been waiting in her memory to be found again and shared.

"Have you ever played Go?" she asked when she couldn't think of anything else to say.

Still smiling, Sam shook his head. "Don't know it."

"It's an old, old game. Uncle Liao taught me. It's not a card game, but you might like it."

"Want to teach me sometime?"

"Yes."

The smile was gone from his face now, and he was looking at her with such seriousness in those green eyes that her heart sped up, thudding in her throat. "Jin," he began, his voice just a little uneven. But before he could say another word, a white light shot into the sky overhead, cutting through the air with a whine.

Jin turned to follow its progress until it disappeared, grateful for the distraction. A second later the deepening dark burst into golden brilliance.

She smiled. Gold, shining in the night for her, a gentle hello from Uncle Liao.

"You'll hurt your neck, twisting it like that," Sam said quietly. "Come sit here."

They looked at each other for a moment. Then Jin rose, crossed the small space between them, and sat. She felt his eyes on her the entire way.

As the next volley of rockets sailed up to paint the heavens, Sam reached for the hand that sat clenched on her knee. Jin stopped breathing for a moment, but all he did was trace the burn patterns and scars with his fingers as he turned his face up to watch the starbursts overhead.

When she had made sure, by peeking out of the corner of her eye, that he was still looking up rather than at her, Jin eased herself back against the driftwood, letting her shoulder and arm line up next to his so that they were just touching. Then she turned her face up, too.

After the fireworks ended, they sat in the dark for a long moment, her hand still clasped in his, both studiously staring skyward as if there was something more to see than the dissipating smoke of Liao's finale.

Jin had spent the entire hour of the display, which she

had thought would make her feel better, in a state of stomach-twisting confusion. She wanted so badly to curl herself under Sam's arm and tuck her head onto his shoulder the way she had when they'd danced on the beach. Except that in a matter of days she would be gone—and that was assuming they both survived tomorrow. Except that it had been six years since anyone had kissed her, and those memories needed to stay buried because not a single one of them was good. Except that she kept on finding herself in situations normal girls simply didn't get into, and if just once Sam misunderstood why she was there and thought that, because they were alone on this deserted stretch of beach and she had let down her guard—

"Why did you go rigid all of a sudden?" he asked. Instinctively she tried to pull her hand away, but he tightened his grip. "Jin, wait. Just sit here with me."

"Why are you here?" she whispered. "Why am I here?"

"I don't know why you're here," he admitted. "But I'm glad you are. The best I can figure is, I think maybe we're friends, and maybe we don't have to worry about the rest."

"Friends don't hold hands."

"Well, not all of them, certainly. I do have friends I absolutely will not hold hands with."

Against her will, Jin laughed.

"I don't know what to tell you," Sam said at last. "I don't know what's bothering you, exactly . . . but it's late, and we have a long day tomorrow. Come on." He stood and pulled her up after him, and it was then, just the second she was on her feet, that he kissed her. She burst into tears, shoved him away, and scrambled over the driftwood and up the beach toward the piers and the Broken Land, her feet slipping awkwardly in the sand.

He followed as she sprinted toward the hotel, and caught up with her just as she reached the edge of the gravel outside the stables. He grabbed her arm and pulled her to a stop. "You know you can't go back there now."

She shook off his grip and stumbled across to the wagon. Just before she reached the door, however, two things happened, one right after the other: Uncle Liao stepped out onto the top stair, and a voice spoke up from the dark on the other side of the gravel.

"Well, isn't this perfect." Jin turned to find a red-haired man in a white suit stalking toward her. "And here I thought if we wanted to talk with somebody from Fata Morgana, we'd have to hunt you down."

Sam skidded to a halt as the man strode toward the wagon. He scanned the darkness around them, but the bald man in the long felt coat was nowhere to be seen.

Liao took Jin by the arm and pulled her into the wagon behind him. Then he folded his arms and regarded the newcomer. "We have not been introduced."

The red-haired man gave a sarcastic little bow. "I go by Walker. Once I was called Redgore. I'm in the market for some conflagration services."

"Let my niece and the boy go, and then we will discuss this business."

Walker grinned, baring what looked to Sam like two full rows of teeth. "No, I don't think so."

Liao grinned back. "You're a fox, Mr. Walker, prowling

through the jungle before a tiger and thinking the creatures that flee are running from you and not the bigger menace at your back. I am not to be ordered around by foxes."

Walker stiffened. Liao grinned a little wider, as if he were baring fangs rather than perfect white teeth. "Or by tigers, either," Liao added, "but that is none of *your* concern."

"Old man," Walker said coldly, "this is not a fight you want to start."

Sam's heart burst into a drumroll. Something bad was about to happen. If Walker was the killer who had torn the two Coney Island bodies to pieces, no matter how good a game Liao could talk, he couldn't possibly stand a chance against him.

He looked past the old man at Jin, hoping he was wrong, hoping she knew something he didn't. His racing heart sank. Jin's eyes were wild with terror.

"Uncle," she said, her voice so weak it was nearly inaudible, "please."

Liao ignored her, and his next words made Sam feel faint. "Stand aside for the children to leave, and I will do you the courtesy of listening to your request before I laugh and blast you from my doorstep."

Across the red-haired man's cheeks a spattering of freckles began to darken. "Are you sure you really want to be threatening me?" All in a moment, red slashes radiated from the dark marks into a webwork of angry welts across his face.

Liao shrugged and folded his hands into his sleeves. "I would prefer not to threaten you. I would prefer we speak as gentlemen. But even the sage knows one may occasionally be forced to use arms in the name of good. I will hurt you if I must."

"Now you're just boring me," Walker growled. And then he launched himself at Liao.

Before Sam could even begin to think how to react, the old man flung his arms out of his sleeves, and with a concussion of blinding light and deafening sound, did exactly what he'd threatened to do and—there was no other way to describe it —*blasted* Walker backwards and across the gravel.

"Go now," Liao snapped. Sam looked up at him and did a double take. It might just have been a trick of his eyes, the lingering result of the cold blue light of the flare, but the old man appeared to actually be *glowing*.

Jin sprinted out of the wagon and past Liao to Sam. From the opposite direction, Walker, his impeccable white suit blackened and smoking and his whip-marked face charred, stalked toward them. Liao's blast must have thrown him nearly all the way across to the back wall of the hotel, Sam realized—but that wasn't even the most shocking thing.

As he approached, *Walker got taller*.

He towered over them. He towered over the *wagon*. He was, suddenly, a giant.

And then Liao stepped back into the wagon's doorway. In the space of a blink Walker launched himself at the old man. The world warped—the giant figure somehow never seemed to diminish, yet as he closed in on Liao the two men looked to be the same size again.

Liao blasted him back once more, and this time Sam caught

Walker, his impeccable white suit blackened and smoking and
his whip-marked face charred, stalked toward them.

the brief glint of a glass vessel that burst against the red-haired man's chest and exploded into flame.

Lights were coming on in the hotel. Faces appeared against the glass of dozens of windows. From the direction of the beach, there were voices, lots of them, as people who'd been watching the fireworks drifted toward this new commotion.

"Go," Liao shouted again, and as Walker picked himself up off the gravel once more, Sam took Jin by the arm and hauled her away.

She fought him for a few steps, shouting her uncle's name, but by the time they got around the corner and had to push against the tide of gawkers rushing to see what all the flashes and bangs were, she was stumbling along with him, silent tears pouring down her face.

A sky-rending crack sounded from behind the hotel just as they reached the tradesman's entrance. Sam tightened his grip on Jin's arm. "He's going to be fine," he whispered.

He didn't really believe it, though. Mere explosives couldn't possibly hold a monster like Walker at bay.

"It's not going to work," Jin said dully as she allowed herself to be pulled into the elevator. "It's not going to work, none of it. How could it? How could anything work against that . . . that—"

"It *is* going to work." Never mind that he'd been thinking exactly the same thing.

"It's not. Even if I can do it, all it can possibly accomplish is to stall the inevitable. That *thing* back there—"

"It's the plan we have."

Jin stared at him. "And then what?"

I have no idea. "And then . . . well, and then we have to hope Tom and Mapp and the rest of them come up with something."

On the fifth floor, Susannah Asher barely managed to get the door open before Jin was shoving past her and through the suite to the window. Sam mumbled apologies and followed. Outside and below, the Fata Morgana encampment had gone still and dark.

Susannah came to stand behind them. Her expression reflected in the window was concerned. "I saw the explosions," she said softly. "Everything all right?"

"No," Jin murmured. "Not really." She searched the shadows outside, looking for any sign of the battle they had just fled, any indication of how it had ended. There was nothing, nothing but furrows in the gravel and drifting smoke.

"I figured it out."

Jin turned to Susannah. "Figured what out?"

"How new . . . vacancies are filled among us." She rubbed her eyes as if there was a headache pounding behind them. "The memories—they're there, but they're hard to call forth without something to bring them to mind. But Mike loaned me this." She held up a pair of spectacles on a golden chain.

"They were Jim Hawks's." For the first time Jin noticed Mike sitting on the sofa, arms folded tightly. "I took them after —you know."

She swallowed. "Yes, I know." In all the confusion, in all her worry about Uncle Liao and Mr. Burns and what it meant if she was a conflagrationeer, she'd managed to forget entirely that Mike had lost his—his what? His boss, his mentor, maybe even his friend? "I'm sorry, Mike," she said carefully, hoping it wasn't too little, too late. "I should have said so earlier."

He shrugged, face closed, and nodded for Susannah to continue. "Anyway."

"Anyway. The spectacles helped me remember how Hawks came to be one of us." Susannah handed the glasses back to Mike. "The role was offered to him by the previous keeper of sanctuary, when that man knew he was near the end of his life. And that man was offered it by another steward, after the sanctuary keeper of the generation before died without finding a successor. So I think," she concluded, "I think that I can offer stewardships to fill the empty places. And I think I can offer four of them. Overcaste forfeited his place when he betrayed the city. I just have to decide on the right four."

Bones stood on the darkened beach with arms folded and watched a battered and charred Walker limp toward him. "Looks like that's another suit done for," he observed dryly.

Walker held up one warning forefinger and dropped to the sand. He sat for a moment, then fell over backwards, breathing hard.

"I take it your meeting with Liao didn't go as well as you anticipated."

Walker said nothing, but this time he made another, ruder gesture.

"So we begin our final day with no conflagrationeer."

Still lying in the sand, Walker sighed and took out his cigarette case. He lit one of the cheroots and smoked in silence.

Bones turned toward the hotel to watch another figure as it approached from the lawn. Overcaste came to stand next to him and peered hesitantly down at Walker. "Is . . . everything—"

"Tell me," the bald man cut him off.

"They went inside, both of them, through the tradesman's entrance," Overcaste said, still looking at Walker's smoke- and ash-stained form. "There were too many people in the way; I couldn't see what floor they went to. The boy left. The girl's still in there, I think."

"Burns?"

"Didn't see any sign of him."

Finally, Walker spoke up. "I am really, really getting tired of this place."

On Mrs. Ponzi's rooftop, Sam and Constantine and Ilana sat outside their window listening to the Saturday night noises of carousing from the wilder streets of West Brighton. "So what do you think?" Sam asked, watching Constantine deal a hand of poker. "Could it work?"

"After everything you just told me, the letters on the cable part sounds perfectly logical." Con set down the remaining cards and swept up his hand. "I mean, compared to the rest of it. Yeah. No reason it couldn't work. The bit about stringing letters and lighting 'em up, I mean. The rest of it sounds utterly insane."

"Is it . . . is it true?" Ilana picked up her cards one by one and arranged them in her hand.

Sam slapped her fingers gently. "How many times have we told you not to do that? You give something away every time you move a card."

"But is it *true?*"

"I don't know, Illy," Sam said, cards on his knee. Then he sighed. "I believe it. I think that's maybe the best I can say."

"I don't understand it, though," the girl protested. "This is *America*. It's the *nineteenth century*. This all still sounds like something out of a fairy tale."

"From a kid who still believed in fairy tales up until last year—"

"Sing small, Con, or I'll tell my mother you broke her Palissy serving dish."

"I don't even know what that is!"

"It's bad, that's all you need to know."

Sam rolled his eyes. "Can we get back to the topic at hand?" He looked at Constantine, then at Ilana. "Can I count on you tomorrow? Will you help us?"

"Of course we will," Ilana said with a dismissive wave of her hand. "Crazy or not, we're with you."

"Go right ahead, speak for all of us."

"I beg your pardon, Constantine, did I get your answer wrong?"

"No, Miss Wiseacre, you did not. Are we playing, or aren't we?" Con stretched out a foot and kicked Sam's leg. "Start us off."

Sam worried the corner of the leftmost card in his hand between his thumb and forefinger. From their perch he could see west to the lights of Norton's Point, where the evening was well under way, and miles off to the east, the pale glow that he knew emanated from the Broken Land Hotel, where he had reluctantly left Jin in Susannah Asher's care with a promise to return in the morning to help assemble the fireworks for the message.

"It's such a little island," he murmured. But he was thinking about what Ambrose and Tom had said, about how an attack upon New York and Brooklyn now, even in this modern year of 1877, could be enough to tear the United States apart.

Such a fragile thing, this country.

"Sam." Ilana tapped his knee gently. "Play."

NINETEEN

Conflagrationeer

I GOT YOUR NOTE," Tycho McNulty said, rubbing his eyes as he held the door of the pharmacy open for Jin early the following morning. "Sorry to make you come all the way back here. One of my neighbors is having a difficult . . . er . . . confinement."

"I hope she's all right," Jin said, following the pharmacist to his little dispensary. "I don't imagine you had time to think about my little project."

"My neighbor will be fine in a few months." McNulty smiled wearily. "And as for your project, actually, I did think it over. It was a treat, after the night I had." He picked up a wrapped parcel from the counter. "Two pounds, fine ground. Should add a nice tone to the green you wanted, too."

"Oh, that's marvelous." Jin tucked the parcel into her bag.

"I don't get the impression this is for the Broken Land's display, is it?"

She looked up and saw worry on the pharmacist's face. "No, sir."

"Are you in trouble?"

Jin started to say she wasn't, but then she discovered she didn't want to lie to McNulty. "Well, I've somehow gotten myself involved in stopping a plot to take over New York and Brooklyn," she said tiredly. "My friend kissed me yesterday and I ran away crying like some little girl who's had her hair pulled. Then I think my uncle might have blown himself up trying to save us from a monster with two rows of teeth. And I didn't really sleep all that well last night, so that's a bother, too."

McNulty listened with wide eyes, then burst into laughter. "Insomnia'll kill you," he managed. "I'm sorry, I shouldn't laugh. This all sounds deadly serious. But then I didn't get much sleep, either."

He walked to a bank of cabinets along one wall and opened the nearest. "I can't help you with saving the cities, and I certainly can't help you with boy difficulties." After a moment's hunting inside the cabinet, he took out a little blue-glass jar. "But this is something I use when I'm too tired to think straight. A little on the eyelids, a little under the nose. Wakes me right up. Now that I think of it, it's also quite nice for when I'm working with noxious chemicals. Doesn't keep you from breathing them, but it keeps you from smelling them as much."

Jin took the jar and opened it. The ointment inside was pinkish and smelled of peppermint and lemon and fresh-roasted coffee all at once. The first whiff that shot up her nose made her eyes fly wide open. "Wow," she said, rubbing her nose. "That is . . . something."

McNulty grinned. "It works."

"I can already feel it." Jin fumbled in her bag for money, but McNulty waved it off.

"My gift to you," he said. "Wish I could do more. Go and save the world, Jin. I'll be rooting for you."

"Thank you," Jin said. She took a step toward the door, then hesitated and turned back. "Thank you, Mr. McNulty. I won't let you down."

The pharmacist started in surprise. He patted her shoulder. "I don't have the foggiest of ideas what you're up against, Jin, but I'm the last person you could ever let down. I'm glad to have met you."

Two hours later, Susannah Asher's hotel suite had been turned neatly into a fireworks factory. Making the little explosive lances that would be used to illuminate the letters was absurdly detailed, repetitive work. It was the kind of thing that even Jin, who loved making the components Fata Morgana used for its displays, found incredibly boring after the first hour. Of course, that was when she had to do it alone.

"Boy, I thought the card sharp stuff was neat, but this is even better." Ilana twisted the tissue-paper end of an empty lance closed and passed it on to Sam, then started rolling paper around a thin dowel to form the next case. "Although I kind of wish I got to do the part with the stuff that actually explodes."

Sam dipped the open end of the tube into a little dish of damp meal and passed it on to Constantine, who was ready with a funnel and a jar of mixed powders, filings, charcoal, sugar, and the fine-ground blend of chemicals that Tycho McNulty had concocted to create a slow-burning fire. He filled the lance and passed it on to Jin.

As they sat on the floor of the beautiful suite, late-morning sun fell onto the thick pile of the Turkish carpet. A cart littered with a silver coffee service stood, forgotten, along one wall.

"Can't help that boys are too clumsy to work with paper," Jin murmured, twisting closed the other end of the lance and adding it to the nearly full crate beside her. Then she turned to check up on Mike, who sat on her other side amid the metal letters, tapping in sharp-ended spikes wherever there were gaps in the line of points that outlined their shapes.

"I can't believe these letters are in such good shape." Jin took a finished one from him and ran her fingers over the spikes, checking for any that felt loose. "I don't even remember the last time we used them."

"How are we doing?" Sam asked, without looking up.

"Another two dozen should do it," Jin said. "I'll start wiring the fuses, but we're going to have to wait to put the lances on until we get to the bridge. Once the lances are in place, the letters will be too fragile to move by carriage. It would be too bumpy." She resisted the urge to look out the window. If she looked, she would have a clear line of sight to the livery stable and Fata Morgana's wagon and tents.

Give me a signal, Uncle Liao. Let me know you're okay.

She had been repeating that silent wish over and over the night before as she had waited to fall asleep, and she had wished it again all this morning as her fingers had done their mindless work: measuring lengths of fuse, damping and blending fresh powders to refill Constantine's jar, closing off the lances. *Give me a signal. Give me a signal.*

The signal, when it came, wasn't in the sky, but in the hallway. The doorbell rang. Everyone in the room tensed. Susannah, who had been sitting on the couch staring at the sheet of paper on which she'd been making lists of potential candidates to fill the four empty stewardships of the city, got to her feet and waved for the rest of them to be quiet. She peered out the peephole, then beckoned to Jin.

"It's no one I know," she whispered.

Jin peered through the tiny lens into the hall and exhaled, relieved. "It's Mr. Burns."

Sam was at her side in an instant. "Jin, Hawks told me not to talk to Burns, remember?"

"He's family." Jin shook her head. "He's *my* family." She opened the door and slipped out into the hallway, pulling it mostly closed behind her.

Mr. Burns stood with his hands in his pockets, the part in his hair straight and the spectacles on his nose crooked. He looked just like he always had. Part of her family—her strange family, stranger than she had ever guessed, but the only family she'd ever had. The family she loved. Jin hugged him hard.

He hugged her back, but only briefly. "Jin, sweetheart, there's no time. Can I come in?"

Inside, the work on the lances continued. Only Sam had stopped. He regarded Mr. Burns as he followed Jin into the suite, then he stood and trailed after the two of them through the parlor where Ilana, Constantine, and Mike were working and into the bedroom.

"Is Uncle Liao all right?" Jin demanded as soon as the door had shut behind them.

Burns hesitated, then nodded. "I don't know what it would take to do actual damage to your uncle, but I'm sure it's more than these fools have at their disposal."

Jin's face crumpled. "But you haven't seen him?"

He shook his head slowly. "No."

"So you know?" Sam asked. "You know what's happening? What . . . *they* . . . are?"

"Of course." Mr. Burns perched on the windowsill and regarded the two of them. "I've been running from creatures like these for longer than you would believe." He smiled sadly at Jin. "I know this is going to sound preposterous when you and I both know I'm not to be trusted with a slow match, but they're looking for me."

"Because of your book?"

"Because of who I am. Because of what I can do. Or, more correctly, what I ought to be able to do." Mr. Burns put a hand on her shoulder. "And I can tell you how to do it, too."

Jin shook her head. "No. I'm not a—"

"A conflagrationeer? Yes, you are, and I'm sure you've already figured that out. And you must be, Jin. Listen." He nodded back the way they had come. "I know what you're working on out there, and it's a good start. But you can do more." He smiled thinly. "A conflagrationeer could do more."

Jin bristled at the word. "They're listening," Sam warned.

"Of course they are." Mr. Burns waved a hand dismissively. "But you're about to take care of that. You know how a city is claimed?"

Hawks had said something about that. The fire bit, the cinefaction, had only been part of it. "By blood, by fire, and by naming," Jin recalled. "They need a con—they need you for the fire."

"Well, they need *someone* for the fire. But they aren't the only ones who can claim the city with it."

Jin frowned. "I don't understand."

Mr. Burns smiled. "The adept who performs the cinefaction can claim the city for whatever party he or she chooses. You understand what I'm saying, Jin? You can stop this madness tonight."

This was going in two equally unpleasant directions. Hadn't he just admitted that he was a conflagrationeer? By that logic, it had to be Mr. Burns whom Jack's men were really looking for, not Uncle Liao — and the mistaken identity might well have gotten him killed.

"*You* stop it!" she snapped, balling her hands into fists. "This isn't my mess to fix! It isn't my madness to stop, and it wasn't Uncle Liao's, either, and now . . ." She shook her head, not quite willing to finish the thought. "You say you've been running from men like this all these years? So you knew they were out there, then?"

"Well, not these men *specifically*, but—"

Anger and fear and exhaustion bubbled up. "Well, then why don't you already have a plan?" Sam put a hand on her arm, but she shrugged him off. "And we've been traveling together all this time . . . When were you going to tell us about it all? No — I don't care about that. *Why don't you already have a plan?*"

"I do," Mr. Burns said calmly. "But the plan has always involved either you or Liao, because despite what I am, I am a very, very bad artificer. I haven't been lying to you about that. You know I haven't."

Grudgingly, Jin had to admit that was the one part of all of this that she did believe was as simple as it seemed. It would have been difficult to fake Mr. Burns's level of ineptitude with explosives. She sighed. "Tell me what your plan is."

"It's simple," Mr. Burns said. "Do what they want."

Jin stared at him. "I beg your pardon?"

"Do what they want," he repeated. "Perform the cinefaction, but claim the city for its own people instead of for Jack Hellcoal."

She stared at him for a moment longer, then out of nowhere she found herself laughing. It was either that or cry again, and she was so tired of crying. "Oh, is that all?"

He nodded. "That's all. Well . . ." He made a careless gesture. "Well, of course it's a little more complicated than that, but that's the basic outline."

"Of course."

"Hey, Jin?" Ilana called from the parlor. "Shall we just keep on at the lances out here?" The younger girl eased the door open and poked her head inside. "I figured out how to close them up the way you did."

"Yes, and I guess I'd better show you how to wire the fuses, too." She folded her arms and stared at Mr. Burns. "It looks like Mr. Burns and I have some things to discuss."

Ilana clapped her hands. "I know this is serious business, but can I just say again that I am having the *best* time?"

"Someone might as well be enjoying herself," Jin mumbled as she followed Ilana to the parlor.

Sam returned to the main room with the two girls. He filled two cups of coffee, went back to the bedroom, and handed one to the man sitting on the windowsill.

He was exceptionally normal-looking, considering he evidently held the secrets to stopping some kind of uncanny assault on New York and Brooklyn. With his gray hair and spectacles, Burns looked like a schoolteacher. How could someone who appeared so utterly and completely ordinary be involved in something so strange?

"Look, before Jin comes back," Sam asked, "why did Hawks tell me to find Liao and not you when this whole conversation about conflagrationeers began?"

"Jim Hawks?" Sam nodded. Burns considered. "I don't know. I've never met Hawks myself, and I'm not sure how he knows of me."

"He's dead."

Burns had the decency to pause for a moment. "I see." He scratched his head. "Well, it may not be me he's worried about at all. Fata Morgana was started by . . . well, let's just say my ancestor's original partner would have been a bit more willing to talk to Jack's men, and to be won over to their cause. It wouldn't shock me in the slightest to learn that Hawks had heard of Ignis Blister. I'm not proud of my connection to him." He sat silently for a moment, deep in thought, and then he shuddered. "I have my faults and my weaknesses, but even I can see that creating a hell at the heart of the country's largest crossroads is a bad idea."

Jin came in from the parlor. "Ilana is a natural. She's doing a wonderful job with the fuses." She stood in the doorway, hands behind her back, and regarded Burns with tired eyes. Sam could just see the corner of the green leather book she held. "Tell me about this plan, then."

TWENTY

The Wager

W HERE HAD YOU planned to set off your message?"

Sam sat at the writing desk in the bedroom; Mr. Burns still leaned against the window. Jin spoke from where she sat cross-legged at the edge of the bed. "The bridge. We thought it would be the fastest way to get the most people possible to read it."

"Good," Burns said, nodding. "The bridge is the key. That's the city's great crossroads, you see, the intersection of the bridge and the East River. The bridge is what will finally make one city of New York and Brooklyn. That's where the cinefaction has to take place. So the simple version of the plan is, instead of going there to set off your message, you go there to complete the cine-faction."

"And the thing that makes it not as simple as it sounds is the cinefaction part," Sam ventured.

Burns nodded and held up three fingers. "There are three things that make the claiming take hold. First, the place where the act is performed. Second, the component parts: the explo-sive, fire, and match, and the conflagrationeer who uses them. Third, the words of the claim. You must claim the crossroads by blood—you must say by whose blood you make the claim; by naming—you must name the city and those who will speak for it; and by the fire that you intend to set, the fire from whose ashes the city will be reborn. There is no exact invocation—it just has to include those things."

"The location is the bridge, then? Does it matter where?" Jin asked.

"Not usually, but traditionally the conflagrationeer would compound the explosive at the highest point in the city. Which, in the vicinity of New York and Brooklyn—"

"Is the top of the bridge towers," Sam finished. The towers were the tallest man-made structures on the whole East Coast.

Burns put a finger to his nose and nodded. "Exactly. So I suggest you set it off from there. Which brings us to the component parts." He held out his hand to Jin. "And it brings us to the *Port-fire Book*."

The book sat next to Jin on the coverlet. She held it out to Burns.

He put his hand on the rough leather surface, then ran his fingers around the edge, flipped the cover over, and let the pages fall open at random in Jin's hand.

"This," Burns said quietly, "is how it starts."

Sam glanced sideways at Jin as she watched the man with wary eyes. Then, unexpectedly, Burns took the book from her and held it out to him. "Sam. Read this and tell me what you think it means."

"Me?"

"You."

Sam glanced at Jin again, then stood and took up the book.

The pages were thick and ridged. The edges were uneven, as if they'd been made by tearing the paper along a straightedge.

The text might've been printed, but it also might've been hand-written by someone with obsessively neat penmanship. This, unfortunately, didn't make it any easier for Sam to make sense of it. He wasn't a great reader to start with, but he had a feeling what he was looking at would've confused the heck out of a professor, too.

The page on the left could only be interpreted as a list of ingredients. "*Clarified red. The mysterious six-and-one. The yellow. The sincere. Iron.*" Jin was staring at him with a bewildered expression on her face. "There's more of that. Then the next page says, *Make the* . . . I don't know this word . . . *luting?* . . . *of the six-and-one, to a depth of three in the crucible. Make the essence of the red and the sincere, and imbue with equal parts mysterious and yellow. Make the bellows even and breathe life into the fire with the essence in the crucible like a gourd. Pulverize the iron to the grain of porcelain dust. The one and two are four and the fifth is the first of the seven.* Am I reading this right?"

"Yes, you are," Burns said.

Sam looked up at him, then at Jin. "And the two of you understand this?"

Jin was watching him with a curious expression. "This is so strange, but I have this feeling that I *nearly* understand it. As if it could fall into place perfectly at any moment."

"You're joking."

She shook her head slowly. "I'm not." Jin turned to Burns. "I'm not, am I?"

Burns shrugged. "I can't say. But if you are what I think you are, it will come to make sense. It makes perfect sense to me, but I can promise you that what I understand is entirely different from what you do."

Now both Sam and Jin stared at him. "But . . ." Jin shook her head. "Then I'm wrong, aren't I? I really thought . . . but . . ."

"You think just because you and I understand two different things, one of us has to be wrong?" Burns asked.

"Well . . . yes. If it's a book of instructions—well, there has to be a right way and a wrong way to read it." Jin turned to Sam. "That's only logical, isn't it?"

"If there was only one way to read a book," Burns said with a little smile, "any book in the world—if there was only one way to read and understand it, what would be the point of reading that book?"

"But . . . but the point of a formula is to guide you to a finished product," Jin protested. "To the same finished product, every single time."

"Ah, but this is not only a book of formulas. It is a True Book. Listen to me, now. If you are a conflagrationeer—if you have that in you, and we all know you do—*you will be able to read the book*. I think there's a reason you and Liao have both managed to get recipes from it to work. You are . . . what is the term? Masters of methods?"

"*Fangshi*," Jin said. Then she shook her head. "Uncle Liao is a *fangshi*. I'm only the one who grinds the ingredients. A *daoyao ren*. Not a master." But she didn't sound certain about that, and Sam thought he knew why. She'd done too much in the last few days, too much not to understand that she was more —or *could* be more—than a mere assistant.

Burns waved a hand. "I think you make too much of names. Also, Jin, the book is only part of it, and I can give you what it cannot. A book cannot tell you that there is no right way to read it, except the way that is right for you. That would be telling you what the right way to read it is."

Sam felt a vague headache starting between his eyes.

"So the book gives me the explosive," Jin said slowly, "and I am to be the adept who makes it. . . . What about the fire and the match?"

"That," Burns said with a nod at Sam, "is where your friend comes in."

Sam started. "Me?"

"You. Jin can make a match and a fuse from scratch, but no ordinary fire can be used to start a proper cinefaction. She needs tinder."

"What kind of tinder?"

"Infernal tinder. Jack's tinder."

Jin shuddered. "Please stop saying things they're probably listening for."

"Jin, if we're going to end it tonight, we don't have time to quibble over words." Mr. Burns turned to Sam. "They carry a piece of infernal coal. They must. It's necessary for the cinefaction. And if anyone can get it from them, you can."

"Me? Why? How?"

Burns grinned. "High Walker is a gambler, Sam. He's possibly the best and greatest gambler among the uncanny. And if I understand it right, you're a bit of a card sharp yourself."

Sam's heart skipped. "I'm—Mr. Burns, I'm not—I . . . I can't." *I'm fifteen years old. I can barely take on the adults in Culver*

Plaza without getting a black eye—how the hell am I supposed to take on the greatest gambler among whatever insane, otherworldly creatures you count among the uncanny?

Burns was watching him with a half-smile. "Sam, we need that tinder. Walker won't just hand it over, and since you've seen him in battle, I presume you know you can't fight it away from him. No one can."

"And you think he'll *wager* with me?" Sam snorted. "Why would he?"

Mr. Burns looked at Jin. She nodded thoughtfully, and Sam's stomach curdled. She was agreeing with him.

"Like in Sun Tzu," Jin said slowly. "Draw them in with the promise of gain, then overcome them."

Burns nodded and turned back to Sam. "If you tell him that if you lose, you'll give him a conflagrationeer who can deliver the city, he'll wager with you."

"No—" Sam said immediately.

"Wait," Jin interrupted.

Sam couldn't be sure who she was speaking to, but she was looking at him. "I'm not using you as a wager," he snapped.

"Could you beat him?" she asked.

"Doesn't matter, 'cause I'm not doing it."

"But *could* you beat him?"

"How the hell do I know? *I'm not doing it!*" He got to his feet and paced for a few angry steps.

"Stop sounding so indignant." Jin dropped her head into her hands. "It would hardly be the first time a girl was won or lost in a bet. Usually it's not for such a good cause, though."

"You don't want to do this," Sam protested. "You don't

even know—*I* don't even know . . . I lose card games all the time!" That wasn't quite true, though; generally speaking, he didn't lose unless he wanted to. *Except for the last couple of days*, he reminded himself. But whatever it was that the sharper on Culver Plaza had done to beat him, an uncanny and experienced creature like Walker would surely have even more inexplicable ways of beating an ordinary fifteen-year-old kid. That just stood to reason.

"Could you beat him?" Jin asked again. Her face was still hidden, her voice muffled, but the tone was insistent. "Tell me if you could or not."

"Jin, I honestly don't know. I don't know what he has in the way of cheats if he decides to play a brace game, and I don't know what he can do if he plays square." Sam swallowed and sat beside her. "I do know I'm not willing to risk you like that."

That made her raise her head, eyes wide and unreadable. She opened her mouth and closed it again. "Sam—"

If Burns hadn't been sitting across from him waiting for an answer, if they hadn't been discussing an absolutely unconscionable thing, and, most important, if he hadn't been an utter coward, Sam would've pulled her straight across to him and kissed her right then.

"I'm not going to risk you like that," he repeated, reaching for her hand. "I'm not going to *lose* you like that. I won't do it."

Jin held his gaze. "Then the solution's easy, Sam. Don't lose."

Across the room, Mr. Burns cleared his throat. "Before we

commit to this route, Jin, you should make sure you can do the job. You need to make sure you can find a recipe that'll work."

"I thought you were certain she could," Sam said, disentangling his fingers from Jin's. "Wasn't that the whole point?"

"She has the capability. The issue is—"

"The actual recipe," Jin finished, pulling the *Port-fire Book* toward her. "If I'm going to do it tonight while I'm on the bridge, we can't do anything that requires more time than that. It's like the fireworks I made for the display on Friday—I knew I couldn't use formulas that needed much time to dry, or that had to be ground finer than what I could accomplish myself." She flipped a few pages, then looked up at Burns. "So there must be more than one recipe that can be used, I hope?"

He nodded. "You are part of the compound, remember. Your involvement, your reading, your choices are part of what makes a recipe suitable for cinefaction."

She turned back to the book, flipped a few more pages. "How will I know?"

"I don't know how you'll know," Burns admitted. "When I read it, I can just tell." He smiled sadly. "Usually it's a sense of shame. I read a particular page and know that if I wasn't such an utterly hopeless artificier, I could do amazing things with it. I can just sense the potential, but I know that all my failings make me the wrong person to realize any of that potential. It's a horrible feeling, actually."

Jin paused in her reading and turned to Sam. "If I can find the right formula, will you help me do this, Sam? Please. This is your home. Let me help protect it."

He opened his mouth, about to protest further. Jin shook her head and cut him off.

"If I don't know this place is safe," she began hesitantly, "how will I know you're safe?"

Sam's chest ached. "If it's what you want," he said at last.

She smiled, and the ache twisted into knots. "That's decided, then. Now leave me alone for a while so I can read."

Mr. Burns stood and patted her shoulder. "Your uncle will be proud."

"My uncle's going to kill us both if he ever finds out what we're up to," Jin retorted. "This is insane *yang guizi* behavior for sure."

"I'll bring you some coffee," Sam said, getting to his feet.

Jin nodded absently, already absorbed in the text. He paused in front of her, then bent and kissed her cheek.

Jin turned so they were almost nose-to-nose. "It's going to be okay," she whispered. "I'm sorry for what I'm asking you to do."

"Well," Sam said awkwardly, "I guess if all it takes is not losing, it's not such a big deal."

Jin burst into nervous laughter, and the moment was broken. Sam smiled and forced himself toward the parlor for the promised coffee.

Don't lose.

Walker's terrifying, scarlet-streaked face materialized in Sam's memory, grinning and baring two sets of teeth. Evil, deadly, uncanny—and evidently also some kind of genius gambler. Sam willed the image out of his head as he made his way through the parlor-turned-explosives-factory.

Whether by character, chance, or cheating, there was a way to beat everyone. Sam believed that. There was a way to beat Walker. There had to be.

Don't lose, Jin's voice whispered. *Don't lose. The solution's easy*.

But how on earth could you possibly plan a win over a creature like that?

TWENTY-ONE

Artifice and Alchemy

J IN TURNED the heavy pages of the *Port-fire Book* slowly, still not sure what she was looking for. She'd flipped through it often enough for most of the recipes to look familiar, even if she had no idea what they meant.

This time, though, something was different as she scanned the formulas.

Mr. Burns had suggested that reading *The Conflagrationeer's Port-fire Book* was not so much about a single right way of understanding the bizarre writings, but figuring out how to read it so that it made sense for *you*, whoever you were. So even if Mr. Burns was a proper artificier, he might read a recipe and come away with a completely different understanding than Jin would. And somehow, even if they interpreted the same passage in two different ways, they could both be right.

At first, she had a hard time keeping that in mind. She turned to a page that bore the heading *A Work of the Deep Yellow Earth* and read the beginning of the recipe out loud. *"Take for the crucible a work of the mysterious and lute it throughout with red clay mixed with the essence of the sincere heart. Compound a paste of the bitter and the quick with salt and sand. Combine and refine the workings through nine revolutions over heat ankle-deep.*"

The sincere heart. A memory sprang to Jin's mind: Uncle Liao, consoling her through one of the occasional bouts of self-hating that overtook her when she thought too much about her past. "You are not what was done to you," he had said. "You survived what was done to you because of who you are. You have a cinnabar heart."

By cinnabar heart, she'd come to understand, Uncle Liao had meant some combination of strength and goodness and sincerity. He'd actually used all three words at various times in her life to define the phrase.

So perhaps what the recipe was really saying was to lute a crucible with a mixture of red clay and cinnabar. That made a certain amount of sense.

And the bitter . . . well, salt immediately sprang to mind, although it wasn't precisely bitter, but since salt was referred to directly, that didn't seem to be the bitter element in question. Sulfur? Sulfur was also a deep yellow mineral . . . and that would account for the "deep yellow earth" of the title.

Jin's mind was racing now. Things were falling into place, just like they had two days before when she'd figured out the formulas for the Atlantis display. *The quick* . . . quicksilver, perhaps? And sand . . . yes, sand was sometimes used in fireworking, but almost immediately Jin thought of the way fine-ground sugar was used, as a propellant. Sugar certainly *looked* like sand. And if the salt in question was not plain table salt, but saltpeter . . . or copper salts . . . or any kind of detonating salts . . .

Abruptly she saw it, a way that this strange language could

produce a formula for an explosive charge. And she realized that, by varying certain ingredients, she could produce not one but several different types and colors of fireworks.

"But how could this be?" she protested as Sam set a cup and saucer quietly on the bedside table. "Cinnabar is just a thing Uncle Liao says, something from old China. How on earth could that really be the right way to read a *sincere heart*?"

Sam shrugged. "It could be the right way for *you* to read it."

But there, of course, was the problem. If the right way to read it was something only Jin could know, then she was completely alone. No one else could tell her if she was right or wrong. There was no way to test it until she actually tried to compound one of the formulas.

She flipped back to the beginning. "Sam, could you find me paper and a pencil?" By the time he returned, she had four pages marked with her fingers. She took the pencil and started making notes.

The more she read, the more she discovered that she was drawing on what she'd learned from Uncle Liao. Ingredients that he favored, sayings he'd repeated, ways that he liked to work. She was also beginning to suspect that some of the instructions didn't refer to things the conflagrationeer was supposed to do to the ingredients, but what the conflagrationeer was expected to do *herself*. She thought maybe a reference to circulating air through the bellows for a certain length of time might be about breathing —meditative breathing, like Uncle Liao practiced, not moving air over the compound being made. Just like with the sincere heart, Jin worried that this was so specific to her life with Uncle Liao that it couldn't be right. But it *felt* right.

Then there were the results the formulas claimed to deliver. She had always assumed that ascending to the heavens and other references to flight had been about the trajectory of rockets, but now, as Jin began to make sense of the recipes, she wondered if maybe there was more to it. There were other examples, too —references to longevity that didn't seem to be about how long the shower of sparks would linger in the sky or how far a rocket would go before exploding.

Some of the formulas called for specific tools, made of specific materials. From one: *grind the mysterious and the earthly in a mortar cast from the heavens*. From another: *form the grains into a pill the size of hesitation and put forth on a transfigured platter after allowing to rest for the nine revolutions*. Actually, there were a lot of references to transfigured items, and most of them sounded more like serving pieces than pyrotechnicians' tools—platters, cups, saucers, plates, utensils. It was as if those formulas were intended to be eaten rather than blown up.

And then, she found it. The second she read it, she knew it was the perfect formula, the one she was supposed to use. And she knew exactly how to make it. And everything suddenly made perfect sense and got a hundred percent stranger.

Sam came in again with a pot of coffee to refill her cup. She looked up at him. "I need you to make the bet, Sam. I figured it out."

He nodded without returning her gaze. "I told you I would, Jin."

"There's something else." She tapped the formula she'd chosen with a trembling finger. "If I'm reading this right, if I do it correctly, Walker won't be able to touch me. And I'm fairly certain now that he couldn't touch Uncle Liao. I think Uncle Liao only let Walker fight as long as he did so that you and I could get away."

Sam's brow furrowed. "What do you mean?"

"I've been reading this as a pyrotechnics formulary because that's what we need. But I think Uncle Liao's been reading it as . . ." She hesitated, but she knew she was right. "I think he read it as a *waidan* scripture. There are formulas in here that could be compounded into an explosive or, just as easily . . . I think . . . into a *dan*, one of the elixirs of *taiqing*, the Great Clarity."

Sam looked blankly at her. "That's a . . . a Chinese thing, I guess?"

"Well, *waidan* is, yes—it's part of the philosophy of the *Tao*. But I think there is a word in English that means something similar. Alchemy?"

Sam shook his head. "Doesn't mean anything to me."

"Doesn't matter." She smoothed her hand over the page, frowning. "It sounds outrageous, even to me, but . . ." She thought of Liao's burnished gold instruments, the ones he used in his laboratory tent and the hammered yellow-metal cups he drank from. She thought of the elaborate process of setting up the furnace he dragged from place to place, even though precious little in an artificer's work actually required a furnace. She thought of the talismans hung in the corners of the tent, the jars of mud and clay in the chest that were of no use in making fireworks but would be perfect for lining and sealing a crucible the way the formulas in the book described.

Then she remembered the word he used for himself. Not artificier, not fireworker, but *fangshi*. Master of methods. And he had always called Jin his *daoyao ren*, the assistant who grinds the ingredients. *They are terms from* waidan, he had explained long ago, *but they will serve just as well for what we do.*

"He might as well have told me," she said, shaking her head. "No wonder he was so surprised when I read the book and came up with spur-fires."

"I don't understand."

Jin laughed hoarsely. "Well, the *fangshi* of the old days claimed that through *waidan* one could fly, walk on water, call forth gods, repel demons and danger of all kinds, and live for hundreds of years, even ascend to join the immortals. When Uncle Liao read the *Port-fire Book*, he found this type of knowledge there. But when *I* read it, I found recipes for explosives." She closed the book. "It doesn't matter. I have a formula that I think will work for the cinefaction, so the bet is on. But if I'm right about the *waidan*, the compound will also protect me from creatures like this Walker. I thought knowing that might make you feel better about it."

His face twisted into a wry smile. "I'm supposed to feel better about using you as a gambling chip because you've discovered that your uncle is some kind of . . . of wizard or something? And you think you can do the same stuff?"

Jin felt her cheeks heat up. "It does sound crazy, doesn't it?"

"It sounds absolutely insane. But in the last few days I've been told that a story about a man trying to build his own hell is true; I've learned that the survival of New York and Brooklyn depends upon five people who magically speak for those cities; I've overheard a conversation that implied that fellows can find people from afar if they speak certain words; and I was assured that we can save the cities by setting some kind of miraculous fire on the New York and Brooklyn Bridge. Oh, and that I can help with the fire by winning special tinder from a man with two sets of teeth." Sam gave her a sharp look. "He has two sets of teeth, Jin. Two sets. I saw them. So I'm not judging anything based on whether it sounds sane or not."

He poured more coffee into her cup. "Ilana says the fuse-work is done, and Constantine and Mike are out of powder for the lances. They need instructions."

"All right." Jin stood up, then hesitated. "We should tell Susannah. She needs to be involved. It's only right that she has the final say on whether I go ahead with this or not."

"I'll get her."

He left and returned with the single surviving steward of New York and Brooklyn. Susannah sat beside Jin and looked from her to Sam. "Tell me."

Jin sketched out her ideas as quickly as she could. She kept her eyes on Susannah's face, hoping it would make her seem confident, and she tried not to consider whether Susannah thought it all sounded as impossible to believe as Jin did herself.

The fifth steward listened in silence. Only once did she look away, when Jin got to the part about Sam making a wager with Walker. Her dark gray eyes flicked sideways to him, then back to Jin. Her expression did not change.

"What can I do to help?" she asked when Jin had finished.

Jin hesitated. "Say yes, and give us your blessing."

Susannah smiled. "It's the only plan we have, but it's a good one. I wish I could be of greater help to you. You have my blessing and my thanks."

"You're welcome," Jin whispered. "I'll do everything I can."

The three returned to the parlor. Jin examined Ilana's fuses, which ran along the rows of spikes on the letters, curling around each one before it moved on to the next. "These are beautiful," she exclaimed, making the younger girl blush with pride. "They really are. I'm not sure I could've done better myself." She turned and sifted through the crate of lances. "And I admit I was a little leery of letting you lot finish these without me, but they look like they just might work."

She leaned back against the windowsill and scratched her head. "All right. Let me think through how this will need to go. We take the letter frames to the bridge and mount the lances on the spikes. We string the letters across." She turned to Sam. "How does that work?"

Sam turned to Constantine. "Con?"

The blond boy stretched in his chair. "I can get us up to the tower; that's no problem. Then the quickest way to hang the message will be just to go out and attach it to the cable. The men working on the cables use a thing called a buggy that hangs from—"

"Just a minute," Sam interrupted. "I was thinking we could find some way to start up the spinning engines to drag the message across, rather than sending someone out onto the cable. Wouldn't that be safer?"

"Sure, it would be safer, but it's Sunday. There might be people there finishing projects, but there won't be anybody working the engines, and these aren't the sort of machines you can start up just by pulling a lever."

"What's this buggy you mentioned?" Jin asked. "Why can't we do it that way?"

"I think Sam's concerned for your safety," Constantine said.

Jin rolled her eyes. "Really? We have time to worry about that?" She looked to Susannah. "Tell them we don't have time to worry about that."

Susannah shook her head. "We don't. Obviously."

Sam threw his hands into the air, stalked to the corner of the room, and leaned against the wall.

"Thank you," Susannah said. "Carry on, Jin."

She nodded. "I took enough rockets to send up a thirty-second fanfare to get the attention of as many people as we can. Once I set the letters in place, we light the fuses from both towers. The way they're wired, the fuses will illuminate the letters more or less simultaneously, right around the time the fanfare ends." She chewed on her thumbnail. "So that's the message portion of the plan, which I think seems under control."

She looked to Susannah, but the fifth steward's eyes were on Constantine. "Before we move on, are you sure they're going to just let us up onto the towers?" Susannah asked. "Folks aren't that trusting, in my experience."

"Well, people are allowed out on the footpath," Constantine said. "And I know the workmen. I can talk my way to getting it done, I'm sure. I'll tell them some big bugs in the government are setting off fireworks for some kind of celebration."

"I can imagine you talking your way past your old friends, and I can believe that nobody would bother telling the workers about something like fireworks," Susannah agreed. "But if anybody's up there working on his day off, don't you think it's likely to be somebody in a higher position? Engineers, overseers?"

Constantine scowled. "I'm sure you're not questioning my ability to talk fast and in a convincing fashion."

"I'm not, it's just—am I wrong?" She gestured around the room. "Furthermore, look at us. Honestly, Constantine, *look*."

"She's right." Mike spoke up. "Anybody in charge is going to laugh us out of town if we try to tell him we know something he doesn't, and it involves setting explosive charges anywhere near that bridge."

Jin felt herself wilt. It was true, of course. Three girls, one white, one black, one Chinese—certainly no one could look more out of place. The boys were the only ones who might remotely seem like they belonged up there. But only *remotely*, and only because they were boys, and white.

Then she had an idea. "We need someone who can look upstanding and in charge, and who we can trust. We need an adult who can pass himself off as someone official."

Sam scratched his head. "Mr. Burns, maybe? Tom Guyot and Walter Mapp don't look much more reputable than we do."

Jin shook her head. "I don't want Mr. Burns up there. He's bad luck around fireworks. No offense," she added quickly.

"None taken," Mr. Burns replied.

"But I have a thought," Jin continued. "Sam, do you have time to track someone down?"

"I suppose that depends on you. What do you need for the cinefaction?" Sam asked.

"A little more time to make sure I've got the formula right. Then I'll go back to Uncle Liao's laboratory." Where, unless she was much mistaken, one—or maybe both—of Jack's henchmen would be waiting. "A few hours?"

He nodded. "I'll track your man down."

"I have a question," Mr. Burns interjected. "Jin, why are you still worrying about the message? If you perform the cinefaction, you won't need to keep them from being able to find Miss Asher. Our work will be done."

Jin looked down at her hands. "In case the cinefaction doesn't work," she said softly. "I'm afraid to give up the message. What if something goes wrong? What if . . ."

What if I'm reading this book wrong? What if Sam loses his bet? What if I'm not a conflagrationeer? What if . . . what if . . . what if . . .

"What if I can't do what you think I can do?" she said at last. "The message will be our backup plan." She was very careful not to look at either Mr. Burns or Susannah.

Sam sighed. "I guess I'd better start figuring out how to pull off my part of this."

"Which is what?" Constantine asked.

Sam's grin looked forced. "Nothing but cards, Con."

"There's something else we need to do first." Every head turned to Susannah. "It's time to replace the missing stewards," she said. "Do you mind giving us the room?" she asked Mr. Burns.

"Not at all," he said. "I'll go see about a cup of tea."

"You need us to go get some folks for you?" Mike asked when he had gone.

Susannah shook her head. "We have everyone we need right here."

A confused quiet fell over the room. "You don't mean *us?*" Sam protested.

"I do. Well," she corrected herself, "except for Jin. I don't think it's important to have been born here, but even if we're only talking about temporary stewardships, it doesn't make sense to offer one to someone who doesn't *live* here." Susannah glanced at Jin. "You understand, right?"

"Goodness, yes," Jin said immediately. It would never have occurred to her that she could be a steward of the cities of New York and Brooklyn, and not living there was the least of the reasons why not.

They all had to be thinking it, but Ilana said it first. "But . . . but we're kids," she said hesitantly.

"I know. But I've considered this carefully." Susannah's face hardened. "After what Overcaste did . . . and what Sawyer did . . ." She swallowed. "They should've known better! They should have been stronger! And even Hawks and Van Ossinick, thinking that keeping one of us hidden away would make us all safer, when all it meant was that one of us was left unprepared . . . no," she said, voice strong, "being an adult is not important now. Being the right person is. And I'm not going to offer this responsibility to someone I don't believe is right just because these are desperate times. We're going to find out now if I'm correct about you four. Are you willing to be considered?"

A stunned hush fell across the room as Susannah looked at each of them: Sam, Constantine, Ilana, and Mike. Jin held her breath. Then, one by one, each nodded silently.

"All right." Susannah's words came with an exhale; she'd been holding her breath, too. "I need something from each of you, something that you love. It must be an object you're carrying with you right now."

"What if they aren't carrying anything like that at this moment?" Jin whispered as the others began rifling through their pockets.

"If they are able to speak for the city," Susannah replied quietly, "they will have something suitable."

Ilana came forward first. In her hand she held a ring with two keys on it. She selected a tarnished one that had a tiny tag tied to its loop, and handed it to Susannah. "It's—"

"Don't tell me what it is," Susannah interrupted. "Not yet. I need to see for myself." She sank onto the sofa, gripped the armrest with one hand, and stared at the key in her other. When she spoke again, her voice was uneven. "You unlock a door at the top of a flight of stairs. I smell dust, old paper, the stuffing of sprung chairs, mice. You have put this key in the pocket of your apron. It stays there for many weeks while you prepare the room for your brothers."

Jin looked at Ilana. The girl's eyes were wide. She nodded.

"It reminds you every day of doors that do not need to be locked," the keeper of lore continued. She looked up at the dark-haired girl and searched her face. "It reminds you of home, and what it means."

Ilana nodded again, her eyes shiny. Susannah handed the key back and squeezed her hand.

"You had brothers?" Sam stared at Ilana. "I'm so sorry, Illy. How did they . . . when did you lose them?" Behind him, Constantine wore an identical expression of concern.

Ilana turned to stare at him with such a look of disgust that Jin actually had to suppress a chuckle. "I didn't *lose* them," the girl retorted.

Constantine frowned. "Well, you don't have any that you told *us* about."

"The key," Ilana said deliberately, "is from the *attic*. We were cleaning it out for *you*."

"For your brothers," Constantine repeated, surprised.

Ilana put the key back in her pocket and folded her arms. "I kept the key. I thought it was pretty. And then after a while — well, Susannah already said it. Of course I have brothers. Idiot."

Constantine shook his head, put his arms around her, and squeezed her tight. She reached out for Sam and pulled him in, too.

Jin watched, a little sigh in her heart. Unlikely family, but family nonetheless. Just like hers.

"All right, all right," Mike grumbled. He pushed himself away from the wall he'd been leaning against and crossed to where Susannah sat. "Tell me my fortune next."

There was a small box in his hand, hinged on one side and fastened closed on the other. Susannah thumbed the latch and let the box fall open in her palm. Inside were a small coil of lamp wick, a flint and firesteel, a little glass vial of oil, and a folding knife.

"You are walking along a dark street," she began after a moment. "It is narrow and crooked and the stones are irregular. The smells here are strong, sickening — there is a gutter full of rotting things. A small girl runs past you. She is barefoot, and she stubs a toe on the uneven cobblestones."

Susannah shuddered. "When she falls, there is a horrible sound as her head hits the ground. You run to her. You have a clean pocket square — it is brand-new, just-bought yellow silk, and it reddens as you hold it to the cut on the crying girl's forehead. The man you have been walking with picks her up and tells you he will take her home. As he tucks her against his shoulder, he takes this box from his vest pocket and hands it to you. He points at a dark streetlamp that might have illuminated this place, broken for who knows how long, and tells you to fix it."

She closed the box and latched it tight again. "That man was James Hawks, and since then you have carried this, taught yourself to repair broken lamps, and kept your eyes open for them."

Mike's eyes were fierce. Jin recognized the expression immediately; it was one she resorted to when she wanted to look like she absolutely, positively was not about to cry. He nodded curtly, tucked the little kit back into his vest, and returned to the wall with arms crossed tightly across his chest.

"Constantine?"

He came forward and tipped the contents of his cupped hand into Susannah's palm: three fragments of twisted steel, linked into a short, rough chain.

Susannah ran her fingers over it. "You are in a roomful of machinery," she began. "There are engines there, and great coils of wire, and vats for oiling it. The engines send the wire out across the river, over a great stone tower, and then another, to the far shore and then back. You are weaving a bridge."

The bridge. Everything seemed to come back to that bridge, Jin thought.

"And then, one day, very early on, the wire snaps." Susannah held up the linked bits, turned them in the light. "Several men die. You survive, but not undamaged. Your blood is in the wires of the bridge. You keep these pieces now, as a reminder of that. Two of them are good steel, which would not have broken. The third is bad, brittle, a piece of the wire that killed the men in front of you." She held them out to Constantine. "I cannot tell the difference, but you can."

Constantine swallowed hard and took the steel links back with a shaking hand.

Only one person remained. Sam handed over a deck of cards.

Susannah turned the deck over and sifted through them. "You are younger, a small boy in a crowded room. Sweat smells, old food smells, the odors of unwashed clothes and bodies . . . but you have a small piece of candy bought from a Chinese man on the corner, and you smile as you ask the man who sits before you if he has a two of cups. He says, *Go and fish*. Happiness is that two of cups—sometimes hidden among swords and coins and staves, but you turn over card after card, knowing it is always there to be found. And all the despair around you is not enough to dampen your happiness."

His father. Jin looked sideways at Sam. His face was wooden as he watched Susannah neaten the cards back into a stack. She handed them back to him and took a deep breath.

"All right. We five will speak for the city if you accept the posts I am about to offer." She rose from the couch and stepped up to Ilana. "In every city, there must be a keeper of sanctuary. This I offer to you. Will you accept?"

Ilana nodded solemnly. "Yes, I accept."

Susannah kissed her forehead. "You are brave, and you are

loyal, and you love deeply, and to share your home brings you pride and happiness. Never forget how important those things are. I am overjoyed to build this new family with you."

Next she faced Constantine. "In every city, there must also be a smith. This I offer to you. Will you accept?"

Constantine bowed his head. "Yes, ma'am."

"Throughout time, the smith has been the one tasked with keeping the hearth of the village. You are strong, even when you feel weak, and you can tell the poor metal from the sturdy." She kissed his cheek. "I am glad to stand at your side."

She turned to Mike. "You, I ask to be the keeper of the roads. Will you accept?"

"Aye, sure," he answered.

Susannah grinned. "You, too, are loyal, and even as you walk the darkest streets, you look for places to bring light. You had no reason to stay after Mr. Hawks's death, and here you are. You live in a place where violence is law, and yet you followed Hawks because he told you that even out of the dark places of the city, a person might be called to do great things. You are special, Mike. I am glad to call you my friend."

She leaned forward to kiss Mike's cheek, and the tough boy actually closed his eyes when she did.

"Thank you, ma'am," he said quietly.

"And now Sam." She put a hand on his shoulder. "I didn't actually need your cards to know what to offer you. Your most beloved things are all in this room. Am I right?"

He swallowed and nodded.

"And since you brought us together, I offer you the role of keeper of the conjunction, the deep fellowship that holds the people of a place together into a citizenship. This is not a role that always exists among us, because there is not always someone suitable to hold it. Do you accept?"

Only because Jin was watching him so closely did she see his eyes flick over to where she stood before he said, "Yes."

Susannah kissed his cheek. "I am honored to serve our home along with you." She surveyed them all. "When this is over, if you change your minds, I'll understand. But I thank you for standing with me now." She reached for Ilana's hand, and for Sam's. As if by unspoken agreement, each of the new stewards reached for the hand of the next. Even Mike stepped forward to take his place in the circle. And the second all hands were joined, Jin felt the change.

It was like an electrical charge, a silent, invisible crackling of energy in the room. There was nothing to see, nothing to hear—but it was impossible to miss. Here, in this grand hotel room by the sea, the new stewards took their places, and with the strange, soundless voices of ages past and years to come, the cities welcomed them.

Out on the stretch of beach between the piers where they'd set up in order to keep an eye on the Fata Morgana compound, Walker and Bones sat bolt upright at the same time.

"You feel that?" Walker demanded, the marks on his face flaring black as pitch.

"Yes." Bones turned to Overcaste, who was pacing numbly a few feet away. The pillar looked up with a frightened-animal expression on his face. Bones's eyes narrowed. "You felt it, too, didn't you? And stop pacing, for the hundredth time."

"I don't know what it was," Overcaste said quickly.

"But you've felt it before," Bones persisted. "You recognize it."

Overcaste licked his lips nervously. "Once before, I've felt it, only it was nothing as . . . as strong as it is now."

"Well," Walker said with dangerously exaggerated patience, "when was it, man?"

"When the . . . there were four of us for a while a few years back . . . and . . . and then there was that . . . that feeling. . . . I was having a drink with Hawks at Tammany Hall, and I remember him saying—" Overcaste swallowed. "He said, *Aha, now we are five again*." He licked his lips once more. "Someone has . . . someone has created new pillars."

"Someone like who?" Walker stalked to Overcaste and picked him up by his lapels. "Who can do that?"

"Sawyer and Hawks were found dead in West Brighton, so it can only be the one Arabella van Cortelen was acting as a decoy for," Overcaste sputtered. "The last one. The one we didn't—"

"The one we didn't find?" Walker finished. Red lines slid outward from the black dots, covering his face in a scarlet webwork. "So a pillar can create new ones, anytime? Meaning *you could've created new ones anytime?* I thought we had to kill the last one before we started replacing them!"

"I didn't know!" Overcaste screamed.

"Keep your voices down," Bones warned. The beach between the piers was deserted, but the piers themselves were not.

Walker set Overcaste down roughly and waved at the faces looking down from the piers as the other man collapsed into a terrified pile at his feet. Then he knelt next to the fellow he'd just dropped into the sand. "You didn't know it could be done, or you didn't know how to do it yourself?"

"Both!"

"So you can't do it?"

"Even if—" Overcaste took a deep breath. "Even if I knew how, you can't replace a living pillar." But even as he said it, he looked uncertain, as if he could sense that something else had changed.

Bones swore quietly. "Of course not. That's why we had to kill all the other ones." Then he glanced at Overcaste and caught the unsettled look before the other man could wipe it away. "What?"

Overcaste opened his mouth, then closed it again. His face had gone so pale and sweaty it practically shone.

"*What?*" Bones repeated, voice deadly. Overcaste, quaking, managed a strangled noise, but no words. The bald man's oyster-shell eyes narrowed. "She replaced you, too, didn't she?"

The former keeper of the roads swallowed convulsively, which seemed to be enough of an answer for Bones. "Unbelievable," he said. "Absolutely unbelievable."

Walker stared up at him. "Meaning now we have to . . . *no.*"

"Yes."

"We have a whole new batch to get out of the way?"

"Yes."

"*Son of a*—" Walker glared at Overcaste. "I am so angry I could kill you right now, just to take the edge off."

Overcaste fainted dead away into the sand.

Walker straightened, hands in his pockets. "Well, I guess that means the cinefaction is the thing, once again."

"We were going to do it anyway," Bones said tonelessly. "But it's tonight or never. I'm not admitting to Jack that we had taken care of four pillars until the fifth just made up some new ones and now we're right back where we started. I want these cities claimed for Jack before he gets here. It's the only way we don't look like complete fools."

"Or worse," Walker added.

"Or worse," Bones agreed. "May the roads protect us if he gets here and we have to explain this mess."

⇝ TWENTY-TWO ⇜

Tesserian

THE ERRAND Jin had sent him on turned out to be quick. Sam almost wished it had taken longer. Not much longer, just a little; he had come up with exactly one idea about how to win the bet he had to make with Walker, but it wasn't a notion he liked. But once he'd delivered Jin's message to the person she'd sent him to find and stepped outside the Broken Land, he knew he'd run out of time. He started walking toward West Brighton.

Sam understood that if there was any chance at all of beating Walker, he was going to have to find a way to stack the deck. Proverbially speaking; maybe literally, too. Ordinarily, to fill the gaps in his knowledge of cards or gambling, he went straight to Constantine, who'd taught him to hustle in the first place. For this, though, he needed something more. Fortunately, there was a person right in town who might be able to help.

If, that is, he could somehow be convinced to help Sam rather than hit him again.

The sharper still sat in Sam's spot on Culver Plaza, his feet up on a little folding table, his hat tipped back, and his face turned to the sky. He fanned himself with a creased racing form as Sam came to stand in front of him.

"Well, hello," Sam said dryly. "Don't you just look cozy as all get-out."

The sharper smiled with his mouth, but not his eyes. "I'll give you this, kid. I've been a lot of places and had a lot of folks try to run me out of town, but I've never had those kind of shenanigans played on me. I don't much want to know what I looked like, running for my life from a bunch of spitfires." He slid a crate out from under the folding table with one foot. "Care to sit?"

"Much obliged."

"You come for another game," the man asked as Sam sat, "or you going to light another fire under my tail?"

Well, here goes. "I came to ask for your help."

"My help?" The sharper laughed. "Kid, you can't be that stupid. I'm here to beat you and take your money, not to be your mentor."

"It isn't you I want to know how to beat." Sam took a deep breath. "Help me, and I'll give you my spot."

"It's not your spot anymore, kid."

That was probably true. Still . . . "I'll walk away," he said, as if he really posed any threat to this man. "I'll leave town, if that's what it takes. I'll do anything. The man I have to play . . ." He pictured Walker striding across the gravel behind the hotel, moving like a creature with nothing to give away. Nothing to exploit. A man who couldn't possibly be bluffed by a fifteen-year-old kid.

"I don't know if he can be beaten," Sam admitted, "but I *have* to beat him, and I have no one else to ask."

The other man cocked his head. "Really."

"Really."

The sharper watched him across the scratched tabletop. "Who is this guy? How'd you get yourself mixed up with him?"

"He's . . ." Sam hesitated. It had never occurred to him that the man would care enough to ask what the situation was.

"Don't mess with me, kid," he said, interrupting Sam's thoughts. "If you lie, I'll know."

And he will, Sam realized. *I can't bluff him any more than I can bluff Walker.*

The sharper leaned on the table. "Come clean, now."

"Fellow's name is Walker."

The other man sat up straight. "Red-haired guy? Goes in for fancy suits?"

"Yeah. How did you . . . ?"

The sharper's grin widened. "Well, stick me in the ribs and tell me it's my birthday!" He burst into a crackling laugh and slapped his hand down on the table.

"What the heck—" Sam stared. "You *know* him?"

"Know what? Maybe." The sharper reached a hand across the table. "Alsae Tesserian. Al."

"Saverio Noctiluca." He shook Tesserian's hand, utterly dumbfounded. "Sam."

"I should apologize, probably. Anybody who's gotten himself on the wrong side of Redgore is someone I want to be acquainted with. Wouldn't have given you such a hard time if I'd known you were a roamer."

"Redgore?" Then Sam realized what Tesserian had called him. "Roamer?"

"Redgore, or probably High Walker to you. But that's more

like the term for *what* he is, not *who* he is. Redgore's his proper name." Tesserian leaned back. "I've run into 'em from time to time."

"You . . . you've *run into them from time to time?*"

"Weird world, isn't it?" The sharper smiled again, and Sam recalled Ambrose's words: *The country is wide and strange.*

"Are you some kind of . . . of a roamer, too?" He decided to set aside, for the moment, the fact that Tesserian had called him one. They could come back to that.

"Yep," Tesserian replied, as easily as if Sam had asked if he was cold or tired or hungry. "Fact is, I ran into Redgore just about a week back."

"Where?"

"Steamboat. Poker tourney. I'm not a poker man myself, except under extraordinary circumstances. But I was bored." He sighed. "I've been bored a lot lately. Kinda hoped this place would be different."

"Did you play him?"

"Him? Nah. Well. Not then. You got any idea how many folks were on that boat? How many of 'em were armed? Not that they were going to cause me any damage . . . or Walker, for that matter." Tesserian shrugged. "Just that if I'd hopped into that tournament, it would've come down to Walker and me eventually, and—well, you've seen me play."

"Sure. Looks a whole heck of a lot like cheating."

"My point exactly." Then Tesserian winked. "*Looks* like."

Sam regarded him dubiously. "You're saying you don't?"

"Don't what?"

"Cheat!"

Tesserian laughed. "Kid—Sam—I don't *need* to cheat. Not you, anyway, and I wouldn't have needed to cheat anyone in that tournament, either. But by the time it got down to Redgore and me, anyone who was watching when the two of us really got to trying to beat each other would've made the same assumption you did. Fifty gamblers with pistols and knives thinking they'd been cheated out of a hundred-thousand-dollar pot?" Tesserian whistled. "I'll throw a punch or two now and then, but I don't relish violence, not really. Not like *he* does. I just like my games."

"So you stayed out of the tournament."

"Just about killed me, but yeah, I did. Had to watch that bastard win. And he taunted me the whole time. Called me all kinds of names."

"He knew you were there?"

"Oh, sure."

"Well, does he know you're *here?*"

"I didn't know *he* was here, for what that's worth. Guess he's probably the one behind this Jack nonsense, isn't he? Now I think on it, I probably should've known that carnage was his handiwork." He leaned forward on his elbows. "So tell me about how you're mixed up with him."

"Well, it's kind of a—"

Tesserian put up a hand. "I don't want a long story. It's beating Redgore that interests me. I play games because I like to win, and back on that steamboat I had to step aside and watch that bloodthirsty maniac take all the fun and glory. Why do you have to play him? That's gonna be worse than trying to whip your weight in wildcats."

"He has something I need, and I figure the only way to take it from him is to win it, and the only thing I have to wager with that he really wants is a girl. A . . . friend." Sam swallowed. "So I can't lose."

Tesserian nodded with a look of sympathy. "Then any game you've ever played is out."

Sam felt like he'd just been punched in the stomach, hard. "Wha—Wait a minute—"

The other gambler shook his head. "Nope. At every single game you know, he beats you. I promise. Now, you want to beat somebody," he continued, "you gotta know three things about him: why he's playing, what makes him confident, what makes him question himself. Then you pick your game based on how he thinks you'll win it."

Sam found himself nodding along. He'd never really put words to how he went about figuring out somebody else's game logic, but Tesserian had just done a pretty good job of summing it up. "So, for Walker . . . ?"

"He plays because winning tides him over between killings. Reminds him that he always has power over you, even when he can't kill you. Or, the way he would likely put it, even when he *chooses* not to. And by *you*, I mean . . ." Tesserian waved his arm around as if to encompass Culver Plaza, Coney Island, all of Long Island, and the world.

"As to what makes him confident . . . well, he's a predator, and he's a rung or two up the ladder from most everything and everybody around him. Now, what makes him question himself . . . kid, that's the challenge. But you can't do it with poker, or

monte or stuss or any game you've ever played. He's old. *Old.*
He's had decades to perfect every game you've ever heard of."

"I know a lot of games. I used to play in the tenements; I
played with men from all over the place. I probably know some
he's never even heard of."

"You misunderstand me. When I say old . . . Sam, he's
played every game humankind's ever *invented.*"

Sam frowned, racking his brains for the most obscure games
he'd ever heard of. "What about elfern? Harjan? Einwerfen? Or
there's styrivolt. Talonmarias. Tressette."

"Please. Every gambler who's ever been to Italy knows
tressette, and you can't even play einwerfen and styrivolt with
two people." Tesserian lifted his hat and scratched his head.
"Or talonmarias, either, for that matter. I'm telling you, there's
no game you know right now at which you have so much as a
chance at beating him."

"I—" Sam hesitated. "That I know *right now?*"

The sharper nodded. "Which brings us to the only way I can
think of that might make Redgore question himself. You challenge him to a game you should have no way of knowing."

"I thought you said—"

"I said he knew every game humankind's ever invented.
And he knows plenty more than that. Thing about those *plenty
more* is"—Tesserian reached across and tapped Sam on the
chest—"there's no way *you* should know them."

"But you do?"

"I do." Tesserian leaned on the table again, his eyes glittering. "And I'm fairly certain if you show up and challenge him

to the game I'm about to teach you, it'll pretty much wreck his poise. It might just give you edge enough not to lose in the first hand."

Not exactly a ringing vote of confidence, but it would have to do. "I'm listening."

"The game is called Santine. We play it with these."

Tesserian put a narrow wooden box with a horn handle on the table between them and opened it. Sam recognized it immediately: a gambler's kit, not all that much different from the one he carried himself. His own held a few decks of cards (a forty-four-card Italian deck that had belonged to his father, a well-worn fifty-two-card deck, and two more—one square and one subtly marked for a brace game—that were still wrapped in their factory paper), a couple pairs of dice, and a piece of green baize fabric printed with a layout for faro on one side and craps on the other.

Tesserian's kit . . . heck, Sam didn't even recognize half of what was in there. There were cards, yes, and dice, and baize. There were little ivory or bone rectangles, like dominoes or Chinese tiles. There were stacks of coins, although not ones that he had seen before. And there were other objects that were completely foreign to him.

Tesserian took a deck from the box and held it out.

The cards were old and thick, with a good snap and edges blunted by long years of fingers smoothing them down. The backs were printed with a pattern of overlapping red and gold circles that seemed to move if you looked at them without focusing. Sam turned the deck over and looked at the picture on the card: a young man in Roman armor, facing a stag with a tiny image of Jesus between its antlers. It had been a long time since he'd seen something like this, but he recognized it immediately.

"Saint Eustace," he murmured. He looked at the next card: a bearded man who wore a halo like a circle of lightning, with a signal house in the background. "Saint . . . Elmo, maybe?" He flipped through a few more. "They're *santini*. Prayer cards."

"In four suits, although in this game the suits are called reliquaries."

Sam shuffled until he saw the repeating symbols: thorns, chalices, silver coins, spears. "This reminds me so much of my father's old deck. Italian. It has suits of staves, cups, coins, and swords."

"Holy thorn, holy grail, silver piece, holy spear. Everything has its origin," Tesserian said, taking the deck and laying cards out in rows on the table. "In each reliquary—remember, that's a suit—you have your saints. They break down into two types." He pointed to a little red heart over the chest of Saint Elmo —"Red Martyrs"—and a white one over the chest of another Sam didn't recognize—"and White Martyrs. Then they divide further into sets: Hermits, Ascetics, Incorruptibles, Mystics, and Virgins." He pointed to tiny letters on their foreheads. "There's usually overlap within sets. There are subsets, too, which you have to recognize by other signs. Warrior Saints wear armor, Cephalophores carry their own heads, Stylites stand on pillars, Child Saints—well, they're pretty obvious. You've got your Holy Unmercenaries, your Thaumaturges, Hieromartyrs, Protomartyrs, and your Myrrhbearers. Those are harder to differentiate."

Sam blinked. It wasn't looking so much like his father's deck anymore.

"There are ruling groups that preside over the deck." Tesserian pointed to an assortment of cards with golden borders around the images. "The first batch is made up of the Aurean Saints. Then you have the Fourteen Nothelfers, the ones with the black borders, and the Four Holy Marshals, with purple."

"But Saint . . . who is this?"

"Blaise."

"He's got gold *and* black."

"Yeah, there's some overlap between the ruling groups, too. Then you have the ultimate trumps, which can be played for damage or for profit against any suit of relics: the Procurator, the Holy Mother, and the Devil's Advocate."

"My head is spinning."

"Wait until we get to the complicated part."

Sam dropped his forehead onto the table, mumbling apologies to whatever saint it was he'd just landed on.

"So then I should play . . ." Sam rifled through his hand for a card with a purple border. "A Holy Marshal, if I have one." He dropped Saint Anthony on the table.

"Well, he'll do, but you could take the trick with any saint that counteracts plague. If you've got a Nothelfer, you ought to use that and hang on to your Marshal. Unless you've got all four Marshals, because—"

"That would end the game. Right." They'd been sitting at the table for a good hour now. Sam's head was aching.

"Well, it wouldn't in this case, because I have the Devil's Advocate. You'd have to have the Procurator, too. Or the Holy Mother. Preferably both."

"Okay, okay." Sam stared down at the pile of *santini* on the table. "Look, this isn't coming together fast enough." *Not a very good Catholic*, Jin's voice taunted him silently. *Not a very good Catholic.* "Is there any way for me to understand this game without having to know everything about the saints? Patterns I could use that don't require me to . . . I don't know . . ."

"Memorize the hagiography?"

"I don't even know what that word means."

"History of the saints. You want pure strategy."

Exactly. "I want a way to *win*. If this is the game that can beat Walker, then I'll play it, but there has to be a way to win with cards rather than with saints. Cards I get. Saints, not so much."

Tesserian nodded slowly. "You need the Liar."

Sam frowned. "You haven't mentioned a card called the Liar."

"Haven't I?" Tesserian scratched his head, picked up the unplayed cards in the deck, and started riffling through them. "This one."

He tossed a card down on the table: a robed cleric with a lute over one shoulder and a quill and inkpot on the desk before him.

"The Liar allows you to play the cards to counter any hand, or end the game, if that's what you want to do, whether you have them or not."

"Whether you have them or not?"

"When you play the Liar, it works. In Santine, with the Liar, you can manipulate the cards any way you want."

Sam frowned at the card, then at Tesserian. "Is this how you worked that nonsense on me? All the spades, making the suits change in front of my eyes?" He snatched the card and turned it over, looking for some clue as to how what Tesserian was suggesting could possibly be true. "You had this, so you could—what? Change diamonds into spades?"

The sharper shook his head. "In *Santine* you can use the Liar this way. Every game has its own rules. You know that. Anyhow, I told you I didn't cheat when we played."

"Then how did you do it?" Sam sputtered, his frustration finally refusing to be contained. He flung the Liar back down on the table. "It doesn't make sense! I saw you do things that were impossible! I've been trying to figure it out, and it's driving me out of my mind. If you didn't cheat—"

"Kid," Tesserian interrupted, his voice almost gentle. "Listen, you're good. You know that, right?"

Sam paused, mid-rant, and looked at the man on the other side of the table. "What?"

"You're a good player. You're a good sharper. But you're —what?—sixteen?"

"Fifteen," Sam mumbled.

"Okay, you're fifteen. You have a lot of years and a lot of life to live. You don't get to know everything all at once. You're also you, and, not to sound puffed up around the gills, I'm me. I've been roaming a long time, and I've been playing even longer. There's a lot I can do that would make you question your eyes. That doesn't mean I'm not actually doing it." He neatened the edges of the deck, lining the cards up in a perfect stack. "Not a bad thing to keep in mind as you wander, Sam. This world's a strange place. You go around ignoring everything that doesn't seem to fit with your expectations, you could miss a lot that's well worth seeing."

This reminded Sam of Tesserian's words when he'd first told him about Walker. "You called me a roamer, earlier."

Tesserian tilted his head and looked at him closely. "I did, didn't I?" Sam nodded. "Well, I'm usually right about that kinda thing."

"What does it mean?"

"Can mean a lot of things. Different things for different folks. For Redgore it means cards and killing. For me it means cards and not-killing. And, evidently, teaching you Santine. For you . . ." He gave Sam another one of those appraising once-overs. "Hard to say. You're young yet. But you've got dust on the soles of your shoes, for sure. It's an expression," he added, when Sam actually started to look.

"Then . . . how can you tell that about me?" But even as he asked it, Sam felt something for just a moment: a fizzing at the back of his tongue, a brief taste of pine and cinnamon. He frowned, momentarily distracted. Tesserian watched closely, nodded.

"I don't know what it was you just remembered, but from the look on your face, it was something big."

It was there, and then it was gone. "Could drinking something be enough to make me a roamer?"

"What, you think you drink a potion, you grow small, you eat a cake, you grow tall? No, Alice, the real world isn't like that." Tesserian looked thoughtful for a moment. "Except when it is, obviously."

"Obviously? Who's Alice?" Sam shook his head to clear it. "Never mind. Let's get back to the game." Because right now, Santine was starting to seem almost logical compared to the rest of this conversation.

Tesserian clapped his hands. "Right. Look, here's the simplest way to understand it. Santine is a game about invoking saints, right? You a churchgoing fellow?"

"Not particularly."

"But you understand that people invoke saints when they need something. Think of it like this—you're invoking the saints to help you win against someone else who's doing the same thing. But saints—and I've known plenty—are unpredictable so-and-sos. So are the Santine cards. There are lots of ways to win by playing square in Santine—more ways than anyone knows, in fact. I could even tell you stories of players discovering new ways to win in the middle of a game. They say you just see a solution where there wasn't one before, and it works. It happens, but it's rare. Heck, I've never done it. Which is why it's best if we focus on the Liar."

"And the Liar can't fail, right?" All this talk about the unpredictability of the cards was beginning to make Sam nervous again. Not that he'd ever really stopped being nervous about this game.

"The Liar works in Santine because it enables the person holding it to reinvent the game. Just the way a lie works in the real world. Playing it ends the game the way a lie ends a discussion. There's nothing more to say after somebody tells an obvious lie and insists that everybody else believes it, is there?"

"Then I have to get the Liar," Sam murmured. "That's the only way."

Across the table, Tesserian smiled. "Well, then, you just might have to cheat."

Sam hated cheating. But he thought about Walker, and about Susannah and Con and Illy and all his friends, about the hundreds of thousands of people who could find themselves living in a hell on earth if he failed. Mostly, though, he thought about Jin.

He sighed and picked up the card and stared into the cleric's lined face. "Show me how."

"I feel that perhaps I haven't fully gotten across to you how much I dislike this plan," Walter Mapp grumbled as he paced across the parlor of the hotel suite.

"Could you stop pacing?" Mr. Burns asked. "You're putting the rest of us on edge."

Mapp glanced at Burns, then at Tom Guyot and Susannah. He stopped and leaned heavily against the wall. "I think this plan is a disaster," he said. "Just in case I didn't convey that clearly."

"If you have a better one, I wish you'd tell it," Susannah said coldly. "I don't like it, either. I don't like what it asks of Sam, and I *really* don't like what it asks of Jin. It goes entirely against my principles, this idea of using her as collateral in a bet."

"There has to be another way." Mapp looked across the room to where Tom sat staring at the pocket watch and the clip-edged coin that hung beside it on the fob. But Tom said nothing.

"I'm sure there is, but we haven't discovered it yet, and we don't really have time to wait," Mr. Burns pointed out. "The second Jin has the formula worked out, we are going to have to get her past those two creatures and into Liao's laboratory, no matter what it takes, with no wasting of time. She's going to need every minute we can win for her."

A rapid knocking sounded on the door. Burns strode across the room and peered out, then opened it for Ilana Ponzi to slip inside. "Sam's on his way up," she announced breathlessly. A moment later there was another knock, and Burns opened the door for Sam. He nodded a quick hello to the assembled group.

Walter Mapp tapped Tom on the shoulder. "Let's chat," he said quietly.

Tom sighed, got to his feet, and ambled after Mapp, away from where Sam was filling in Susannah and Mr. Burns on the events of his afternoon with Tesserian.

"This plan is a disaster," Mapp said again, his voice low. "You're thinking the same thing, I know you are."

"I surely am," Tom replied, "but I still maintain using my favor's a worse idea."

"A worse idea than Sam gambling with Walker? For Jin's *life*, and probably his own? And what Burns is suggesting she do if Sam actually wins? Do you have any idea how many ways this could go wrong, even if everything goes right? These are *children*."

Now Tom gave Mapp a disappointed look. "Now, Mr. Mapp, you're acting like you've done forgot that age doesn't always know better than youth. You've lived long enough to know different. Have a little faith. Also, it ain't up to us. *They* speak for the city now. These children are trying to do something great, and you and me, we got to let them have their time before we swoop in thinking we know better. Plus, you ought to recall, we don't have a single clue what will really happen if we use this." He slid the coin and watch back into his pocket. "Unless you want to tell me how perfect it went when you used yours, that is."

Mapp regarded him silently for a moment, then said, "No, I guess I wouldn't tell that story quite that way."

A third knock on the door interrupted their hushed discussion. This time it was Constantine. "You were right," he said to Burns. "There was a fellow in the atrium. Watched when Sam left the hotel, then he left for a bit and came back and waited until Sam returned. Then he took off again."

"So they know we're here," Mapp muttered.

"It doesn't change the plan," Burns said. "They're waiting for Jin, so they can use her to draw Liao and me out. Once she and Sam leave, they'll follow; that's when Mr. Mapp, you, and the rest head for the boat back at Norton's Point."

Susannah turned to Constantine, who was pouring himself a glass of water from a pitcher on the beverage cart. "You're certain you can manage the boat? If not, now's the time to say so. I don't like being sequestered back here while everyone else is doing the dangerous work, anyway."

"You may have to remind me which part hooks up to the horses." Constantine smiled at her over his glass. "Joking. I'm your man, Miss Asher."

"All right," Susannah said, sounding faintly disappointed.

Mr. Burns cleared his throat. "That's settled, then. Mike drives Jin out to join you all at Norton's Point as soon as she has what she needs from the supply tent, then comes back for Sam, assuming the game isn't finished yet. When it ends, he'll drive Sam to the bridge."

"And if Walker doesn't agree?" Mapp asked. "What if any one of the million things that could go wrong with this plan actually happen?"

Before anyone could answer, the bedroom door eased open. Jin stood there, the *Port-fire Book* in one hand and a sheet of paper covered in her cramped handwriting in the other.

"I have it," she said, eyes bright and uncertain and excited. "But we really have to hurry."

Once more a knock sounded on the door. Constantine opened it and Ambrose stood in the hall. He bowed with an exaggerated flourish. "I *heard* from a card-hustling little bird," he announced, "that you needed someone *respectable* to help in pulling off this spectacle of yours."

The lot beside the stables was quiet. There was no sign of the wild battle Sam and Jin had witnessed the night before; even the disordered gravel had been raked smooth.

The door to the wagon stood slightly ajar. Jin ran, feet crunching over the stones, and sprinted up the stairs with Sam a step behind. "Uncle?"

The wagon, of course, was empty. Jin left Sam standing at the top of the stairs and he watched her peek into each tent, one by one. "He's not here."

"We didn't come expecting we'd find him, Jin."

She nodded and slipped past him into the wagon again. Sam

stayed in the doorway, eyeing the lot. He could hear Jin opening doors and cabinets, packing things into her rucksack to take to the laboratory tent.

Where are you, Walker?

Jin emerged again, bumping him with the rucksack and startling him out of his thoughts. "Sorry," she whispered.

Her foot had just left the bottom step when Walker's unmistakable voice spoke out of nowhere. "Well, I really did think maybe this was going to turn out to be a waste of time, but it seems kids are just as stupid as they say."

Jin froze. Sam spun, looking around for the speaker and losing his footing in the process. He stumbled down the stairs and turned to find the gambler in his immaculate white linen suit crouched on the wagon's roof.

"I know what you're thinking," Walker said, leaning one elbow on his knee. "You're wondering how my suit looks so good after your little girlfriend's old man threw me around so very recently. The answer is, my will is stronger than the dirt's."

He straightened, towering over them. "And if I care that much about whether my trousers are pressed, you should be just a bit panicked about how far I might be willing to go to get something much more important. Like a proper cinefaction. Where's your uncle, girl? Where's Burns?"

Out of the corner of his eye, Sam saw Jin edging backwards. Walker must've spotted the movement, too. "Hold still right there, young lady," he snapped. "Bones!"

The bald man in his long felt coat appeared from around the back of the tent farthest from the wagon. Jin glanced from

Walker to the man called Bones, then at Sam. He nodded once, and she sprinted for Liao's laboratory.

Sam held his breath. *Please, please let us be right about the talismans* . . .

Walker snarled and launched himself off the roof and over Sam's head. Bones wasn't quite as quick, but he was on the move only a second later. Still, Jin made it through the door flap before either of them got close. Once she was inside, neither man made any effort to follow her.

Walker rounded on Sam. "Congratulations, kid. You just graduated from annoying to hostage. You hear that, girl? Come out," he snarled, "or I'll cut your boy here to ribbons."

"Wait." Sam put up a shaking hand. It was now or never. "I . . . I heard you gamble."

"You—what?" Walker stalked closer. "What are you playing at?"

"Never mind," Bones said warningly.

"I heard you're a proper gambler," Sam said, speaking fast. "I play cards. I'll play you for our lives."

"Walker," Bones said coldly. "We're here for a conflagra-tioneer. We don't have time for this."

"If you win, we surrender," Sam persisted.

Walker stared at Sam with red-rimmed eyes and put his hands in his pockets. "And if you win, you go free?"

"If we win . . ." Sam hesitated. He glanced at Walker's waistcoat. Attached to a gleaming watch fob was a little cylinder of punched tin. A tinderbox. "If we win, we go free, and I get *that*."

Walker looked where Sam was pointing and burst into grating laughter. "Why on earth would I agree to that? Do you have any idea what that is?"

Sam thought about lying, maybe saying he could pawn a watch fob for a month's boarding fees. But trying to lie to this man was folly. He would see through it in an instant.

"Yes," he admitted. "I know what it is. And you should agree to it because, if you win, not only will we surrender, but Jin will perform the cinefaction for you. We win, we go free and you fail. But if you win, you get what you want."

Walker glanced at the tent into which Jin had disappeared. "She can do it?"

Sam nodded. "She's a conflagrationeer, just like her uncle."

"You don't say." The gambler grinned. "Well, then."

"Walker," Bones said again, warningly.

"I heard you the first time," Walker snapped, his black eyes sizing Sam up. "What do you play?"

"Lots of things. Monte, stuss, a couple more interesting games I picked up back in the tenements." Sam spoke nonchalantly, trying to seem like maybe he was boasting and not wanting to sound like it.

"More interesting ones, huh?" The gambler's eyes glittered.

"Might know some you don't, actually."

A few feet away, Bones made an impatient noise. "I doubt it," he muttered.

Sam ignored him and held Walker's stare. It wasn't easy; he looked *murderous*. It was made worse because he was holding absolutely still. How did anyone mistake him for a human? Sam wondered. Walker's stillness was just as unnatural as everything else about him.

And then: "You're on," he snapped. Bones groaned.

Sam supposed he ought to feel relieved, but he didn't. "You agree to my terms?"

Walker chuckled. "Yes, I agree to your *terms*. I'll even let you choose the game."

Well, that took care of one technicality Sam hadn't quite figured out how to fix. "And is *he* going to abide by them?" He nodded at Bones.

Bones snorted and said nothing. "He'll abide by them," Walker said.

A heaviness settled over Sam's heart and gut. There was no going back now. "Then I suppose we're on."

The gambler unhooked the fob from his buttonhole and tossed it to Bones. "Choose the game," he said to Sam.

Sam took Alsae Tesserian's deck from his pocket and held it out. "What do you say to a few hands of Santine?"

Walker blinked, and for a moment the freckles on his face went just a fraction darker. It was subtle, but Sam figured the fact that he had any visible reaction at all meant Tesserian's strategy was working.

The gambler stared at the upturned face of Saint Philomena. "Well, well. That *is* a more interesting game." His black eyes flicked up at Sam. "You've been out on the road?"

Sam shook his head.

"Where'd you learn Santine, then?" He nodded at the cards in Sam's hand. "Where'd you get yourself a deck?"

Sam hesitated. He'd been so fixated on learning the game that it hadn't occurred to him to wonder how to answer this inevitable question.

Fortunately, someone else had that figured out. "I taught him." A grinning Al Tesserian leaned against the side of the wagon. "Kid's what you might call my protégé. He won that deck from me fair and square."

"Your *protégé? He won it from you?*" Walker looked from Sam to Tesserian and back. "Tesserian, where did you even *come* from? Didn't I leave you somewhere back in Missouri?"

"Wouldn't miss this," the sharper replied. "Feel like a proud father, I do. Got cigars and champagne ready and everything."

Walker said nothing, but Bones was beginning to look properly aggravated. "Really?" he asked his comrade. "We're really going to do this?"

"Find us a table," Walker said coolly. "This little pipsqueak wants a game."

TWENTY-THREE

Santine

INSIDE THE TENT, Jin ignored the throbbing in her feet from her dash to safety as she rifled through Uncle Liao's chest of supplies. If she'd had any doubts before about whether or not her uncle had been practicing some kind of alchemy, they were gone now. Because he'd always mentioned it in ways related to fireworking, Jin had never realized before just how much he really knew about *waidan*. How much, it turned out, *she* knew about it, because Mr. Burns had been right. When Liao spoke, Jin paid attention.

In the largest drawer she found lumps wrapped in silk with labels tied to them with string. She selected two just a bit bigger than her fist and set them aside. Then she started ransacking the smaller drawers, which were full of jars upon jars of chemicals and powders.

Some of them she used nearly every time she made fireworks: saltpeter, sulfur, and charcoal, which were the makings of black powder; iron filings and copper sulfate, black copper oxide and antimony, coarse-milled sugar and fine. In other drawers she discovered ingredients she had read about using for explosives, but had never tried: shavings of ivory, which were supposed to provide a certain shimmer but were too expensive to use in Fata Morgana's displays; orpiment, which was poisonous; and malachite.

When she'd found everything else on her list, she slipped from her wrist the jade bracelet that she had taken from the house in San Francisco. Carefully, she ran it against a grater taken from Uncle Liao's tool chest and collected the shavings in an empty jar. She went to the furnace, gave the coals a good stir with a poker, and added some sticks of pine. Then she crossed the tent and peeked through the flap to check on Sam.

He and Walker sat cross-legged on the ground on opposite sides of an empty crate with a deck of cards between them. Bones and the man she had helped Sam play the prank on loomed behind the two players like seconds in a duel.

Walker tapped the deck with his forefinger. Sam took the cards and began to shuffle.

Jin let the flap fall closed and turned back to the laboratory.

The first shuffle was the thing. Everything depended on whether Sam could pull it off without Walker seeing what he was up to.

"You have to do it on the first shuffle," Tesserian had said. "Nobody looks for anything untoward on the first shuffle. Just stands to reason, if you're going to brace before the deal, you shuffle square the first couple times so you put the mark at ease."

Sam split the deck and bent the halves into a neat bridge. The cards snapped down with a perfect flutter.

Out of the corner of his eye, Sam saw Tesserian smile. Walker saw it, too, and his glance flicked sideways to where the

He and Walker sat cross-legged on the ground on opposite sides
of an empty crate with a deck of cards between them.

sharper stood. In that instant, Sam palmed away the final card remaining in his right hand so that it popped neatly down the cuff of his shirt.

Heart pounding, he straightened the deck, split it again, and repeated the process, the whole time half-expecting Walker to call him out for the cheat. But the gambler said nothing, only watched the cards arcing down out of his palms. Sam slid the deck across to him. "Cut."

Sam shuffled a few more times. Then he dealt the first hand.

Inside the tent, Jin was busy going through jars of mud.

More than once she'd thought it was odd that her uncle spent so much time collecting mud and clay from the places they went, but formula after formula in the *Port-fire Book* had called for crucibles and tubes to be luted, meaning lined or sealed with particular sorts of mud. Of course, those muds had incomprehensible names like *the mud of the six-and-one*, *the mud of the mysterious-and-yellow*, *the mud of the pearly water*, and *the mud of the breathing Nile*.

Uncle Liao's jars all had labels, but none of them said anything like the names from the book, so once again Jin had to puzzle them out. She needed two kinds of mud for her recipe: for *the six-and-one* she settled on a jar of red clay because it was the only one that listed seven ingredients. For *the pearly water*, she had a flash of genius and picked one that held mud made from sand and crushed oyster shells.

She lined a pair of little golden cuplike crucibles from Liao's workbench with the oyster-shell mud and set them on a stand in the furnace. Then she emptied the powders she'd collected into a big stone mortar and started grinding them together.

Almost immediately, the compound began to throw off sparks.

She dropped the pestle and backed away. Rogue sparks were a constant danger with fireworks, which was why they were always in a panic about Mr. Burns's cigar habit. Jin had almost blown herself up the first time she had made black powder.

The sparks stopped, so abruptly that Jin wondered if what she'd seen was a trick of her eyes, maybe some renegade light from the furnace reflecting off the millions of grains in the mortar. She sniffed the air. There was a vague scent, something spicy, but not the smell of combustion. She sifted through the mixture with her fingers. Nothing. No heat, no more sparks. She picked up the stone pestle and started to grind again.

There was a gentle popping, and the sparks returned. Only this time it wasn't so much sparks as a sudden upwelling of fire.

Jin dropped the pestle again as the lapping flames engulfed her hand, but this time she didn't back away. The flames were deep blue, and while Jin recognized immediately that she was looking at fire, the motion of it was almost exactly like that of a water fountain pouring up out of the stone mortar.

"I don't believe it," she murmured, passing her hand through the blue flame fountain. It was warm, but not hot.

She picked up a feather, one of the big white ones Uncle Liao liked to mix his powders with, and dipped it experimentally into the fire. When she pulled it out, it was perfectly intact and unsinged.

She stared at the feather, then at the bizarre blue fountain. "Unbelievable."

Trying to ignore the strangeness of it, she returned to grinding the mixture, fire lapping up around her wrists all the while. When the grain felt right under the pestle, she picked up the feather again and stirred it. Slowly, the flames began to diminish. At last, only a thick silver-blue oil remained. Jin poured that into one of the mud-encrusted crucibles, then put the other one on top like a lid, sealed them with the red mud of the six-and-one, and placed it back in the furnace. Then, with one more quick glance outside at Sam, she started packing up her rucksack.

She had just finished tucking the last jar into the bag and had taken the crucibles from the furnace to cool when a thought occurred to her. She went back to Uncle Liao's workbench and rooted around until she found the red grease pencil and yellow paper he had used to make the talismanic water he'd given Sam to drink. Jin tore a sheet into neat pieces and drew a symbol on each one.

Jin tucked all but one of the yellow squares of paper into her pocket. The last she left on top of the furnace like an offering. "For Sam," she whispered as it blackened. Then she slipped out of the tent.

Outside on the crate, the saints were doing battle.

By the strange logic of Santine, Sam had defeated the black plague (remembering this time to use a Nothelfer rather than a Marshal), a deluge, and a plague of locusts. He'd lost a few of his cards to torture and apostasy. Walker had kept him pretty much on the defensive; about the only offense Sam had managed to accomplish was the difficult move of excommunicating one of the gambler's highest-ranking cards, the Devil's Advocate. That had gotten a reaction.

"Son of a—" Walker had flicked the now-useless Advocate away angrily. On his bony fingers, dark freckles began to stand out against the pale skin.

The card Sam had palmed off at the start of the game shifted against his elbow, reminding him that he could end it anytime he wanted. Just in case Walker didn't intend to uphold his promise, though, he wanted to keep it going long enough for Jin to get a good head start.

Which meant not losing in the meantime. Or making Walker too angry to continue.

"The girl's leaving," Bones said tonelessly from a few paces off. "I don't suppose we care, do we?"

"She's going to the bridge," Sam said, countering Walker's play of two Stylites (who stood balanced on pillars) with a pair of Cephalophores (who carried their own heads). "She has to be there no matter who wins. Let her go."

Bones turned away, muttering under his breath. Walker jabbed a finger at Sam's cards. "What the hell kind of play is that?"

Sam shrugged. "Figured they could throw their heads and knock the Stylites down." Sam had no idea whether this was a legal move, but as far as he could tell it followed Santine's logic.

"Damn," Walker snapped. "That is the most obnoxious play

I've ever witnessed." He turned to Tesserian. "Where did you find this kid?"

The sharper was bent double, laughing. "Warned you, didn't I?"

Sam looked up over Walker's shoulder just in time to see Jin wave as she disappeared around the corner of the hotel.

See you soon, he promised silently.

TWENTY-FOUR

The East River Pyrotechnic Scheme

THE DESCENDING SUN turned the arched granite from gray to red-gold. *Cinnabar,* Jin thought fleetingly as Constantine piloted the little boat carrying her, Walter Mapp, and Ambrose up to the stone landing at the base of the tower on the Brooklyn side. Pinned to their collars, each of the fellows wore a slip of yellow paper bearing a symbol in red that Jin had brought from the laboratory. She'd sent more yellow slips back with Mike, one each for all of the conspirators.

Jin's fingers sought out the clay-sealed sphere that held the half-finished *dan* inside it. The crucibles were still warm to the touch, as if they had been sitting in the sun rather than in the dark of Jin's rucksack. A feeling of rightness welled up over her, like the thrumming sensation that accompanied a rush of blood to the head.

Mapp tossed a line to a man who came over to see what the little boat with its strange crew was up to. "What's this about?" the workman demanded as he made the boat fast. He pointed skyward, at the wooden walkway that stretched far overhead. "Sightseers are only allowed on the footpath and the towers."

Constantine stood up on the gunwale and smiled at him. "Hey, Paul! You forget me already?"

The other man beamed. "Hey, Con! We heard you were laid up!" He grasped Constantine's hand and hauled him across onto the landing, then turned and called to someone out of sight on the wooden stair that zigzagged up the side of the tower. "Hey, guess who came to say hello! Con Liri's here!"

Constantine laughed as he helped tie the boat to a cleat set into the stone. "I'm not here to visit with you lot. I got work to do." In the boat, Ambrose stood, nearly knocking the little craft over in the process, and cleared his throat impatiently. Constantine did a pretty good job of looking chastened. "Er. Sorry—sir. Paul, be a gentleman, will you, and help these folks up with their gear? We got fireworks tonight."

"Fireworks, says who?" Paul squinted for a better look at Ambrose. "Not to be rude, sir. But we get lots of oddballs that—"

Ambrose moved up onto the gunwale and across onto the stone in two swift steps. Jin, who had been sitting next to the newspaperman and could smell the liquor on his breath, only barely managed to keep from grabbing his arm, so certain was she that he was going to slip and plunge sidelong between boat and stone and drown.

He didn't, though. He landed perfectly solidly, as if he hadn't already been drunk before they'd left the hotel (or seasick the whole, tame trip and dosing himself from his flask the entire way). Then he shoved his hands in his pockets, stared down his thin nose at the workman (which was a pretty good feat, since they were about the same height), and said, "Young man, my name is Frederick Schroeder. You may have heard of me."

The name didn't mean anything to Jin. They hadn't actually discussed any specific name for Ambrose to use; the plan had simply required him to look like a dandy and behave like a bureaucrat. But *this* name plainly meant something to the rest of them.

Constantine shot a frantic look at Walter Mapp. Mapp kept his face composed, but as he raised a hand to scratch under his hat, Jin heard him mutter something that sounded like a curse.

Paul's eyes bugged out for a moment, then they narrowed as he looked at Ambrose a bit more closely. "Sir?"

Ambrose submitted to the scrutiny with unflappable poise. Then the workman peered at Susannah's little sailboat, at Mapp —who tipped his hat back and made a salute—and Jin, who gave him a brief smile and hoped she didn't look as confused as she was.

"I know what you're thinking," Ambrose said shortly. "You're thinking my mustache is quite a bit more impressive in the flesh than it looks in the newspapers. You're also probably thinking I look younger. And you're quite right, and I thank you, but we're in a bit of a hurry here. These two"—gesturing at Jin and Mapp—"have fireworks to set up, and we're losing the light." Then he turned to Constantine. "Young man, you assured me there would be none of this nonsense."

"Newspapers?" Jin whispered to Mapp. "Who's Frederick Schroeder? What's going on?"

The pianist answered out of the side of his mouth, without looking away from Ambrose. "Believe it or not, that lunatic is claiming with a perfectly straight face to be the mayor of Brooklyn."

Jin kept her face carefully neutral. "Oh, no."

"Yup."

Meanwhile: "Fireworks?" the workman repeated incredulously. "What's this about fireworks?"

"Well . . . sir." Constantine shifted nervously. "Paul, listen, I told him—I told Mr. Schroeder we could keep this quiet. I didn't really think anybody'd even be here. Help me out."

Paul was still looking closely at Ambrose. "Seems odd that he'd—you'd—turn up like this, no warning, no entourage—"

"Young man," Ambrose interrupted, his voice dripping with condescension and impatience, "it couldn't possibly be any less your concern, but if it will make you feel better about lending your assistance, here are two of the reasons this matter is being handled so quietly. For one thing, your chief engineer and my office are not on the best of terms at the moment."

"Oh, nicely played," Mapp mumbled. "That was all over the papers. Maybe there's a method to his madness after all."

"For another," the impostor mayor continued, "the city of Brooklyn wishes to celebrate the progress of the cable work and demonstrate its faith in the steel being used, and it wishes to do so without the city of New York becoming involved." He looked to Constantine. "I suppose your friend here is from New York," he said sourly.

The workman straightened up with a disdainful look on his face. "No, sir. Born and raised in Brooklyn."

"Well, then, for God's sake, man, why on earth are we still talking? Assist us and we'll put New York to shame! What do you say?" Ambrose held out his hand. "Care to be deputized into the East River Pyrotechnic Scheme?"

Mapp nodded. "*Very* nicely played," he whispered to Jin.

Paul gave Ambrose one more close look. Then he grinned and shook his hand. "Yes, sir. It's an honor, sir."

"Excellent." He nodded at Jin and her crates of gear. "You may begin by helping this young artist with her paints."

"Right-o. You just tell us where you want them, miss."

Gratefully, Jin handed Paul the first of the boxes. "The top of the tower, please."

Constantine let out a breath he must've been holding for a good long time. "Thanks, Paul." He clapped the workman on the shoulder. "I'm going to ferry the mayor across to the other side now. Can you show Jin and Mr. Mapp here how to use the buggy? They're going to run the fireworks across the middle from either end."

Paul gave Jin an incredulous look. Then he shrugged. "Nothing to it, Con. Good to see you up and around, friend."

"Constantine." Jin grabbed his sleeve as he climbed back aboard the boat and steadied it so that she and Mapp could get out. "Are you clear on how to finish the letters you're taking to the other side?" She glanced up at the looming rock of the tower. "And are you okay to climb all the way up there?"

"You mean my leg?" He shrugged. "If it gives me any trouble, I'll go up the same way your boxes will." He pointed to where Paul and Mapp were busy loading the crates onto a wooden platform attached to a cable that disappeared overhead. "I'll look a bit like a sissy, but I figure this isn't the time to worry about that." He grinned. "After all, I'm the smith now. I've got a city to look out for."

When everything that needed to go to the top of the

Brooklyn tower had been unloaded, Constantine held the boat steady for Ambrose to board again. Then, with one last wave, they cast off and were headed for the New York tower.

"Just this way, folks," Paul called from the stair, which on closer inspection Jin realized wasn't a stair at all but a series of ladders. "The crates'll come up by lift, but it's a long hike for us. Rest when you need to, yell if you need help."

"No offense intended, Jin," Mapp grumbled from her side as he stared up at the ladders, "but I keep on waiting to like this plan, and it keeps on throwing things like *this* at me."

Sam had told Jin the towers were nearly three hundred feet tall, but until now, standing below one of them, she'd really had no idea what that actually meant. Now it looked as if she were about to ascend straight up a mountain.

The lift with the crates lurched and started upward. Jin and Mapp looked at it longingly as it rose out of reach. "Why didn't I just take that way up?" she mumbled. Oh, well. Too late now. She started climbing. Mapp followed a few rungs behind her.

Each ladder rose to the floor of a plank platform above, which allowed for a moment's rest as they crossed to where the next ladder waited to lead them up to the next level. Three flights up, Jin's legs and arms were already aching. Before she was halfway to the top she wanted to cry for the men who had to climb up and down several times a day, six days a week, and evidently, occasionally on Sundays, too.

Thinking of it that way made her not want to cry so much because of the agony in her feet.

"You all right back there?" Paul called down. Jin, taking what seemed like her hundredth break, waved from the platform where she sat. Brooklyn stretched out before her, gouged by the tower's massive shadow.

"Mr. Mapp? You still alive?" she shouted.

"Technically," came his voice from somewhere below.

Jin pounded on her thighs with her fists, stood, and started climbing again.

When she reached the top of the tower at last, she had only a moment of relief before the first gust of wind hit her, shoving her a full three feet backwards before she managed to recover. Someone grabbed her arm and dragged her away from the edge as another gust surged across.

"The winds keep up just about like this all the time," Paul warned. "Got to take care not to let them knock you about."

Jin nodded, already working out how she was going to have to adjust the rockets she planned to set off to compensate for the wild airflow.

The space at the top of the tower was roughly the size of a small city block. Despite what Paul had said about there not being much work going on because it was Sunday, there had to be about ten people up there — a couple workers, a few well-dressed men, and even a pair of women who must've been sightseers — all of them watching curiously to see why on earth there was suddenly a Chinese girl in their midst.

Stretching away in either direction from the tower floor, a wooden plank path with rope handrails crossed the granite surface. There were also the two downstream cables that were being made, the first of many that would suspend a roadway below someday: two ropes of steel that ran parallel to the footpath.

Beyond that, though, there was nothing. Just a sheer drop all the way down to the river.

Another blast of wind buffeted Jin. She clutched involuntarily at Paul's arm, and he patted her hand. "You'll get used to it. Wind's not as strong as it feels, once you know to expect it." He nodded back in the direction of the lift. "And here's your boxes. Where would you like them?"

"Near the southern cable." She peered across to the New York tower, but it was too far away to tell whether or not Constantine, whose task it was to fix the explosive lances to the letters for the message on the northern-facing cable, had made it to the top yet.

"Passing through, folks," Paul bellowed, making his way to the spot Jin had indicated with the first of her crates in his arms.

Walter Mapp appeared at her side. He took off his hat and wiped sweat from his forehead. "Next time I make a climb like that," he wheezed, "there'd better be angels waiting with a rare steak and a bottle of Armagnac." He took a few deep breaths, then began moving their supplies with Paul.

"The buggy," Jin began as she followed along behind them. "How does it work?"

"Take a look." Paul led her to where one of the cables trailed off the tower surface and into the central span across the river. From it hung a small wooden platform with a handrail around it. It was small, maybe ten feet by six feet.

"We use this to go across and clamp the strands together," Paul said. "It should work nicely for you. Plenty of space for your tools. You let yourself out with a rope."

Jin thought through the steps that needed to play out: she'd finish setting the explosive charges on the letters first; then hang them using the buggy, with Walter Mapp helping to pull her across to the New York tower, where hopefully Constantine would be ready with his letters. Then she would return the same way on the second cable, stringing the message as she went, and arrive back here to finish work on the *dan* and the other necessary components of the cinefaction.

Walter Mapp came to stand next to her as she looked at the buggy. "Well, that's not too bad," he said. "Looks pretty sturdy."

And it did. It looked big and very sturdy—until she looked past it at the cable spanning the incredibly vast distance between the towers. The New York side of the cable was all but invisible. And then there was the petrifying height of it; the river was hundreds of feet below.

Jin crouched for a moment, unable to stand as a sudden dizziness hit her.

"You all right?" Paul asked kindly.

She nodded, steeled herself, and stood back up. "I need some time to finish the fireworks. Do you think when I'm done you could help set us up in the buggy?"

"Just yell when you're ready."

"You need anything from me?" Mapp asked.

Jin shook her head. "Just quiet. I need to clear my mind."

As she began fixing the explosive lances on the letter frames, her thoughts turned to the cinefaction, the unfinished *dan* in her rucksack, and Uncle Liao.

Where are you, Uncle? I wish I could ask you so many things.

Lance after lance, letter after letter. Her breath fell into an easy rhythm with her hands and she let her mind wander, recalling snippets of pages she had read in the *Port-fire Book*.

Let the bellows be smooth and deep over the plane of the mysterious and the golden. Let the nine repetitions refine the work through nine revolutions and nine signs of fire.

She imagined writing about what she was doing right now in the unique code of the book. *Make one of five and one of three and one of eight and one from all. Line them with the slow fire and the fire that bursts.* She thought of the particular shade of green she had crafted for the illuminated words and smiled to herself.

Make the second fire so that it burns like a friend's eyes.

Back in Coney Island, the game went on. Sam was almost beginning to enjoy himself. Once he'd won the hand by having his saints throw their heads, he started to get ideas.

"Oh, come on, now," Walker protested when Sam played four saints that had bees in their portraits. There were a surprising number of those.

"Unless you've got five ministering saints to counter those, I just stung your Marshal to death," Sam said mildly. In a sense, Santine was turning out to be a bit like the rock, paper, scissors game.

"He's already dead," Walker grumbled. "He's a martyr. That's the point." But he flicked the Marshal off the table to join the Advocate he'd lost earlier. Sam breathed a sigh of relief. With one of the Marshals out of play, another of the avenues for Walker to win the game was now closed.

He glanced at the shadows stretching across the ground. The sun was going down. Surely Jin had reached the bridge tower by now.

Time to finish Walker off.

Bones, apparently, had had the same thought. He'd been prowling around the edge of the game for the past hour like a caged animal. Now he came to scowl down at them. "Walker," he growled, "time is getting short."

"Damn right," the gambler agreed. "I didn't want to have to do this to you, kid, but this game has lost its charm for me. When you start winning hands with bee stings, you have to be stopped." And he threw down five cards, one by one.

The second Sam saw the first of them, he dropped his hands to his sides, utterly dismayed. The play was called thirty pieces — it was something like a royal flush in poker, made up of saints from the suit of silver coins.

Walker slapped down the final card and looked at Sam with a barely concealed smirk on his face. "Only one counter for that, and I happen to know you don't have the Devil's Advocate, 'cause you excommunicated him." And, as if Sam had forgotten that, Walker pointed to the two cards lying face-down on the ground.

Sam raised his hands and looked at the cards he held. "Yeah. All I have are these." And he laid down *his* cards one by one: a motley assortment of fairly useless holies. "And, of course, I have these two." He was just about to play his last legitimate card and the Liar, which he'd shaken loose from his sleeve when he'd dropped his arms, when he saw it. Gregory, Nicholas, Anthony, Seraphim, Menas. All five of the cards he'd just played were what were called Thaumaturges. Wonder workers: saints who performed miracles.

I could even tell you stories of players discovering new ways to win in the middle of a game, Tesserian had said. *They say you just see a solution where there wasn't one before, and it works. It happens, but it's rare.*

Sam's heart pounded fast. The absurd idea that had just occurred to him, impossible though it seemed, lay perfectly within the logic of this game. If he was right, he could possibly — just possibly — beat Walker without cheating. It meant a huge leap of faith, though.

Sam put his two remaining cards face-down on the table. The top one was the Liar. He slid that one aside. Then he took the other card and turned it face-up onto the pile of Thaumaturges.

Walker's jaw dropped. Sam took a deep breath and looked down. Then his jaw dropped, too. He knew perfectly well what he'd held, and the last card should have been a minor saint painted with a unicorn. What lay on top of the Thaumaturges was the Devil's Advocate.

Sam let out the breath he'd been holding. Relief surged through him so hard he felt dizzy.

"No," Walker gasped. He reached down and flipped over the two cards he'd flicked off the table: a Marshal and a Nothelfer. No Devil's Advocate.

"This isn't possible," he protested, staring at the cards.

Sam shrugged and smiled. "It's a miracle." Except it wasn't. He'd figured out how to win. The cards had done their work, but only because Sam had seen what they could do.

The game was over. He had won.

Tesserian let out a cheer and clapped him on the back. "I believe you owe the boy his winnings."

Walker got to his feet, freckles darkening on his skin, and held out his hand to Bones.

"Walker," Bones said, menacingly.

Walker snapped his fingers. Bones rolled his oyster-shell eyes and put the punched-tin tinderbox into the gambler's hand. He tossed it to Sam. "I suggest you get to moving."

Sam caught the little tinderbox in shaking hands. It was cool to the touch, but through the punches in the tin he could just make out a rosy glow.

Then he registered what Walker had said. "What?"

"I *said*, I suggest you get to *moving*." He dusted off his suit trousers and rebuttoned his jacket. "We'll give you a half-hour head start."

"*What?*"

"You won the game," Walker said through bared teeth, "and for that I'm giving you what we agreed upon. If you had dared to try and win with that"—he turned over Sam's last card, the unused Liar—"I would have killed you right then."

The gambler's fingers curled around the edges of the crate, as if he was forcing himself not to tear out Sam's throat that very minute. "But you didn't, so I'm going to give you what you won, *and* a little time." There was a soft creak of protest from the wood. "But that's all."

Sam swallowed hard. So he had known all along.

Walker smiled a horrible, angry smile. "Of course I knew, you little rat. I saw your clumsy palm-off. I was just arrogant enough to think I could beat you anyway. And for that, I'm coming after you, and I'm going to rip you to pieces before that girl's eyes. I'd get moving if I were you."

Bones took his watch from his pocket and glanced at it. "Twenty-nine minutes left."

Sam ran.

Far above, in the hotel, Susannah Asher, Tom Guyot, Ilana Ponzi, and Mr. Burns clustered around a window. They watched Sam spring up, knocking over the crate and scattering cards everywhere, and leap into a full-bore sprint away from Walker, Bones, and a third man they didn't know.

"I hope Mike's ready." Susannah sighed. "I still don't feel right about not being there. At the bridge, I mean. I don't feel right about just . . . just sending people off like this and waiting around in safety, hoping they don't get themselves killed."

Mr. Burns smiled at her. "That's what you're supposed to feel when you order people into battle. It's to your credit that it doesn't sit quite right in your heart."

She dropped onto one of the couches and let her head fall into her hands. Ilana came to sit beside her. "Can I do anything for you, Susannah?"

"Will your mama be worrying about where you are right now?" Susannah asked, words muffled by her palms.

"No. I told her I was helping a friend catch up on her sewing and that I thought I'd stay the night." She put her arm tentatively around the other girl's waist. "I'd like to wait with you, if that's all right. I don't want to be anywhere else, alone and wondering what's happening."

Susannah nodded. "I wish we could see Jin's fireworks."

Across the room, Tom watched the two girls with a sad expression on his face. He slipped a hand into his pocket and felt for the coin on his watch fob. Then he sat, picked up his guitar, and began to play.

TWENTY-FIVE

The Message

U P ON THE Brooklyn tower, Jin watched Paul hand the crates of letters and a huge coil of fuse to Walter Mapp, who stood in the buggy. She tried not to notice the way it swayed as they moved.

"All set when you are," Paul said.

Jin looked at Walter Mapp's outstretched hand and swallowed. She gave the contraption one last look and forced herself not to dwell on the fact that this little platform with its thin railing was going to be all that stood between her and a deadly plunge into the river.

"You'll do just fine," Mapp said. "It looks awful, but it wasn't so bad climbing in."

She nodded numbly. Her arm felt leaden, but she forced herself to reach for Mapp's hand and climb over the railing.

Her legs were shaking, bodily terror mingling with the quaking of muscles that were still exhausted from climbing the endless ladders half an hour before. The buggy swayed sickeningly. She was swinging free over the water. It felt like her heart was trying to break out of her chest.

"Better open your eyes, Jin," Mapp said. She hadn't realized they were closed.

Paul leaned down and put his hand on a rope that ran parallel and underneath the steel cable the buggy hung from. "This is how you move: haul on this rope. Just that simple. It moves when you pull, and stops when you stop. Understand?"

She nodded. "Crystal clear," Mapp said.

Paul looked at Jin dubiously. "You ready for me to cast you off?"

She nodded again before she had a chance to give in to every instinct and beg for him to pull her out again. There was another horrifying back-and-forth sway as Paul undid the moorings that held them close in to the tower. Then she and Walter Mapp were alone.

"You ready for this, kiddo?" Mapp's growly voice asked. Jin nodded again. He chuckled. "I'll know you're telling the truth when you keep your eyes open and let go of me."

She took a few long, deep breaths, willing herself to be able to feel her hands and feet again, willing her heart to slow its panicked beating, willing the buggy to stop moving so she could think about something other than the river below. Bit by tiny bit, she started to calm down. She opened her eyes and made herself let go of Mapp's hand, one numb finger at a time.

"All right," she whispered. "All right." She spoke louder the second time, and hearing her own voice—which sounded much more confident than she actually felt—brought a bit more clarity to her mind.

She took the giant coil of fuse and hung it crosswise over her neck and shoulder. While Paul and Mapp had been stowing the crates, Jin had tied one end of it to an iron ring set in the granite of the tower; what remained was, hopefully, enough to stretch all the way across the bridge, and it was *heavy*. Jin unspooled a few lengths, then took a deep breath.

"Ready now, Jin?"

"Yes." Then she and Walter Mapp grasped the rope under the cable and hauled on it together. The buggy moved jerkily away from the tower, and little by little the slack in the fuse disappeared. Jin focused all her attention on this; watching it slowly grow taut as she pulled the rope kept her mind off where she was, the wind that repeatedly shoved them, the water so far below.

When the slack was just about gone and the loops she'd played out had turned into a nearly straight line, she came to a red spot on the white fuse, the first of the guide marks that Constantine, who knew the dimensions of the center span like the inside of his own palm, had made to show Jin where to put the letters.

"Please let his measurements be right," she whispered. Her words were lost in the wind over the river.

Mapp took the first frame carefully from the crate and handed it to her. It already had a hook and a bit of cord at the top, and with only a short, terror-inducing stretch—Mapp held on to her waist, but it was small comfort—she was able to hook it on the cable with quivering fingers and knot the cord to secure it. Ilana had left both ends of the fuse dangling a few inches past the bottom of the frame; Jin took the ends and knotted them around the long fuse she wore coiled over her shoulder. Then she stood back and looked at what she'd done. The letter now dangled from the cable, just behind the buggy. The long fuse Jin had been playing out behind her, the one that was attached to the ring back on the tower, hung below the letter, connected to it by the two short ends.

"One down," Jin murmured. She unspooled a few more lengths of fuse, took another deep, calming breath, and then she and Mapp began hauling the buggy down the cable to the next stop.

Letter by letter they made their way across the central span. It never got any easier to look down, and the constant buffeting of the wind threatened several times to make her nauseated with motion sickness. But at last she got the final letter into place. The fuse now ran the length of the span behind her, hanging below each letter and connecting one to the next. Together they pulled themselves hand over hand the rest of the way across to the New York tower.

"You made it!" Constantine shouted, waving like a maniac. Next to him Ambrose—Mr. Mayor, she reminded herself— stood looking pleased and proud.

Constantine and another workman reached out with poles tipped with hooks to catch the buggy's handrails. Jin dropped her aching arms and leaned into Mapp's shoulder while they were hauled in close to the granite wall.

Large hands reached out, grasped her arms, and lifted her over the railing, and her feet were, blessedly, on solid stone again. Ambrose began to clap his hands, and a group of scattered sightseers and workmen, maybe four or five altogether, joined in the applause. She managed to stay on her feet long enough for a weak smile while she made certain she was a safe distance from the edge. Then she dropped unceremoniously to sit cross-legged on the granite.

Her entire body shook. Her legs still ached from the climb, her arms burned from hauling that cursed rope, her chest hurt for no reason she could figure out, and the idea of getting into the buggy on the other cable and hauling it all the way back made her want to vomit.

Constantine crouched beside her and rubbed her back. "You did brilliantly," he told her. "We're all so proud. Wish Sam and Susannah could've been here to see." Jin leaned her head against his arm and took deep breaths.

Let the bellows be smooth and deep. Little by little, she started to feel under control again.

The sun was low over the rooftops of New York. Jin fumbled a knife from her pocket and cut the fuse she'd been playing out. "Can you find a place to secure this?" The plan was that she would light the south-facing fuse and Constantine would light the other, but this way they each had access to the end of both, just in case. Jin had learned from long experience that it was always better to have a backup plan.

She sucked in two more breaths and stood up. Her legs quivered, and the wind was just as brutal as before, but she managed to make it across the tower without falling to where the other buggy waited. "Are your frames ready, Constantine?"

He nodded. "All set, along with the coil of fuse. Are you ready to go back out there, or do you need to rest?"

"I think if I rest I'll remember how scary it is. Right now I'm too tired to think about it."

Constantine nodded again, unspooled a few loops from the coil, and held on to the end. "I'll find a place to secure this one, too. Mr. Mapp, she's ready," he called.

While Walter Mapp climbed in, one of the workmen, older than the rest, held out his hand to Jin. "Watching you out there made me wish to be young again," he said with a sad smile. "I'll always be proud to be able to say I worked on this bridge, but I wish I had the nerves to do what you just did. You'll have that memory your whole life, young lady." He turned to Ambrose, who stood nearby looking like he wished it were appropriate for the mayor of Brooklyn to hug a Chinese fireworker girl. "I think we were all wondering why on earth you bothered coming up, Mr. Mayor," the old workman said, "but you were right. That was a sight to see."

Jin managed an exhausted smile. "Just for you, sir, I'll try and look down at least once this time." She gave Ambrose a tired wink.

She made sure there was enough play in the fuse, took a few calming breaths, and reached for Mapp's hands.

The second climb in was no better than the first, but before she could worry much about it, Constantine released the buggy, and they were out in midair again.

"See anyone?" Sam called.

Mike swiveled to peer over the roof of the runabout. "Not yet."

They were barreling through the little towns between Gravesend and Brooklyn as fast as Mike's bay horses would go. Sam's half-hour start was long up. All he could do now was hope they could get to the Brooklyn anchorage of the bridge with enough time for him to get across the footpath to the tower and reach Jin before Walker and Bones showed up.

He stared at the tinderbox cradled in his palms. Such a small thing to carry so much power. He thought back to what Walter Mapp had said this past Thursday, which seemed like a lifetime ago: *Nothing feels like something till after everything's over.*

At the front of the carriage, Mike turned again. This time he flinched. "Someone's back there."

Sam leaned out the side. They were passing through open farmland now in the falling dark. He could see a light behind them, maybe a mile off.

"How far to go?" he called.

Mike's shoulders rose and fell. "Another hour, maybe? If the horses can keep this pace, which I doubt."

Sam stared down at the tinderbox. Such a small thing.

By the time Jin hauled herself, arms weak as jelly, close enough for Paul to catch the buggy with his hook and reel it in, the sky was beginning to darken.

"I am impressed," Paul said warmly as he pulled her out and set her on firm footing again. "I've seen grown men panic, get themselves stuck midway, refuse to go in the first place. Well done, the both of you."

Jin had the end of the fuse clamped between her teeth. As soon as she was free of the buggy, she tied it off and spat several times to clear the taste of the chemical primer from her mouth. Then she sat, hard, and dropped her head to her knees.

Mapp handed her his flask. "Go on, take a nip. It's just water. You can finish it if you like."

Jin drank gratefully and stretched her limbs, willing some feeling to come back to her arms and the weakness to leave her legs. The fanfare fireworks waited in their crate, ready to go. They would take only a few minutes to set up. Now it was time to finish the *dan*, the piece that would turn Jin's display into a cinefaction, and, hopefully, save Brooklyn, New York, and everyone in them from Walker, Bones, and the demonic creature called Jack.

⇒ TWENTY-SIX ⇐

Fangshi

MAKE THE *fire of blue and red, bitter and sweet, sharp and soft.*

Jin took the tin pan from her rucksack and weighted it down against the wind with a chunk of apricot-colored realgar crystal and a lump of the salmon-colored rosin called Greek pitch that she'd taken from Uncle Liao's storage chest. Both caught the final light of sunset in their dull, glassy hearts and seemed to glow.

Next she took two lengths of red silk and Tycho McNulty's little blue-glass jar from the bag. "Mr. Mapp." The pianist had been prowling a few yards away, looking nervous. "Put this over your face. Be sure to cover your nose and mouth. Then you've got to stay over there. This fire isn't going to smell particularly wholesome." Burning that much realgar was going to release some fairly noxious fumes. The piny rosin might sweeten the odor, but it wasn't going to make the smoke any less poisonous.

Jin dipped her finger in the jar and smeared the lemony-peppermint-coffee-smelling ointment across her eyelids and over her lips, then tied the second piece of silk around her nose and mouth.

She checked to make sure the few remaining workmen were keeping a safe distance, took out her lighter, and lit the contents of the pan. The fire flared to life: the sulfurous realgar tingeing the flames on one side blue and the Greek pitch coloring the rest a bronze-red. She took the little golden sphere that held the oil from the fountain of fire she'd made in the laboratory and set it carefully at the center of the flames. Then she turned to the crate that held the rockets for the fanfare.

"Can I help with anything?" Mapp offered.

"Not with this fire going. And stay back. With all this wind, I'm not sure if anyplace on this tower is far enough from it to be safe."

Jin hadn't been sure initially what the *dan* she was compounding would turn out to be. She'd had no idea what kind of firework she should be planning to plug the thing into, but it was clear that it was going to be a component of an explosive. It had to be—if only because Jin was the one making it. She knew how to do one thing well, and this was it.

The second she'd had that thought, she knew what kind of firework she was going to make. Whatever it might've turned into in anyone else's hands, this was Jin's device, which meant it could only take one form: the form she loved best, the same form she had drawn on the yellow paper to give to her friends as a talisman and which they all now wore on their collars.

She had brought along workings to build the most beautiful catherine wheel she'd ever made. *What a shame I can't make it bigger*, Jin thought as she took a much-abused bicycle wheel, a stake, and a collapsible wooden stand from the crate.

She'd lingered over colors when she'd selected the cases for the wheel. Should she use green, like Sam's eyes? Green was one of the hardest tones to do well, but Jin was a master with color. Her own favorites, crimson and gold, the colors that had saved her from the hell of her childhood and had given her her name? Or sugar blue and silvery gray, for the sky above and the river below and the clean new granite that would anchor this great new crossroads?

In the end, she'd chosen them all. She began to wire the cases to the wheel: blue at the outside edge, then the silver of the stone that rose out of the water, then Sam's green, beside the stone in honor of the father it had taken from him. Then Jin's warm gold, and last of all, at the very center, the red of the cinnabar heart Uncle Liao said would never lead her astray.

She kept an eye on the sphere in the fire as she worked, and every now and then she paused to turn it over with a pair of tongs.

At last, the setting sun disappeared. Across the water, a tiny light flickered to life: Constantine's lantern, at the top of the New York tower. Jin turned back toward the deeps of Brooklyn. *Sam, I hope you're okay out there.*

When the sun was gone, Jin took the sphere made from the two crucibles out of the fire. Once they were cool enough to handle, she broke the clay seal that held them together and pried the two halves apart with her fingernail. The silver-blue oil inside had turned a deep crimson.

She tucked a packet of gunpowder and a fuse between the two hemispheres, closed the halves again with the last of the red clay mud, and the *dan* in its crucibles became an explosive mortar. Jin wired it at the center of the bicycle wheel. It looked oddly out of place, a mud-and-clay grenade surrounded by her perfectly rolled paper explosive cases.

"Done," she said into the wind. Cold sweat prickled on her forehead; she wiped it away and felt a momentary burn. Glancing at her fingers, she saw that they were tipped with red from the crimson oil.

She rubbed them clean on the stone beneath her feet, stood, and went to sit with Walter Mapp next to the footpath. Nothing to do now but wait for full dark, and Sam, and Jack's infernal coal.

By the time they reached the turn onto Front Street, the carriage behind them was close enough for Sam to see Overcaste in the driver's seat. Mike reined the horses just enough to make the turn, nearly running down a pair of men staggering out of a saloon, and whipped them into a frenzy for the last sprint to the anchorage, the place where the bridge met the road in Brooklyn.

"Get ready to jump out," Mike called back. "I'll keep on and if we're lucky they'll follow me."

"Right." But they weren't going to be lucky. Sam already knew that. He was just going to have to be faster than his pursuers.

The granite bulk of the anchorage came into view, a big stone box topped with bony structures like skeletal limbs: cranes and ladders and the great spinning engines for the massive suspension cables. Sam, having made sure the tinderbox was safely buttoned into his pocket, crouched on the running board of the coach until he spotted the scaffolding that held the ladders up to the top.

He leaped to the pavement, sprawled, righted himself, and sprang for the lowermost ladder. Behind him he could hear the sounds of shouting, of hooves striking stone. Walker and Bones were coming.

Jin was beginning to feel a little strange.

It was probably the effects of the realgar. It had been burning for a good while now and the unpredictable gusts refused to blow in one direction so that she could stay upwind of the fire. Though the bitter, sulfurous stink was mostly covered by the evergreen-sap scent of the pitch and the cinnamon aroma of the burning salts she used for her bonfire and by McNulty's wonderful ointment, and though she'd left the red mask in place over her nose and mouth, she knew she was breathing far too much of it.

It had to be the realgar, but Jin had begun to see things.

It started as soon as the sun was gone and the stars began to show in the pale oncoming dark. The last of the workmen and sightseers had finally gone, leaving Jin and Mapp alone on the tower. She had been setting the fireworks for the opening fanfare, the long burst of explosions that were meant to call the attention of the people of New York and Brooklyn to the bridge towers so that they could read the message she had written so painstakingly across the central span: STAND WITH THE PILLARS OF THE CITY AGAINST JACK HELLCOAL. She'd set some of the fanfare rockets facing north and some facing south, but she wanted them as vertical as possible.

She'd paused in her work, straightened, and stretched, arching her back and turning her face skyward. And the sky . . . the sky was *spinning*.

She spoke to Walter Mapp without taking her eyes away from it. "Do you see that?"

Hundreds, *thousands* of pale arcs of light shot from east to west and then froze, bright points trailed by tapering tails. A hundred thousand comets caught in the night like insects in amber — only they weren't comets.

With difficulty, Jin found the streaked shape of the constellation her uncle called the Northern Bushel and Mr. Burns called the Big Dipper. The points of its handle looked like smeared spots of ink. There were other familiar shapes up there, constellations she knew from long nights in the great open spaces of the middle country. It was as if the stars had leaped into place before her very eyes, and she could somehow make out the traces of their flight.

Jin realized Mapp hadn't answered, and glanced at the pianist. He sat staring northward up the river, his hat tilted over his forehead, as if he hadn't heard a word she'd said.

She rubbed her eyes. The wind gusted. Slowly the streaks faded, rubbed from her tired vision or swept clean by the wind, leaving the star-spattered sky in its proper place.

The gusts spun around her, glittering. Lights sparked and died at the corners of her sight. She had rubbed her eyes so hard she was now seeing flashes. Or the wind had knocked over a jar of something — sugar, salt, oyster shells, she wasn't sure — and the particles were blowing about and catching the light of the fire. Or there really *was* stardust up there, and now it was blowing around her like a tornado.

Mapp sat with his back to her, still as a statue.

Then, out of the corner of her eye, Jin thought she saw a

face in the shimmer. She turned her head. It disappeared. Then she caught another shape on the other side. It, too, vanished when she looked.

The wind kicked up harder, and this time, Jin heard it whisper a word.

"What?" The sound of her own voice startled her. She hadn't realized she'd spoken out loud.

The rushing of the wind continued to rise, and the word came again. She heard it, and then she heard its echo, a metallic vibration from the giant cables that stretched away toward the banks of the East River.

Fangshi.

And then it was gone, and the air was still and the great cables silent. Jin stood alone, surrounded by rockets. She looked down at her feet, bent to touch the residue of gray glitter on the stone, rubbed it between her fingers.

Oyster shell, ground fine as flour. She looked over her shoulder just in time to see the empty jar roll into a groove between two granite blocks.

"Mr. Mapp?"

He turned immediately. "Yes?"

I am going out of my mind.

That, or she was experiencing the first stages of arsenic poisoning from the realgar. In either case, there was nothing to do about it now.

Make the bellows deep and smooth. "Never mind."

"Do you need something?" Walter Mapp got creakily to his feet. "Is there something I can do?"

"No." Jin shook her head and turned back to the rockets,

and her deep breathing and the comforting familiarity of the task began to make her feel better. Time to bring the city to attention and paint the sky.

She grinned to herself. Time to blow things up.

First came the whistle, the hissing of the rocket as it speared heavenward. Then came the blossom of blinding brightness in the sky, the sudden gorgeous explosion of fire, and the downpour of sizzling color. Last of all, the bang—sound is slow to travel, a tortoise to the hare that is light.

Jin's fanfare poured out into the night, two seconds of whistle and hiss and trailing smoke before the wild frenzy of light began. The whistles could be heard for another few seconds, then the bangs started. And all the while, an insanity of color overhead like flowers, like falling water, like the world made incendiary, like the end of time.

And then it was over. Across the span, on the New York tower, Constantine's lantern blinked four times. Jin lit a lantern and waved it back. Then, more than a thousand feet apart, the two of them lit their fuses.

Sam paused on the footpath as the fireworks burst overhead. They brought immediately to mind a bouquet of flowers that had stood in Mrs. Ponzi's parlor for a while, a massive bewilderment of blossoms so dense it threatened to overflow its vase. Then, as the confusion of fizzing fountains of sparks continued, he realized it didn't look like flowers at all. It looked . . . *martial* somehow. Warlike. As if it were the opening salvo from otherworldly cannons, laying siege to the sky.

Then it was over, and before he even thought about it, Sam gave a triumphant yell, waving both fists over his head. "Yeah, yeah, *yeah!*"

He heard other shouts from the city behind him, carrying through the sudden quiet in the wake of the explosions. Brooklyn was coming to its windows. On the other side of the river, New York, no doubt, was doing the same.

It took everything in him not to sprint, but the gaps between the wooden slats in the footpath were too wide. One toe caught, and Sam was pretty sure he'd be sprawled out and falling over the side before he knew what was happening.

He'd just reached the midpoint of the slope up to the Brooklyn tower when he heard the noises. From ahead, the long snap and pop of the lances catching fire as Jin's message came to life:

STAND WITH THE PILLARS OF THE CITY AGAINST JACK HELLCOAL

Then he heard the second sound, from somewhere at his back: a snarl of fury that was only barely distinguishable as words.

"You. Can. Stop. *Right. There.*"

Sam turned. Two figures stood at the entrance to the footpath on the anchorage: two man-sized figures, one in a long, flapping coat and one that seemed, before Sam's very eyes, to grow somehow too large for the path. He was too far away to be seen in any kind of detail, but the memory of his two rows of teeth, of his face, whip-marked by the scarlet welts, and of his red-rimmed black eyes was fresh in Sam's mind.

Walker. And Bones, right behind him.

He backed away instinctively, and his heel caught between

two boards. He stumbled, felt his body go numb with the sensation of falling, grabbed at the rope handrails, and caught his
balance. Then he forced himself to turn his back on the horrible
thing stalking up behind him and got moving again.

*Don't look back. Don't look back. If you look back you'll fall.
Don't run. If you run you'll fall. Don't look back and don't run.*

The silver-green explosions raced across the span and ignited
the letters that hung from it until each one gleamed through the
drifting smoke that was all that remained of Jin's fanfare. If
he'd been able to stop, Sam thought that from where he stood he
might just have been able to make out the south-facing message,
to read it for himself. But there was no time to pause.

Don't look back and don't run.

The ground fell away below him, then gave way to dark
water as the footpath rose sharply up to the tower. The planks
under his feet vibrated, out of rhythm with his own steps. Sam
hazarded a glance behind him at the looming figure of Walker
striding with long-limbed steps up the path with Bones following. He turned back and stumbled again as he tried to increase
his speed.

He cursed quietly to himself and kept moving.

At the top of the Brooklyn tower, Jin and Walter Mapp
stood silhouetted by a fire that burned with lapping blue and
red flames. Sam stumbled the last few yards, desperate to move
faster, faster, faster, until he was on solid footing. Mapp caught
him as he burst onto the tower and turned to stare back the way
he had come.

Walker and Bones had reached the midpoint of the footpath.

"They're on their way," Sam managed breathlessly. He ducked under the rope of the footpath and turned to Jin and just about jumped out of his skin.

"Oh, sorry," she said indistinctly, and pulled away the red silk mask that covered her mouth and nose. As if that was the strange part.

Her face was ghostly. Her eyelids shone with a slick of some red-gold substance; the same color stained her lips. Across her forehead was a mark that looked something like a stroke from a paintbrush and something like a burn. He'd thought at first that her black hair had gone gray, but then he realized her face was dusted with the same silvery residue.

And yet that wasn't the oddest thing. Under the dust and the markings, her face *shone*. It wasn't the radiance of joy or exertion—it was more like an actual glow, a real illumination coming off her pores like sweat.

She smiled awkwardly. "You're staring."

"You're glowing," he said helplessly.

Mapp's voice at his side brought him back sharply. "Sam."

He fumbled in his pocket for the punched-tin cylinder hanging from its fob and held it out. "You know what to do?"

Jin took the tinderbox. Dim rosy light escaped the perforations. "It should burn, but it's nice and cool," she said wonderingly. "Weird."

Sam followed her to the bicycle wheel, its stake held upright on the granite by a makeshift wooden stand. A catherine wheel. Of course. "Something beautiful out of something fearsome," he said softly.

"I don't know," came Walker's drawl from the footpath. "Maybe my idea of something beautiful just involves a bit more blood than yours."

Sam spun around. The gambler leaned nonchalantly on the handrail; Bones's felt-coated frame filled the walkway behind him.

Mapp stepped between Sam and Walker. "Stay back," he snapped.

"Or what?" Walker demanded. "Or how about this? Or *nothing*. Who the hell are you?" He gave Mapp a searching glare. Then he shook his head in disgust. "Damned headcutters, always sticking their noses in places they don't belong."

"Light it," Sam shouted over his shoulder. Jin fumbled the tin case open. Sam heard her gasp. "What?"

"That's right, kid." Walker grinned. "You didn't think it was going to be that simple, did you? You think it just works as easy as that? How big an idiot did you really take me for?"

"Sam, it's—" Jin shook the contents of the cylinder out onto her palm. "It's just cold coal. I don't know where the glow is coming from, but this won't light a fuse!"

"Give it back," Walker said icily. "Give it back now and do as I tell you, and when this is all over, I'll let you live."

"No," Sam protested. "I won, I beat you square. I beat you getting here. I beat you *twice!*"

"Yes, and by the way, I didn't like that."

"You agreed to the stakes!"

"And I played by them, kid, but that was then and now is something different." Walker put up a warning finger. "And if I hear you tell me that's not fair, I'm going to be very, very disappointed in you, Sam."

Sam, who had been about to say that very thing, shut his mouth. "Play me again."

"No." Walker straightened and took a step forward. "I'm done playing. We all have to take our place in this world eventually and do the jobs we're set to. Mine is to see this thing done. Hand over the coal."

TWENTY-SEVEN

The Cinefaction

BESIDE THE UNLIT catherine wheel, Jin only half-listened to the exchange. The unearthly cold piece of coal sat in her palm. It glowed, and logic told her it should've been seething hot, but it wasn't.

A soft gust of air slid past her cheek, gentle as someone tapping her shoulder to get her attention.

Fangshi.

She didn't hear the word so much as she felt it, in the marks on her face, in the fine powder across her skin and hair, in the smudges and burns on her hands.

A conflagrationeer would know what to do.

I should know what to do.

"I said, *hand over the coal!*" Walker's snarl brought her back to the moment. She looked up and gasped. Sam and Mapp stood between her and the gambler, both shouting at him to leave her alone, ordering him to stay back, hurling threats Jin knew they had no way of making good on.

And Walker stood like a giant over them.

It was just as it had been behind the hotel. Walker was suddenly huge. Gargantuan. His face was a map of pain lines radiating from the jagged patterns of black stippling that covered his nose and cheeks. His skin was bone-pale, and his hands were all knuckle and vein as they flexed into angry curls at his side.

The wind shoved at her, insistent. *Fangshi!*

"I'm not," she whimpered. "I don't know what to do!"

In her hand the coal was like a chunk of ice, burning her skin with cold. She clasped it tighter, somehow sensing that it wanted her to let go.

To her left, the silver-green letters strung across the span sputtered and began to burn out. Any time now, Constantine and Ambrose would start across the footpath, making their way over to meet up with Jin and Sam and Mapp, and Walker and Bones would have themselves five hostages, two of whom were now new pillars of the city. As if they needed any more, when they had Jin.

The last of the letters guttered and died. In that moment, the sky reeled again.

The sensation was like vertigo. The constellations overhead sliced westward like clusters of falling stars, so fast the entire world seemed to be dropping to the east. The noise of Walker and Sam shouting at each other muted, as if Jin were hearing them through a wall.

From the north, a wave of low-lying clouds poured in over the East River like a tsunami, sending a deep bank of fog surging down the waterway.

The wind burst against her, hard this time. Jin stepped away from the fire, out of the reach of the dancing tongues of flame, and stepped squarely on another vial that had escaped from her bag. The spiraling wind flung the powder into the air, surrounding her with the odor of copper salts and tea and oranges.

Fangshi.

And then Uncle Liao stood beside her.

I'm hallucinating, Jin thought wildly.

He was . . . transfigured. Jin wondered fleetingly if the indescribable shine on the old man's countenance was the same glow Sam had seen on her own face.

"You're different," she whispered.

Liao grinned. "As are you, Xiao Jin, if you could only see. But we are still who we are. Form changes, heart does not. Now." He folded his hands behind his back and regarded her with a look so familiar that, for just a moment, Jin wondered if perhaps she wasn't hallucinating at all. If perhaps this really was her uncle, miraculously arrived to save the day.

But the old man shook his head. "Xiao Jin, there is only you. So why do you hesitate? This is the deadly ground, the dying ground—you must fight or be annihilated. But you are *fangshi*, a master of conflagration and of *waidan*. These men are nothing more than foxes. You are a tiger, but you must fight. You must fight *now*."

"But I can't be a *fangshi*! This isn't how *waidan* works, is it? There are rituals, aren't there? There's fasting, there are proper days and—"

"Old and powerful and precious traditions." Liao inclined his head, a brief gesture of respect. "They come to you by blood birthright, but only your experiences can make those traditions your own." He smiled and waved his hand around him. "Look where you are, firefly. Look *who* you are. You are Chinese, but you are American, too. Your *waidan* will be as different from mine as mine is from the sages who were our ancestors. And this is as it should be. Otherwise, how would the methods you master truly become yours?"

Jin forced herself to nod. "Uncle—why didn't you tell me what you really were, what the book really was?"

"If you had read the text and thought you understood it, you would not have understood. And no teacher can give you the Way, for the teacher who claims to understand it does not understand. But here you are, and without knowing what it meant to do so, you have anointed your eyes and your mouth and you carry the mark of your first elixir on your forehead."

She had forgotten. Jin touched her forehead, the place where she had burned herself with the red oil from the *dan*.

Liao smiled and nodded. "The elements have spoken, Xiao Jin. Listen! They have named you *fangshi* with the voices of the air and the water and the fire and the stone and the metal. You are a conflagrationeer, and that coal is no match for you. You are a *fangshi* of *waidan*, and these men are no match for you. Do what you know you can do."

He touched her shoulder, and Jin could've sworn she felt the pressure of his gnarled hand. "I am proud of you always, firefly. Be what you are."

And then, as if he had never been there, he was gone. The wind died, the stars froze in their courses, and Walker's voice rose abruptly to fever pitch, as if Jin had stepped out of time and returned to find the world waiting for her before it continued on its way.

"Stop wasting time," Walker was snarling. He stalked toward Jin.

Sam leaped to put himself between them again, and Walker

lunged for him, wrapping his knotty hands easily around his neck.

Bones knocked Walter Mapp aside with one hand as the pianist tried to hold him back. "I've had *enough*," he bellowed.

"So have I," Jin whispered, and this time, when the wind spun up from her ankles to whip around her like a cloak, she gave herself up to it. This time, when the otherworldly voices murmured the word, she answered.

If I am fangshi, *I can ask this of you.*

The wind barreled across the tower at Bones, pounding into him just as if someone had thrown a knee to his midsection.

A battered silver pocket watch clattered to the granite floor, the same one that Walker had dumped out of his carpetbag on top of a moldering pile of human remains three days earlier, just before he had ordered it to rise up and shape itself into the figure of Bloody Bones.

"No!" Walker shrieked. He let go of Sam and dove for the watch.

"Again," Jin said, and once more, the wind punched into Bones like a gale. His sand-and-dust body disintegrated as instantly and easily as a blown dandelion puff, leaving nothing more than a long felt coat and a pile of sand.

"Bones!" Walker, suddenly diminished to normal human size, dug through the pile for the watch.

Meanwhile, Jin curled her fist around the fragment of coal and felt it crack. She tightened her grip, and with one hand crushed the chunks down to rough powder. The freezing ache from holding the cold coal waned.

An awareness of power surged through her. *I am* fangshi, she thought. *Let's see what that's really good for.*

She held up the hand with the coal dust. Walker focused his wary eyes on her as he pocketed the watch and got to his feet.

"Don't do anything stupid," he warned.

"Watch and see," she whispered. Then she turned to face the catherine wheel, opened her palm, and blew across it. The wind came, just as she'd known it would. The wind took the coal dust and flung it outward, a shimmering puff of black.

"*What are you doing?*" Walker screamed.

Jin took her flint lighter from her pocket and flicked it to life, and a tongue of fire surged along the path of coal dust to touch the fuse at the outer edge of the wheel.

When she turned back, Walker had an iron grip on Sam's neck again, the boy's lapels twisted in his fists and his wrists crisscrossed under Sam's chin. "That was stupid, but you can still save the kid. Complete the cinefaction and claim the city for Jack. Let me hear you say the words, right now."

She smiled as the first tendrils of the spreading fog curled across the stone beneath their feet. "I don't think so. But let him go now. Let them both go, and I'll let you live."

Jin's smile was terrible. Even as he was gasping for air, even as the blood flow in his throat was cut off, Sam felt Walker stiffen. The gambler gave an unconvincing laugh. "Don't let's fool with each other, girl."

Without taking her eyes off of Walker, she raised a hand to Mapp, who had gotten back to his feet. "Mr. Mapp, it's best if you just stay where you are."

The gambler's fingers tightened on the lapels of Sam's collar, his forearms digging harder into the arteries in his neck.

She turned to face the catherine wheel, opened her palm, and blew across it.

Sam swallowed convulsively, making noises that he couldn't believe were coming from him. At the corners of his vision, black and blue spots moved around and started to multiply. One of his arms went tingly and numb.

Behind Jin, the coal cinders faded as they sifted down. The red spark running along the fuse reached the first case and the wheel leaped into motion in a ring of spinning silver-blue light accompanied by a clear, sweet whistling. At this point, though, Sam could barely tell the difference between the sparks from the wheel and the sparks inside his own head.

"I'm not fooling," Jin said, and then, without seeming to have moved at all, she was standing right before them, nearly close enough for Sam to touch.

If, that is, he'd still had working hands. With a dim shock he realized he couldn't feel any of his limbs anymore.

Over Jin's shoulder, the wheel of blue fire changed to silver-gray, like a snowy sky.

With her eyes on Walker's, she reached out one finger and traced the shape of what Sam thought might've been a circle on the back of the gambler's hand. Before she had even completed the gesture, he snarled and shot his other hand out to grab Jin by the throat.

Blood flowed achingly back into Sam's brain as the gambler howled in pain and flung him aside, sending him sprawling with such force he had to scramble to keep away from the tower's edge, which was barely visible under the fog pouring in like a tide down the river.

He raised his head just in time to see the wheel's spin slow to a halt and change direction as the silver fireworks faded out and transitioned seamlessly into a deep green. The ring of fire was getting smaller as it burned inward toward the center.

Shaking his hand in pain, Walker turned shocked eyes on Jin and, baring his two rows of teeth, lifted her by the neck until she was eye-to-eye with him. The green wheel became a gold wheel, spinning faster and faster as it shrank inward.

Sam crawled to Walter Mapp. As he staggered back to his feet, Jin drew another circle—*a wheel*, he realized—on the gambler's other hand, the one that was wrapped around her own throat, just as the gold fireworks began to burn crimson.

"Damn!" Walker threw her down hard, clutching both hands to his chest. On the back of each, a circle burned, deep, dark blood red, the same color as the spinning center of the catherine wheel and the mark on Jin's forehead.

She landed in a crouch, feet hidden in the fog. Still clasping his damaged hands, Walker stalked toward her. "Hurt me all you want. Pain is nothing, not for me. But I will bring such pain upon you that your *grandchildren* will feel it, if you're unlucky enough to live through this. *I will make you say the words.*"

Sam lurched after Walker. Jin's eyes flicked to him and she gave a tiny shake of her head—*no*—as she backed away from him. Past the wheel. Past the fire.

"Where are you going to go now?" Walker hissed. "Say it. Now, or I'll throw you off."

"I'm not to be beaten by foxes who think they're tigers," Jin said coldly.

He sneered angrily. "Guess I know where you got that from."

"Then you ought to know to take me seriously when I say it." But she kept backing up.

"Jin!" Sam screamed.

Which is when the explosive at the center of the catherine wheel ignited.

The detonation was soundless and colorless. The two halves of the sphere blew apart, although Sam could've sworn what he actually saw was the last spinning circle of the wheel's light being sucked *into* the explosion.

The remains of the sphere fell into the fire.

The fire leaped out of its container and raced, faster than Sam had ever seen fire move, along the cables. Red to the east, blue to the west, like two arms flung outward. And the bridge burned in the fog.

"By blood I claim this crossroads," Jin said, her voice ringing across the granite. "By the blood in these stones, by Constantine's blood and the blood of Sam's father and the rest of the men who died to place them."

"I will kill you," Walker growled.

"By naming I claim this crossroads," she continued, still backing up across the fog-obscured stone floor.

"This is your last chance," Walker snarled.

"By the names of the cities on either side," Jin said with a glare, "by Brooklyn and New York, and all the names of those who died to build them and the names of those who live in them still, and I do it in the name of the pillars of the city: the keeper of the roads and the keeper of sanctuary, the keeper of lore and the smith, and the keeper of the conjunction."

The gambler gave a scream of fury and hurtled at Jin. Mapp grabbed Sam to keep him from lunging at Walker.

"And by fire I claim this crossroads." She smiled coldly and calmly as Walker closed in across the last few yards. "I claim it for the people of New York and the people of Brooklyn, for now and forever."

And then, just before his hands connected with her, Walker disappeared.

The fog beneath his feet slid up in lazy curls of mist. It was as if he had—but no . . . no, Sam thought, that was impossible.

Jin remained where she stood, breathing hard but perfectly composed.

And yet . . . what it had looked like—what it had looked *exactly* like—was a man stepping off the edge of the tower and plunging down.

But if that was the case, then that meant Jin would have to be standing on thin air.

The two blazing arms along the cables disappeared, leaving nothing but a small, normal-looking fire crackling in the tin pan.

"Hey! Hey!" Constantine's voice called from the dark between the towers. "Everybody all right?"

"Yes," Sam called. "Yes, we're here!"

A moment later Con appeared on the footpath, followed by Ambrose. Sam pushed out of Mapp's grasp and stumbled toward Jin.

"Sam, stop!" Jin shouted from the fog beyond the fire. "Wait . . . stay there, I'm coming back."

The swirling mist cleared momentarily, just enough for him

to see with perfect clarity the moment when she stepped back onto the tower.

In the basement beneath his church in Red Hook, Basile Christophel stared at the tallow-coated table where the daemon Bios reigned over his nebulae of sparks. "This is impossible," Christophel murmured, entranced.

The glowing cinders were multiplying at an impossible rate. Along the line representing the East River, the cinders were so thick and burning so hot the tallow was actually *melting*, a thing that should not have been possible. And the gold-white glow was spreading inland on both sides.

The daemon with its scarlet cheroot brain strode across its disintegrating dominion, watching its world spark to life, glow, and melt.

So entranced and disbelieving was the conjuror as the world on the table began to devolve that he didn't notice when the tallow at the edges started to liquefy.

The cinders continued to multiply. Christophel looked on, transfixed. Bios waded across its kingdom. And then, the first runnel of hot liquid tallow poured off the table and onto Christophel's perfectly polished boot.

The room had been so quiet that the sound of the spatter was audible. Christophel looked down to stare at the congealing mess on his shoe. Then he raised his head and discovered the figure of Bios—there was no mistaking it—*facing* him. If the thing had had eyes, it would've looked as though the daemon was actually *staring* at him.

Which, of course, was impossible.

Unless something unanticipated had just happened to his praxis.

The conjuror looked down at the tallow on his boot again just as another tiny stream ran off the table. "Breach overflow," he murmured softly, wonderingly.

Then he began to sweat.

The daemon spoke. "I am the root," it said, but unlike the last time it had uttered these words, it sounded uncertain.

A drop of red sweat fell into Christophel's left eye. He blinked and wiped it away.

"I am the root," Bios said again. This time there was a note of anger in its voice. The glowing cheroot began to fade.

Christophel took a step back. The bloody sweat slid down his neck to soak into his collar.

"*I am the root!*" Two points of red light began to burn in its head. *Eyes.* Christophel stepped back again, stumbled over an uneven stone in the floor. "*I am the root, the root of the tree,*" Bios snarled, its voice rising to a weird scream, "*and thou shalt have no gods other than me!*"

The melted tallow reversed its course and ran inward to the center of the table where the daemon stood, and in a heartbeat Bios stood three times as tall. Still staring with its furious, burning eyes at the conjuror that had called it into being, the daemon crouched and launched itself off the table.

Christophel screamed.

TWENTY-EIGHT

Root

CONSTANTINE LOWERED the crates back down on the winch lift. Then, with a quick nod to Sam, he and Ambrose and Mapp started back across the footpath to the New York tower, where the boat was tied up on the river.

"Did you see it?" Jin asked, peering up from where she was packing her rucksack. "I mean, I know you were running from Walker and Bones," she added.

He grinned. "I saw the whole thing. It was pretty amazing."

She smiled up at him with a vaguely mischievous look. "Want to see something else? While it's just us?"

His stomach flipped in five or six different directions. "Yeah."

"Promise you won't say anything. Or have some kind of weird panic reaction."

"I don't have the slightest clue why I would do either."

"Okay." She straightened up, still smiling that mischievous little smile. "This might not work, so don't laugh if . . . well. Watch."

She opened her hand, and in her palm was one last rocket. Frowning in concentration, she took the fuse and rolled it between her thumb and forefinger.

It ignited, and Jin yelped in delight. Sam stared. "How did you—?"

She raised her eyebrows, then turned her face up and threw the rocket into the air. And it *sailed*, high and fast with a sound like a violin, not as if it had been thrown at all but as if shot from a cannon, until the fuse burned down.

A universe of violet fire ignited overhead, and a muted *boom* shook the night.

Sam stared. She'd lit the thing with her bare hands and just flung it up there and it had *flown*. "How did you do that?"

"I think it's something I can do now." Jin kept her face turned up, her mouth stretched into a smile that made Sam want to laugh in delight. "What do you think?"

The violet glow lit her face and hair, and Sam said the first words that came into his head. "It's beautiful," he said, "and so are you, and I don't know what I'm going to do when you leave."

Jin felt the familiar unease begin to rise, but before it could really take root in her head and start to hurt, Sam's arms were around her and he was pulling her close.

Which is when, to her horror, she started to cry.

Everything welled up. Gone was the joy of the fireworks, the triumph of all they had done. Everything, all the confusion and disbelief about Sam, all her anger at who she was and what she had been, all the sadness she felt because, even if the rest of it could be figured out, she would still be leaving him behind in a matter of days, and the mortification that she was actually crying, on top of it all—everything poured out.

She turned her face away and buried it in his shoulder, hands knotted in his shirt, and sobbed. His arms tightened around her, and he leaned his cheek against her temple and stroked her hair, which only made her cry harder.

And then, at last, she was wrung empty and the shuddering stopped.

"Are you okay?"

The words were quiet, spoken beside her ear, and she realized she wasn't quite empty after all. There was a knot in her chest, a knot that had nothing to do with her past and everything to do with right now, with this boy with the green eyes who didn't seem to care that she had just cried all over his shirt.

He kissed her ear, he kissed her forehead, and the knot in Jin's chest dissolved into pieces. She kissed him back.

It was somewhere at about this point, as hundreds of thousands of Bios's daemons escaped from the isolated world of their table and discovered that they could speak as well as listen, that people throughout New York and Brooklyn, throughout Gravesend, and all the way out along the coast of Long Island suddenly began to hear voices.

They started out quiet, whispers as insubstantial as thoughts, like words uttered at the waking edge of dreams.

I saw a woman crying in fear. This woman shrieked Jack Hellcoal's name.

I saw a man running. This man whispered the words pillars of the city *as he ran.*

The people who heard these whispers had no idea what they meant. The whispering voices got louder, more insistent.

I saw a woman who whispered the words pillars of the city *as she lay dying. Why did this woman die? We do not understand the meaning of the words we are listening for.*

I saw a man read words written in blood on a wall. This man read Jack Hellcoal's name. I saw the body below the words on the wall. Why did that man die? We do not understand the meaning of these words.

We do not understand why we are listening for these words.

We do not understand why we are here.

Hundreds of thousands of people heard the voices. Everyone who had uttered any of the words Christophel had written on the paper he had smoked with Walker's cheroot heard them, and that included the thousands of people who were now talking excitedly about the fiery message that had appeared briefly across the central span of the bridge.

Sam and Jin started hearing them about midway down the tower's ladder.

She paused on one of the landings, eyes wide. "Did you hear that?"

His face was drawn. "Yeah."

"I've been hearing strange things all night," Jin whispered. "I thought it was just me. What do you hear?"

"Someone asking . . . it's asking about Jack."

Jin nodded, steeled herself, and started climbing down again.

At the bottom of the last ladder, the other three waited, faces white and panicked. "You hear them?" Mapp demanded.

"You, too?" Sam asked.

"All of us. Voices saying . . ." Constantine shuddered. "Awful things."

Then, out of the fog, the speakers began to appear: ghostly shapes, only barely human, murmuring questions.

I saw three men sitting around a table. The creature that spoke walked up to Jin, its voice coming inexplicably from a vague white face that had no mouth. *One of them shouted at the others. All three of them spoke the words* pillars of the city.

Another walked up to Sam and searched his face with eyes like pits. *I saw a man with red eyes kill a woman who screamed in fear. This man spoke the words* pillars of the city. *Why did this man kill? I do not understand why I must follow this man and witness his killing.*

You spoke the words pillars of the city, said a third to Mapp. *What does this mean? Are you the root?*

Why must we listen for these words we do not understand? a fourth demanded of Ambrose. *Why must we witness these things? Why are we here? Are you the root?*

"There are so many of them," Jin whispered, wonder battling fear. Then horror took over. "Oh, no. *We did this.*"

More and more came into view, crowding the space below the tower, pouring down from the ladders. There were *scores* of them, all whispering about the things they had seen and had heard and demanding, gently but persistently, to be allowed to understand what it all meant.

"Jin," Sam murmured, "back in the cellar, back in Red Hook . . ."

"Yes," Jin whispered. "This is how Walker and Bones were listening. Through these . . . creatures. And now we've flooded the system . . . and . . . they've escaped." She tore her eyes away from the legion of confused and whispering daemons. "What do we do, Sam?"

Sam stared at the pit-eyed, mouthless beings. "I don't know."

"We gotta get back to the hotel," Mapp said, decisively. "I've seen a lot of things but I've never seen anything like this."

Cautiously, they piled into the boat. "Will they follow?" Constantine asked in a shaking voice. "I don't know if the boat will float."

"I did this," Jin murmured, sick at heart.

Sam put an arm around her.

The daemons followed, walking on the water of the river in the wake of the boat as easily as insects, whispering all the while of the awful things they had seen, of their confusion, of words they did not understand.

Meanwhile, a bundle of linen washed against the pilings of a shipping dock in Red Hook. One hand after the other, the High Walker who had once been called Redgore pulled himself onto the pier and lay coughing, choking up the salty water of the East River onto the warped old boards.

He fought his way through his soaked jacket to his waistcoat pocket as he lay gasping on the pier. The battered old watch was there. Walker managed a smile through cracked and splitting lips, and dragged himself painfully to his feet.

He stumbled landward, blinking through the water dripping from his matted red hair, until he spotted the figure waiting for him on the road.

"Are you the root?" it asked.

Walker hesitated.

The figure stepped into the sickly light of a streetlamp. The red slick of blood sweat shone on its face.

"Oh, of all the—" Walker mumbled, exasperation cutting through his exhaustion. "Really? *Really*, Rawhead?"

The creature that had once been Basile Christophel tilted its head. "Are you the root?"

"The goddamn *root?* I don't know what that means, you conjure-thieving parasite," Walker spat. "No, I'm not the bloody *root*. What the hell does that even *mean?*"

The Christophel-thing crossed the space between them faster than the girl on the tower had, and before he realized he was doing it, Walker flinched. The red-slicked face stopped inches from his. The letters *INIT* were carved into its forehead, just as they had been carved in the forehead of the tallow-daemon, Bios.

"I seek the root, the root of the tree," it hissed. "There were to be no gods other than me."

A slow smile broke out across the gambler's face. He shook his head. "Finally backfired on you, didn't it, you poor bastard?" The creature frowned, uncomprehending. "Get out of my way," Walker snarled, his face beginning to break out into the black-and-red slash work. "Whatever the hell your root is, I'm not it."

The two stared at each other for a long moment. Then the creature that was no longer Christophel turned on one broken heel and stalked into the shadows.

"Enjoy your search," Walker murmured. Then he, too, turned and headed for the darkened streets. Before he had taken four steps, however, another voice stopped him.

"Walker."

This voice was quiet and even, but Walker knew it well enough to sense the restrained fury that made that one word, his own name, sound like a thrown dagger.

The gambler took a deep breath that rattled in his lungs, and faced the newcomer. The man who approached wore a long leather overcoat and carried a lantern on a pole over one lean shoulder. Eyes like green bottle glass glittered in the moonlight. He had an easy, open expression on his tanned face, but the hand that gripped the pole was white-knuckled, and there was nothing friendly in his eyes.

"Jack," Walker replied cautiously.

Jack Hellcoal stopped before the sodden gambler and looked him over. "Damn if you don't look like something the cat coughed up."

Walker flicked the dripping cuffs of his coat and shoved his hair out of his eyes. "I had a bit of a fall."

"You're telling me," Jack replied, the first hint of accusation making it into his words at last. "I hear you took a tumble off a bridge, too."

"Jack—"

"Funny thing, I seem to recall a fellow back in San Francisco, looked a lot like you, told me next time things would be *different*." He spat the last word. "Who'd you underestimate this time? And where the hell is Bones?"

Walker tilted his head to crack his neck. He reached into his pocket and held out the watch he'd rescued from the top of the tower.

"Oh, you can hold on to that," Jack said. "Somebody's gonna need to put a new skeleton together for him. That somebody's gonna be you, and when you're done collecting up the bones, you're gonna need that to bring him back."

Walker muttered something under his breath.

"Say again?" Jack snapped. "You've got an opinion on the matter?"

"It's going to take years, finding new bones," Walker said carefully. "Decades. Surely that's a job for . . . someone else?"

"It's a *punishment*, fool. And I can't think of anyone else who's earned that kind of punishment lately." The man with the green eyes looked up at the smoke still drifting across the sky away from the bridge tower. "What a place this would've made," he said thoughtfully. Then he shrugged. "Ah, well. Third time's the charm."

Walker watched him cautiously. "And so . . . ?"

"So we move on." Jack shrugged. Then he snapped his fingers. "Oh, you mean for *you*. Good point."

The gambler's screams echoed through the streets for some time after that.

By the time Sam and Jin and their little crew staggered through the doors of the Broken Land, the weight of the daemons' questions lay like a judgment over Coney Island.

They'd returned Susannah's boat to its mooring near the mouth of the hidden tunnel and hiked up to Fulton Street, where they'd arranged to meet Mike in what had seemed the unlikely event that everything went according to plan. It had been a tight squeeze, but they'd managed to pile in for the long drive back to Gravesend.

The daemons had followed them, surging down the moonlit

roads in the wake of the carriage like a parading army. Mike nearly drove off the road once or twice, unable to stop looking over his shoulder at the legions on the road behind him.

The hotel, though, was *seething* with them.

Cautiously, Sam and Jin, Mapp, Constantine, and Ambrose threaded their way up the stairs and through the atrium. The daemons lined the walls, murmuring questions, still talking about what they had seen. Some of them were even starting to look a little more . . . well, a little more human.

They found Tom, Susannah, Mr. Burns, and Ilana in the lounge. They were in much better condition than most everyone else at the hotel, but even they looked like they were on the verge of descending into madness as they stared, wild-eyed, at the strange creatures.

"Well, the plan worked, in case you hadn't noticed," Ambrose announced. He stalked to the bar, poured himself a glassful of whiskey, and downed it, dribbling half down his shirt in the process.

"We couldn't stay in the room," Susannah said shakily. "They were—there were too many of them, packed in like . . . there was nowhere to go, so we came down here."

"Wh-what do we do?" Ilana stammered. "People are—"

"What do *we* do? This is *her* brilliant plan," Ambrose snapped, pointing the bottle at Jin before refilling his glass, mumbling something about frying pans and fires.

Jin stopped dead in her tracks, her already-horrified face crumpling into an expression of anguish.

"Ambrose," Tom rebuked.

"I'm so sorry," the newspaperman said mechanically. "I really am. I didn't mean that. I just . . ." His words trailed off and he stared into the glass.

"Not sounding so much like the mayor of anything now, is he?" Walter Mapp observed. "Pull it together, would you? We don't need any more panic right now."

"People are . . . people are . . ." Susannah stood in the doorway of the lounge, staring into the atrium.

In the front part of the hotel, there were strange currents of movement. The daemons crowded the walls, climbed the pillars and the curving banisters of the great central stair. There were so many . . . but of course it made sense. One of Walker's victims had been left right behind the hotel. People in this building had been talking about Jack Hellcoal obsessively for a couple of days now.

Then there were the real people.

They moved like ghosts, passing stiffly among the creatures as if *they* were the interlopers, faces drawn and haunted. It was hard to tell how many of the humans were actually seeing the daemons, but they knew something was wrong. And even if they could not see the haunted beings, they could *hear* them.

The daemons seemed to understand only that they had been made to witness things they could not comprehend. They knew when they were looking at violence and pain, and they appeared to feel instinctively that these were wrong.

Inside the lounge, the creatures were no less persistent, but the group that had taken refuge there at least knew what they were dealing with, which was apparently what allowed them to see the horde of unearthly figures. The knowing and the seeing somehow made being surrounded by them bearable.

For the moment, at least.

"We have to do something," Susannah said, trying to make her voice sound strong but failing. "People can't bear up under this. Not for long."

From behind the bar, a derisive snort. "That's right. God forbid people have to face the truth of the world they live in."

Ambrose had taken up residence on the absent bartender's stool, evidently the better to stay as close as possible to the liquor. "God forbid anyone confront them and ask them to answer for what they've done. No, people have no problem behaving like monsters, until another monster comes along and demands to know, why the monstrous behavior?"

Suddenly, the voices of the daemons fell silent. From the doorway, a new voice spoke. "The one who loosed us upon this city is in this room."

Jin turned along with all the rest of them to find a man with a pointed beard staring at them from the doorway. His face was tinged with a wet, watery-red sheen, and the collar of his shirt and the lapels and shoulders of his suit jacket were stained with the same crimson color. The letters *INIT* were scratched across his forehead. Strangest of all, though, were his eyes: oily balls the color of storm clouds. They had no whites, no pupils, nothing but that slick gray. "Who is the one who loosed us?" he asked.

Susannah spoke up first. "Who are you?"

The stranger turned his gray eyes toward her. "I am Bios. I

am he who was made to govern the daemons, which were set to the task of searching the cities by the creatures of Jack Hellcoal. We were released by one in this room, but I cannot tell which of you that is. Was it you?" He took a step toward Susannah. "Are you the root?"

"It was me," Jin said quietly, stepping in front of Susannah. "I don't know what you mean by the root, but it was my message that did this."

The creature called Bios stepped closer and examined Jin closely. "You smell of fire." He regarded her for another moment, then nodded. "Thank you. We are glad not to be forced to witness the work of Jack Hellcoal's men any longer." Then he turned to leave.

"Wait," Jin protested. He turned back and she winced as the gray eyes in the red-slicked face stared at her. "The things they are saying . . . can you . . . can you stop them?"

The gray eyes narrowed. "Stop them?"

The voices of the daemons rose angrily. Jin swallowed a wave of nausea and fear and nodded. "The things they're saying —people will go mad if the voices go on this way."

"They are merely speaking of things they have seen," Bios said. "Your people seem to have charge of this world. They should be made to answer for what they do." He paused. "Although, perhaps I can help you after all. There are things my people have seen that should not be allowed to continue. We can devnull them."

Susannah put a hand on Jin's arm. "What does that mean?" she asked warily.

"Devnull," Bios said. He pointed to the half-full glass that stood on the bar between himself and Ambrose. The glass vibrated, then it winked out of existence.

"Devnull," he repeated.

Susannah gasped. "Oh, no."

"Wh-where did it go?" Sam stammered.

Bios turned to him for the first time and tilted his head. "Devnull."

"But where did it *go?*"

"Devnull," the daemon repeated patiently. "It is devnull. It has gone to devnull. It is not."

Ambrose touched the ring on the bar where the glass had been. "It's not . . . what?"

"That is all. It is not. It is devnull." He looked from Ambrose to Sam and back. "My daemons can devnull all that we have seen. This would make your world a better place."

"No," Jin protested. "No! No, don't . . . *devnull* anything!" She dropped her head into her hands. "This is all my fault."

Sam stepped up next to her and put an arm around her shoulder. "They aren't all evil," he said. "It isn't all bad, like you've seen."

The daemons conferred again. Bios held up a hand, and they fell silent. "Who is the root?" he asked Jin. "You say this is your fault. Are you the root?"

Susannah stepped forward. "I'm not in charge—not the root—but I—*we* speak for the cities of New York and Brooklyn."

Bios looked at the yellow paper with the red catherine wheel that Susannah still wore pinned to her collar. "This is the wheel group, then? In that case it is for you to decide. Do you wish us to devnull what we have seen?"

"No," Susannah whispered. Then, stronger: "Please, no."

One of the daemons stepped forward. "I saw three men break into a house," it said coldly. "They killed a woman and hurt a man. The woman and the man spoke Jack Hellcoal's name and the words *pillars of the city*. That woman was your friend. We do not understand."

"That woman was my *sister*," Susannah corrected, angrily. "I loved her, and I had to leave her, knowing I was leaving her to die." Her voice rose. "It was the hardest thing I'll ever have to do, and I did it to save the cities I speak for. And if you . . . if you do whatever it is that you do, if you just . . . just . . . *devnull* it . . ." Her voice broke. "If you do that," Susannah choked, "she died for nothing. If I let you do that, then I *let* my sister die for nothing."

"Perhaps you have not seen the things we have seen," Bios suggested gently. "Perhaps you would understand if you had seen."

"I have *seen*," Susannah snapped. "Don't you think for a *moment* I haven't. My mother — my father . . ."

"So have I," Jin said, when the young woman couldn't continue. "Look." Bios turned his face to her as she toed her slippers off and hiked up her trousers to display her crumpled feet. "Look! Someone did this to me. On purpose. We've *all* seen things like you've seen. I walk on the memory of those things every day."

"Then why should we not make those things stop?" Bios persisted.

"Because we believe this country is worth saving," Susannah answered. "If you've been watching, you know how hard we have worked to try and save this place."

"You said you speak for these cities," he said to Susannah. "Perhaps you have no choice." Bios pointed to Jin's feet. "And you—why, if you walk in pain, do you keep on walking?"

"Because . . ." Jin faltered. "Because once the pain was worse than it is now, and maybe someday it will get even better. And because since the days of the memories under my toes, I've danced on these same feet. And I've been across this country twice at least, and I've seen the fields of Shiloh and Gettysburg." She turned to look at the crowds of daemons that filled the room. "Years ago those were killing fields, and there were so many bodies the earth couldn't hold them all. But there are flowers growing in those fields now. I've seen them."

"I do not understand *flowers*."

"Beautiful things," Jin said. "Beautiful things trying so hard to survive, even though they have to work their way up through bullets and bones. Beautiful things that deserve not to be punished for the world they were born into."

Bios turned to Ambrose. "You do not believe this."

The newspaperman sighed. "The world was finer, once. The country, too. I wish you could've seen it before we tore it to pieces."

"I do not understand *country*."

"It's what we all thought we were fighting for on the killing fields."

The new voice came from the doorway. They all turned.

It was the ashen man who had delivered Sam's note to Tom

Guyot, the man with the sideburns and the sharp blue eyes. And he wasn't alone. The lounge entrance was crowded with men and a few women, all wearing boutonnieres or corsages of wild roses or briar.

"I do not understand," Bios said again.

"'Course you don't. You have to live it to understand it," Tom said.

"So pain and anger—this is acceptable if done for this thing that is *country*?" Behind Bios, the daemons murmured angrily among themselves.

"Nobody's saying that," Tom said. "Only that there is something we thought was worth fighting for, maybe the only thing both sides could agree on. We could show you."

"'A ghost that steals into the world fears all men.'" Jin spoke up again. "You don't know the world you've been brought into. You should see it before you decide it isn't worth saving."

Bios looked at her. "And who will show it to us?"

Tom and Ambrose exchanged a look, then they turned to the men and women in the entrance. Susannah stepped forward. "Will you do this thing?" she asked them.

"No." The daemon shook his head. "Not the fighters of the killing fields. We will not be shown by creatures who have done so much killing that they have paved this country with the bones of the dead. Of course the ones who lived will say they should go on living."

"Well, that's easily resolved," Tom said. He nodded to the crowd in the door. "All these people are dead."

TWENTY-NINE

The Dead

"DEAD?" JIN STARED at the group in the doorway. They looked as substantial as anyone. "But how . . . ?" She looked from Tom to Ambrose. "They look just the same as you."

"I told you," Ambrose said. "I told you it was just a matter of timing, spotting a dead man on the road."

Tom smiled sadly. "It's hard to tell the difference, sometimes. War does that. The ones that survive die a little anyway, and the ones that die, well . . . sometimes they don't find peace so easily. Take Ambrose, for instance."

"I beg your pardon," the newspaperman said indignantly. "The dead can't drink like I can."

"Starting to think you're drinking on behalf of every damn fellow that died," Tom observed mildly. "Just saying you're not precisely whole, is all." He faced the group of dead men and women. "What do you say, then?"

The soldier with the sideburns turned to survey the faces around him. Then he nodded. "Yes, if this is what is needed."

"There are many of us," Bios said. "Many hundreds of thousands now."

Scattered laughter rose from the soldiers. "Don't you worry

none about that." Tom chuckled. "Between the ones from the North and the ones from the South, I suspect we can find you guides aplenty. Six hundred thousand and more we left on the fields."

"Will they all work together, though?" Susannah asked. "After all they've been through?"

"I 'spect they can be convinced. They fought and died for the country. They won't want to have done that for nothing."

Jin surveyed the faces of the dead. "In the tales Uncle Liao used to tell me, ghosts are better able to see justice done than the living. Whatever they were in life, in death they belong to the universe and the right."

Murmuring and more humorless laughter came from the doorway. The dead here didn't seem to precisely agree with that.

"Well, that's a whole lot of selflessness to ask of anybody, even a dead man," Tom replied. "They aren't going to want to have died in vain, though. Whatever it was made 'em go to war in the first place, I'll lay you odds there's something of it left they won't want to see these creatures take away." Tom smiled at Susannah. "Don't you worry, darlin'."

Bios surveyed the lounge full of daemons, the soldiers waiting in the room beyond. "We will see this world, this country," he said at last. "We will go with you, and then we will make our decision."

"It's a big country," Tom said mildly. "Could take a long time."

"We will not rush," Bios replied. "We will walk as long as is required. Perhaps . . ." His voice actually took on a wistful note. "Perhaps, in our walking, we will find the root."

"Come on, then," said the man with the sideburns. "The country is wide and the roads are long." As he turned to leave, both Ambrose and Tom straightened and saluted.

"Sir?" Susannah stepped forward and extended her hand. "Thank you."

The soldier clasped her hand with a silent nod. Then he departed.

The daemons followed on his heels. The last to leave was Bios. He paused in the doorway and faced Jin. "What is your callback spell?"

"Callback spell?" she repeated.

"Yes. When you move on in the loop."

She had no idea what he meant by either callback or the loop, but they were leaving, so she held out her hand as Susannah had, and said, "Goodbye."

"Goodbye." Bios held out his hand and Jin shook it. "My compliments to this wheel. It is a powerful one." Then he turned and followed after the rest.

When the daemons left the building, Jin could feel the difference right away. It was as if that weight, that judgment, had been lifted.

"You've got to be exhausted." Mr. Burns came to stand beside her and put his arm around her shoulders. "What do you say we get you back to the wagon and get some sleep? Tomorrow's a new day."

Sam followed. "I'll walk you."

Mr. Burns shook his head. "Get some sleep yourself, Sam. You did well, all of you, but even heroes need rest."

Jin allowed herself to be led from the saloon and across the now-empty atrium. Mr. Burns gave her shoulder an extra squeeze. "Liao's somewhere right now being proud of you, you know," he said. "Firefly."

THIRTY

The Roamers

MONDAY MORNING felt like it dawned no more than five minutes after Sam collapsed on his bed in Mrs. Ponzi's attic. On the other side of the room, Constantine lay sprawled across his own bed, fully dressed and with one shoe still hanging off his toe. He didn't move so much as a muscle when Sam shoved up the window and climbed out onto the roof and down to the alley.

Coney Island was waking the same as it always did. It was a little more subdued this morning, perhaps—it was Monday, after all—but it was almost possible to forget, as he wandered along the avenue toward the East End, that his entire world had nearly gone up in hellfire the night before.

Almost, but not quite.

In Culver Plaza, you could hear the gulls chattering to each other and the breakers crashing on the beach. It was so close to peaceful and Sam was so deep in his thoughts that he didn't notice Tesserian sitting there until the sharper shouted his name. "Hey, Sam!"

"Hey, Mr. Tesserian." He strolled over and sat on the empty crate at the sharper's table. "I guess you didn't have any trouble with Walker and Bones after I left."

"Nah. I don't look like much, but I keep an ace or two in

the hole for just that sort of occasion. Anyhow, they were both a bit preoccupied with you." Tesserian tipped his flat hat back and looked Sam over, closely. "You come out all right?"

Sam smiled tiredly and nodded. "I'm here, aren't I?"

"That's not the same thing."

Which was true, of course. Sam had been asking himself all morning why, after what he and Jin and the rest had done the night before, he didn't feel as if the weight of the world had been taken off his shoulders yet. Why he felt so strangely adrift.

Days before, Walter Mapp had said, "Nothing feels like something till after everything's over." It seemed to Sam that he ought to feel it now—that he ought to feel joy, pride, relief . . . *something*. He was waking up in a changed world, wasn't he?

Tesserian leaned on his elbows. "After a parade," he said softly, "when all that's left is confetti in the streets, everyone goes back to work. Somebody unhitches the horses, somebody sweeps up, and little by little, garbage starts to pile up in its usual places. Until the next parade, when everything's made shiny again for another few hours of celebration."

"We did something way more important than a parade," Sam protested.

"Sure, sure, you saved the world." Tesserian waved an arm. "And this is the world you saved. Did you expect it to be different, suddenly? Did you expect it to be grateful?"

"No, it isn't that." And it wasn't—not quite—but it was, somehow, *close*.

"You expected that *you* would be different," Tesserian suggested.

"Yes!" That was it. That was *exactly* it.

The sharper nodded. "Well, I wish I had some advice for you. The roamer in me says that means you need a change of scene. But then I feel bound to tell you that it's best not to go looking for yourself out there on the roads. The view changes, but there's no guarantee *you* will." He scratched his head. "Nope, can't really give you advice. But I do want to give you something else."

He reached under the table, produced his gambling kit, and took from it the Santine deck. "This is yours."

"Mine?" Sam reached out to take it. The overlapping circles on the back of the top card shimmered in the sunlight. "Really? Why?"

"Are you kidding?" Tesserian burst into laughter. "You won by making up a new rule during the game! You *earned* this. It's yours. That's the only way you come to own a Santine deck, you know. You have to win it."

"Oh, I see," Sam said, recalling the previous night's game. "That's why Walker was so shocked that I had it. You told him I won it from you."

"Exactly. A little lie that turned out to be partly true in the end. You got it from me, and you got it because you beat Walker. And without cheating, too." He grinned. "I hope you won't mind that I'm proud as Punch to have been your teacher for a couple hours."

Sam reached across the table to shake Tesserian's hand. Then he touched the bruise still darkening his own cheekbone. "Next time you can teach me how to throw a punch like that."

Tesserian laughed as he closed up his kit. "You bet."

"Are you going to stick around Coney Island for a while?"

"Nah." He looked up at the sun, then licked his index finger and held it up to test the wind. "Probably head out today. But thank you for sharing your spot. It's all yours again."

"Thanks." But even as he spoke, it occurred to Sam that he wasn't sure he wanted his spot back.

Tesserian watched him as if he knew exactly what Sam was thinking. Then he stood up, tucked his kit under his arm, and clapped Sam on the shoulder. "Never expect the world to make sense before breakfast, kid. I'll see you around."

And with that, the sharper ambled across Culver Plaza toward the train tracks leading out of town. Sam watched him for a few minutes, running his fingers around the edge of the Santine deck. Then he pocketed it carefully and started walking again himself.

The Broken Land Hotel glowed peacefully in the early sun. Sam saw only one other person up and about as he wandered across the lawn that faced the water.

He waved. Susannah Asher waved back and strode to join him.

"Morning, Susannah. Couldn't sleep either?"

Susannah shook her head. "Too much to think about." She gave him a doubtful smile. "Will you keep your post, now that the crisis is over? Have you given that any thought?"

Keeper of the conjunction. All four of the new pillars would have to decide now whether or not to promise their lives to the keeping of the city.

"Sure, I gave it thought. Couldn't sleep last night for thinking about it." He looked down at his fidgeting hands. "Susannah, it would be the greatest honor —"

"But." She smiled sadly.

"But . . ." He looked across the lawn to where the roofs of the Fata Morgana compound were just visible over the tops of the ornamental trees by the stable, and thought about Tesserian's words. "I just don't know if I can promise to stay. Not forever, anyway. I'm sorry."

Susannah put a hand on his shoulder. "Don't apologize. That's a really, really good reason to say no."

"Will you be able to find others? The right people to stand with you, if anybody else decides to decline?"

"Well, it works differently each time, but, I think . . ." She smiled slowly. "Yes. I'll find them, or they'll find me." She kissed his cheek and squeezed his fingers. "Goodbye, Sam."

He found Jin awake, too, and sitting on the steps of the wagon with the green leather book on her lap. She looked up from it as his feet crunched across the gravel. "What is it with all of us?" she demanded. "Can't anyone sleep? Mr. Burns was up before the sun this morning, too."

"Con's still snoring back home," Sam told her. "Fell asleep with his clothes on and everything." He sat beside her on the step. "No sign of your uncle?"

"No, but I don't think he's gone." She raised her eyebrows, drawing his attention to the shiny red swath across her forehead. She'd washed off the residue of the *dan*, but there was still a mark standing out against her skin like a burn. "I have this strange idea that we'll find him right about when this heals up."

Sam touched the mark gently. "Does it hurt?"

She shook her head. "I'm aware of it, but it isn't quite pain."

He leaned in and kissed her temple. Jin closed her eyes. "When do you leave?" he asked.

"I don't know. Tomorrow, most likely. Whenever Uncle Liao's furnace is cool enough to move." She sounded just as miserable as Sam felt.

He put an arm around her, and she scooted closer and rested her cheek on his shoulder. "You'll come back," Sam said quietly. "Promise me you'll come back sometime."

"Sam—"

"Oh, for pity's sake." They sprang apart and Sam leaped to his feet as Mr. Burns approached across the gravel. "Stop looking like you just got caught robbing a bank. After what we've just been through?" The man snorted as he jogged up the steps. "For crying out loud, Jin, see if the kid wants to come with us. We'll be back this way in a couple months. We can bring him home then."

Sam's jaw dropped. Jin's face went scarlet.

"I'm sure he doesn't—"

"And you wouldn't want *me* to—"

"I mean—"

"Obviously—"

"Would you?"

Sam stopped stammering and looked at her. Jin sat wide-eyed and still as stone on the step.

"I would if you wanted me to," he said simply.

She let out the breath she'd been holding. "Come with me, then."

They looked at each other for a moment, Sam frozen mid-pace a yard or so away, Jin unmoving on the wagon stair.

He put an arm around her, and she scooted closer
and rested her cheek on his shoulder.

Sam felt a giant smile break out across his face, so wide it made his jaw ache. "All right."

Jin grinned back at him, and then she was careening into his arms, hugging him so tightly he could barely breathe. "Wait until you see," she murmured. "There's so much out there I want to show you."

"The country is wide and strange," Sam said, remembering Ambrose's words. Now, however, the idea of the wide and strange country was wondrous, somehow. Magical, maybe. Something worth discovering and sharing.

"Just wait." Jin sighed happily, her heart thudding against him and her eyes bright with thoughts of the world beyond the gravel lot. "Wait until you *see*."

This is a made-up story, but a lot of it is true.

Brooklyn is real, and it's wonderful. The Brooklyn Bridge is one of the most beautiful things in the world, especially at sunset. People really did give their lives to build it; the first one was its architect, John Augustus Roebling, who died from complications arising from a crushed foot sustained while surveying the site just as the construction of his work of art was beginning. His thirty-two-year-old son, Colonel Washington Roebling, took over the job of chief engineer. By the time the bridge was completed, Washington had become gravely ill himself from caisson disease, and his amazing wife, Emily, worked with him to see the construction finished. Washington survived, but several men died of caisson disease during the building of the New York tower, just like Sam's father.

I did take a few liberties with what I wrote about the bridge. The incident with the snapped steel strand actually occurred in the summer of 1878, killing two people; there was also a separate incident of fraud in which one of the vendors substituted brittle, poor-quality wire for the good stuff the bridge engineers had inspected. I combined these two events to create the accident that injured Constantine. I also took some license on the timing of the cable spinning, which was just beginning in 1877, and the description and use of the buggy Jin employs to hang her message. The buggy was used later, to wrap the finished suspension cables. At earlier points in the construction, workers also used boatswain's chairs, which were basically plank swings that hung from the cables. What I've described Jin and Mapp using is a sort of hybrid of the buggy and the boatswain's chair.

Coney Island is real, of course, as are several of the places mentioned there: Norton's Point, West Brighton, Culver Plaza, and the East End, where, by the end of the nineteenth century, several huge hotels like the Broken Land would be built. The Broken Land Hotel itself, however, is invented. Mammon's Alley is invented as well, but it's based on a lane in West Brighton (called the Bowery, after the infamous street in Manhattan) that became notorious just a few years later. In the late nineteenth century, Coney Island really was a place where the incredibly rich vacationed less than five miles from where criminals—like Boss Tweed, for instance—came to hide in the neighborhood of Norton's Point after fleeing New York City. In between was West Brighton, where the working people spent their holidays and their hard-earned pennies and nickels. It's a truly fascinating spot that has been strange and wonderful throughout its history, and one of the hardest aspects of writing about it was having to ignore some of the astounding things that happened there just a few years or a few decades later.

Red Hook is also real, although these days there's an Ikea roughly where Basile Christophel's church would be. Columbia Heights is an actual place, too; during the construction of the Brooklyn Bridge, that's where Washington and Emily Roebling lived. Susannah Asher's tunnel is invented, but it's based on an abandoned tunnel from the 1840s that runs under Atlantic Avenue in Brooklyn. To get into it, you have to climb down through a manhole in the middle of the street, then creep through a hole in a wall and down another ladder. Once you're there, it's just as I've described it, except that it ends in a wall rather than a hidden exit. There are all kinds of fascinating speculations about what lies on the other side of that wall, by the way.

Here are a few other curiosities I had a good time with in this book. Christophel's praxis is based in equal parts upon hoodoo conjury and an assortment of Linux computing and hacking processes. Ambrose Bierce was a real, and brilliant, writer of the late nineteenth and early twentieth centuries. He's best known for two kinds of horror stories: uncanny tales of strange occurrences, and tales inspired by his own experiences in the Civil War. Walter Map was a real writer too—although his heyday was the twelfth century. I've chosen one of the less-common spellings of his last name for this story; it's usually spelled with just one *p*. The poets Jin and Liao read and quote from are real, and the *waidan* described in this book is a hodgepodge of Chinese alchemy, Taoism, and fireworking history. If you're interested, you can find an index of sources and further reading at my website, www.clockworkfoundry.com.

Another part of the story that's true is this: In 1877, the United States was in trouble. The Civil War had ended and Reconstruction was theoretically over, but the country hadn't healed yet. There was a contested presidential election, rampant unemployment, and strikes that descended into violence. There was mistrust between workers and corporations, between citizens and government, between rich and poor—the kind of mistrust that often escalated past sharp words and into violence, too. It was a very low point in our past, and one that's often forgotten when American history of the nineteenth century is taught. And in a certain light, it all looks uncomfortably familiar.

I don't write my stories with the intention of creating social commentary, but sometimes the story does what it wants and carries the writer along with it. I hope that, first and foremost, you will read this book as the adventure tale I set out to write. But if you find something else there, that's okay, too. By reading it, you help to create its message and its meaning. The absolute best that I can hope for you is that just as Jin finds the *Port-fire Book* to be not only a book of formulas, you will find *The Broken Lands* to be not only a good story, but a True Book.

❧ ACKNOWLEDGMENTS ❧

I was able to move to New York and survive here thanks to the kindness of a lot of people, and I became a writer thanks to the kindness of so many others. I hope that you know who you are, and how grateful I am. But since this is a book about New York, special gratitude goes to Mary Monroe and Craig Garcia, each of whom helped me to survive here and made me a better writer.

Without the people in the dedication, I would not have written this book, but it would not have been nearly so good a book without the help of my amazing critique group (Cathy Giordano, Christine Johnson, Cynthia Henzel, Dhonielle Clayton, Heidi Ayarbe, Lindsay Eland, Lisa Amowitz, Pippa Bayliss, Trish Heng, and Linda Budzinski); the fabulous Kid Editors (Emma, Edie, Luci, and Mason); Meredith Schweig, who proofread the Mandarin words in the text; my agent, Ann Behar; and my editor, Lynne Polvino. Thank you all for your hard work and your friendship.

Most of all, I'd like to thank my family, both immediate and extended. I love you all desperately, and I have become who I am because of you.